TAKE WHAT YOU CAN

HEATHER GARVIN

TAKE WHAT YOU CAN

ISBN: 9781734908244

For information contact : Heather Garvin
heathergarvinbooks@gmail.com

Cover Design : Sam Palencia, Ink and Laurel
Editor : See Acknowledgments
First Edition: 2020

Published by Tuskan Publishing LLC

TAKE WHAT YOU CAN

TUSKAN PUBLISHING LLC

DEDICATION

To you, and every reader who picks up this book, I can't thank you enough.

I

My ears flood with the rhythmic resonance of pencils drumming on wooden desks and feet tapping against the bland, linoleum floor. Even with no summer plans, my heart pumps with anticipation for the school bell to ring. My eyes narrow at the round clock above the whiteboard. I can't tell if it's broken or just moving slowly enough to torture me. Struggling to pass the time, I resort to doodling in my art notebook that, as of today, I'll no longer need. *Paige Lawson*, I write in the top corner. Habit, I guess. Despite my best efforts, my eyes always find their way back to the clock that I've decided *must* be broken.

Over the hum of everyone's excitement, my ears catch a dry cough in the corner of the room. My eyes peel away from the must-be-broken clock and land on a short woman with her nose pressed against the paper she vigorously reads. Mrs. Beal has tiny rectangular glasses at the end of her nose, giving her a haughty appearance.

I watch mindlessly as she drags a finger from left to right. She only stops every few seconds to push her glasses up the slope of her nose, but they always slide back down again.

She looks innocent enough, but she's the type of older woman who creates a constant shadow over her students' lives—like mine. It's ironic that I only took art this year because I thought it would be easy. As it turns out, *this* was the class I had struggled with the most.

Her judgmental gaze drifts upward to meet mine, and it takes me a moment to realize we're staring at each other. As soon as it registers, I dart my eyes down to my notebook. My doodle had potential, but the more I try to draw a sleeping dog, the more it looks like a lumpy sack of potatoes… with a tail.

I'm about to salvage the potato dog when I jump in my seat, startled by the sound of the bell. Books slam shut, backpacks zip, and feet pound against the floor as everyone stampedes to freedom.

Summer is here.

I decide to hang back and wait for the masses to clear before gathering my things. As I make my way to the door, some kids linger in the room a few paces behind me. They're loudly talking about a party at the beach tonight, making the corners of my mouth pull into a smile. There's always a beach party to kick off summer. I guess you could say it's a Jessup High School tradition—even though Jessup High School is nowhere near the beach.

The city of Oviedo doesn't have much to offer in the entertainment department. Our options are a mall with more murals of storefronts than actual stores… and orange groves.

So, the forty-minute drive to the coast is well worth it.

My dad and I live on three acres in the neighboring town of good ole Chuluota, Florida. Oviedo may only have a depressing mall, but Chuluota only has Chuluota's Food N' Stuff. It's basically a cross between a grocery store and a concession stand, but it's our staple, and we're proud of it.

There are still a few people cleaning out their lockers by the time I leave the classroom. It's an odd feeling knowing I'll never walk these halls as a junior again. Next year, the school will proudly hang banners of light blue and black that read: "Class of 2004, Hear Us Roar!" It makes more sense when you know our mascot is a lion. I may not have much school spirit, but the school is practically dripping with it.

Austin and Leah head in my direction as I make my way down the hallway. Leah moved here six months ago and has quickly become one of my best friends. Between her clothes and her personality, she always has a way of brightening the grim high school experience.

I smile as I watch her skip to me wearing a tie-dye jacket with matching sneakers, she likely made herself. Compared to my plain black shirt and jeans, she looks like she's made of happiness and rainbows—and she practically is. Her blonde curls, dazzling smile, and sparkling, blue eyes can brighten anyone's day.

Austin's style is more reserved, like mine. His clean-cut, light-brown hair goes perfectly with his baby blue polo and khakis. He's quiet most of the time. I guess you can say he and I are similar in that way, too. Our conversations usually end before they begin.

From the other end of the hallway, Leah yells, "Paige! It's summer!" She never has the patience to wait until we're at a normal speaking distance to begin a conversation. It's one of the things I love about her, though. And I've learned to just wait for her to get to me before answering.

Once Leah bounds up to me, I answer her with a grin. "It's summer."

Even though we're both looking forward to the break, our excitement stems from completely different places. She's ready for summer because "academia is limiting her life," while I look forward to a break from the high school social hierarchy that *is* Leah's life.

"So, a few of us are going to the beach tonight. Want to come?" *A few of us* is her way of making sure I'll go. I know by *a few of us*, she means at least the kids who sit at our lunch table—and all the tables surrounding it.

"Sounds fun," I answer, even though I'm not convinced. Parties are hypothetically great—emphasis on *hypothetically*.

The junior year comes to a close with a final slam of my locker, and I sling my backpack over my shoulder. Leah hooks her arm through mine and tries to make me skip with her down the hallway. I let out a laugh, but I don't budge.

We walk outside where the rest of the gang waits for us. Josh, Anna, and Luke stand in the middle of the courtyard, all talking about the party tonight, too.

Josh McCormick is the Joey to my Phoebe—we watch a lot of *Friends*. He and I met when I first moved to Florida over three years ago. My dad had no idea what to do with a teenage daughter, so as any responsible father would, he tried to pawn me off on a teenage boy. To be fair, my dad has known Josh's parents for years, but he's also the only kid on our street who's my age. I think my dad saw him as a Hail Mary. He pretended to need Josh's help with everything that first summer, hoping he would pull me out of my shell. It was awkward at first, but my father's scheme ultimately worked.

Standing over six feet tall and made of lean muscle, there's no doubt Josh is a ladies' man. He's good-looking, I guess, but it's safe to say that we've only ever seen each other platonically. The idea of us being anything more than friends is… well, gross.

We still have a small habit of doing everything together. Looking back at that first summer, it's funny remembering how much of a nuisance I thought he was. Luckily, he's matured since then… a little.

I hate to say it, but Luke, on the other hand, still annoys me. This has less to do with his maturity level and more to do with his unyielding, unwanted infatuation with me. It would be one thing if he just had a crush on me, but everyone *knows* he has a crush on me, and that somehow makes it so much worse. He gives me a head nod as we walk up, but I'm not sure if he's greeting me or just trying to get his shaggy blond hair out of his eyes.

His gaze shifts to the ground after we make eye contact, but he peeks up at me. "Um… hey, Paige. Will you be there tonight?" he asks as he smooths down the front of his hair.

I keep my voice casual as I answer, always determined not to lead him on or give him the wrong idea. "I think so. How about you?"

This is a stupid question, but I ask it anyway for the sake of being polite. Luke has gone to every get-together with our group of friends this year.

"Of course! Are you kidding? It'll be awesome. I was talking to Dan last night, and he said they'll have a bonfire."

Rocking back on my heels, I nod to Luke's excitement. Dan is his older cousin who lives at the beach. I'm not sure how old he is exactly, but it's old enough to make me question his hanging out with high schoolers. He knows Luke has a thing for me, so every time I'm around them, he tries to foster our nonexistent relationship.

The six of us make our way to the parking lot where a few beat-up trucks and cars are still parked. Most of the people who live here are the type of people who wake up extra early on Sundays to go fishin' before church, so my 1991 Ford pickup with its faded red paint and rust on the back fender fits in just fine. I thought I would hate driving a truck, but in this town, I'd stick out more driving something small and quiet.

Anna is the only one with a newer car, and she always seems to flaunt it in subtle ways. She likes to flaunt most things. Anything from her salon-bleached hair to daisy dukes. Even now she twirls the keys to her new Honda around her freshly manicured finger for everyone to see.

She makes a point not to look at me as we all stand in the parking lot. Anna pines over Luke for reasons I'll never understand, so she probably thinks I'm the reason they haven't ridden off into the sunset together. If only she knew how happy I'd be if she took him off my hands.

I'm considering how to divert his attention to her when she eyes Luke with a flirtatious smile. "Hey, Luke. Do you think you can give me a ride to the beach tonight?"

She holds her breath in anticipation, and I hope he'll indulge her. As much as I think Anna is high maintenance, she's a bombshell, which is why every guy at our school is into her.

Any guy except Luke apparently.

His eyes flicker in my direction before answering, and she catches it. She only lets her face fall for a moment before she recovers, showing us her award-winning smile.

I have a feeling he's hoping I'll twirl my hair and say I need a ride too—which I do, but that's beside the point.

Luke gives Anna a half-hearted smile. "Yeah, I can give you a ride."

Her face lights up. "Thanks! Give me a call, and we can figure out what time. See you guys later!" As Anna walks to her car, she repeatedly presses the unlock button. Her headlights flash, making them look more like two attention-seeking strobe lights.

Leah sneaks an eyeroll in my direction, and I stifle a laugh.

With no desire to stay at school longer than necessary, I turn to everyone and wave. "I'm going to head home, too. I'll see you tonight!" Halfway to my truck, I turn around and call out to Josh. "Hey Josh, want to ride together since I'm on the way?"

He's in the middle of a conversation with Austin, but he throws me a thumbs-up without looking my way.

He knows all too well how much I hate parking my truck at crowded parties. Someone always blocks me in, and I usually want to leave early.

Turning back around, I head toward my truck, feeling Luke's gaze on my back the entire way.

☠ ☠ ☠

Our gravel driveway crunches under my truck's tires as I pull up to our quaint two-story ranch house. I cut the engine and the radio along with it. The silence that follows is one of the things that's great about living here. It's always quiet out in the country.

The wood-grain front door creaks as I push it open, adding to the house's charm. Setting my keys down on the entryway table, I step around the staircase. My dad sits on the edge of the couch in the family room watching television. Decked out in all things Under Armor, he always dresses more like one of the players than the sports analyst he is.

He greets me with his eyes glued to the screen. "Hey there, kiddo."

I sit in the massive recliner next to the couch and say, "Hey."

"How was the last day of school?"

"It was okay. Nothing special. A few of us are going to the beach tonight if that's okay." The irony of my using Leah's sneaky *few of us* isn't lost on me.

He nods, still not breaking his gaze. "Sure thing. Riding with Josh?"

"Yup," I answer with a nod of my head.

On more than one occasion, Josh has come over to hang out with me, only to end up on our couch yelling at the Miami Dolphins with my father.

Dad holds sports above all else, and I sometimes wonder if that's the reason his marriage suffered. My parents divorced when I was six. I had spent most of my life living with my mom. She's a great mom, just a little all over the place and a lot over the top. For most of my childhood, my mother dictated when I would see my dad, which only amounted to a couple of weekends a year.

For my thirteenth birthday, I told her I wanted to visit my dad for the summer. She let me go with the constant reminder that she was "just a phone call away" and could come to get me early if I wanted her to.

After that first summer, I decided to stay a little longer. Now, over three years later, my mom has finally given up on the idea of me living in Atlanta again. As much as I used to make fun of this dinky, country town, I can't bring myself to leave it.

I head upstairs to put my school stuff in my room. Opening the door, I take a moment to admire the natural light that pours in through the back window. Decorating isn't exactly my dad's strong suit, so my room is simple, but I wouldn't change it. Setting my backpack on my twin-size bed, I admire the books on their mounted shelves. Dad says I'll make the shelves too heavy if I keep it up, but I don't buy it. They're bookshelves; they're literally *made* to hold books.

In my adjoined bathroom, I study myself in the mirror. Leaving the windows down on my drive home left my hair a little wild. I lazily comb my fingers through it, not wanting to do anything requiring actual effort, and it eventually calms down. My hair falls to the middle of my back with ends that curl. I was blonde when I was younger, but over time my roots have gradually gotten darker. The natural ombre makes it look like I spend more time at the beach than I do.

Heading back downstairs, I try to think of what to cook for dinner. Ever since I moved here, I've been the one to cook most nights. It was either that, or my father's bachelor diet of Hot Pockets and Pizza Rolls would have killed me by now.

"Hey, what do you want for dinner?" I ask him, leaning over the back of the couch.

He finally pulls his attention away from the television and turns to me with a grin. He always acts like the only thing he lives for is his next meal, and I love that about him. He always seems happy regardless of his workload, too. He's never in front of the TV without a notepad and pen, taking notes on everything happening in the world of sports. He has his dream job, but it doesn't leave much time for anything else.

"I trust the chef!" He gestures toward me with both hands, making me laugh.

I think for a minute and remember the large pot of pasta sauce I made earlier this week. My mother, being the Italian woman she is, made sure I knew how to make her sauce by the age of ten. I used to dread the mandatory cooking lessons, but now I'm grateful for them, and I think my dad is, too. When I told him I knew how to make her famous recipe, he had me cook only that for two weeks straight.

Tonight, we agree on a simple spaghetti dinner. Just as the water starts to boil, the house phone rings behind me, and I reach for it.

"Hello?"

"Hey, Paige!" Leah's bubbly voice comes rushing out of the phone.

"Hey, what's up?"

She starts rambling, her words almost unintelligible. "I'm pretty sure Luke has a plan to make a move on you tonight. I heard him talking to Josh and Austin about it, and when I walked up to them, they all got quiet. Dan is probably in on it, too. I don't know what they're going to do, but I'm sure it involves you and Luke having some *alone time.*"

My forehead falls against the wall, and I let out a groan. I guess my response isn't good enough for her because she presses further.

"So, what are you going to do about it?"

I shrug even though she can't see me. "Try not to let it happen, I guess?"

"Just stick with me. I got you, girl!" She's bounced back to her usual self.

I laugh knowing Leah will likely be the life of the party, and I'll be lucky if I see her at all tonight. "Josh might be a better bet."

I can hear the smile in her voice as she answers. "You might be right." She giggles knowingly and says, "We'll figure it out. I just figured you should know. See you tonight!"

I'm still laughing a little as I say goodbye and hang up the phone.

Tossing a box of spaghetti into the pot, I run upstairs to check my email, expecting I'll have at least one from my mother. She would never admit it, but I know she doesn't want to call the house and get my father on the line instead of me. My old computer comes to life, and I see the email from her in bold, unread lettering.

Paige,

Congrats on ending the school year with honor roll! I'm so proud of you. Let me know how you're doing and what you've been up to.

TTYL Mom

I'm thankful this email doesn't take twenty minutes to read like her last one and write back a few lines of text.

Mom,

Thank you! Dad and I are fine. I'm going to a beach party later tonight with Josh, Leah, and a few other people. I'll let you know how it goes. How's everything with Trevor?

Xo Paige

Trevor married my mother a year and a half ago. He's a nice guy, I guess. He's a loving, doting husband like she deserves, but he's a little bland—like if oatmeal were a person. My mother may be many things but unattractive is not one of them. Trevor doesn't care much for sports; I think that's what sealed the deal for her.

I make it back downstairs just as the water threatens to boil over. Tilting my head back, I test one of the noodles and call out to dad that the food is ready.

Dad and I eat together the same way we always do. He goes on about something sports related as if I'll understand, and I nod along, pretending to understand. Once we're done, I hurry upstairs to get ready for the bonfire. Josh will probably be here any minute, so I leave on my same outfit from earlier and add a touch of mascara.

Grabbing my babysitting money from a few weeks ago, I run downstairs to find Josh standing in the kitchen—overly punctual as usual.

"You're early," I say, a little out of breath from running down the stairs.

"I'm on time," he corrects, and I playfully roll my eyes at him.

"You've got to respect a guy who doesn't keep a girl waiting," Dad chimes in as he dries one of our dinner plates.

Josh raises his eyebrows as if to say, *See?* He tosses his keys in the air and catches them. "Let's get going. I don't want to miss anything."

I hear a hint of irony in his voice, and I have a feeling he's thinking of the plan involving Luke. There's no way I'm going to this party without knowing what to expect.

Giving my dad a quick kiss on the cheek, I follow Josh out the door.

His grey Chevy Silverado sits on the gravel driveway out front. Yes, Josh drives a Chevy. I try not to hold it against him… too much.

"Hop on in!" He yells when I hesitate to open the truck door.

"Are you sure you don't want to drive my truck?"

Without missing a beat, he says, "Hell no. I can't be seen driving a Ford." He fastens his seatbelt and stares at me expectantly. "Now, hurry up and get in. Like I said, I don't want to miss anything." His last words are followed by a mischievous grin that makes me uneasy.

Rolling my eyes, I get into the passenger seat and brace myself for the night ahead.

2

Josh makes sure not to drive over the front yard as he turns his truck around. His Silverado bumps its way down the driveway, the sun brightening and dimming as the rays shine through the canopy of trees overhead. Just before turning onto the main road, I catch sight of our mailbox. Rust speckles the black metal now, but *Lawson,* painted in my childhood writing is still visible.

I was eight when my mom brought me to see my dad that weekend. He never tried as hard as she did when it came to planning things for us to do, but I never cared. I always had fun at his house. For this visit, I remember my mother had recently put in a custom mailbox for our house in Atlanta. Looking back now, it was gaudy, but being eight at the time, I commented to my dad that his mailbox was boring in comparison. That same day, he took me out to get all the paint colors I wanted. When we came home, we decorated the mailbox together. It's one of my favorite memories, and considering the mailbox still stands, it must be one of his, too.

Josh bops his head along to *Carry on Wayward Son*. Another reason he and my father seem to get along so well. They both share the same taste in music despite the generation gap.

I watch, waiting for him to come out with Luke's plan. We usually share everything, so it's annoying that he hasn't mentioned it.

He glances my way with furrowed brows. "What's your problem?"

Letting out a sigh, I cut to the chase. "Leah said she overheard you and the guys talking about something?" The words come out more like an accusation than a question.

"Huh." He looks out the window to hide his smirk, but I can see his face in the reflection of the glass. He thinks he's hilarious.

I prompt him again. "Something that involves me?"

"It's nothing," he says as he looks back at me with a grin.

Studying him, I frown. "Listen, if I'm getting ambushed tonight, I think I deserve a heads up."

He leans back with both eyebrows raised. "Ambushed?"

Throwing my hands in the air, I say, "You don't even like Luke! Why are you helping him?"

The corner of his mouth pulls into a knowing smile. "I never said I was helping him. I just told him the truth." He focuses in front of him as he turns onto the main road.

Refusing to back down, I ask, "And what truth is that?"

A sly smile creeps across his lips. "That you've filed a restraining order against his stalker-ass."

My mouth falls open. Luke annoys me, but he's still a good guy.

Not to mention, he's a little on the sensitive side.

Last year, Luke hadn't filled out yet. He was still lanky and awkward like most middle schoolers and a few of the guys were making fun of him for it. He had laughed along with them, but I could see it bothered him. That was when I told the guys to knock it off. It wasn't a big deal, but now that I think about it, that incident probably started Luke's crush. Maybe I shouldn't have gotten involved.

I can just picture the look on his face when he thinks I've filed a restraining order against him. He'd be so hurt.

"Josh, that's mean! You can't do that to him. I can't believe you—" I cut my sentence short at the sound of his bellowing laughter, realizing he's joking.

My eyes narrow, and I look for something to throw at him. I only see an old, half-drunken water bottle, but it'll do.

"Hey!" He tries to dodge the bottle but fails as it smacks him in the shoulder. He gapes at me, wide-eyed. "Can't you see I'm driving?"

The corners of my mouth twitch, glad I hit him. "You deserved it." He glances at me, so I redirect his gaze to the windshield with a point of my finger. "Hey, pay attention to the road."

He rubs his shoulder where the bottle hit. "If I can manage the rest of the trip without being assaulted."

He stays quiet for a moment, and I know he's hoping I'll drop this. We've known each other long enough for him to know better, though.

"Josh," I push.

He rolls his eyes hard enough to make his head fall back. "Alright, fine!" Straightening in his seat, he says, "You already know Luke likes you." His eyes flicker in my direction to make sure I'm following.

I am.

"Well, Dan is going to try to help him tonight," he says with a shrug.

My lips purse at the thought of trying to avoid Dan and Luke all night. "What does that mean *help him*?" I ask.

Josh pauses, carefully gauging my reaction. He takes a deep breath and says, "It's not exactly a master plan—it is Dan, after all—but he'll ask the two of you to collect more firewood at some point."

I imagine being in the woods…alone…with Luke.

No, thank you.

"I'll just tell him I don't want to go," I say with a shrug as I look out the window at the passing trees.

Josh gives me a pointed look. "I know how Dan can be, and I know how you are. You'd probably marry Luke before you'd stand up to Dan's stupid-ass."

I give him a heavy-lidded stare, unamused by the picture he's painting. "Okay, that's dramatic."

A breath of laughter leaves his lips as he gives me a sideways glance. "You're telling me you're going to stand up to Dan?"

I picture Dan, tall and ominous, as he towers over me with his arms crossed. The thought alone makes me swallow my nerves. "Well, I guess this will be interesting," I say, surrendering to my fate.

He's quiet for a moment, and I can tell he's weighing the options in his head.

Finally, he says, "Don't go."

His response catches me off guard. "What?"

"Don't go," he says again.

I turn in the passenger seat, looking at him head-on. "Isn't that what I just said?"

He gives me a leveling look. "*You* won't be able to turn Dan down, but I can."

I mull it over in my mind. "Okay...?" The corners of my mouth dip as I consider how tonight will go. "What are you thinking?"

He drums his fingers on the steering wheel before shrugging. "I'll go instead. No offense, Paige, but you're a wimp." He flexes one arm as he steers the truck with the other. "I'll just have to be careful not to get these guns too close to the flames." He watches me, hoping I'll fawn over his oh-so-clever comment. When I roll my eyes, he brushes it off. Josh is never embarrassed and never discouraged.

Don't get me wrong, Josh has muscles in all the right places, but I'll never tell him that. I feel like it's my civic duty to keep his ego in check.

It seems like I've failed, though. He's currently wearing a tank top that reads, "Suns Out, Guns Out."

His words replay in my head, and I wonder if Dan will argue with him on the matter. The two already hate each other. The thought sends more anxiety bubbling in my stomach, but I try to ignore it. I try to just be thankful for my best friend stepping up and hope that tonight will be fun.

☠　☠　☠

Unfamiliar cars and trucks pack the beach parking lot. I see a few bumper stickers I recognize from school, but word of this party has spread.

Josh lets out a slow whistle. "Little crowded, huh?"

My eyes scan for a space in the gravel lot. "Yeah, just a little," I mutter sarcastically.

Finally, Josh manages to park his truck. I'm not convinced it's an actual parking space, though. Worn gravel makes up most of the lot, but we're on a raised grassy median at the end of a row.

He throws the truck in park, opens the door, and hops out. As he's about to close the driver's side door, he notices I'm still fastened in my seat.

I peer over the dashboard. "I don't think this is a spot."

He rests his arm on the doorframe, and his next words come out slow and deliberate. "Paige, get out of the truck."

Twisting to unbuckle, I say, "Fine, but if you get a ticket, don't say I didn't warn you."

I can practically hear him rolling his eyes as he closes the driver's side door. "Yes, Mom."

Meeting him on the other side of the truck, I nudge him. We walk through the maze of overparked cars until we finally see the ocean in front of us. Regardless of the early hour, the party has already taken over the beach. I feel like I'm walking through the school cafeteria. The only difference is that everyone here is half-naked and three-fourths drunk.

Where the white, fluffy sand becomes wet and packed, a large bonfire takes up most of the ocean view. The flames blaze tall even though we still have some lingering daylight. I can only imagine how bright it will look once the sun sets.

As we pad through the deep sand, shoes in hand, the music selection changes from group to group, with everyone playing their version of "great music." I hardly see anyone without a red cup filled with some type of alcohol. Imagining what would happen if the cops showed makes my heart pound. Josh has told me more than once that my "worst-case scenario" outlook on life holds me back, but I like to think it saves me a lot of trouble.

"Don't go too far," I whisper as I catch a glimpse of Luke's blonde hair headed our way.

"Why?" he says with a blank expression, and I know he's trying to make me panic. I only have time to shoot him a pointed stare before Luke comes running up to us.

"Hey, Paige! Isn't this great?"

Josh answers the question for me. "Yeah, man. It's great." He doesn't look at Luke. He has his eyes on the bonfire. I try to look more enthusiastic than I feel. Even though Josh and I have a plan, the task of dodging Luke and Dan all night still weighs on my mind.

Just when it starts to feel awkward with the three of us standing there, I'm relieved to see Leah practically skipping up to us. "Paige!" She crashes into me with a hug. "Hey, Josh!" She greets him over my shoulder, her arms still around my neck.

A grin spreads across my face. I can already feel Leah's excitement rubbing off on me. "Who else is here?" I ask, letting go of her.

"Just about everyone! It's still early, so I'm sure more are on the way." She grabs my hand and pulls me toward the massive group by the water. "You have to see this party, Paige!"

As she drags me to the crowded beach, I glance over my shoulder at Josh and Luke. I try to give Josh an apologetic look for leaving him with one of his least favorite people, but he still narrows his eyes at me as I'm dragged away.

Near the shore, I can see what Leah meant. I didn't recognize most of the cars in the parking lot, and I don't recognize most of the people here.

Leah interrupts my observation when she asks if Josh told me about Luke's plan.

"Yeah, it's dumb," I say.

This doesn't dissuade her. Her blue eyes widen with anticipation. "Well, what is it?" She bounces on her heels, making her curls come alive with movement like a chanting audience demanding entertainment.

I finish telling her the plan, and she stops bouncing, her crowd of curls falling silent and still. She frowns. "Because you're bound to realize you've been in love with Luke this entire time thanks to voluntold manual labor?" She shakes her head. "That's an interesting theory."

I dig my toes into the cool sand. "Yeah, I don't get it. At least Josh said he'll offer to go with Luke instead."

She forms a fist like she's holding a microphone. "Josh saves the day, yet again!"

I playfully roll my eyes. "Right."

She smiles at me as we walk toward a group of familiar faces. It looks like in the time it took Leah to show me the bonfire, Josh and Luke found our other friends from school. They're with Nick, Juri, Anna, and Austin near one of the kegs. Nick and Juri are stepbrothers who look like actual brothers. With their similar facial features and black hair, you'd never know Nick's mom only married Juri's dad a couple of years ago.

From what I understand, Josh and Juri have been playing sports together their whole lives. They're almost too competitive, though. I think that's why Josh considers Austin his best friend even though they seem to have less in common. Austin does drumline for the school, but he lives a few streets over from us, so they've been friends since they were kids.

Anna smiles at Leah, keys twirling around a finger before her eyes overlook me entirely to settle back on Josh to continue their conversation.

Leah gives me a look, reading my mind before turning to Nick. "Where's Jenna?" she asks.

"Sick." He looks down at the red cup in his hand, swirling its contents halfheartedly. Nick and Jenna have been dating for about five months and are usually inseparable. Their relationship is how we acquired Anna in the first place, and now we have no choice but to be forever grateful.

Juri makes a sad face to mock his lovesick brother before looking up and laughing at something behind me, making him laugh. I follow his gaze over my shoulder and see a group of shirtless guys throwing around a football.

"Aw, that's cute," Juri says sarcastically. I look back at him and can see his wheels turning. Being one of the school's top athletes, I'm sure he can't resist a game.

Josh jogs toward the crowd of guys, calling out to them, "Want to make it a real game?" I always admire Josh's fearlessness when it comes to approaching people he doesn't know. I swear he can make friends anywhere. The guys in our group follow, leaving Anna, Leah, and me behind. We watch for a few minutes, but once the guys divvy into teams and start a new game, we lose interest.

"What now?" I ask.

Leah shakes her head disapprovingly. "Paige."

I stare back at her. "Leah."

"There's a great party going on! I'm sure we can find *something* to do." She holds out her arms and spins in a circle to showcase our surroundings. My eyes fall on a group of people holding up their fingers as a guy with black hair and a cocky smile calls out, "Never have I ever wanted to have sex with me!" The girls in the group cry out, pretending to take offense, before giggling and taking a drink.

I don't belong here.

The fact that I don't drink always makes me feel a little out of place at parties—especially ones with this many people.

Anna laughs at Leah's outstretched arms but keeps glancing at a group of girls a few feet away. I'm not surprised when she says, "I'll catch up with you guys later!" She waves goodbye and heads toward her fellow cheerleaders, all sitting like a model might pose for a photoshoot.

I glance over at Leah. "Do you think they're comfortable like that?"

She throws her head back with laughter. "Oh, not a chance." Her eyes wander toward them again before she shrugs. "But they look good."

I scrunch my nose a little at that, and it only makes her grin wider.

The setting sun casts long stretching shadows that mirror our movements. People take shots and roast marshmallows near the fire, so we decide to head back that way.

A blond guy who just graduated from our school walks over to one of the coolers and opens it. From where I'm standing, I can see countless brightly colored, individually capped Jell-O shots. Leah trots over when the guy offers to share, but I hang back.

Looking around, my eyes land on Josh and Luke who have already stopped playing football. Josh winks at me, and I know he's following Luke in case there's a sudden need for a couple of amateur lumberjacks.

My stomach flips.

Their scheme may be juvenile, but it still makes me uncomfortable.

"Done with football?" My voice reveals some of my surprise. I know Josh could easily play all night.

"Yeah, got sick of playing," Luke answers in a matter-of-fact tone as he dusts the sand off his pants. I catch Josh looking back at the game as he rubs his palm over his chest before half-heartedly agreeing.

As if on cue, Dan comes out of nowhere. Even with a party this size, he usually stands out in a crowd. I'm always thrown off by how much older he looks compared to the rest of us, his black goatee and buzzcut giving him a rugged look. His dark eyes add years to his age, putting him aesthetically in his late twenties when he must be only a few years older than us. With a diamond stud in one ear and the skull tattoo on his forearm, he's the opposite of Luke in every way.

The tattoo only shows the skull from the nose up. Where the teeth should be are thick black lines in the shape of an X, giving off the vibe that the skull is sworn to secrecy. Even though I've seen Dan and his tattoo countless times, my eyes always find their way to his forearm.

Dan tilts his cup back, emptying it. "Is this a killer party, or what?"

"Hell, yeah. Thanks for setting up the fire pit." Luke nods over his shoulder to the flames, and my heart sinks. The once-high flames are already dwindling. I stare up at Josh for any sign of reassurance, but he isn't looking at me. He keeps his gaze locked on Dan; his mouth set in a hard line.

Dan's eyes meet mine, a Cheshire Cat smile on his lips. "Well, hello, Paige." There's nothing wrong with his smile, but it gives me an empty feeling in the pit of my stomach.

"Hello," is all I can bring myself to say.

His harsh gaze gives the impression that he can see straight through me. I shudder at the thought of him knowing anything I'm thinking right now. Unfortunately, he takes notice of my involuntary shiver, and his smile widens.

"Hey, Luke. Paige looks cold. Why don't the two of you get some wood to bring this fire back to life?"

"I'm not cold," I blurt, hating that I let him get to me.

Dan considers me carefully with a slow arch of his brow. The way he's looking at me makes me wish I wouldn't have said anything at all. "The fire's still dying."

I swallow the lump in my throat. Here it is, the moment capable of ruining the entire evening. I freeze, waiting for Josh to intervene. The mention of gathering firewood snaps Josh back to reality. He turns away from Dan to look down at Luke. "Why don't I come with you instead? I can carry more, anyway." He sneaks me a wink, and I grin up at him, desperately hoping he'll be able to see the thanks behind my eyes.

Dan clenches his jaw and shakes his head. "She'll be fine. We don't need much."

Luke's wide eyes flicker between them as he watches their exchange.

"No," Josh waves his hand as if offering a favor. "Why make the girl work? She's at a party. Have fun, Paige. I'll help them."

Before Dan or Luke can argue with him further, I back toward the bonfire and call out, "Thanks! I'll see you guys later," with a wave.

I turn and try not to listen to the instant arguing that breaks out behind me. After creating enough distance between us, I glance over my shoulder. They're headed toward the woods. Luke stands in the middle with his shoulders slumped while Dan and Josh have a heated argument over his head. My mouth goes dry, and the emptiness that plagued my stomach is now filled with a knot.

I take a seat next to the dying flames. There are a lot of things I would rather eat than a hotdog, but for the sake of looking busy, I put one on a skewer.

My eyes land on the crackling flames in front of me, and my mind wanders. Maybe it would be easier if I were blunt with Luke. Maybe it would be better if I flat-out tell him it's never going to happen—that I only see him as a friend. I abandon the thought as soon as I play the scene out in my head. I hate conflict, and I know as soon as Luke looks at me with wounded eyes, the guilt would probably make me ask *him* out.

I'm pulled from my thoughts when I realize I'm no longer alone. Out of the corner of my eye, I see someone sitting next to me. A guy with dark brown hair. His eyes are on the flames like mine had been a moment ago. Unknown Guy must sense me staring at him because he glances at me and flashes a small smile.

Taking a closer look, I see that he's roasting a hotdog. And that I'm no longer roasting a hotdog? Did he—no, I would have noticed, right? Sure enough, he holds the now-roasted hotdog that had been in my hands only moments ago. I look down to double-check. Empty. When I look back at him, my eyes are wide. *How did he do that without me noticing?*

He looks at my face apologetically. "It was too easy." He goes to hand me back the skewer, but I shake my head.

"It's okay. I'm not hungry."

Shrugging, he says, "If you insist." With that, he pulls the hotdog off the stick and places it in a bun, finishing it in a matter of bites. "You know," he says, still half chewing. He swallows before finishing his thought. "You should pay attention to what's going on around you. There are a lot of people here."

I shoot him a side-long glance. "Well, I didn't think anyone would have the audacity to steal my hotdog."

The corner of his mouth quirks. "That's fair." Before I can say anything else, he leans forward and looks around me for something. "You didn't have a purse, did you?"

I shake my head. "No, why?"

Resting his elbows on his knees, he says, "Just making sure someone didn't come by and grab it while you were *away*." He taps his temple as he says this. The stranger holds his hand out for me to shake. "Fredrick Pryce."

I meet his outstretched hand and offer my name politely in return. "Paige Lawson."

He nods and looks back at the fire. His gaze doesn't break from the smoldering flames when he speaks again. "Are your friends the ones in charge of this?"

Something in his voice makes me want to say no, but I can't figure out why. I look around at the large crowd of people and answer truthfully. "I don't think anyone is in charge of this, but I guess you could say my friends helped."

"Then why are you alone?" He shifts his attention back to me, and the intensity of his stare has my mouth opening and no words coming out. He has the type of eyes that draw you in, and I can only break away when he looks back at the flames.

I pause. Honestly, I'm not sure why I'm alone. When Leah went to do shots, I could have gone with her. "I like being alone," I say with a shrug.

His expression hardens as he stares into the dying flames, the light ricocheting off him. "You don't know what kind of people hang around here. You shouldn't be alone at a party this big."

This snaps me out of my daze. Who does he think he is? I don't even know this guy, and now he's telling me what I should and shouldn't do. To avoid rolling my eyes, I glare back into the flames. "I'll keep that in mind."

I can feel him looking at me again, but I'm determined to ignore him. Eventually, he mutters under his breath, "Better hope no one wants your twenty."

I sit up straight and frown at him. "How do you know I have cash on me?"

Raising his eyebrows expectantly, his gaze drops to my hip.

My eyes follow his, and sure enough, my folded twenty hangs halfway out of my pocket. Shoving the cash down deeper, I look up to find him watching me intently.

He's extremely good-looking. It surprises me that it wasn't the first thing I noticed about him. Then again, I was a little preoccupied with the fact that he had stolen my hotdog. But now, I let my eyes scan over him, noting his short, mussed hair and his jawline that could cut glass. How one moment his molten brown eyes hold more warmth than the fire before us, and then the next, they look colder than the deepest depths of the ocean. There's something foreboding in those eyes as they reflect the illuminating flames, but it doesn't give me a feeling of unease. If anything, it makes him more intriguing.

I find it odd that he's wearing jeans. His t-shirt may have a beach-worthy boating logo, but most people would never wear jeans to the beach.

I realize my eyes are moving over him, lingering shamelessly, and my cheeks flush. "Well, I appreciate the help, but I doubt anyone here would have stolen from me."

If he noticed my staring, he hides it well. He looks down at his hands and mutters, "You'd be surprised."

Unsure of what to say, I face the fire, and he does the same. Neither of us says anything for a while. The pointedness of our silence stands out in contrast to the party going on around us. The fact that we're not talking makes me anxiously trace my finger through the sand. When I can't take it anymore, I blurt out, "So, what school do you go to?"

Fredrick looks at me with mild surprise as if he had forgotten I was sitting next to him. "This was my last year."

"Here? You live close by?"

"Yeah," he says. "What about you guys?" With a nod of his head, he gestures to the group of kids I recognize from school dancing to country music.

"Oviedo." It's always easier to say I'm from Oviedo because even though most people have never heard of it, even fewer people have heard of Chuluota.

The edge of his mouth pulls up into a smirk. "Figures."

I raise my eyebrows but can't help smiling at his reaction. "What's that supposed to mean?"

"I'm familiar with Oviedo," he says with another glance at the group dancing. "People who go out of their way to throw this big of a party at the beach are rarely from the beach."

I think about that for a moment. "I guess that makes sense."

The sound of Josh and Luke's familiar voices gets my attention. Looking over my shoulder, I see them walking back with piles of wood and get up to help.

"Where's Dan?" My voice sounds breathless as I grab a large log from Josh's pile.

His words come out more like a growl. "Ended up not coming with us."

I toss my log onto the fire and watch the sparks float to the now-darkened sky.

"Why?" I ask as he throws his log onto the fire. I have to step back to avoid the explosion of sparks.

Josh shrugs, but his movements are tense. "Had something more important to do, I guess." His eyes are ruthless, and the knot in my stomach returns. Maybe I should have gone instead. It would have been better than Josh having a short fuse for the rest of the night.

Luke slowly makes his way up to the fire with his two smaller logs. Josh walks away without offering to help, leaving me standing alone in front of Luke.

"Here," I say as I grab the top log.

"Thanks, Paige." He sounds defeated and out of breath.

Once we throw the new wood on the fire, the flames reach for the sky once more. The heat sweeps across my face, forcing me to step back a few feet.

Suddenly, I remember I had been talking to Fredrick and turn to look where we were sitting, but he's gone. My eyes scan the party for him until I spot him walking along the water.

Even from a distance, he intrigues me. I can't help studying him, my head tilting slightly. His shoulders are tense, his hands are in his pockets, and he keeps his head down. His walk somehow seems casual yet determined, and I want to know where he's going.

Luke's voice behind me pulls my attention back to the present, but I can't tear my eyes away from Fredrick. "I'm glad Josh offered to help. He's right, you should be able to enjoy the party. I don't know why Dan wanted to ask you of all people."

Maybe it's because I know he's lying, or maybe it's because he's Luke, but I mutter, "Yeah, Josh is great. I'll talk to you later." Without looking back, I hurry to catch up with the hotdog thief.

I have to jog to catch up to him. "Hey, why did you leave?" When I look at him, I realize his eyes are tense, leaving his expression hard. He doesn't stop to talk to me, so I struggle to keep up with his long strides.

"You had company." He uses the same matter-of-fact voice as earlier.

"I know…I'm sorry, should I have introduced you?"

He stops and pivots so that he's blocking my path. I nearly crash into him, stumbling back on my heels. The added closeness makes me feel like the air around us has been pulled away by the waves. I take a step back to clear my head, but it doesn't work.

He hesitates but says, "No." Shaking his head, he adds, "And don't apologize." His face relaxes, but something behind his eyes remains on edge.

"Then why did you walk away?"

He glances at the fire pit and runs a hand through his hair.

I'm not asking him anything difficult. I know his silence shouldn't get to me. I don't even know him, but my fingernails still dig into my palms as I wait for him to say something. "You know what, forget it," I turn to go back to the fire alone.

With one giant step, he cuts me off. "What are you doing?"

Caught off guard, I blink up at him. "Going back to the fire." I try to sidestep around him only to have him block me again.

"I'll come with you."

My eyebrows pinch together. "Why?"

He looks over his shoulder at the flames before answering. "Because I want to."

I stare at him, waiting for a better explanation. He looks like he's about to say something but changes his mind.

When raising my eyebrows doesn't pull more from him, I huff and start back up the beach. A faint laugh echoes behind me before Fredrick matches my stride. Glaring at him, I see that even though his eyes are straight ahead, there's a trace of a smile on his lips.

When we reach the bonfire, the flames illuminate his appearance once more. This time, something around his neck catches my attention. I hadn't noticed it earlier, but now the firelight reflects against a thin gold chain. He has the necklace tucked into his shirt, and I can't help wondering what the rest of it looks like.

I push the thought aside and sit down, Fredrick taking a seat next to me. I'm surprised no one took our spots considering how many people are here. My eyes are on the flames, but he's staring at me. I can feel it.

"You're staring at me," I say as I look over at him.

"I'm looking at you," he says with a light laugh.

"Well, your version of looking is very stare-ish."

He shakes his head, a tight-lipped smile forming. "You're blunt."

I make sure not to break my eyes away from his. "Yeah, well…" My voice trails off because I'm usually not blunt. "I don't get you."

His eyes scan the party behind me before finding mine again. "You weren't alone anymore. You didn't need me."

Is he serious? "To be honest, I don't really need you now, either." *Who does this guy think he is?* I never asked for his help. And what type of name is Fredrick anyway? He's probably the only person with that name to experience working electricity and the worldwide phenomenon known as running water.

"Okay," he mutters but still doesn't leave my side.

"Who are you here with anyway?" I cross my arms as I wait for his answer.

His eyes remain on the flames as he says, "Myself." He leans back, his hands and feet outstretched. Nudging me with his foot, he says, "But now, I guess I'm here with you."

My heart jumps when his sneaker taps my leg, and I try not to let the way he's looking at me affect me. "You came to a party alone?"

He drops his gaze, shaking his head slightly. "I live here."

I take inventory of the party now that some time has passed. People are laughing, dancing, stumbling, and making out with each other. You know, the usual behavior brought on by underage drinking. It's funny how you can find yourself around so many people and still feel completely alone. I often feel like this at parties. Sobriety has a way of doing that, I guess.

A sandy-haired guy I've never seen before suddenly blocks my view. He lazily grins down at me and says, "You look miserable."

Fredrick goes from leaning back on his hands to sitting forward with his elbows on his knees. His eyes trail up to the guy passively, but he doesn't say a word.

Meeting the stranger's gaze, I say, "Well, I'm not."

He leans down, putting his mouth near my ear. I can smell the beer on his breath and wonder how many red cups he has already emptied. "Well, I promise you'd have more fun with me."

His words douse the heat of the flames, sending a chill down my spine. My body freezes, and my heart starts to race like when you're daydreaming in class, and the teacher calls on you. My cheeks flush with the embarrassment of not knowing what to say and the discomfort of being spoken to in the first place.

As this stranger straightens, his hands wrap around my wrists to pull me up with him. Frederick gets to his feet and the guy releases me to put his hands in the air. "Whoa, whoa, man. It's all good. We were just talking." Fredrick doesn't do or say anything. He just looks at the guy, but it's enough to make him step back. "You need to relax, man." He turns on the spot and stumbles away, his intoxicated feet struggling to pad through the deep sand.

I can feel Fredrick's body relax next to mine, but his eyes follow our drunken visitor even after he takes a seat again.

My jaw drops. "Uh, what was that?"

Fredrick rubs the back of his neck. "He put his hands on you."

I stare at him, at a loss for what to say. He's not wrong, but why would he care? My mouth opens, but I can't seem to land on anything coherent to say.

Josh comes up behind me. "Hey, Paige, we better get going."

My eyes find his, and even though I'm a little confused, I nod anyway. Josh usually doesn't drink at parties. He cares more about sculpting his six-pack than drinking one. It's not uncommon for us to leave parties early—usually when everyone else gets sloppy. This is early even for him, though, and I can't help wondering if his argument with Dan put him in a bad mood.

"I'll meet you by your truck in a minute." I smile at him, but his hardened facade doesn't crack.

He gives Fredrick a careful glance before adding, "Don't take too long."

When I turn back to Fredrick, he no longer looks embarrassed. His dark eyes follow Josh for a moment before he recovers and brings his gaze back to meet mine, his expression softening. "Do you think you'll be back?"

"It's the beach, and it's summer," I say as I stand up. "There's a good chance."

With a crisp nod, he says, "I guess I'll see you around, Paige

Lawson."

I don't bother stopping the smile from spreading across my face. "See you around."

With that, I turn and head toward the dark parking lot where I'll find Josh. As I walk, I try to remember where we parked. I never remember where I park. It's a problem. I'm thankful that Josh left his truck on a median because it narrows down my search. Compared to the party, the silence of the parking lot feels eerie. My heart rate speeds up as my eyes scan the rows of cars.

Once I see Josh's familiar figure leaning against his pickup, I relax a bit and hurry over to him. He greets me with a pat on the back. "Have fun tonight?"

"Yeah, I did," I say carefully. "What about you?"

"Yeah," he says curtly. His movements are stiff as he yanks open the truck door. He seems like he wants to say something but isn't sure how to say it. Josh never holds back, usually to a fault. This is weird. We never have awkward silence. We may bicker, argue, and get on each other's nerves, but we're never quiet.

Luckily, we've only been driving for a few minutes when he clears his throat. "So, I saw you talking to Fredrick."

I tilt my head. "You know him?"

"I knew him," he says, "or at least I thought I did."

I lean back against the headrest and roll my head to look at him with a sigh. "Don't be cryptic."

Josh clenches his fists around the steering wheel. "He's bad news, Paige. If you're smart, you'll stay the fuck away from him."

The anger in his voice makes my head snap up. "Why?"

"Just trust me."

I run my hands through my hair, putting it in a ponytail. "Well, if I see him at the beach this summer, I'm not going to run the other way."

"I'm serious, Paige."

I give him a pointed stare. "Me too, Josh." Shaking my head, I turn to look out the window. "You're being weird."

"Damn it, Paige, would you just listen to me for once?" His voice bites through the air between us, making my head snap back to him.

I throw my hands up in the air. "Okay! I'll probably never see him again. It's not like I'm going to go out of my way to hang out with him. What's the big deal?"

As he looks over his shoulder to change lanes, his eyes meet mine. "Just be careful. He's not someone you want to be associated with."

"Why?" The question spills out automatically.

His lips are a thin line as he turns on the radio. I know Josh won't say anything more about Fredrick, but for the entire drive home, he's all I can think about.

3

The first official day of summer vacation feels like a blank page. I turn over in my bed, blinking until my vision clears. My eyes adjust, and my alarm clock reads 9:13 a.m. Sounds about right. Regardless of how late I stay up, I usually can't hibernate for twelve hours like some of my friends can. It's like my body has an internal alarm clock. Even when I have the perfect opportunity to get hours of uninterrupted sleep, my body insists I be productive no later than 9 a.m. I guess I should be thankful for the extra thirteen minutes.

I roll over and stare at the ceiling. The house is quiet, letting me know Dad has already left for work.

Getting out of bed, I head into the bathroom to brush my tangled mess of hair. After the bonfire last night, I took a shower but was too tired to dry my hair. Now, I'm stuck dealing with the consequences of my poorly thought-out actions. Going to bed with wet hair is never a good idea. My usually tame waves have broken into a full-blown rebellion.

When I finally tame the tangled mess, I look out the small circular window in the bathroom. The sun has decided to stay out of sight today. To replace it, thick white clouds take over the sky, meaning only one thing, rain.

I make my way downstairs to get something to eat. In the pantry, my limited options are peanut butter, cereal, or a few cans of Campbell's soup that have probably been on this shelf since before I was born. I don't have any plans today, and with the weather looking bleak, I add grocery shopping to the docket.

The kitchen holds a serene atmosphere as I eat my bowl of cereal. I don't think my dad is ever home without the television on, but I like the quiet. This is my favorite time of day to be home. On sunny days light pours through the window over the kitchen sink, giving the entire room a golden glow, but this morning the dark kitchen matches the gloom outside.

The wooden stairs feel cool against the bottoms of my feet as I set out to get my day started. Today's shopping list expands further than what Chuluota's Food N' Stuff can offer, so I'll have to go into Oviedo for Publix. I want to get my shopping done first. On the off chance it doesn't rain today, at least the rest of my afternoon will be free. This is Florida, after all. Here, the weather forecast of heat, humidity, and rain is to be expected.

Throwing on a pair of denim shorts and a black tank top, I put my hair in a ponytail, grab two twenties from the jar in the kitchen, and head out.

☠   ☠   ☠

I wander through the store, making sure to hit every aisle. I'm usually strict about sticking to our grocery list, but a tub of strawberry ice cream catches my eye. It *is* the first day of summer—might as well splurge on ice cream.

Closing the freezer door and putting the tub in my cart, I hear the same smooth voice from last night.

"Paige Lawson?"

I turn to see Fredrick leaning against one of the freezer doors. His dark blue jeans are now paired with a plain white t-shirt, and I can't help appreciating the contrast of the light shirt with his dark features.

"Fredrick?" I tilt my head, feeling mildly confused. "What are you doing here?"

He walks over to my cart and raises his eyebrows expectantly. "Grocery shopping?"

My eyes scan over him. "Where's your cart?"

He puts both hands in his pockets and shrugs. "I don't need much."

"Wouldn't you go to a grocery store near the beach?" I ask with narrowed eyes.

He grabs a can of soup from a nearby shelf, studying the label as he turns it over in his hand. "Prices are cheaper here."

I doubt that. Deliberately lowering my head to stare at him, all I offer is a skeptical, "Really?"

He looks up from the can in his hand before placing it back on the shelf. "Yeah." I'm about to object further, but he cuts me off. "Mind if I join you?"

I raise my eyebrows. "You want to join me… at Publix?" It seems odd, but at the same time, there's something about him that makes me glad he asked.

He looks up and down the aisle. "You're here alone, right?"

"Um, yeah?" I don't mean for my words to come out as a question, but he seems to find my response amusing with the way his mouth quirks.

He takes the shopping list from me and says, "Good." With my list in hand, he pushes my cart down the next aisle. "Any plans this summer?"

My fingers run along the different brands of canned tomatoes on the shelf beside me, and I let out a breath of laughter. "No." He glances at me, wanting me to say more. "My summer will probably be uneventful," I offer, not sure if I should be embarrassed by the lack of excitement in my life.

He doesn't make fun of me, though. Instead, his eyebrows pull together as he asks, "Well, what do you like to do?"

"Read." My cheeks flush again. He's going to think I'm a hermit.

"Ah, she reads." I catch him glancing at me from the corner of his eye, a small smile forming on his lips.

"You don't?"

He rests his elbows on the handle as he continues to push the cart. "Oh, I do. I want to escape my reality just as much as the next person." Something darkens behind his eyes, but he shifts his gaze forward before I can study what it might mean. Muttering under his breath, he adds, "Maybe more."

Watching him, I wait for more of an explanation. When he doesn't say anything, I let my eyes trail over the many brands of packaged cookies. Dad's a sucker for Oreos, but they aren't on sale this week. Even as someone content with their reality, I read to escape, too. I think everyone does. But there's something ominous behind his words. Something I can't put my finger on.

Before I can inquire more, he asks, "What do you like about reading?"

His question catches me off guard, and I have to think before I answer. People usually ask for my favorite book, or who my favorite author is. Nobody asks why I enjoy the general act of reading. "I guess it's to have an escape… but my favorite thing is the feeling it gives me throughout the day while I'm not reading. Having the characters in the back of my mind, knowing the rest of the story is waiting for me. It's a way to feel less alone, I guess." I give him a quick glance and backpedal slightly. "I don't know if that makes sense."

Fredrick takes in my words. "I know the feeling."

His response puts me at ease, and I notice he's a lot more relaxed here than he was at the beach last night. We make our way up and down the aisles and talk about our favorite books. He loves Stephen King, which leads to me confessing how easily I get scared.

"You won't watch scary movies?" He's looking at me, bewildered.

I shake my head definitively. "Nope."

Fredrick runs his hand over his face and groans. "You're missing out on *so many* good movies."

"I'll be fine," I say as I look at the baskets of Publix fried chicken. I'm tempted to grab one because they smell amazing, but I already impulsively picked up ice cream. Even though I ate cereal this morning, the smell wafting through the store makes my stomach growl.

"Do you want to get lunch?" The words fell out of my mouth before I even realized I wanted to say them. *What is he doing to me?*

He opens his mouth like he's about to say something but stops, his expression hardening. "I can't." My face falls, and he must see it, because he quickly adds, "But one day, we're watching a scary movie. Non-negotiable."

I laugh, trying to brush off my disappointment. "No. We're not."

"It's already in motion, Paige. No stopping it now." The corner of his mouth pulls into a crooked smile, and I have to admit, the thought of watching a horror film suddenly doesn't seem so bad.

As we pass another aisle, he points over his shoulder with a trace of humor in his eyes. "Hotdogs?"

I scrunch my nose and wave him off. "No thanks, not a fan."

Fredrick cocks his head. "You're telling me the hotdog girl from the bonfire doesn't like hotdogs?"

Grimacing, I say, "Please don't tell me you think of me as *the hotdog girl.*"

His eyes are bright as he answers. "Well, not anymore. Now

that I know you're a liar."

I playfully push him away from me, and he laughs. Fredrick has the type of laugh you can't listen to without smiling.

Turning to me, he asks, "Is that everything?"

For the first time since I ran into him, I look down at the cart. The few things I had written on my list are now neatly collected. As we were talking, I never saw him put anything in the cart. My eyes jump to meet his, and I feel like he knows what I'm thinking. If he does, he doesn't say anything.

I mutter, "Yeah… that's everything," as I stare at the cart, trying to figure out when he filled it.

"Okay, let's check out." A fleeting look of amusement crosses his face. I know I didn't see him put anything in the cart. In fact, I was about to ask for my list back, so I could start shopping.

I must look as puzzled as I feel because he studies me carefully as we stand in the check-out line. "Are you okay?"

Blinking a few times, I recover and say, "Yeah, I'm fine." To my surprise, my voice sounds convincing.

The cashier barely acknowledges me, her eyes never leaving her register screen, "That'll be $34.27. Cash or card?"

"Cash," I respond, fishing the money from my pocket.

Holding out her hand, she finally looks up, glancing over me to land on Frederick. Her entire demeanor shifts as she comes off her "customer service" autopilot. Smoothing her long, blonde hair, she leans over the counter to zero in on him. The green of her apron makes her eyes pop as she pins Fredrick with a flirtatious stare. "And did you find everything you were looking for today?" She bites her lip like she's suggesting his list is incomplete without her.

I can't blame her. I'm sure most girls would want to add Fredrick to their shopping lists, but I still get the urge to roll my eyes.

To my surprise, Fredrick acts like the girl is as attractive as a middle-aged balding man, not a stunning cashier that could pass for Miss Teen USA.

He looks at me to redirect her question. "Well, Paige?"

The girl flashes her eyes in my direction, but her smile is less genuine. "Yes, ma'am. Did you find everything okay?" The way she asks makes it sound like she's saying something completely different.

"Um, yeah. Thanks," I manage to stammer as I hand her money.

She bags my items with her head down, so she can sneak peeks at Fredrick through lowered lashes. I don't think she cares if I see. I'm not usually a threat to girls as picturesque as her. Once the receipt prints, she pulls it behind the counter. I swear I see her scribble something before dropping it into the bag.

Fredrick helps me push the cart out to my truck and load the bags into the cab. After placing one onto the back seat, he stops and turns to me. "What else are you doing today?"

I give him a wry smile. "What does it matter? I thought you were busy." Before he can answer, I reach past him to grab the receipt out of the bag. Sure enough, there's a phone number in pink marker with the words:

Call me—Heidi

I show Fredrick the small piece of paper. "Heidi," is all I say.

He smiles, pushing the receipt back into my hand. "I'm good."

We both look back at the girl through the glass storefront. Sure enough, she gives Fredrick a little wave. The sight makes me roll my eyes before I can stop myself.

Fredrick doesn't seem to notice my reaction, but he abruptly asks, "Do you know what time it is?"

I lean into the truck to turn the key. The engine roars to life, and the clock on my radio lights up. I read, "12:15. Why?"

At the sound of my answer, Fredrick recklessly tosses the bags into my truck, causing items to spill all over my backseat. "Shit, I'm late."

I stare at him wide-eyed. He notices but doesn't seem to have time to explain. After making a quick mess of my backseat, he turns and gives me an earnest look. "Paige, I'm sorry. Really."

With that, he takes off down the street at a jog, rounding the corner and disappearing. I stare in the direction he went, unmoving. *What just happened?*

I listen to the radio on the way home but barely hear the music. I'm too busy comparing Fredrick's running off to Josh's warning. Is randomly running off with no explanation one of the things that makes Fredrick so terrible? I still can't decide if I should heed Josh's warning or let Fredrick set his own reputation.

I want to know how the two of them know each other. *Does Fredrick feel the same way toward Josh that Josh feels toward him?* I try to remember seeing them around each other last night, but I can't. As soon as Josh returned with the firewood, Fredrick took off down the beach. Then, when I sat down with Fredrick again, Josh immediately wanted to leave. I rack my brain, trying to figure out if it's a coincidence or correlated.

By the time I pull into the driveway, I've exhausted my thoughts. I park and open the back door of my truck, only to stand there and take in the mess. Items are strewn all over the back seat, leaving most bags empty. It looks like a tornado tore through every-thing—a tornado named Fredrick Pryce. If he had to leave that sec-ond, he could have left the bags in the cart for me to load myself. It probably would have been easier than repacking everything.

I throw the items back in the bags and storm into the house. I'm reaching up to put the flattened bread on the top shelf of the pantry when the doorbell rings. A glance out the kitchen window shows a grey Chevy Silverado parked out front. Josh has a tendency of being impatient when it comes to doorbells, so I drop everything and run to the door. By the time I reach it, he's already rung three more times.

"You're so annoying," I say as I yank the door open.

He pushes past me. "So, what are our plans for the first day of summer?"

I gesture toward the grocery bags still on the counter. "You're looking at it."

He grimaces, shaking his head in disapproval. "Only you, Paige."

Josh's mom does all the shopping in his house, so when he hears about me doing "mom chores," he thinks I'm wasting my youth. What he doesn't realize, is if I were to let my dad do the shopping, I'd be stuck eating his recipes every night. I love my fa-ther, but he thinks a good meal is one part bread, one part cheese, and two parts butter. "Yeah, I know. Only me. Do you think you can help me put them away?"

He sighs. "I knew I shouldn't have come here."

I place both hands on his back and push him toward the kitchen. At first, he resists, but I inevitably win.

Unpacking the bags, I take a deep breath and say to him over my shoulder, "I saw Fredrick at Publix."

I sneak a peek to check for his reaction, but he's just staring off at the space in front of him with furrowed brows. "What was he doing out here?"

I keep putting away groceries as I answer. "He said something about cheaper prices?"

Josh scoffs and says, "Right… because prices matter to him."

"What?" I ask, not sure what he means.

"Nothing," he shakes his head, but I have a feeling something's still bothering him. "I'm just surprised he stuck around long enough to tell you that."

That gets my attention. "What do you mean?"

"Forget it," he mutters with a shake of his head.

I hate that he won't just come out and say whatever it is. Glaring at him, I say, "Yeah, he stuck around long enough to have a full conversation with me."

He nods, making a face as if to say, *Well, good for you.* "And how did this invigorating conversation end?"

My cheeks flush, knowing the point he's about to make. Josh takes note of my reaction and points at me. "Exactly!" He doesn't help put away any of the groceries. Instead, he pushes himself up on the counter and eats unwashed grapes out of a shopping bag. "He always did that," he says, popping another grape into his mouth. "We would have plans to do something, and he would back out last minute saying something came up."

I put away my ice cream. "First of all, those grapes are dirty, and did you ever ask where he was going?"

He throws a grape in the air and catches it in his mouth. "First of all, when was the last time you heard of someone dying because of a fucking unwashed grape?" He slaps a hand on his forehead. "And damn it! I never thought of that!" Turning serious, he adds, "Of course, Paige. Do you honestly think I didn't try that?" He doesn't wait for my response but lazily pads to the living room and plops down on the couch.

I put the last few items away and follow. "So, what did he say?" I sit down in the recliner in the corner of the room.

He shrugs.

"Josh," I press.

He sighs and sits up. "He just made it clear it was none of my business."

My heart pounds at the thought of finding out what happened between them. "Is that when you guys stopped talking?"

He leans back against the couch, closing his eyes and putting his hands behind his head. "Nah, that was more of a gradual thing."

"Oh."

He squints an eye open at me. "Why so interested?"

I shift in my seat, not wanting to seem *too* interested. "I'm just trying to understand."

He sits up, and his eyes are harsh. "Don't waste your time trying to understand Fredrick Pryce."

Leaning forward, I take a moment to study him. His reactions aren't matching up with his reasons. "What aren't you telling me?"

His jaw clenches and his eyes dart past me to the window. I expect him to lash out, but he sighs and says, "You know he used to live here, right? Then, he moved out to the beach and started hanging out with some sketchy people. They're weird, too. Always picky about who they hang out with. I guess Fredrick fit the fucking mold because he dropped Austin and me and never looked back."

Not sure what to say, I mutter, "Oh." It takes me a moment, but I add, "Wait, he used to live here?"

Josh has a stony expression as he says, "Yup. We're better off without him, trust me."

He turns on the TV, and I know it's his way of ending our conversation. Something doesn't add up, but I'm not sure what else to ask without setting him off.

I don't feel like watching TV, but when I look outside, I see the inevitable summer afternoon rain has started.

Surrendering, I turn my attention to *Friends*. With two spoons and no bowls, we finish the pint of strawberry ice cream. Well, Josh hogs most of it, but I don't mind.

I can't help wondering what this afternoon would have been like if Fredrick had taken me up on my offer. I wouldn't be sitting at home, that's for sure. He and I could have gone somewhere or done something. It would have been nice to break away from the ordinary.

After watching more episodes than I'd like to admit, Josh sighs. "The rain looks like it's letting up. I should head home. Are you doing anything tonight?"

I look up at him and ask, "Does reading count?"

He crosses his arms and looks down at me. "On a Saturday night? Fuck, no. That's sad even for your lame-ass."

I laugh and throw the nearest pillow at him. "What plans do you have tonight, then?"

"I have to watch Jacob, so Austin's coming over."

"Well, at least Austin will be there with you. Have fun with the seven-year-old." Josh is great with his younger brother, but I know how much he hates to babysit.

He sighs, nodding as he walks out the door. "I'll see you later."

With Josh gone and the TV off, I'm struck by how quiet the house feels. I decide to go upstairs and check my email. Sure enough, there's a new one from Mom.

Hi Honey,

I'm glad to hear you're having fun with your friends! Yes, let me know how the beach went. Trevor and I are great! You should see the house now that it's being remodeled. It's beautiful! A lot of work, but it's beautiful! I love you and miss you a ton. Write back soon.

G2G Mom

I smile at her abbreviated sign-off. My mother makes a point of being very *hip*. When I try to think about my first day of summer and what to tell her, I find my thoughts clouded by Fredrick. I know it seems crazy, and maybe it's because I can't quite figure him out, but he's all I've been able to think about. I decide to leave this out of my email, though. Knowing my mother, she will vastly blow things out of proportion. It took her a solid two years to stop asking when Josh and I would start dating. The last thing I want to do is introduce a new male figure for her to obsess over.

Hey Mom,

I'm glad you're doing well. The beach party was a lot of fun. There was a huge bonfire, and everyone was dancing all night. Josh came over today, but we were stuck inside because of the rain. I don't have much to report other than that. Talk to you soon.

Xo Paige

My email ends shorter than I had hoped. As soon as I press send, I hear the sound of the garage door opening. Dad must be home. Halfway down the stairs, he sees me and grins.

"Hey there, kiddo. How was your day?" he says as he loosens his tie.

He watches me until my feet hit the landing of the first floor. I give him a quick kiss on the cheek and say, "I went grocery shopping, and then Josh came over for a little bit."

He nods in response and goes into his bedroom off the living room to change. I head to the kitchen and grab bread and cheese. "Is grilled cheese okay?" I call out, even though I already know he'll be fine with it. Bread, cheese, and butter: three of his favorite things.

His voice sounds upbeat as always. "Sounds good to me!" I hear him collapse on the couch and turn on ESPN. The sound of sports anchors' banter joins the sizzling of our sandwiches on the stove.

Once the bread turns golden and the cheese has melted, I bring both sandwiches to the living room. I may not enjoy watching sports, but watching my father verbally dispute the call made on-screen keeps me entertained as I eat.

The phone rings in the kitchen, and I jump up from the couch to pick it up. "Hello?"

"Hey, Paige!" Leah's energetic voice comes out of the phone speaker in full force.

I realize I never said goodbye to her when I left the bonfire. "Hey, what's up?"

"Who's the guy?"

I frown. "What guy?"

"At the party last night!"

"The one sitting with me?" I didn't even think Leah saw me with Fredrick.

"Yes." Her voice is all business.

"I don't know much about him other than his name is Fredrick." I peek around the corner to make sure my dad isn't listening. He's leaning forward on the edge of the couch, clearly wrapped in whatever the anchors are saying. I keep my voice low regardless. The last thing I need is my father asking me who Fredrick is, or even worse, he might ask Josh.

Her voice turns to mock seriousness. "Paige, he's beautiful.

Learn more about him. Please."

I let out a laugh with a shake of my head. "So, what did you do today?"

The other end of the phone falls quiet for a moment. I know she's contemplating whether she should continue her interrogation or drop it. Finally, she sighs, and I'm grateful she took the bait. "This morning I had to watch the little bro while my mom was at work, but then I went to check on Jenna."

"How is she?" I want to keep the conversation focused on anything but Fredrick.

"Better. I don't think she's contagious anymore. What about you? Do anything fun today?"

As I describe my day, I leave Fredrick out. Leah would only want a play-by-play of my trip to Publix, and I'd rather not get into it.

She cuts me off. "Hey, Paige. There's another call coming in. I have to go, but I'll talk to you tomorrow, okay?"

I say, "Okay, talk to you then," and we both hang up.

Peering around the corner, I see my dad hasn't moved an inch. "Dad, I think I'm going to turn in early," I say as I peer around the corner at him.

He nods without looking up from the television. "Okay, sweetie. I'll take care of the dishes. Goodnight."

"Goodnight."

I take my time as I get ready for bed. I'm not tired yet, but boredom gnaws at me. Scanning my bookshelves for something to read, I settle on *The Perks of Being a Wallflower*. I have a habit of re-reading the books I love and rarely adding new ones to my library. Most of the time, I grab a book I've already read, open it to a random chapter, and don't bother bookmarking when I'm done. There's no point saving the page because, next time, I'll grab a different book and do the same thing. Picking up an old book feels like visiting an old friend, and it's been a while since I've checked in on Charlie.

4

The week flies by with cleaning, reading, and kidnappings by Josh and Leah. I haven't been back to the beach since the bonfire, and Fredrick hasn't popped up anywhere else unexpectantly. After meeting him, I could picture his conflicted brown eyes effortlessly. I used to try to figure out the meaning behind those eyes, but now all parts of him are an enigma, and thoughts of him fade with each passing day.

Dad and I have finished our Sunday breakfast and now sit at the table. Sunday breakfast is my father's specialty. I may have to cook most of our other meals, but when it comes to pancakes and scrambled eggs, he's your man. He stretches his arms above his head as he leans back in his chair. "What are your plans today?"

I clear the table and walk over to the sink to wash our dishes. "Not sure. What about you?"

Before I turn to the sink, I catch his brows furrowing, and I know he's concerned. He worries about me the same way most extroverts worry about introverts. Despite his long days at the office, my dad has always been a social guy. I can't remember him ever having a day off without plans. He clears his throat and says, "Figured I would go to Jim's... don't you have plans with Josh or Leah?"

Drying one of our recently washed breakfast plates, I lean against the sink to look at him. "It's not even 10 a.m. I like to live my life on the edge, Dad, you know that." I give him a dubious look before turning back around to wash the second plate.

Even though I'm not looking at him, I can hear the amusement in his voice. "Of course, you do."

It's no shock that he has plans with Jim. I can hardly remember a race day without Jim and Miller Lite. He isn't a spokesperson for them yet, but I'm sure his loyalty will pay off someday. If I'm home, I usually make homemade nachos. I've tried curling up with a good book on days like these before, but it's hard to pay attention to the words on the page with a constant chorus of cheers and boos coming from downstairs. I guess the saying holds true: if you can't beat em', join em.'

My dad picks up the phone and dials what I'm assuming is Jim's number. When I listen to the one-sided conversation, I confirm my assumption. I can't help laughing at the enthusiasm emulating from this end.

"Jim! Race day!"

I hear Jim's muffled but equally excited voice on the other end.

My dad looks at the clock on the stove before responding.

"Okay, I'll be over there in about an hour… Yeah, yeah, I know. I'll pick something up."

They exchange goodbyes, and my dad hangs up the phone. He hurries into his bedroom only to reappear seconds later in a black NASCAR t-shirt and khaki shorts.

"Paige, I'm headed to the store and then straight to Jim's. I'll see you later tonight."

I've finished cleaning the pan he used to make eggs and set it on the counter rack to dry. "Okay, have fun!"

"You, too! Try to find something to do today, okay?"

I smile at him reassuringly. "Okay."

After he leaves, it takes me a few minutes to settle on something to do. When I know I'll have the house to myself, I usually do laundry to pass the time. There's nothing like multiple loads of laundry to kill a day.

After starting the first load, I sit cross-legged at the kitchen table and open *The Perks of Being a Wallflower* again. This time, I open it to the chapter where Charlie first meets Sam and Patrick at the football game. The way books keep a story frozen in time makes me nostalgic for people and places only real within the pages.

I jump, startled out of my book when the phone rings behind me. Not wanting to get up, I stretch out my arm to answer it. I can barely reach it, but my fingers brush the bottom, tipping it off the wall mount. It nearly falls on me, but I catch the phone just in time, nestling it in the crook of my neck so I can keep reading. "Hello?"

"Hey, Paige, did I wake you?" Luke's voice comes through the speaker, dragging me further out of the story. Luke never calls. He might try to talk to me at school, but he's only called my house once to ask if he could borrow one of my textbooks.

"No, not at all. What's up?" My voice comes out monotone as I multitask—trying my best to stay in the world of wallflowers. Part of me feels bad about not giving Luke my undivided attention, but reading makes talking to him a little easier.

"Oh, okay. Good. I haven't talked to you in a while. I think the last time I saw you, we were at the beach, right?" He's trying to sound casual and failing.

The nerves behind his voice only heighten my own, and I glare down at the page in front of me to block the feeling.

Charlie, Sam, and Patrick are at Big Boy after the game. The way Charlie wholeheartedly appreciates his new friends wanting to learn about him brings a smile to my lips. "Yeah, I think you're right."

His voice comes out sounding higher than usual. "Yeah. So, anyway… I was wondering if—well, maybe you'd want to get something to eat tonight?"

The book falls closed as I grab the phone with my hand. My mouth goes dry, and I wish I hadn't answered his call. I now understand why he sounded nervous. He has never asked me out on an actual date.

Date.

The word echoes in my mind making me cringe. I try to think of an excuse to say no without panicking, but ideas are generating too quickly. My mind feels like a blur, and excuses aren't sticking in the forefront long enough for me to even consider them.

Finally, I blurt, "We should get a bunch of our friends together for dinner tonight. Who were you thinking of inviting?" and wince as I wait for his response.

Luke stammers on the other end. "Oh, um, I don't know." His voice no longer trembles with hesitation. "Maybe we can ask…" he pauses for a moment, "everyone?"

I feel the color return to my cheeks. "That sounds great! I'll check with my dad to see if I can go, okay?"

I know my dad would let me go—actual date or not. He would even encourage it, but the more Luke can think my dad is a perpetual hard-ass, the better.

I try to ignore the dip in his voice as he says, "Okay, Paige… I'll let you know as soon as I find people. So, what have you been up to?"

I don't want to do this. I don't want to sit here talking to Luke on the phone. The more I talk to him, the more he might get the wrong idea. My mind reels for more excuses, but my thoughts are interrupted by the doorbell ringing.

Perfect timing.

"Hey, someone's at the door. Keep me updated about tonight, though!"

I jump to my feet and hang up the phone, practically running to the door to avoid Josh's follow-up rings. Yanking the handle, I'm about to boast that I've beaten him, but it isn't Josh standing on the front porch.

It's Fredrick.

He takes me in, his eyebrows furrowing before he cocks one,

and I immediately feel flustered. "Sorry, I thought you were some-one else."

He looks me up and down, making me overly aware of the fact that I'm still wearing the black leggings and oversized t-shirt I slept in. I'm sure I look like a mess, but all he says is, "Expecting some-one?"

My stomach flutters at the sight of him standing on my front porch. "I uh—no, not really." He eyes me curiously, and my cheeks run hot.

"Just not me," he says, still watching me carefully.

I let out a breath of laughter, willing my cheeks to return to their normal cover. "No, not you." He looks down, but I catch a smile pulling at the corners of his lips. "How did you know I live here?"

A laugh escapes him as he points over his shoulder. "I'd recog-nize that truck anywhere." He adds, "And your last name is on the mailbox."

"Oh, yeah." Starting to regain control of my facial expressions, I give him a small smile without my cheeks flushing… I hope. "So, what are you doing here?"

He shrugs, breaking my gaze and running his hand along the back of his neck. "I know I ran off on you last week. I thought I'd make it up to you."

My eyes linger on the muscles in his arm, but at the mention of our last meeting, I frown, unsure of what to make of everything. "You don't need to make anything up to me."

"I want to," he says, and my attention snaps back to him. "I figured we could have lunch or something like you suggested."

My thoughts snag on the *or something,* and my eyes flicker to his mouth, betraying me. My neck warms and my eyes jump back to meet his. "Yeah, we can do that," I croak, clearing my throat to mask it.

He flashes his award-winning, crooked smile. "Okay." Tilting his head, he adds, "It might be easier if you let me in."

His answer leaves me frozen for a moment, but when he raises his eyebrows, I snap out of it. "Oh, sorry. Come in." I look out at my driveway, but only my truck sits on the gravel. "Where's your car?"

As he steps past me, he says, "I parked on the street."

I crane my neck to see, but like most of our three acres, thick oak trees block my view.

Closing the front door behind him, I walk into the kitchen with Fredrick in tow. Not sure where to lead him, I take a seat at the kitchen table, and he does the same.

"So, no more running off?" I meant it as a joke, but his expression hardens. Trying to lighten things, I add, "Or smashing my bread?"

"I can't promise that." I must look confused because he adds, "Running off, I mean." The corner of his mouth quirks as he adds, "Future bread should be safe."

Before I can think twice, my eyebrows pinch, and I ask, "Why?"

He thinks for a moment, resting his arms on the table. "Because things come up, and it might happen, but I wanted you to know I didn't want to leave so soon last week. If I could've had things my way, I would have spent the day with you." I raise my eyebrows, but before I can ask anything, he adds, "Which is why I came here today. Today is a day of no obligation. I'm all yours if you'll have me."

I open my mouth to say something, but I'm not sure what to say.

He's looking at me like I'm funny to him again, making me self-conscious. I'm relieved when he asks, "Read any books at the beach yet?"

The fact that he remembers our last conversation lands a fluttering feeling in my chest. "Not yet. I've mostly been spending time with my friends Josh and Leah."

Fredrick drops his gaze to the table. "Right… How is Josh?"

"You know Josh?" I ask, hoping my voice doesn't give me away.

His dark eyes shoot up to meet mine, and I shrink. "He's talked to you about me," he says with a knowing realization.

I stare down at my hands in my lap and try to think of what to say. "No. Well, not really… a little maybe." I tentatively lift my gaze.

To my surprise, as our eyes meet, his mouth quirks with amusement. "You're a bad liar."

I glare at him. "I wasn't lying. We've only had one conversation about you." He raises his eyebrows, and his dubious stare prompts me to add, "Two very short, insignificant conversations about you."

He's full-blown smirking now. "Two? That's hardly insignificant."

I try to remember what Josh and I had talked about last weekend. It seems so long ago. "I know you used to be friends, and now you're not." He nods slowly. I can tell he's uncomfortable with the topic, but I ignore it. "What happened?"

Something in his eyes turns cold. "People change."

I hitch my leg up and rest my chin on my knee. "Which one of you changed?"

"I don't know. Both of us? People drift apart. It's not a big deal," he says, and there's an edge to his voice that wasn't there before.

I know all the flags are up, and I should heed his warning, but my curiosity—and maybe my stubbornness—get the better of me. "According to him, you were the one who did most of the changing."

Fredrick's jaw ticks. "If he told you what happened, why are you asking me about it?"

Josh's warnings are playing on a loop in the back of my mind, but all I feel is annoyed—annoyed at Josh for being right about everything and at Fredrick for living up to his reputation.

Before I can come up with a solid course of action, my scattered thoughts are tumbling out of my mouth with no filter in sight. "You know, I'm starting to think Josh was right about you. He told me you went off on him whenever he asked you anything about your friends. You can't expect people to accept ignorance. If you're going to be so closed off, what's the point of you even being here?"

Fredrick sits there watching me, his expression unreadable. My words hang between us, thick in the air, and I wring my hands in my lap.

"Are you done?" he asks, oddly calm.

I give a small nod.

Fredrick leans forward across the table, and my breath catches under the intensity of his stare. "Listen to me, Paige. I'm here right now because I want to be—or at least wanted to be." He pauses, and I swear I can see the corner of his mouth twitch. "And I don't think Josh told you everything." He looks thoughtful, like he's debating if he should continue but decides against it.

I stay quiet, but I know my eyes are pleading for him to say more.

Eventually, he says, "Things got out of hand… Austin handled things fine, but Josh?" He shakes his head. "Josh took things too far."

His words give me pause. "What do you mean?"

Before answering, he fixes his gaze on the table and scratches his cheek. "It got to a point where he was following me. He even started to follow my friends."

"That doesn't sound like him." Josh has a temper, but he's not the type of guy to put that much effort into something.

He shrugs. "If you don't believe me, ask him about it."

My next question eats at me, but I know it's something he won't want to answer. "Can I ask you something?"

His expression falters for a moment but then he sighs, nodding his head. "Yeah, what is it?"

I choose my words carefully. "What were you doing with your friends? You know, that looked so suspicious to Josh."

His eyes freeze. "Nothing," he says almost too quickly.

I purse my lips as I consider how to get more information out of him.

Before I can say anything, he adds, "You're never going to let this go, are you?"

I shrug. "Someone who has a lot of secrets is bound to get a lot of questions."

"Well, give it a rest. It's better for both of us if you stop."

I sit up straight. "What's that supposed to mean?"

He rolls his eyes, but a nervous laugh escapes him. "You're not listening to me, Paige. Stop." He looks around the kitchen. "Aren't we supposed to have lunch?"

I think about ignoring his question to keep the conversation going, but I find the break in the tension welcoming. "Oh, um… yeah, sure. What do you want?"

I stand and walk over to the pantry to consider our options. Now that I think about it, I am starving. After taking inventory, I look back at Fredrick, but he's gone.

"I can make us something." The sound of his voice makes my head whip back around to find him a few feet from me near the kitchen sink. My mouth opens with the realization that I didn't hear him get up from his chair or walk across the kitchen. "How did you do that?"

Pulling his eyebrows together he says, "Do what?"

"Sneak up on me!" I think of all the times I didn't notice

Fredrick doing something. At the bonfire, he took my hotdog without my noticing. At the grocery store, he loaded my cart—again unnoticed. Now, in my kitchen, this guarded, intriguing boy stumps me again.

A crooked smile pulls at the corner of his lips, nearly taking my breath away. "Practice."

5

After lunch, Fredrick and I are in my room. I've had boys in my room before. Josh, Austin, Nick, and even Juri have all been in my room at some point. They're all guys. Fredrick is a guy. So, why does this feel different? Seeing him in my room makes me realize my bedroom—with its light purple walls and twin-sized bed—looks like it belongs to someone under the age of ten.

Fredrick's eyes travel past me, and I know he's scanning my bookshelves on the wall behind me. He sits, straddling the back of my computer chair, and his lips twitch. "You weren't joking when you said you like to read."

Sitting cross-legged on my bed, I twist to glance up at the shelves stocked with my favorite novels. I've never been one for libraries, always finding it too difficult to part with books after I've read them. It might sound extreme, but the books I've cultivated feel like an extension of myself. I am me because of them, and they represent me in a way nothing else can. Not to mention, the most uneventful chapter in any of those stories still holds more excitement than my entire existence. I turn back around to find Fredrick studying me and say, "Those are my favorites."

He crosses his arms over the back of the chair and rests his chin. "You have a lot of favorites."

Still feeling self-conscious about my bedroom, I hug my knees to my chest and try to change the subject. "What do you usually do?" I rest my chin on the tops of my knees. "You know, on 'days of no obligation?'"

Fredrick picks his head up, looking more alert. "Sailing."

"Really? Like boats?"

I detect a trace of a smirk on his lips. "Yeah, like boats." He grips the back of the chair and drums his thumbs against the top. "I'll take you some time."

"I'll hold you to that." I've never been sailing, but I like the idea of going with Fredrick. Even though I haven't known him long, I feel like I can trust him—or at least I want to.

He shakes his head. "You won't need to."

His eyes lock on mine, and his words hang between us. His unwavering stare makes my cheeks burn, and I hope he doesn't notice.

"Do you have any siblings?" I ask in a pathetic attempt to bring the conversation back to my comfort zone.

His eyes break from mine, and he lets out a breathy laugh. "Yeah, an older brother and a younger sister."

My mind is still stuck on the way he looked at me a moment

ago. I stop hugging my knees and go back to sitting with my legs crossed, hoping to seem more casual. *Get it together, Paige.* "How old are they?"

He looks at me with less intensity and seems more relaxed. It's good to know he's not guarded with *everything*. "My sister, Nicole, is fourteen. And my brother, Ben, is nineteen. What about you, any siblings?"

I shake my head. "No, it's just me. My parents split when I was six."

Fredrick nods. "My dad left a few years ago." Something tenses in his features, but it's gone as quickly as it appeared.

I open my mouth to say something, but the sound of the doorbell cuts me off. There are only two people who ever show up to my house uninvited, and I desperately hope that today it's Leah.

Getting to my feet, I walk over to the window overlooking the gravel driveway. Sitting in the driveway below is a grey Chevy pickup. I freeze, suddenly feeling like there isn't enough air in the room. Having a conversation about Josh was bad enough. The possibility of what can happen with Josh and Fredrick in the same place makes me sweat. What will Josh think if he sees him here? I told him I'd stay away from Fredrick, but the fact that he's sitting in my bedroom is bound to raise questions.

The doorbell rings four more times, and I turn to Fredrick. "Um, hold on."

Before he can say anything, I'm halfway down the stairs, flustered and out of breath by the time I crack open the front door. "Hey."

"Uh, are you okay?" Josh's eyebrows pull together as he takes me in.

I put on my best grin. "Of course!" *Too eager.* "I mean, yes, I'm fine. What are you doing here?"

The crease between his brows deepens, and he speaks slowly. "A group of us are going out tonight. I figured we could watch a movie or something and then ride together."

I shake my head, perhaps too quickly. "No, no. I can't right now. Sorry. Maybe another time?"

Josh lowers his head to study me, his eyes narrowing. "Why?"

"Um, well—" My head whips around to find Fredrick standing at the top of the steps. He pauses and cocks his head, mirroring Josh's confused expression at the door.

Josh says my name, and Fredrick must figure out who's at the door because his face hardens. He takes another deliberate step, this time with a thud, and my eyes narrow.

My head whips back to Josh when he goes to step past me.

"Who's there?" He tries to crane his neck over me to get a better view, but I keep the door cracked and push against his chest. He steps back so he can look me in the eye. "What the hell, Paige?"

My mouth opens, but I struggle to find the words.

Unfortunately, there's no need for any explanation. Within seconds, Fredrick pulls the door open further and stands at my side. My eyes flicker to Fredrick, expecting to see him standing tall and threatening. To my surprise, he doesn't look angry at all. Fredrick leans against the doorframe with his arms casually crossed.

Josh's face contorts with anger as soon as Fredrick steps into view. His jaw clenches which is never a good sign, and his lips press into a hard line.

I search for something to say, but neither of them are looking at me, anyway. Josh glares at Fredrick, breathing hard, and even though Fredrick's face is a stoic mask, it's clear he isn't thrilled about the reunion. I knew they didn't like each other, but as I take in the scene before me, I feel like I'm missing a vital piece of the puzzle.

The only thing clear to me is that they shouldn't both be here right now. I anxiously bite my thumbnail. If I tell Josh to go home, he'll never forgive me for putting Fredrick before our friendship. On the other hand, telling Fredrick to go seems a bit unfair, and if I'm being honest, I don't want him to leave.

Josh doesn't feign pleasantries. He turns to me and speaks through gritted teeth. "What the hell is he doing here?"

I'm not sure why I have a sudden urge to apologize, but I do. Before I can say anything, though, Fredrick steps in.

"I was in town and thought I'd stop by. Paige didn't know I was coming."

Josh's eyes burn into me, and he crosses his arms over his chest. "And what have you two been up to?" His judgmental gaze flickers to Fredrick before settling back on me.

Josh's unwarranted anger fuels something inside of me, and my eyes narrow. "We ate lunch." He looks at me and raises his eyebrows as if to say, *And?*

Who does he think he is, my father?

Still glaring at him, I snap, "And then you showed up." Letting my frustration fuel me further, I add, "I think you should go. You're angry. Nothing good will come of this."

He takes a staggering step backward, like my words physically hit him. His brows furrow and the hurt on his face makes me question myself. I've only seen Josh like this once before—it was with Dan, and it was when I first moved here. He tried to punch Dan, who was much bigger than him back then. So, I know this type of anger makes him irrational.

At the time, I didn't know Josh well enough to ask him what caused it, but his relationship with Dan never recovered. The few times I've tried to ask him about it, he always shuts down. It's one of the few things in our friendship that I've learned is off-limits.

Josh's eyes keep traveling back and forth between Fredrick and me, and the tension behind them grows each time they fall on Fredrick. "You're right. Nothing good can fucking come of this." He gestures to the two of us.

My jaw drops, and my heart pounds in my chest. As I'm about to say something I'm sure I would regret later, Fredrick cuts me off by taking a single step toward Josh. He's less relaxed, but his voice remains steady. "What's the problem?"

Josh scoffs, momentarily glancing at me before returning his attention to Fredrick. "Seriously? You don't see the problem here?"

Fredrick's only response is a shrug.

Josh stares at Fredrick for a beat too long. "The problem is that you're a scumbag, and Paige has no business hanging around you."

Fredrick cocks an eyebrow, his eyes never leaving Josh. "I'm not saying she does. But either way, it doesn't concern you."

I'm surprised Fredrick doesn't object to the *scumbag* comment.

"Josh, enough." I try to interject.

He balls his hands into fists at his sides—another bad sign. "He's no good for you, Paige." He looks at Fredrick and spits the words, "He's no good for any of us."

"Josh!" I can't take this anymore. I can't take him being so rude.

"It's okay." Fredrick's eyes meet mine for a moment, and there's clarity behind them like he's seeing me for the first time. I hope Josh's cruel words aren't getting to him. The moment passes as quickly as it came, and Fredrick's attention is back on Josh. "Don't worry. When I'm with Paige, I'll tell you where we are." He leans forward and lowers his voice. "You know, so you don't have to follow us."

Josh grits his jaw. "You're asking for it."

Fredrick keeps his composure, but something in his voice darkens. "Is that supposed to be a threat?"

At the stroke of his last word, Josh swings at Fredrick's face with enough force to make me turn away and yelp.

"Fuck!" The word is full of anguish, making my eyes dart up to Fredrick. I expect to see him holding his face in pain, but he stands there, untouched. He's looking at Josh with his jaw set.

"Josh!" My skin prickles when my eyes land on the blood coming from Josh's hand. I can only assume Fredrick must have dodged the punch, which means Josh just slammed his fist into the front of our house. I reach out to him. "Are you okay?" When he doesn't say anything, I take it as a no and let out a sigh. "Come inside."

Buckled over in pain and clutching his hand to his chest, he shakes his head.

"Josh. Get inside." I'm relieved when my voice comes out stronger than I feel.

"Shit. No, Paige. It's fine." He's still shaking his head in protest, but when I lightly pull on his arm, he follows me.

I lead him to the kitchen, and Fredrick hangs back, giving us space. The cold water runs over Josh's hand, and I watch his knuckles bleed, new blood replacing the old. I steal a glance at Fredrick to find him watching from a distance, running an anxious hand through his hair.

Looking back at Josh's hand makes the room spin momentarily. The blood-stained water spirals down the drain, and I try to control my breathing to avoid passing out. The water washes away the blood, and I can see how deep the cuts are across his knuckles. "Can you move your fingers?"

He opens and closes his hand, each movement releasing fresh blood from the cracked skin. I stare up at the ceiling and take a deep breath. My vision speckles and my fingers grip the counter to steady myself. *Breathe.* In a matter of seconds, I hear Fredrick's voice ask, "Are you okay?" I know he must be standing next to me, but he sounds far away.

Peeling my eyes away from the ceiling, I nod my head in response.

Fredrick shakes his head, laughing slightly. "No, you're not. Come sit down." He leads me to the couch in the living room where I slump into the cushion.

"I have to help Josh," I halfheartedly protest.

"I'll help him," he says flatly, and a moment later, he's gone.

I crane my neck over the back of the couch and try to catch a glimpse of what they're doing. The last thing I need is more bloodshed. I see Fredrick handing Josh paper towels. Josh refuses to look at Fredrick as he snatches the roll from his hand.

Fredrick doesn't look at Josh either. His gaze stays fixed on the injured hand. It only takes the sight of Josh's bloodstained shirt to make me woozy again, so I let my head fall back onto the couch and contemplate everything that happened today.

Minutes pass before Fredrick's face comes into view.

"Is it over?" I ask.

Despite everything, his mouth quirks with amusement. "It's safe."

I sit up and look around. "Where is he?"

"By the front door. He wants to talk to you." Fredrick glances in that direction and adds, "Alone."

"Okay." Taking a steadying breath, I push myself up from the couch. Even as I walk to the door, I can feel Fredrick's eyes on me like he's worried I might spontaneously collapse.

Once I reach Josh, I make sure not to look at his busted knuckles. "How's your hand?" My voice comes out small, and I hate the way it sounds.

He shrugs. "It'll be fine."

My chest tightens, and I get the urge to wrap my arms around him and tell him I'm sorry. On any other day, I probably would have, but not today. He took it too far today. All I manage to mutter is, "That's good."

Josh nods and drops his gaze. "Listen, Paige. I came here to see if you wanted to join the group date tonight, but I don't think it's a good idea." His eyes pierce past me. "Especially if you'd consider bringing him."

"Okay." I don't know why I can't bring myself to say what's on my mind. I want to yell at him for being an idiot. I want him to know how mad I am at him for trying to start a fight on my porch. I want to tell him that if I wanted to bring Fredrick, he'd have to deal with it. But instead of saying any of these things, I say, "Wait, who are you going on a date with tonight?"

His expression softens, but only slightly. "Kimberly. A bunch of us are going to eat at that restaurant on the river. I hope I can still hold a fork." He grimaces and looks down at his hand.

Relaxing my shoulders, I give him a faint smile. "Kimberly is sweet. I hope you guys have a great time."

His wary eyes pass over me again. "Are you sure you'll be okay here with him?"

His question makes my heart swell a little. That's Josh for you, though. An egotistical, bad-tempered ladies' man with a heart of gold. "I'll be fine," I assure him.

"Well, I guess I'll see you later."

"See you," I say.

As he walks to his truck, his arms are limp at his sides. I hate the tension between us, but I know we can't fix it today—not with Fredrick here.

When I turn around, Fredrick startles me. He's leaning against the wall only a few feet away, and of course, I didn't hear him. The

Fredrick who was here before Josh's visit has vanished. To replace him is his anxious and disheveled clone.

"I'm sorry."

I shrug as I walk past him to the kitchen. "Why? You're not the one who threw a punch." I look over my shoulder to make sure he's still behind me before continuing. "Josh has a bit of a temper, as I'm sure you know. It's not your fault."

"I know, but I don't want to be responsible for you two fighting."

Shaking my head, I lean my back against the counter so I can look at him. He's standing in the kitchen entryway, and I can tell his mind is busy. "You're not going to ruin any friendship of mine. Josh overreacted, and in the end, he got what he deserved. You didn't do anything."

His eyebrows stay drawn together, but he gives me a nod before looking at the clock on the stove. "I should get going."

I don't want him to leave, but I know he's right. As we walk to the door, I say, "I'm sorry… for today. I can't believe Josh tried to hit you." I can't help imagining what would have happened if Fredrick hadn't dodged the punch. I bite the inside of my cheek at the thought of a full-blown fight breaking out.

He shrugs and says, "It was somewhat expected."

"Still, he shouldn't have done that."

Once we're standing in the doorway, Fredrick turns to face me. "He has his reasons—and no, I'm not going to explain what those reasons are."

I let out a light laugh. "Fine. Another time." My chest tightens when I realize he probably won't want to see me again after this. Letting my gaze fall, I say, "I think he thought something was going on between us. I'll tell him there isn't. Maybe that will calm him down."

His warm, brown eyes search mine. "Something going on between us?"

My cheeks burn. "Josh is like an older brother—an overprotective older brother. I'll make sure to tell him you and I are just friends… it might help."

Shoving his hands in his pockets, he shrugs. "Or don't." He turns and starts down our long driveway. Calling over his shoulder, he says, "I'll see you around, Paige Lawson." I'm thankful he doesn't look back because I'm pretty sure my mouth is open.

Clamping my jaw shut, I close the door and stand there for a moment, feeling light-headed. *Or don't?* I shake my head to clear my mind and take in the empty house. The quiet that felt so calming this morning now feels forlorn. It's times like these I'm reminded of one major drawback to being an only child: there's no one to break the silence.

I check the kitchen, expecting to see evidence of blood. To my surprise, it's spotless. I get a tight feeling in my stomach when I think of Fredrick going out of his way to clean up the blood that was supposed to be his.

I go upstairs to email my mom, knowing I won't include anything about today in my message. I love my mother, but she has a way of turning things on me. I'm sure if I told her what happened, she would pinpoint something I should have done differently.

Sitting down at my computer, I'm numb as I watch it slowly come to life. I try to bury any thoughts of Fredrick or Josh, but they continue to creep into the forefront of my mind.

Once the computer turns on, I notice two emails from her. The first reads:

Hey Paige,

I'm glad Josh is keeping you busy! How is he doing? Trevor and I are thinking of taking a trip to see you. I don't want to make your father uncomfortable, though, so nothing is set in stone. I'll keep you updated!

TK Mom

I try to figure out what her sign-off means. She gets so wrapped up in the abbreviations that she sometimes abbreviates things most people wouldn't. I think this one means "take care."

Every summer, my mom promises to visit me in Florida, but it hasn't happened yet. She always has plenty of excuses, at least one of which involves my father. I know having the two of them under the same roof would be uncomfortable, to say the least, but it would be worth it. As much as I wish she could push past her negative feelings to come here, I can't say I blame her. In high-stress situations, she has a way of unintentionally making things worse.

Before answering, I check the second email.

Paige,

Are you okay? I haven't heard from you in a few days. You're making me nervous. Let me know what you're up to.

Love, Mom

Her sign-off lets me know she's worried. It's like the fears generated by not hearing from me remind her that she does love me. I check the date of my last email. It was nearly a week ago. I didn't realize so much time had passed, and I feel a stab of guilt. On the other hand, nothing happened during my week worth writing about—well, until today.

I skim over the words in her first email again. Of course, today of all days, she wants to know about Josh.

Still feeling numb and actively trying not to think about everything, I whip up a halfhearted email that I hope doesn't come across that way.

Hey Mom,

Sorry I haven't been writing. Nothing exciting has happened this past week, and there wasn't much to report. Josh is fine. He hurt his hand today, though. That would be great if you and Trevor could come down for a visit. It would be nice to see you. Let me know if you're coming, and I'll tell Dad.

Xo Paige

I watch the green progress bar until it's full and my email sends. Turning off the computer, I head downstairs, knowing Dad will be home in about an hour.

As I try to think of what to cook for dinner, the phone rings.

"Hello?"

"Hi, Paige! It's Luke."

I almost let out a groan after the day I'd had. Taking in a deep breath, I try to sound convincing. "Hey, Luke. What's up?"

"Well, I could only get Anna and Dan to come to dinner."

Dinner!

"Oh, Luke, I'm sorry! I forgot all about the dinner, and I'm already cooking something. Do you think the three of you can go without me?"

His voice sounds quiet coming from the other end of the phone. "Oh, sure. Don't worry about it, Paige. I'll talk to you later."

"I'm sorry. Maybe ask Josh? He said something about a group date tonight, too."

"Oh, okay. Maybe Anna invited him already. Bye, Paige."

"Bye."

Even though part of me feels terrible, I'm ultimately relieved. Dinner with Dan trying to set me up with Luke while Anna gives me the stink eye all night doesn't sound like a good time.

It takes me three times longer than usual to pick something for dinner. I stand with the pantry open for a solid ten minutes, but my mind keeps going back to my angry best friend and the dark-haired boy who makes him that way.

6

Three days have passed since the Fredrick-Josh debacle, which means three mornings of waking up with a tight chest. Not knowing where I stand with Josh makes me think about him constantly.
And if I'm not thinking about Josh, I'm almost always thinking about Fredrick.

Across from my bed, I check the calendar over my computer desk. June showcases a black and white photo of The Beatles during their mustache phase. I wasn't alive when they were popular, so I usually dictate the point in their career by how much facial hair they have.

My dad has always been a fan of The Beatles. I used to gripe every time he would play one of their albums—yes, *albums*. He still has the record player and everything. But eventually, I started to love the songs just as much as he does. Today's box is vacant, aside from a small number eleven in the upper left corner.

I pad to the window on my back wall and open the curtains. Warmth hits my face, and I have to shield my eyes from the glaring sun. The fact that it's still early and already this warm tells me today will be hotter than most. I'm not talking about your typical hot summer day where your forehead glistens, and you grab a popsicle. I'm talking about the type of heat only native to Florida. The type that makes the air feel too thick to breathe and the humidity feels too dense to walk through.

Downstairs, I find my dad passed out on the couch. He must have fallen asleep while taking notes because he has papers scattered around him.

I try to wake him, knowing he's already late for work. After the fourth or fifth nudge, I know he's awake and ignoring me. I kneel next to him and say, "Dad, you're late for wo—" Before I can finish my sentence, he jolts upright and looks at his watch. "Paige! Why didn't you wake me?"

Really? This is my fault? I throw my hands up defensively. "I was in my room, and the house was quiet. I thought you left!"

He nods his head frantically. "Right. Right, of course." Without another word, he rushes into his bedroom, slamming the door behind him.

I know he's already having a bad morning, so I gather the scattered papers and stack them on the coffee table.

Back upstairs, I shower and get dressed before peering over the railing to see if he's left for work yet. Nope. I glance into the living room and see him tossing aside pillows and looking under the furniture. I know he's looking for his keys, so I call out, "They're on the hook by the front door!"

He runs over, cursing under his breath, and grabs the keys off the hook. "Bye! Have a great day!" He yells over his shoulder before slamming the door behind him.

The abrupt calm that fills the house takes a minute to get used to. After the morning chaos, it's like being at the beach after a hurricane. Still standing on the staircase, I turn and go back up to my bedroom. The sun pours through my window, making my light purple walls look almost white. I gaze at the bulletin board on my wall next to the Beatles calendar. It's covered in pictures from last year. Most—if not all—have Josh in them.

I lock on a picture of Josh and me from last summer and have to swallow the lump in my throat. Leah didn't live here then, so Josh and I did everything together. The picture is from a day at the lake. I don't remember who took it, but Josh and I are standing side by side. He's holding up two fingers behind my head to give me bunny ears in the photo. At the moment the picture was taken, I'm glaring up at him because I figured out what he was doing. Josh's head is tossed back in a crow of laughter. Nick is in the picture, too. Sort of. You can only see part of him and he looks more like a blur of dark hair because he tried to jump into the frame at the last minute, but it's him.

I hate that I haven't heard from Josh since he left here with busted knuckles. It feels like the more time passes, the more distance grows between us. I can't let Fredrick, who I barely know, ruin my closest friendship. Without giving myself time to overthink things, I run down to the kitchen and pick up the phone to dial Josh's number.

The phone only rings twice before I hear his groggy voice on the other end. "Hello?"

"Josh." My relief carries in my voice, but I don't care.

"Paige?" he says, sounding more alert.

"Yeah, it's me." I balance the phone in the crook of my neck and hug my torso.

He pauses, and the silence nearly kills me.

"Why are you calling?"

I take it back. *That* nearly kills me.

When I don't say anything, he must realize he's hurt me because he backpedals. "I mean, why are you calling so early?"

I let out a breath, and my words come out in a rush. "I just feel bad about this whole Fredrick thing, and I wanted to know how your date went the other night." Before he can answer, I add, "Is your hand okay?"

After a moment of hesitation, he says, "It's fine. The swelling has gone down a bit, and I can use it again. I just have to wait for the cuts to heal. Mom flipped when she saw it, though," he adds with a laugh.

Josh constantly gets hurt—usually sports-related—and his mom doesn't take it lightly. With his injured hand being obviously not a sports injury, I can only imagine her reaction.

"Did you tell her how it happened?"

"Nah, she would've called me dumb for trying to take him on." Even at the indirect mention of Fredrick, I can hear a change in his voice.

"Your mom knows Fredrick?"

"Yeah, the dick practically lived here before… well, before he was a dick."

I roll my eyes, and I'm thankful he can't see me. "Right." I try to picture the two of them being friends, but I can't.

Josh clears his throat. "So… have you talked to him?"

I wind the phone cord around my fingers. "Fredrick? No. He left right after you on Sunday. He feels bad about everything, though."

He scoffs. "Yeah, I know. He told me."

I nearly drop the phone. "He did? When?"

"When he was helping me in the kitchen." His voice muffles, and I picture him running a hand over his face. "He wouldn't shut up about it. It kind of took the fun out of hating his ass."

"Oh." I'm not sure what to say. My eyebrows pull together as I try to remember the two of them in the kitchen. "I didn't see you two talking. You didn't even look at each other."

He forces a laugh. "You weren't exactly in your right mind, but no surprise there. If there's one thing I know about Fredrick, it's that he's good at hiding shit."

All the times I never noticed Fredrick doing things come to mind. "Yeah, he is," I say quietly.

"But, like I said, you were out of it."

Leaning my head against the kitchen wall, I groan. "I hate blood." The memory of Josh's busted knuckles alone is enough to make me woozy.

I expect him to laugh, but he doesn't. Josh falls quiet for a moment before saying seriously, "Why was he at your house?"

I turn, leaning my shoulder against the wall. "He said he was in the area and wanted to stop by. I guess he recognized my truck."

"I'm telling you, he's bad news," he says in a tight voice.

Staring up at the ceiling, I say, "He's been fine, Josh. I know you don't want to talk about what ended your friendship, but that was *years* ago. Maybe he's changed."

"Doubtful," he mutters. "You don't know him like I do."

His comment ignites a defensiveness in me. I'm not sure why it bothers me so much, but I know I need to change the subject. "So, how was your date with Kimberly?"

Luckily, he welcomes the shift as much as I do. "She's shy, but we had fun. She's beautiful."

His words pull at the corners of my mouth. People at school call Josh a player, and he does date a lot of girls, but he genuinely likes every girl he dates. I think he's secretly a hopeless romantic. "Yeah, she is pretty. I hope it works out for you guys."

"Thanks. Uh… I actually have plans to meet up with her for lunch, and Mom left a list of chores a mile long for me to do before then. Talk to you later?"

"Alright. Bye, Josh."

"Later, P."

On a day as hot as today, the only relief I'll find is near the water. Going upstairs, I grab my beach bag, a good book, and a towel. I'm about to change into my swimsuit when the doorbell rings. Even though I know it isn't likely, my heart hammers at the possibility of it being Fredrick. I peer out my bedroom window, but it's Leah's bright red Nissan parked out front.

Running downstairs, I hear her bubbly voice yell, "Paige!" before I even answer.

I open the door, laughing. "Leah! Why are you yelling?"

She walks past me into the house. "Uh, because I haven't seen you in *for-ev-er*, and I don't have to babysit today." She bounces on her heels, and adds, "So, we're doing something."

Leah usually gets stuck babysitting her younger brother every summer. The gig limits her freedom to afternoons and weekends. "Why don't you have to babysit?"

She grins. "Mom has a cold and stayed home from work. Pretty great, right?"

"So sympathetic," I say with a laugh.

She talks to me over her shoulder as she makes her way to the kitchen. "Let's go to the lake!"

I know better than to challenge any plans made by Leah, especially on a day she's brother-free. "Sure, just let me change."

I go upstairs and settle on wearing grey drawstring shorts and a navy tank top over my black bathing suit. Leaving my beach bag and book on my bed, I head downstairs toward my new plans. "Okay, ready to go."

"Sweet!" Leah flips her heart-shaped sunglasses down from on top of her head. "Let's hit the road."

In my truck, Leah shifts in the passenger seat to face me. "So, have you heard from the mysterious bonfire guy?"

"Fredrick?" I ask to stall the conversation.

"Of course, I mean Fredrick! Who else would I be talking about?"

I shrug. "I don't know. There were other people at that party."

She rolls her eyes. "Have you heard from him?"

I shake my head, keeping my eyes on the road ahead, so she can't tell I'm lying. "No, not really. I ran into him a couple of times when I wasn't expecting to, but that's about it." *Technically not a lie, right?*

She lets out an exasperated sigh. "Such a shame. He is seriously so beautiful." She pauses and adds, "Kind of scary, though."

I choke back laughter. "*Scary?*"

Leah flips up her sunglasses, and her eyes are wide with enthusiasm. "You don't think so?"

I answer easily. "No. You do?"

She gets a far-off look on her face. "I don't know. He's the type of guy you know could wreck your world, but you still get on the back of his motorcycle anyway. You know?"

With a trace of lingering laughter, I say, "I don't think Fredrick has a motorcycle."

She lets her head fall back against the headrest as she waves my comment away with her hand. "You know what I mean!" She sighs again, snapping out of her daze. "I guess we'll never know for sure, will we?"

"We'll just have to leave it to your imagination." Eager to

change the subject, I ask, "So, how has your summer been so far?"

She shrugs. "Babysitting. Austin has been coming over to hang out, though."

I tilt my head to glance at her. "Hang out?" I ask with air quotes.

She drops her gaze, a small smile pulling at the corners of her mouth. "I don't know." Something in her voice tells me she *does* know, but before I have a chance to say anything, words are spilling out of her. "He's nice, and funny, and sweet, and cute! Do you think he's cute? Because I think he's cute, but sometimes we have different tastes, so I wasn't sure if you'd think he was cute, too."

I've never felt attracted to Austin, but I don't have to think twice about my answer. "Yeah, he's cute. You guys would be good together."

Leah wiggles in her seat as I park my truck on the grass near the lake. There aren't many people here today because it's a weekday. On a Saturday, countless cars and trucks take over the grassy lawn. People set up portable grills, and overlapping music plays from all directions. Today, however, there are only a few people here. A group of guys play hacky sack near the dock, and two guys toss a football back and forth.

My heart sinks. Luke and Juri are the ones throwing the football. I shoot Leah a look of dread. She grimaces, but it doesn't comfort me in the slightest.

Luke's face lights up when he spots Leah and me by the truck. He catches the ball and runs over to us, leaving Juri behind to throw his arms in the air.

"Hey, guys!" Sweat has soaked through his shirt, letting me know they've been here for a while.

Leah speaks to him first. "Hey, Luke. What are you guys doing here?"

He lifts his hand with the ball and breathlessly says one word. "Football."

"Are you thinking of trying out this year?" I ask over my shoulder as I walk past Luke to Juri.

Luke laughs behind me. "Are you kidding me? The guys on our team are douchebags."

Being one of the guys on the team, Juri gives Luke the finger as he walks up to us. "You're just mad because you'd never get picked." Luke laughs as Juri snatches the football out of his hands. "Way to run away with the ball, dumbass."

Luke brushes off the comment with a grin and turns to me. "It's too bad you couldn't come to dinner Sunday. Josh and Kimberly were in their own world, so it was weird sitting there with Anna and Dan."

I try to look genuine as I say, "I'm sorry about that. So, was Anna your date or Dan's?"

Luke manages a weak smile. "I wish I could say Dan's, but that's not exactly how it felt."

"What do you mean?" The words are out of my mouth before I can stop myself.

He brushes his hair out of his eyes like a nervous tick. "She acted like my date, but I didn't want her to be."

I know this is the perfect time to tell him I know how he feels, but I can't bring myself to do it. "Anna is great," I lie through my teeth. "It might be worth it to give her a chance." Anna may not be my favorite person, but I'll advertise her all day to Luke.

"She is… but I sort of like someone else." His cheeks flush, and I interpret them as red warning flags. *This conversation needs to end. Now.*

Looking over at Juri holding the football under his arm gives me an idea. So, even though I hate sports, I snatch the ball from him and walk backward toward the water with it.

Juri whips his head around in surprise before giving me a slow shake of his head. "Oh, you should not have done that," he says with a mischievous glint in his eyes. He heads straight for me, and I have to turn and make a run for it. Laughing, I stop and turn when I reach the lake, ready to admit defeat. There's no way I can outrun him. I hold out the ball for him to take, but he doesn't stop when he gets to me. His arm hooks around my waist, and before I know what's happened, we're underwater. I gasp as I come up for air, and my ears are met with his laughter.

I splash him before making my way to the edge of the lakeshore. My eyes land on Leah, and I grin, about to pull her in. She takes a step backward, shaking her head. "Oh, no, no, no." She's not quick enough, though. I wrap my fingers around her wrist and pull her into the water.

As she stumbles into the lake, she squeals, "Paige!" Her bouncing curls are plastered to her face when she comes to the surface. Pushing her hair back, she glares at me, but it doesn't last long. Her face breaks into a grin, and she tosses her head back with laughter.

Juri smacks water in Luke's direction, making him jump back. "Come on in. The water's fine."

Luke puts his hands in the air and retreats backward. "I'll take your word for it, man."

"Luke, get in here!" Leah yells playfully.

I flip my head over and try to wrangle my wet hair into a bun. When I lift my head, I'm met with Luke's stare. His blue eyes peer into me, and I suddenly feel exposed in my wet clothes. I try to shrug off the feeling and say, "You'll end up in here one way or another."

He sighs, his shoulders sagging. He seems to accept his fate soon enough because, with a running start, he does a cannonball off the dock.

When he comes up for air, Leah cups her hands on either side of her mouth and whoops in approval.

A little while later, we all make our way to the sandy edge. My soaked clothes help to keep me cool in the blazing sun. I sit with my legs stretched out in front of me and watch as the shallow water rocks up against me.

Juri shakes the water from his hair, taking a seat next to me. "You girls are trouble."

"You guys just can't handle us," Leah fires back.

Juri lazily splashes her, and she sticks her tongue out in response.

Luke gazes upward, blocking the rays with his hand. "Man, that sun is brutal."

I nod in agreement. "At least we're cool now… thanks to Juri." I jokingly give him a pointed look.

He grins with a sense of pride.

Luke pushes his wet hair back with his hand. "You've been kind of MIA ever since the bonfire. What have you been up to?"

I use my hand as a visor, so I can look at him without squinting. "Mostly spending time with Josh and Leah—well, occasionally Fredrick, I guess. How about you?" I don't even realize I've said it until I register the look on his face.

His demeanor changes at once, and his voice goes flat. "Pretty much the same but with different people." He tilts his head. "Fredrick?"

I look at Leah for help, but she's wrapped up in her conversation with Juri. Bringing my attention back to Luke, I say, "I met him at the bonfire. I don't know him well, but I've bumped into him a few times since then." I shrug it off as no big deal.

He looks down and digs a small stick into the sand. "Oh."

Using his short answer as an escape, I turn to the conversation next to us. "Hey Juri, where's Nick?"

He rolls his eyes. "Today is one of those stupid monthly anniversary things with Jenna."

Leah beams at his response. "He's seriously such a good boyfriend. Where's he taking her?"

Juri scoffs and leans back on his hands. "Who knows, he's already taken her to every restaurant in this town."

I sense something in his tone and ask, "Do you not like them together?"

He frowns. "That's not it. I mean, they're good together. It's just that everything with him involves her now."

His response reminds me of how it felt when my mom first met Trevor. The walls closing in around the life we had until all that's left are memories. I don't think it matters if the change in our lives is good or bad. To some extent, change makes us long for how things used to be.

Juri thinks for a moment before continuing. "And he's always trying to set me up with someone. He thinks I feel left out." He wrinkles his nose at the thought.

Leah slants her head. The large red-rimmed hearts framing her eyes hide most of her face, making it impossible to see her expression. "What's so bad about dating someone?"

Juri shakes his head. "Nothing. I just don't want him to find someone for me. I can do that myself."

Luke blushes. "Yeah, I know what you mean. Dan is always trying to help me out. It's embarrassing."

I frown at Luke, and he gives me a weak smile. I knew most of the schemes were Dan's idea, but I always thought Luke supported it. Now, I'm not so sure.

Leah breaks the awkward silence. "Dan is creepy."

We all laugh, even her.

Luke looks at her, bewildered. "What?"

She gapes at him. "You don't see it? I know he's your cousin, but you have to see it."

I may not be able to agree with Leah about Fredrick being scary, but I have no problem jumping on board when it comes to Dan.

He stares at us with wide eyes. "I can't believe you guys think that. I mean, I get that he's older, but I don't think that makes him creepy."

I think about all the times I've seen Dan over the years. "I don't know. He always looks like he's sneaking around."

Juri laughs. "Yeah, sometimes I'll be at a party, and I'll turn around to find him just standing there watching people. Creepy as shit."

Leah and I nod in agreement before she stands up. "Listen, Luke, we're not trying to gang up on you or anything, promise."

Luke gets to his feet as well. "I guess I just never saw it."

"I'm starving," Leah says as she hugs her torso. "Anyone know what time it is?"

Juri looks down at his watch. "One-thirty."

Brushing the sand off my legs I stand and say, "Leah and I should head home and eat something. Do you guys want to come?"

As Juri gets to his feet, he says, "Can't. I promised Mom I would help clean out the garage at some point today. Nick gets to have all the fun with his monthiversary bullshit while I'm stuck cleaning. Maybe I *should* get a girlfriend." He winks at Leah and me.

Leah and I look at each other, holding back laughter before looking back at him and shaking our heads.

He waves us off. "Your loss."

Luke seems reluctant at first but ends up saying he needs to get home too, which I'm thankful for.

Back at my truck, Leah and I lay towels on the seats to help soak up the lake water. Our wet clothes keep us cool on the ride home with the windows down.

☠   ☠   ☠

After taking turns showering and changing into comfortable clothes, Leah and I make turkey sandwiches for lunch. She sits in the chair with one leg hitched up. "I didn't know Luke had nothing to do with Dan's stupid matchmaker plans."

"Yeah, I didn't either. It doesn't make sense, though. Now that I think about it, we knew about Dan's plan before the bonfire, which means Luke knew, too."

She considers this for a moment. "Do you think he was lying?"

"Who knows." I set down a sandwich in front of Leah and take a seat across from her with my own.

She takes a bite and frowns. "Do you think there's a reason Austin hasn't asked me out?"

"No," I answer before taking a bite.

Leah purses her lips at me. "Then why hasn't he asked me out?"

I shrug. "I don't know, but I don't see why he wouldn't. If he's spending that much time with you, he's probably feeling the same way."

"Or maybe he's just bored," she says, her eyebrows knitting together. I lower my gaze at her, and she laughs. "Okay, okay!"

When Leah first moved here, all the guys at school wanted to ask her out because she was new and exciting. Josh included. He used to send me out to do intel on her because her locker was next to mine. Once the two of them got to know each other, it was clear there would be no romantic future, but that whole charade is what brought us together. It's funny how the people you least expect can impact your life the most.

7

This morning might be hotter than yesterday. I made the mistake of trying to read on our front porch swing. It only took fifteen minutes for my cheeks to turn pink and my hair to stick to the back of my neck. Giving up, I put my hair in a messy bun and head inside for some relief.

Checking my email in the central air sounds better than reading outside anyway. My computer takes its time turning on, but as soon as it's running, I see a new email from Mom.

Paige,

Is Josh okay? How did he hurt his hand? We're still not sure if Trevor and I are coming down. I'll let you know as soon as we sort everything out. Don't worry about not writing. I just get nervous! Is your summer good so far? Don't forget to do any summer homework. It's better to get it out of the way early than to let it pile up.

ILY Mom

I always do my summer assignments early. I've already finished half of the book and completed the questions for the corresponding chapters. The problem is, even though I love reading, I'd rather spend my time reading the books I want to read. *Death of a Salesman* just doesn't do it for me.

I type my response.

Hey Mom,

Josh is fine. I think he hurt it while playing football with the guys or something. I've been keeping up with the summer reading and doing the assignments. Leah and I went to the lake yesterday. It's way too hot to do much else this summer, so I'm sure my emails will start to sound repetitive. I hope you have a great day.

Xo Paige

Claiming Josh hurt himself in a football-related injury is almost too easy of a lie. Unlike Josh's mom, my mother will never see his busted knuckles to know the difference.

My long dresser is where folded clothes, crumpled receipts, and anything else I acquire throughout the day collects. Usually, more than one book ends up stacked there, and I have to return them to the shelves on my wall.

I pick up a knocked-over picture frame to reveal a shot of Leah and me sticking our tongues out. We're making faces at the camera, but I remember Josh taking the picture, so chances are we were making faces at him.

Under the frame hides a silver link bracelet my mom gave me for my seventeenth birthday in March. I think I wore it once before forgetting about it. I've never been one for jewelry, always finding it more annoying than anything else. I frown at the forgotten bracelet and clasp it around my left wrist. The delicate silver chain is beautiful, yet simple. If I did wear jewelry, it would be my taste. I should make an effort to wear it more.

I turn on the radio for two seconds before turning it off. They're only talking about the miserable Florida weather. Every day it's the same thing: a heat index of an obnoxiously high number with a chance of afternoon thunderstorms. I can literally *feel* the heat, so listening to someone talk about it is just redundant.

Walking across the room, I put one of my Harry Potter books back on the shelf. Movement outside catches my attention, and I slowly set the book down before peering out my window. A black Jeep sits on our gravel driveway below, and my adrenaline spikes. I don't know anyone who drives a Jeep, and I'm not expecting any visitors. My eyes stay glued to the driveway, anticipating the stranger stepping out of their vehicle. A small voice in the back of my mind wonders if I locked the front door, but I don't abandon my lookout to check.

I've always had a fear of being home during a break-in. They don't happen often around here. Chuluota isn't exactly crime-ridden, but you never know. Sometimes I lie awake at night thinking about what I would do. I can usually come up with a step-by-step plan, but now that the moment is possibly here, I'm useless.

Fredrick steps out of the Jeep, and my relief is quickly followed by confusion. Tilting my head, I watch as he casually strides toward the front door.

My front door.

I run to look in the mirror above my dresser and take in my appearance. It's not great. I'm wearing a faded Toby Keith concert t-shirt two sizes too big, and a pair of grey cotton shorts. My hair still rests in a somewhat sweaty bun with flyaways and shorter strands falling around my face. I groan as I try to smooth some of the rebellious pieces.

Giving up, I head downstairs. I don't see a point in waiting for him to knock, so I pull open the door as he steps foot onto our porch. "Fredrick?"

He slants his head, a bemused smile pulling at his lips. "Hey, Neighborhood Watch."

Leaning against the door frame, I cross my arms and shrug. "Just doing what I can."

Every time I see him, it's as if I'm meeting him for the first time. Today is no exception. His dark hair is windblown, giving him a more rugged look, but his eyes are bright. He's wearing his usual dark jeans, this time with a light grey t-shirt. Leah's comments about Fredrick being *seriously so beautiful* run through the back of my mind. I try to ignore them.

He smiles when he reaches me at the door, and it's a real one—the type that reaches his eyes. "If we plan on going sailing, today's the day."

I falter briefly. "Right now?" I didn't expect him to make our hypothetical conversation about sailing a reality.

He lifts an eyebrow as he takes me in. Those molten eyes are burning through me, and my heart rate rises. His mouth quirks, my only clue that he finds me mildly amusing. "I told you we'd go sailing, didn't I?"

I swallow, trying to hide the fact that my heart pounds beneath the surface. "Yeah, I just didn't—" I shake my head. "I mean, I just have to get my stuff together."

Turning back into the house, I glance at him over my shoulder before heading up the stairs. "I'll be right back." The words come out awkward and stilted, and I want to slap a palm to my forehead.

With both hands in his pockets, he rocks back on his heels. "Take your time."

I nod before hurrying up the stairs, but I don't want to take my time. I want to get this day started as soon as possible.

My black bathing suit is still damp from yesterday, so I put on my blue one. I try to look for something cute to wear over it, but at the same time, I'm afraid of looking like I'm trying too hard. I give up and settle on denim shorts and a dark grey tank top.

A look in the mirror shows my cheeks are rosy, but now I'm not sure if it's because of the lingering heat or Fredrick waiting downstairs. My hair is already in a messy bun. If I take it out now, it will be kinked and bent, so there's no hope for much else. I leave it as is and reach for my aviator sunglasses, resting them on my head.

Back downstairs, I spot Fredrick looking at baby pictures on the mantle—*my* baby pictures. I bite my lip and hope he hasn't seen anything too embarrassing. I'm about to announce my entrance into the room when the sight of his right hand stops me. His knuckles are bruised and scabbed over. I wonder what might have happened but can't bring myself to ask. Eventually, I just say, "Hey."

"Hey," he says, still examining the pictures. When he turns around to face me, his eyes linger. After a moment, he follows my gaze down to his knuckles and jerks his hand out of sight. "Ready to go?"

His reaction confuses me, but my excitement for sailing makes me let it go. "Definitely," I say with a smile. "I can drive if you tell me where we're going." I walk over to the entryway table and reach for my keys.

Fredrick beats me to the punch and scoops the keys up effortlessly. He holds them up for me to see and says, "You lock up. I'll drive." He drops the keys in my hand and walks out the front door.

"But you already drove all the way here." I protest after him. The beach isn't exactly around the corner, so I want to make sure I'm being fair.

Fredrick stops on the front porch and raises his eyebrows, ignoring my comment. "Coming?"

I lock the door and turn around to find him already leaning against his black Jeep Wrangler, waiting for me.

"Of course, the guy who lives at the beach drives a Wrangler." I don't say it in a mean way. I love Wranglers, and I don't hate how Fredrick looks standing next to his. *Seriously, what is wrong with me?*

He smirks, his eyes shifting to my truck. "Do you really want to talk about driving stereotypes?"

I let out a laugh because I know he's right. I have the most

Chuluota-looking truck imaginable. Walking past him, I get in the passenger seat, but before I've even buckled my seatbelt, he's already gotten into the car and started the engine. *How did he beat me?* I'm about to ask him just that, but a beam of sunlight creates a halo effect around him as he glances in the rearview mirror, making my breath catch. I flip my aviators down and look straight ahead, staring out the windshield. *I need to get a grip.*

I keep my eyes fixed on the space in front of me as a precaution. The last thing I need is for Fredrick to catch me staring. I ask, "So, where exactly are we going sailing?"

His arm rests on the back of my seat as he looks over his shoulder and reverses. The added closeness between us makes it impossible not to look at him. Not to mention, the scent of coconut and sandalwood consumes me. I've always loved the beachy smell of salt and sunscreen and combined with Fredrick's looks, it's almost too much to handle. He keeps his focus out his back window, but I can see the corners of his mouth twitch. "You'll see."

"Aren't we going to the beach?"

He gives me a sideways glance. "You'll see," he says again. With a fleeting look in my direction, he smiles and accelerates down the gravel road.

I playfully roll my eyes and surrender to looking out the window. I have a feeling that's the most I'll get out of him.

Riding with Fredrick is different than riding with Josh or Leah. Fredrick seems to enjoy the silence when he drives. He doesn't blast music or try to fill the quiet with small talk. Josh and Leah usually crank up the music and provide a dynamic performance along with it. For Josh, it's always *ACDC*, and for Leah, it's usually songs from Broadway musicals. I'm not a huge fan of either, but watching them sing and dance in the car is enough to keep me entertained.

Driving with Fredrick feels like a void in comparison. After taking as much quiet as I can handle, I say, "Can I at least turn on the radio if you're not going to talk?" I make sure to play it off with a smile, but I'm hoping he takes the hint.

The look he gives me makes me feel like he had forgotten I was in the car with him. "Oh, sorry. Uh, how's Josh's hand?"

Not exactly the topic of conversation I was hoping for. "He says he can use it again. Just waiting for the cuts to heal now."

Fredrick glances at his own busted knuckles, but he just nods. More silence.

"So, how long will it take for us to get to this mysterious place?"

"Not long. We should be there in about twenty minutes."

"Oh, okay." I rack my brain for something else to ask him. "What do you usually do when you're not harassing me?" *Is this my best attempt at flirting? Pathetic.*

A wry smile pulls at the corners of his mouth. "Harassing you? Is that what I'm doing?"

"I mean, you pop up at my grocery store and my house, so…" I let my voice trail off as I look over at him. He shakes his head and laughs to himself. I add, "Do you bother all the girls you meet like this?"

"The other girls don't usually complain." His words catch me off guard. He glances in my direction, watching for my reaction. When I don't say anything, he asks, "Jealous?"

My eyes narrow. "No." I go back to staring out the window until I hear a breath of laughter that makes my head whip back around. "What's so funny?"

He keeps his eyes on the road, but I can see him fighting back a smile. "You."

"Yeah, hilarious," I say with pursed lips.

"You are. And you know what else you are?"

Alright, I'll bite. "*What?*"

He lowers his voice and playfully whispers, "Jealous."

I scoff and cross my arms before returning my gaze to the roadside wetlands. "Hardly."

"I only cause trouble with you, Paige. Consider yourself lucky."

Even though I don't fully understand why *I do* feel lucky. This, however, doesn't stop me from coating my voice with sarcasm as I say, "Lucky. Sure."

My eyes find Fredrick, and he gives me a crooked smile. How he's looking at me makes my cheeks flush, so I change the subject. "Have you always lived near the beach?"

He shakes his head. "No, I used to live only a few streets over from yours."

I already knew this, but I'm not sure how Fredrick would feel about me getting my information from Josh, so I pretend we have a clean slate. "Why did you move out to the beach?"

His eyes don't leave the road, but even from here, I can see that something has shifted. His jaw ticks. "My dad has always loved the ocean more than anything, but I never thought he'd choose it over us. I guess I was wrong because he's out there somewhere living on his 30-footer with a crew of his friends, 'living the life,' as he would say." There's a trace of bitterness in his voice, and he pauses before continuing. "My mom was crushed and knew if there were any chance of him coming back, it wouldn't be inland. She knew she would have to live by the ocean, so now we do. Sometimes he'll stop by for a day or two, but we all know he's never coming back for good."

I don't know what to say. My voice comes out meek, but I manage to offer an apology.

Fredrick shifts in his seat. "I'm not sure why I told you that." He looks at me briefly like he's trying to gauge my reaction. "And it's alright. Honestly, we're better off without him."

"It must have been a lot, though. Having a parent who doesn't prioritize you sucks." My thoughts flash to my mother, but I shut them down. She would never do what Fredrick's father did, and anyway, I'm the one who left her.

Something in his expression hardens. "I can handle him not giving a shit about me, but I'll never forgive him for what he did to my mom." He shakes his head at the thought.

The way he spits out the words sends chills up my spine. There has to be more to the story he's not telling me, but I don't want to pry. "I'm surprised your mom moved to the beach. That's so… accommodating."

Fredrick forces out a laugh. "Yeah. Well, that's my mom. I know she did it to give us a chance to have a relationship with the guy, but it's pointless. The only thing he's ever given us is his old bait shop business—well, that and I got stuck with his name."

I think back to the night I met Fredrick and how I had felt so frustrated by everything about him, even his name. *What type of name is Fredrick anyway?* I had thought. The memory brings a small smile to my lips, and I say, "If it's any consolation, I think you have a great name."

His mouth pulls into a crooked smile, and I can see his eyes are lighter again. "If you like it, I guess it's not so bad."

My cheeks blaze, and I bite my lip to stop myself from breaking into a grin. Reining it in, I ask, "So, is that where you work? At your family's bait shop?"

Something flickers in his expression, but he recovers and says, "No, my brother Ben took that over. My mom and sister alternate helping out because there's only enough business to have two people on the payroll."

"So, where do you work?"

He shrugs. "I don't need to." I open my mouth to inquire more, but he cuts me off. "We're here."

I look up as Fredrick pulls the Jeep into a parking space overlooking the water. My jaw drops when I see where we are, even though I have no idea where it is. Thick trees cast shade over sparsely placed picnic tables. Beyond that, sunlight sparkles against the water's surface like shattered glass. To the right, a small dock houses a handful of sailboats. Each has its own unique, brightly colored sail, except for a solid white one at the end. I feel like I'm inside a picture taken for a calendar.

"Where are we?" I don't take my eyes off our view as I ask.

I feel him watching me. "The spot where your friends threw

the party is about five miles that way." He points to my right.

I nod to the collection of sailboats. "One of those is yours?"

Fredrick points to the boat with white sails at the end. "That one."

I beam at him. "It's beautiful!"

There's a gleam in his eye as he says, "Thanks. I've put a lot of work into her."

"Really? What did you do?"

He nods in the direction of the dock as he opens the Jeep door. "I'll show you."

We both step down from the Jeep and weave through the scattered tables toward the dock. The sandy soil beneath the trees is cool against my toes as my flip-flops pad through it. I follow him to the end of the dock, taking in each boat's detail up close. Most have chrome accents and railings, giving them a modern aesthetic. This only makes Fredrick's classic sailboat stand out even more. The benches and trim of the small boat are all made of wood, the grain visible beneath the stain.

"Did you do all this woodwork?" I ask.

A small dip of his chin is his only response as he stands back, watching me marvel over his craftsmanship.

From where I'm standing, I reach out and run my hand along the wood trim. It's glass beneath my fingertips, not an imperfection in sight. My voice comes out as a whisper. "Incredible... How did you do this?" I look up to find Fredrick still studying my reaction intently.

He puts his hands in his pockets and meets me by the edge of the dock. "My dad only ever had two passions: sailing, and carpentry. Before he left, he taught me both."

His voice doesn't hold any bitterness like it did in the car. There's no emotion behind his words at all now.

"How long did it take you?"

He shrugs. "About two years, I guess. It's a small boat, but I had to rebuild from the ground up."

I break my gaze from the boat and gape at him. "Two *years?*"

He nods to my hand on the railing. "If you had run your hand down that two years ago, you would have needed surgery to remove the splinters."

I grimace at the thought. "Well, I guess it's a good thing you fixed that."

Fredrick steps up into the boat and gets a pair of gloves out from one of the compartments onboard.

"Won't you be warm with jeans on?" I know I've never seen him wear anything else, but jeans and water don't exactly mix.

The corner of his mouth quirks. "I'll manage."

"And what are the gloves for?"

"Can't let the lines destroy my hands. Are you coming, or are you going to stand there and ask me questions all day?" He holds out a gloved hand for me to take and helps me on board.

In the boat, I point to a rope and ask, "So, this is a line?"

He shakes his head, his amusement shining through. "No, that's the sheet." Gripping one of the other nearby ropes and tugging it, he says, "This is a line."

"Right," I say slowly, "because calling them all ropes would make too much sense."

He locks eyes with me, a small smile forming on his lips, but he doesn't say anything. Taking a seat on the wooden bench, I watch as he untethers the boat from the dock.

☠ ☠ ☠

Fredrick has to stay behind to steer the boat, but once we're out in open water, he takes a break to sit across from me. "If you see a dock you want to stop at, just let me know."

"Okay." I look around but don't see any yet. Everything around us is a painting of blue and green. The water, and the natural shoreline flooded with trees. We're going in the opposite direction from where he pointed out the bonfire had been. Residential homes take up most of the beach on this end which, as it turns out, preserves a lot of the natural beauty.

The ocean breeze cools my skin while the sun bakes it. We sit together, listening to the waves crash against the boat, and the silence is in no way awkward.

When I look back at Fredrick, he has two wrapped sandwiches in his hand. Holding one out to me, he asks, "Hungry?"

I look down at the sandwich before bringing my eyes back to meet his. "You brought food?"

He gives me a funny look like I shouldn't be surprised. "It's only PB&J."

Frowning, I mutter, "Thanks," as I take the sandwich from him. My mouth opens to ask something, but I change my mind at the last minute, clamping it shut.

Fredrick notices and tilts his head, the crease between his eyebrows deepening.

"I didn't see you bring a cooler on board." My thoughts go back to us at the dock earlier, and I try to recall him carrying anything. I distinctly remember him not having a cooler.

His tight-lipped smile grows. "I came earlier this morning and got everything packed."

Taking a bite, I try to hide my blatant relief. Sometimes when I'm around him, I feel like I'm losing it. Swallowing, I say, "If I knew we were sailing today, I could have helped you."

He shrugs. "Ben hasn't come out here with me since Dad left, so I'm used to handling the prep work."

I debate asking my next question, but Fredrick has been so open with me today. I feel like I need to take advantage of his mood. "When did your dad leave?"

He thinks for a minute before answering. "It's been about four years now."

Thinking aloud, I mutter, "That was right before I moved here."

"Yeah, I know." He finishes his bite before continuing. "It's a good thing you moved here, too. I don't know how bad things with Josh would have gotten if you hadn't shown up. You gave him something else to focus on."

"I don't understand why things are so bad between you two. I mean, isn't it expected to lose touch with someone when they move to another town?"

Fredrick nods, considering my question. "It is, but he didn't like the crowd I started to hang with... and honestly, I didn't either."

His second remark gets my attention. "You didn't?"

His eyes harden before he diverts his gaze back to the water ahead of us. "My friends are kind of a packaged deal. Some are cool, and others are..." His voice trails off until his eyes find mine again. "Well, the others are the reason Josh was losing his shit."

I try to think of what Fredrick's friends must be like. I can't imagine him hanging out with people much different from himself, and he's not so bad, but he was alone at the bonfire. "I don't think I've met any of your friends," I say.

His eyebrows furrow. "Yes, you have."

I shake my head, trying to remember if I've seen Fredrick talk to anyone other than Josh or myself. "I don't think so."

He leans toward me and says, "I thought you said you knew the people who threw the beach party."

I nod slowly, unsure of where he's going with this. "I do..."

"Then you know Dan?"

My eyes widen. "You're friends with *Dan?*"

Fredrick's jaw clenches. "*Friends* is generous."

Of all the people Fredrick could be friends with, Dan was not who I expected.

"He's so... different than you," I say, choosing my words carefully.

Fredrick's lips press together, but something softens behind those brown eyes. "You don't like him." It's not a question.

I look down at my sandwich, not wanting to say the wrong

thing. "I don't know him other than that he's Luke's cousin."

Fredrick glances down at what's left of his sandwich before tearing off a piece of bread and tossing it into the water. A seagull swoops down to snatch it within seconds. "Right," he says as he watches the bird fly off into the distance. "You and Luke."

"I'm sorry. What?"

Ignoring my question, he asks, "What's going on between you two anyway?"

I blink. "Nothing's going on between us."

He shrugs, "That's not what I heard."

My face runs hot, but I don't let my eyes leave his. It's hard to keep the anger out of my voice when I say, "Who told you that?"

Fredrick looks at me with an unsure expression and answers slowly. "Dan saw me talking to you at the party and wasn't happy about it. He said you guys had something going on."

My eyes narrow. "And you believed him?"

Fredrick, looking far too casual, gets up and goes back to steering the boat. "Why wouldn't I?"

I have no idea why he wouldn't believe Dan. Dan's his friend, so I guess it makes sense, but my blood simmers anyway. Turning to face him, I say, "Maybe because I spent most of the party talking to you—not Luke." I raise my eyebrows at him expectantly.

"So you're not involved with Luke," he says, his intense gaze burning into me.

"No."

Fredrick's stare is unwavering. "At all?"

This conversation is making me breathless. "Not even a little."

I expect some type of reaction from him, but his face reveals nothing as he turns over a can of soda in his hands.

I've kept my eyes on him through this whole conversation, and I have no idea where he got the can of soda.

My eyes narrow. "Is that your trick or something?"

Fredrick shifts his stare from the can to me, an eyebrow cocked. "What?"

Marching over to him, I bend down and open the cooler. "This is me getting a soda." Once I retrieve the can from the cooler, I slam the lid and hold it up for him to see. "You just saw me get something to drink, but I never see you do *anything*."

Fredrick laughs but avoids my stare. "I told you, practice."

I shake my head. "No, it's not practice. It's something else."

His smile falters. "It's practice."

Taking a hard seat back on the bench, I let out a huff. "Okay, whatever. Let's say it's all practice. Why would you need to be good at something like that anyway?"

Fredrick's voice sounds gruff as he mutters, "It's nothing."

"Clearly." I give him a dubious stare before cracking open my soda and taking a sip.

He sits across from me, forcing me to look at him. "You're just going to sit here?" he asks.

I roll my eyes. "You're the one with the secrets."

"I don't know what you want to hear, Paige. Let it go," he says with an edge to his voice.

His tone carries a warning, but I ignore it. "I don't understand why you can't tell me." Shaking my head, I add, "No wonder it drove Josh insane. It's making me insane, and I've only been with you for an hour."

His eyes lock on mine. "You wouldn't understand."

Getting to my feet, I throw my hands in the air. "Oh, yeah? Try me."

Fredrick looks up at me, the same impassive look on his face that he gave the guy at the bonfire. "No."

My chest rises and falls. "What's the point of me being here, then? What's the point of bringing me here if you're not going to talk to me?"

Fredrick rubs both hands over his face, but when he looks up at me again, his expression softens. "I do want to talk to you but not about this."

"That's not how it works," I say, crossing my arms.

He gets to his feet, matching me. "Christ, you're infuriating, you know that? Why can't we have fun and get to know each other?"

"I'm trying to get to know you!" I didn't mean to yell, but my voice comes out louder than expected.

He runs a hand through his windblown hair. "Trust me, you don't want to know."

My eyes narrow as we stand facing off, literally toe to toe. "I can't trust you if I don't know you."

Fredrick throws his arms in the air. "Shit, Paige. I swipe stuff, okay? Is that what you want to hear? Are you happy now?"

My brows furrow because I don't understand. "You what?"

"Steal." His eyes are equal parts angry and anxious. "I'm a fucking thief, Paige."

I stare at him, unsure of what to say.

He raises his eyebrows. "A con, pickpocket, crook, whatever you want to call it, that's what I am."

At first, I think he's joking, but the way he's staring at me tells me otherwise. I might be in shock because I can't believe the words coming out of his mouth. There's no way Fredrick could be a criminal. Isn't denial the first stage of shock? Oh wait, that's grief. What's the first stage of shock? Does shock even have stages? Never mind, not important. What's important is it turns out Fredrick is mysterious for ugly reasons.

I can't contain my laughter. Maybe laughing is a stage of shock? Either way, I'm completely cracking up.

Fredrick rubs the back of his neck, clearly unsure what to make of my reaction.

When I finally catch my breath, I wipe my forehead with the back of my hand. "Okay, let me get this straight. You live on the beach, have a boat, and steal from people?"

He keeps his eyes locked on mine, but neither confirms nor denies.

I choke back my relentless laughter. "Wouldn't that basically make you a pirate?"

A stressed laugh escapes him, sounding more like a cough. "You're joking, right?"

My lips twist as I try to fight my smile. "I mean... I don't know exactly what you do, but if the shoe fits," I say with a shrug.

Fredrick shakes his head. "I'm not exactly out here with a peg leg, shooting cannons."

I roll my eyes but can't help the corners of my mouth from twitching at his comment. "I was thinking more modern-day."

He frowns, watching me carefully. "You think I'm a pirate."

I think Fredrick is a lot of things, but I don't think his confession has sunk in yet. My mind can't wrap around the thought of him being any of the things he listed. So, pirate, it is. "I think you could be," I say with a nod as I take a seat.

The ocean seems louder than before, and I'm suddenly more aware of the waves rocking us.

"Have you ever stolen anything from me?" I blurt without thinking.

He looks at me, bewildered. "What?" he says, as he slowly sits across from me again.

The way he's looking at me makes me want to take it back. I glance down at my hands in my lap. "I feel like it's a valid question under the circumstances."

"No," he says adamantly.

I study him, looking for sincerity. His brown eyes are almost molten as he stares back at me, but I can't help thinking of all the times he made himself nearly invisible through ways of stealth. "You took my hotdog at the bonfire."

Fredrick rolls his eyes, but I can see a smile tugging at the corners of his mouth. "How will you ever forgive me?"

I try to wrap my head around everything and feel haunted by the mention of Fredrick's friendship with Dan. "Does Dan steal too?"

His body stiffens at the mention of Dan's name. "You could

say that."

"You don't like him," I say, mirroring his words from earlier.

Fredrick locks eyes with me. "He's a prick." Earlier Fredrick didn't show any feeling when I told him Dan was lying about Luke and me, but I heard his feelings on the matter loud and clear in those three words. As if reading my mind, he goes on to say, "I planned on staying away from you after the bonfire."

"Why?" I demand. It feels like I've finally pried open a locked door, and I want to see everything that's been hiding behind it.

Fredrick pauses, and it looks like he may not answer my question, but then he rests his elbows on his knees, leveling with me. "Because Josh is right. You're better off without me."

Our knees are almost touching as we sit across from each other, and I can't help staring down at his hand. It's resting just outside my bare knee, and just the thought of him touching my leg makes me swallow hard. "I don't think that's true," I say, but my voice comes out as a whisper.

Fredrick registers everything. His dark eyes shift to the base of my throat, to his hand, to my knee, and when he shifts in his seat and sits up straight, disappointment floods through me. "Well, I do."

With a little more conviction this time, I ask, "Then why am I here?"

He stares at me for a long moment, and I squirm under the intensity of his gaze. I notice when his eyes fall on my mouth for half a second, and that alone is enough to make my breath catch. Lifting his gaze to meet my stare again, he says, "Because I'm being selfish."

My head swims with too many thoughts. Taking a deep breath, I try to let the salt air still my mind. "Fredrick, you can't steal to get by in life," I finally say, unsure how he'll react.

"I know. When I started, I felt like I had no other choice. I'm not saying it will be like this forever, but this is my life for now."

His casual response to everything makes my mouth go dry. "That doesn't make it okay."

He nods, seeming to agree with me, but then he asks, "Would you notice if a five-dollar bill went missing from your wallet?"

I let out a laugh in disbelief. "Yes."

He shrugs. "Well, a lot of people wouldn't."

"How would you know? You don't know what people are going through. That five dollars might be all they have to buy food."

He sits up straight. "I know that a lot of people don't notice because I've been doing this for years, Paige. I always take small amounts, and no one has the slightest idea." He pauses before adding, "And I don't steal from just anyone."

I try not to dwell on the fact that he's been stealing from innocent people for years. Even thinking it sounds far-fetched. "You mean, you choose your victims carefully," I sputter.

Unfazed, he just says, "If I need to, I can return it as easily as I took it."

He can't be serious. I roll my eyes and lean back against the side of the boat. "Fredrick, you can't do that."

He sighs. "I know what I'm doing. I only take a small amount of cash from people who won't notice."

I sit up straight and look at him directly. "Does Josh know?"

He hesitates but says flatly, "No."

"Well, no wonder he thought your friends were sketchy. It's because they are!"

His usually soft eyes harden. "You don't know what you're talking about."

We glare at each other, neither one of us saying anything.

He gets up to do whatever you do while sailing a boat, but eventually, ends up sitting across from me again. The waves that felt so relaxing before, now emanate aggression. A heaviness sits in the pit of my stomach as I imagine all the unlucky people Fredrick has encountered over the years.

Finally, he says, "I know you don't understand, but I can't stop… not right now."

When I speak, my voice comes out rough from lack of use. "What does that even mean? Why can't you stop?"

"It's more complicated than what you're thinking." He opens his mouth to say more, but instead, reaches down and pulls up his jeans, exposing his calf. My eyes widen when I recognize the same skull tattoo Dan has on his forearm. The two lines forming an X where the skull's mouth should be taunts me like they've been holding back Fredrick's secrets all along.

"Th-that's Dan's tattoo," I stammer.

Fredrick drops his pant leg, concealing the black ink. "We all have one. Some of us just advertise it more than others."

They all have one? Questions reel through my mind, but I find myself unable to speak. Between the tattoo and Fredrick's busted knuckles, I'm starting to think this isn't just a stealing habit. Everything he's saying makes it sound like he's in a gang… and there's a lot more that comes along with that lifestyle than pickpocketing people.

Fredrick has a pained expression when he continues. "Everyone in my group has this tattoo. It was sort of an initiation, I guess. We all have the same tattoo, and we all keep the first thing we stole with us at all times."

"What's yours?" My voice is barely above a whisper as I try not to think about rituals being a sign that he's in a gang… a gang of pirates? My head spins at the thought.

Reaching into his shirt, he pulls out the gold chain necklace. At the end of the chain hangs a small gold medallion, about the size of a dime. When I look closer, I can see the shape of a geometric sun engraved on the small circle.

"This," Fredrick says as he loops his thumb around the chain and holds the tiny medallion out for me to see.

I study the necklace. The hammered gold doesn't look new. Its weathered edges are dull from age.

Breaking my stare away from the necklace, I meet his gaze. "What's the first thing Dan stole?"

His shoulders relax now that I'm talking again. "Have you ever noticed he has his ear pierced?"

I nod. It's almost impossible to picture Dan without the diamond stud in his ear. "The first thing he stole was the diamond?"

The corners of his mouth quirk. "Dumbass stole the actual earring." He shakes his head. "Right after he stole it, he had to go get his ear pierced. Nobody knows if the diamond is real, even though he swears it is. He won't let any of us look at it closely enough to find out."

I gape at him. "He had to get his ear pierced just so he can always have it with him?"

Fredrick shrugs. "Rules are rules."

I try to hold back my laughter, but it comes out anyway. He laughs too, and it feels good to know we both have the same opinion of Dan.

Music from a nearby dock catches our attention, and Fredrick turns to me. "Want to check it out?"

I know I shouldn't. He's a thief, a crook, a pirate—all of it. He's not the person I thought he was. He's not a good person—he can't be, but before any of that can stop me, I hear myself say, "Sure."

8

Fredrick leaps out of the drifting boat, effortlessly tying it to the dock. He's more careful around me now. Gone are the bright eyes and snarky attitude. He's guarded again.

I hesitantly take his hand as he helps me onto the dock. Fredrick admitted he's a criminal, and if he's in a gang, that's not even the worst of it.

But I'm still here.

Not only that, I still *want* to be here.

Part of me knows I should tell him to take me home, accept that he isn't who I thought he was, and never look back. But it's not that simple. Being human is multifaceted and messy. I may have one small piece of me trying to err on the side of caution, but the rest of me feels alive with new energy—an energy I'm not willing to give up just yet.

Fredrick nods in the direction of a shaded path. The sandy

ground turns out of sight with thin wispy trees lining each side. "It sounds like a party. Are you sure you want to go?"

I look down the secluded trail. Bass thumping from an amp in the distance thuds in my ears, and I know it must be a live performance.

"Yeah, I think it will be fun." I smile reassuringly. I don't like that Fredrick steals, but he's been honest with me today—and that alone has me intrigued.

He nods, but his expression remains a stoic mask, hiding away anything he might be thinking.

Holding out his hand, he gestures for me to take the lead, which I do cautiously. I know he wouldn't leave me here, but I'm still compelled to look over my shoulder to make sure he's following. Even my own steps are muffled in the sand, so any hope of hearing him walking behind me is lost completely.

The end of the path reveals a beachside restaurant to our left with a big sign that reads, "Moe's Seafood Shack." The smell of fried shrimp and burgers wafts from the "shack." It looks like someone renovated an old boathouse into a place of business. The fact that I've never heard of the name tells me Moe's must be family-owned. No one would put a chain restaurant back here—not enough foot traffic. Even with its quiet location, the outdoor tables are packed with people enjoying the afternoon.

To our right, near the water, a small stage is set with a country band playing covers of popular hits. It looks like the lead singer doesn't take himself too seriously with his flannel vest and Crocodile Dundee-style hat. He's singing a cover of Brad Paisley's "I'm Gonna

Miss Her," a funny song even without the lead's added dramatics, but it's nice to see he's having fun. Everyone in the audience sways and sings along to the tune, clearly having a great time. The restaurant must be hosting an event, and from the looks of things, there's a strong turnout.

Fredrick scans the beach like he's looking for something. Watching him gives me a flashback to how he did the same thing at the bonfire the night we met. Looking back, I think he was trying to avoid Josh then. I doubt he's looking for Josh here, though, so I wonder what he's searching for… or who?

"Do you know the band?" I ask to get his attention.

He shakes his head, his eyes still looking straight ahead. "No, they're not bad, though."

"You like country music?" I don't bother hiding the surprise in my voice.

The corners of Fredrick's mouth twitch. "I *don't mind* country music."

Standing at the back of the crowd, I'm tempted to move to the beat of the song like everyone else enjoying the show. The only reason I don't is that any movement on my part would look like a violent outburst compared to Fredrick's stoic frame.

I stand on my toes and lean closer so Fredrick can hear me over the crowd and music. "Okay, so how does this work?"

He looks down at me with his eyebrows raised. His eyes search mine for a moment, and his entire demeanor relaxes. "You want to see what I do?"

I shrug, unsure of what to say.

"Here's an obvious one," he says as he nods his head toward someone standing off to the side of the crowd. "See that girl?"

I look to find an attractive blonde who might be in her mid-twenties and nod.

As he explains his tactics, he leans closer to me. I try not to notice our arms touching and how close his face is to mine. "Every single thing on her is a recently released pattern from an expensive designer."

"You know the latest designer releases?" Frowning, I look at the girl. She reminds me a little of Leah.

Happy. Bubbly. Blonde.

Fredrick watches me intently as I study her. I can feel his eyes on me when he says, "I do." The words make me look up at him, and the earnest expression on his face is enough to make me swallow.

I return my gaze to the girl, my eyebrows pinching. "What if they're all gifts?" Fredrick rolls his eyes, and I scrutinize him further. "What if they're all gifts?" I ask again.

He sighs. "Then her sugar-daddy can spot her the petty cash I'd take. We don't steal a lot from one person. We take a little from lots of people. It's how we stay under the radar. I wasn't kidding when I said most people we steal from don't even notice."

I gape at him. "She's not even distracted. She's going to see you!"

Fredrick eyes me seriously. "Calm down. I won't take anything from her." Relief washes over me, but the feeling doesn't last because he adds, "I'll take something from him." With a slight bow of his head, he locks in on someone in the middle of the crowd.

I follow his gaze to a man, also seeming to be in his mid-twenties, dancing and enjoying the show. Turning to Fredrick, I say, "You're not—" My voice drops off when I realize I'm suddenly alone.

I stand behind a group of strangers and try to blend in. My hips move to the music as I crane my neck, looking for him. Everyone in the crowd keeps shuffling and blocking my view, and finding him is more difficult than I thought.

The idea of being caught here with him makes my heart pound. *Does this make me an accomplice?* The longer I scan the crowd for him, the more my anxiety grows.

Finally, I see him standing about three feet away from the man. He sways to the music, but it's obvious he doesn't care for dancing. His movements are stiff compared to the sea of carefree limbs surrounding him, bringing a twinge of a smile to my lips.

I try to watch him, but it's impossible to see through all the people. Once they clear out of the way, I briefly see Fredrick holding a wallet. He looks so casual with it. Anyone passing would assume he had taken out his own wallet, not lifted one off a stranger. In a matter of moments, people block my view once more, and I'm unable to see him take anything.

And when those people clear, he's gone.

He catches me off guard when he flashes a folded ten-dollar bill between his fingers before pocketing the cash.

"I get it. You have a talent for this, but..." My eyes narrow on the pocket he just put the money in, and I bite the inside of my cheek, not sure how he'll react to what I'm about to say. I shift my focus back to him. "You have to give it back."

Looking down, he shakes his head, but I catch his mouth quirking. Lifting his gaze to meet mine, he nods. "Okay. You're the boss."

As he walks away, I push myself up on my toes, straining to witness the return, but he disappears into the crowd too easily. I sway along to the music and anxiously scan the countless faces for him with no luck.

"There. Happy?" His voice behind me makes me jump. He raises his eyebrows at my startled response and adds, "Go on, keep dancing. Don't stop on my account."

Without giving myself time to feel embarrassed, I mutter, "I don't like it, but I get it… you're good."

A sly smile is his only response. Fredrick glances down at his pocket, noticing something. He pulls out a small piece of paper and unfolds it. His brows furrow as he reads, and when he looks up again, he tenses next to me. "Let's go." He grabs my wrist and attempts to pull me with him.

I stand my ground. "Why? What's on the paper?"

He's looking past me, his face serious before his eyes fall on me with a pleading stare. "Now."

I look over my shoulder at the crowd, but everything looks the same. There are people drinking, dancing, and having fun—exactly how it looked when we got here.

He cups the back of my neck with his hand, pulling me to him, and guiding me in the direction he wants me to go. His grip is firm but gentle, and the warmth of his hand on my skin makes it harder to think straight. "Don't look. Just go," he says in my ear, and goosebumps prickle my spine.

Trying to get my bearings, I take one last look over my shoulder. In the distance, three figures stand separate from the crowd. Two guys and a girl, staring directly at us.

My head snaps forward. "Who are they?"

Without looking at me, Fredrick murmurs, "Quiet."

When I look back again, the figures are gone. My heart jumps to my throat, and I quicken my pace. Once I start cooperating, I can feel Fredrick's body relax next to me.

Back on the dock, he flicks the folded piece of paper into the boat before offering his hand. I step up and kneel to collect the page. Opening the yellow-lined note, I see the word *leave* scribbled in sloppy writing.

Looking up after untethering the boat, Fredrick freezes at the sight of me holding the paper. It only lasts a moment, though, and once he recovers, he pushes us off the dock.

I watch him intently until the sound of thunder makes me glance up at the darkening sky. The rain starts slow, a teaser of what's to come. Rain always follows Florida's heat. I guess to control a perpetual fire, you have to douse it with water. I glance down at my bracelet from my mother and feel a stab of guilt. She would never approve of me wearing it so carelessly. I can hear her voice in my head, accusing me of not taking care of things and being irresponsible.

Sure enough, the heavy clouds crack, and the sky opens above us. My voice sounds like a muffled yell, drowned out by the pounding rain against the water. "What is this?" I lift the wilted paper.

Fredrick walks over and kneels next to me, his voice strained against the sound of the storm. "We have…" He thinks for a moment, and I know he's choosing his words carefully. "Territories." When my blank stare continues, he adds, "They must have thought I was tampering with what's theirs. It doesn't make any sense, though…" He trails off looking deep in thought. Before I can ask any questions, Fredrick gets to his feet and steers us in the direction of his Jeep.

I stare at the small page in my hands, with its smudged ink and water-logged shape. *Is this a warning or a threat?*

I try to picture the faces of the three figures who had watched us from the edge of the crowd. Maybe I didn't get a good look at them, or maybe I didn't think to pay attention, but I only have the vaguest recollection of what they looked like. One guy had light hair, the other had dark hair and a skinny frame, and the girl was petite with jet-black hair. *Do they know Fredrick?*

There are so many things I want to know. I watch Fredrick adjust the sails and think of all the questions I want to ask, but I'm afraid of what his answers might be. The rain makes his shirt cling to him, highlighting the muscles in his back as he stands to adjust the sail. He must feel me watching him because his eyes land on mine. My breath catches, and I dart my gaze back down to the soggy paper in hand.

After the sails are set, and we're back on track, Fredrick sits on one of the bench seats. It isn't until he sits that I notice I'm still kneeling on the floor of the boat. I get to my feet and take a seat next to him. With a deep breath that gets lost in the rain, I bring myself to ask the one question that has been eating at me. "What would they have done?"

"Hard to say."

I turn my head to look at him, wiping the rain from my eyes. "But you think they would have done something?"

His lips are a thin line as he says, "They may have."

"Life-threatening?" I press further.

Fredrick looks at me and shakes his head slightly. "No, not quite."

A shaky sigh of relief escapes my lips, and I lean back against the side of the boat. Thinking out loud to myself, I mumble, "They were pirates too…"

He laughs lightly and squints at me through the pouring rain. "Isn't there a different name you can give us?"

I think for a minute but shake my head. "That's what you are… a modern-day pirate."

He sighs before calling out over the storm. "Fine, and yes. They were uh, what I am." He looks deep in thought like he's wrestling with something.

"What is it?" I ask.

Fredrick brushes wet hair out of his eyes. "As far as I know, that part of the beach isn't claimed by anyone. Our group is the only one in this area. I don't know who those people were, but something doesn't feel right."

I stare down at the note in my hand. The paper has ripped

from the rain, but I can still see the faded writing. A shiver runs down my spine, but I'm not sure if Fredrick's words are to blame or the wet clothes clinging to me.

Minutes later, I feel a knock against the side of the boat as it gently bumps into the dock. Fredrick jumps out and ties the boat to the wooden post with ease. Once it's secured to the dock, he extends a hand for me to take as I step down.

Lightning flashes in the sky, making me jump. I've never been a fan of Florida's lightning. It's hard to be a fan of anything so powerful and unforgiving. Fredrick motions toward the Jeep with a nod of his head, and we run for cover.

Closing the door to the Jeep behind me, I welcome the break from the rain. My arms wrap around my torso as the water on my skin turns cold.

Fredrick looks over at me. "Are you okay?"

"Y-yeah I'm… good." I study him for a moment and notice he doesn't look cold at all. I shouldn't be cold. It's summer in Florida, but between the hidden sun, cool rain, and feeling of unease, I'm practically shaking. "Aren't y-you cold?"

He laughs lightly. "No. Here, take this." Reaching into the back seat, he hands me a dry black t-shirt with a bait shop logo on the front pocket.

I stare down at the shirt, unsure of what to do. I know I have a bathing suit under my shirt, but changing in front of him still feels oddly intimate.

He seems to understand my hesitation because he looks out the driver's side window and doesn't look back until I swap shirts and say, "Thanks."

When his eyes land on me again, they linger, making me self-conscious.

"What is it?" I ask as I look down, checking for anything out of place.

He rubs the back of his neck and lets out a nervous laugh. "Do you have to ask?"

Fidgeting in my seat, I say, "You're looking at me." I glance down at myself again, but everything looks normal.

Fredrick puts the Jeep in gear. "Jesus, Paige. You're soaking wet, and you're wearing my shirt. Of course, I'm looking at you."

My eyes widen, and my heart feels like it just dropped into the pit of my stomach. I'm relieved when he starts to drive because I'm not sure how I would handle those eyes taking me in again.

After a few minutes of driving in silence, I finally find my voice again. "So, you have a territory?"

He answers without looking away from the road. "I don't, but I guess you could say that our—Dan's group does."

"Your territory is the beach where the bonfire was," I say the words more to myself than anything else.

He nods. "It's convenient because we all live there."

"Wait, Dan's group? How many people are in the group?"

He gives me a weary look at the mention of Dan's name. "Dan started the group in our territory, so he's the leader… even if he's a shitty one. And there are five of us."

I try to imagine the other faceless criminals in my mind. "Do I know any of them? Other than you and Dan?"

Fredrick shakes his head. "I don't think so. There's Dan, Jason, Melissa, Carter, and myself." There's a playfulness in his eyes when he adds, "Speaking off the record, of course."

His added remark brings a smile to my lips. He's trusting me with not only his secrets but his friend's secrets too.

I hold up three fingers to show the scout's honor like they teach us when we're kids. "Off the record," I confirm. The mention of a girl's name surprises me. It's my own bias, but I never thought a girl would get wrapped up in something like this. "There's a girl?"

His lips twitch. "She's tougher than most guys I know, but yeah, Melissa is Carter's sister. Our group is small compared to most, but I like it better that way."

I raise my eyebrows. "Small?"

Fredrick nods. "Usually, they're made up of at least ten people."

My thoughts take me back to the three figures on the beach today. "But the group back there had only three."

His eyes tense at the mention of our encounter. "I have a feeling that wasn't all of them."

Aside from his charm and good looks, there's something dark about Fredrick. I watch him drive in silence and try to pinpoint what it is, but I can't.

The word *gang* pops into my mind again, and I blurt out, "Are you guys dangerous?" I immediately regret my question when I hear how ridiculous it sounds spoken out loud.

I expect him to laugh, but he considers my question seriously before saying, "Depends on the person."

Not exactly reassuring. "Meaning?"

"Look," Fredrick says, his fingers flexing around the steering wheel. "The larger the group, the more complicated it is. People get greedy. That being said, I've met people in smaller groups who would take things pretty far to get what they wanted."

My desire for answers makes me sit up straighter. "How far would one of you go to get what you want?"

His glance tells me I don't want to hear the answer, and I bite my lip as I turn toward the window.

I think about the first night I met Fredrick at the bonfire. Things seemed so simple then. Knowing what I know now, I look back at the memories with newfound clarity. The pieces click into place, and I suck in a breath. "You were going to steal from me the night we met, weren't you?"

He runs a hand through his damp hair and mutters, "I thought about it."

My jaw drops, and I'm not sure what to say. Should I be angry? Does it even matter? My head is swimming with too many thoughts, and I'm struggling to make sense of it all.

"I did what I always do, Paige. It wasn't about you."

When I look over at him, he seems sincere, but I still have to ask, "Did you take anything from me that night?"

He frowns. "No. I already told you, I've never stolen from you. I took your hotdog to see if you were paying attention, and by the time I was about to grab your money, you noticed me." He hesitates, and his voice is lower when he speaks next. "Once I talked to you, my plans changed."

140

A heavy silence falls between us. I don't want to ask any more questions. I don't even want to continue this conversation. Without asking, I turn on the radio for a break. I watch the passing trees, my thoughts spiraling until we drive by the lake Leah and I went to yesterday.

We're getting close to my house, and I don't want to end our day like this. I try to think of something to say as I turn down the music. "So," At the sound of my voice, Fredrick blinks a few times and sits up straighter, keeping his eyes on the road. I take a deep breath and say, "Thanks for taking me sailing. I… learned a lot." He nods but doesn't say anything, so I add, "I didn't know it was so complicated to sail a boat. With all those ropes…" My voice trails off as I study him. He doesn't appear to be listening at all. His eyes stay locked on the road in front of him, his mind elsewhere.

"What's wrong?" I ask.

Fredrick's jaw ticks as he glances at me. "Nothing. Just remember, you can't tell anyone."

The Jeep bumps its way up my gravel driveway, and I gape at him. "You think I would tell someone?"

He runs a hand over his hair, his eyes shifting to me again. "I don't know what to think."

I glare at him as he parks the Jeep. "I would never tell anyone." I need to get away from him. I need to clear my head. My thoughts and emotions are already all over the place, and the fact that he thinks I'd tell someone his secret only adds anger to the mix. Opening the door to the Jeep, I hop down. "But if you're that worried, let's forget today ever happened." Without another word, I slam the door shut and march up my driveway to the front porch.

I hate that he has affected me to the point of slamming doors. Even as I did it, it felt like a tantrum, but I don't know what to make of everything.

As I turn to close the door behind me, I steal a glance at Fredrick just in time to see him bang his fist against the steering wheel.

I turn around, pressing my back against the closed door, to find my dad sitting on the couch watching TV. Seeing him home startles me. "You're home early."

He sits up and looks over the back of the couch to see me standing in the doorway. "No, you're late." Turning his attention back to the TV, he adds, "You look a little wet, kiddo."

"Yeah, I know," I mutter. If he's home, it must be after six. I'm surprised I didn't keep track of time better.

I'm halfway up the stairs when I hear him call out. "Want me to order pizza?"

"Yes, please!" I yell back.

I grab clean shorts and a t-shirt from my dresser and hurry into the bathroom. My appearance startles me. I had forgotten about wearing Fredrick's shirt. As I pull the soft black t-shirt up and over my head, his scent floods my senses, making me wish he were still here. I feel a conflicted pang in my chest as I hold the shirt up to my nose, breathing him in. Why do I still feel so drawn to him? Everything I learned today—everything that *happened* today should have snuffed out any feelings I may have had for him.

But it didn't.

If anything, the smell of salt air and sandalwood makes me wish for a do-over. It makes me wish for another chance to set things right with him.

After a long shower, I get dressed and comb my hair. I consider shutting my bedroom door and diving into a book. Escaping today is almost too tempting, but my growling stomach leads me back downstairs.

We put on *That 70's Show* to kill time while we wait for the pizza to arrive. I would normally find myself enthralled in the gang's shenanigans, but my day with Fredrick runs through my mind on repeat.

The doorbell brings me back to reality, and I offer to get the pizza as a welcome distraction. The spare change always sinks to the bottom of the money jar, so I jostle it as I pull open the wood-grain door with my spare hand.

"Paige?"

My eyes dart up to find Josh standing in my doorway with no pizza. He looks terrible; his hair is a mess, and he has dark circles under his eyes.

"Josh? Is everything okay?"

He takes a deep breath and says, "We need to talk."

9

"Did I give you enough money, bud?" My dad calls from the other room as I let Josh inside.

"No pizza yet. Just Josh." I hold my breath and listen for any sign of him getting up from the couch. It would only take one look for him to know something is wrong. If that happens, the three of us will end up sitting at the kitchen table until my dad thinks he's fixed the issue.

Luckily, his answer comes from the other room. "Josh! How's it going, man?"

"Can't complain, Mr. L! Just came by to talk to Paige about something." Josh's voice sounds more convincing than I thought it would.

Before their conversation can continue, I interrupt. "We'll be upstairs, okay?"

"Sure thing."

In my room, I sit on my bed and wait to hear what Josh came here to say. I try to keep my eyes on him, but his intense stare makes me drop my gaze. I resort to twisting the silver bracelet around my wrist, trying to ignore the tightness in my chest.

Josh shuts my bedroom door and looks back at me. "You promised, Paige."

"Promised what?" The bracelet slides around my wrist again.

He walks to my desk and pulls out the computer chair, positioning himself directly in front of me, so I have no choice but to look at him. "You promised you'd stay away from him."

I immediately know where he's going with this conversation and have no desire to talk about this. The thought alone is enough to give me a headache. Rubbing my fingers against my temples, my voice comes out as a groan. "Why do you care so much about this guy?" I stand and aimlessly organize one of my bookshelves, if for no other reason than to avoid his glare. "It's a little over the top, don't you think?"

Josh sighs. "No, I don't. You don't know him like I do."

After learning about Fredrick today, Josh's comment makes me drop my copy of *Tuesdays with Morrie*. I quickly bend down to get it, putting it back on the shelf. With my back still facing him, I say, "Maybe I haven't known him as long as you have, but that doesn't mean I don't know him."

Frustration bubbles in Josh's voice, and it only makes me want to avoid this conversation more. "No, it's more than that. Paige, I promise. You. Don't. Know. Him."

Looking over my shoulder, I stare at him for a long moment,

trying to see all the things he isn't saying. With a huff, I walk back to my bed and sit across from him. "Fine. Why don't you help me get to know him better? Tell me all about big, bad Fredrick."

Josh's eyes drop to the ground, and he mutters, "Now you're just being annoying."

"I'm the one being annoying? What did you do, Josh? Follow me to see if I was hanging out with him?"

He doesn't lift his gaze. "It's not like that, Paige. I've seen..." His eyes lift to meet mine but only for a second before he shakes his head.

"What did you see?" I ask as I sit up straighter.

Josh closes his eyes and pinches the bridge of his nose. "Paige, I've seen him steal... a lot."

I know under normal circumstances, I should look surprised. But I'm not surprised, and today has been long, and I feel numb.

Once Josh is convinced I'm not going to say anything, he adds, "And he did it so casually like it was no big deal. He's a sketchy guy who hangs out with sketchy people."

I'm at a loss for words. *How had Josh seen Fredrick steal something? And when?* Earlier today, I knew he would take something, but even though I watched closely, I still missed it.

"You *saw* him take something?" I can't help that my voice sounds full of curiosity.

He scowls at my response. "Yeah."

"Oh." Luckily the doorbell rings, saving me from having to fake my reaction. I jump to my feet, and he looks up, taken aback by my sudden movement. I may sound a little too eager to get away from him when I say, "Pizza. Hold on."

My feet pound against the wooden stairs, getting my nerves out with each step. I thought if I left the room, I'd be able to think clearly, but my thoughts are still all over the place. I hear Dad get up from the couch, so I shout, "I'll get it!"

I'm not in any hurry to get back to my conversation with Josh, so the longer I can drag out this pizza retrieval, the better. My mind, numb as it may be, has resolved to deny knowing anything about Fredrick and the other pirates. I reach for the door handle just as the doorbell rings a second time.

I open the door to a grumpy-looking kid around my age with a name tag that reads Preston. "That'll be sixteen-fifty." Pizza Guy Preston has an unfortunate uniform. The red hat and red polo shirt only accentuate his bright red hair and freckles. He holds out a hand. "Er... money?"

"Oh, right. Sorry. Here you go."

He snatches the money out of my hand and mutters, "Thanks."

Closing the door, I pick up the pizza off the entryway table and call to Josh. "Josh, want pizza?"

He appears at the top of the stairs. He looks uncomfortable like he'd rather continue our conversation, but eventually, he clears his throat. "Sure."

A few minutes later, we're all sitting around the kitchen table with paper plates. My dad, oblivious to the tension between us, nudges Josh with his elbow. "I hear you're dating Kimberly, that true?"

Josh nearly chokes on his bite before shooting me a questioning look.

I put my hands up. "I didn't say anything."

Dad eyes us and laughs. "She didn't." When we both stare at him, he raises his eyebrows. "What? I know things."

Josh eyes my dad suspiciously before surrendering and letting out a sigh. "Well, I'm not dating her." He takes a bite of pizza, not looking at either of us.

Surprised by his answer, I say, "You're not?"

He hesitates before answering. "Well," he turns toward me, "you know how she's really quiet?"

I nod slowly as I chew my bite of pizza. "Yeah…"

"She's like that *all the time*. At first, I thought maybe she was just shy, but it never changed. She's gorgeous, but I couldn't take it."

Dad laughs, and I do too. It feels good to laugh with Josh until I remember why he's here.

Patting Josh on the back as he grabs another slice, my dad says, "On to the next, right? I'm sure a strapping gentleman like yourself must have the ladies lined up."

Josh smiles, and he almost looks bashful as he shakes his head and takes another bite. It's nice to see him like this. This is the Josh I know—well, usually know.

For the rest of their dinner, Josh and Dad talk about sports. I know them both too well to fake my interest, so I sit while they finish the rest of the pizza. My thoughts spiral into an endless cycle of feeling intrigued by Fredrick and prioritizing my friendship with Josh. It would be easier to pick the latter if I didn't feel so drawn to Fredrick in the first place.

My attention snaps back when I feel Josh stand from the table next to me. I quickly get up as well, mirroring his action almost too perfectly.

Dad raises an eyebrow at us. "You kids going back upstairs?"

I glance at Josh. The light that shone through his eyes moments ago has vanished, his expression now slack.

"Yeah, we'll be upstairs," I say as I grab Josh's wrist before Dad can start prying.

"Alright, I'll just be down here…" His voice trails off in mild concern, and I'm relieved when he doesn't ask questions.

Once Josh and I are behind closed doors, I don't hesitate to pick up where we left off. "Okay, so you saw Fredrick steal… but what? Why didn't you tell him you saw him? Why didn't he tell you if he knew you saw?"

Josh watches me with a careful expression. "Paige, if you'd just sit for a minute, we can talk about this."

I hadn't realized I was pacing the room. Pausing to look at him, I scoff. "We can talk about this?" I shake my head as I head toward my bed, sitting on my mattress with my legs crossed. "Josh, I've been *trying* to talk to you about this. You won't give me straight answers!"

Pullings his head back to look at me, he mutters. "Okay." Grabbing my desk chair to sit in front of me again, he adds. "You're right. I'm sorry, but that's why I came here tonight—to tell you that he steals shit." He opens his mouth like he's about to say more, but I cut him off.

"What did he steal?"

Josh blinks. "Everything."

I frown at the memory of Fredrick's claim to only pocket cash. "What do you mean by *everything?*"

Josh squares his shoulders, thinking. Finally, he shrugs. "A lot of stuff, I guess. I've seen him shoplift more times than I can count." He pauses for a moment, so I wait for him to say more. Eventually, he adds, "Yeah, I guess it was mostly shoplifting."

The pit of my stomach tightens into a knot, and my cheeks burn. *Did Fredrick lie to me? And if he did, shouldn't I expect as much from someone like him?* Josh studies me, and I know he's trying to gauge my reaction. "What did he shoplift?" I ask in a tight voice.

"Whatever he wanted," he answers flatly.

The room feels warmer than it should. "How often did it happen?"

I must seem angry because he lifts his chin, looking smug. He knows he's getting through to me. What he doesn't know is that I'm not angry because Fredrick steals. I knew that. I'm angry because he lied to me about what he steals and how—which I'm aware doesn't make sense.

"Almost every time we would walk into a store, I'd watch him take something."

"Didn't you talk to him about it?"

Josh looks at the ground. He appears torn for a moment until finally saying, "Yeah, I tried to talk to him about it, but he wouldn't admit to anything. At first, I would wait until we were out of the store and ask him how he got what he stole. He never told the truth, though. That's why you need to stay away from him, Paige. He only cares about himself. I was his best friend, and he lied to my face."

My voice comes out as a whisper. "So, he's bound to lie to me, too."

"Exactly, and I don't want to see him hurt you."

I soften at the sound of these last words. He cares about me—he always has, and I'm thankful for him. But as much gratitude as I feel toward Josh, I feel twice as much anger toward Fredrick.

I stand up, causing Josh to lift his head. "You know where Fredrick lives, right?"

10

The drive to Fredrick's house helps clear my head, and I find myself losing momentum. The burning anger that drove me to come here has dwindled to a flickering flame—hesitant and wavering.

But I'm here.

Ultimately, it's my unanswered questions that drive me forward. I don't exactly have a plan. All I know is that I want the truth, and I'm not leaving until I get it.

I hate how Fredrick and I left things today. I hate that he thought I would tell someone. I hate the tension between him and Josh. And I hate that the only reason I'm standing here right now isn't that I'm mad about him stealing but because he lied about *how* he steals.

I can't see the beach from here, but the sound of the ocean lets me know I must be only a few streets over from the blanket of sand and sea. The sky has already started to darken, casting long shadows in soft light.

The street is quiet as I take in the house in front of me. It isn't much different from other older Florida homes. A small, square frame made of concrete block. White stucco and bright blue shutters make the house stand out more than the others on the street. The house is worn in some areas, probably from years in this salt-rich environment, but they are overshadowed by a beautiful flower garden that seems to surround the house. This house feels like a home, and a loved one.

The fresh ocean breeze sends a chill down my spine. I left my truck parked around the corner to avoid drawing attention. The last thing I need is Fredrick confronting me before I've gathered my thoughts.

Josh took quite a bit of convincing for him to give me Frederick's address, but once he finally relented, I then had to persuade him not to come. I told him I needed to talk to Frederick alone. I think he finally understood after I locked my doors and left him standing in my Chulutoa driveway. I'd like to avoid another fight between the two of them if I can help it.

I hug my arms around my waist as another seaside breeze sends goosebumps across my skin. The air felt warmer at home, but here by the coast, my shorts and t-shirt leave my limbs exposed to the brisk night air.

I take a deep breath and make my way up the driveway. The glass front door gives me a clear view of Fredrick sitting in the living room, reading a book. Relief floods through me when I don't see anyone else. For the first time since meeting him, he's wearing black basketball shorts instead of his usual jeans. I wish I could say the casual attire takes away from his appearance, but if anything, I might like seeing him dressed this way more. The only thing keeping me grounded is the sight of the skull tattoo on his calf, reminding me of all the things I wish weren't true about him.

Hesitantly, I tap on the glass, and Fredrick's head snaps up, his eyes locking with mine. The corners of his mouth dip, his eyebrows furrowing.

Maybe I shouldn't have come here.

He closes his book and strides toward me, his face revealing nothing. My heart pounds in my chest, and I wipe my sweating palms on the denim of my shorts.

I take a step back as he opens the glass door, his head cocked. "Paige, what are you doing here?"

The longer I look at him, the harder it is to think straight. I drop my gaze and fidget with the bracelet around my wrist, spinning it the same way I did while talking to Josh. "I need to talk to you." Daring to bring my eyes back to meet his, I add, "Josh came to my house tonight and—"

"Do you want to come inside?"

I look past him at the seemingly empty house. "Is anyone else home?"

"They will be later, but we have time," he says as he steps aside.

I let out a breath and enter the house. Light hardwood floors, cool white walls, and oak bookshelves give the house a simplistic comfort I wasn't expecting.

Fredrick runs a hand through his hair and gestures toward the couch with a slight nod.

We take a seat, and I turn, hitching one leg up to face him. I could tip-toe around why I'm here, but I decide to come out with it. "Josh said he's seen you… take things." I check for his reaction, but he doesn't blow up like I thought he might. He's calm as he stares back at me, waiting for me to continue. "Why am I getting different stories from you two?"

Fredrick nods as if he had been expecting this, and the knot in my stomach tightens. "Josh told you," he says with an unreadable expression.

His response confirms Josh's accusations, and the warmth of my anger returns. "He's seen you take a lot more than a little cash, Fredrick." I know I'm speaking louder than I should; all the pent-up frustration finally has an outlet. "Not that stealing anything is okay. I'm just trying to understand."

His gaze is unwavering, and his voice remains calm. "Paige, that was a long time ago. That was when I first started, and I thought it was cool. I felt like I could get whatever I wanted, whenever I wanted, and I didn't care who I hurt in the process. It was all a game."

My eyes widen in disbelief. "A game?"

Fredrick watches me curiously. "Have you ever gone against what you're supposed to do? Broken a rule? Given into an impulse without thinking about the consequences?"

His questions give me pause. I wasn't expecting him to turn the conversation on me. I honestly can't think of a time I've ever done any of those things. The thought had never occurred to me. Now that I think about it, my first act of rebellion was probably going sailing with him, even though I told Josh I would stay away… but I can't say that now.

When I don't say anything, amusement flickers across his features. "I thought so."

"What does that have to do with anything?" I deflect.

He leans toward me like he's about to tell me a secret, lowering his head so I'm looking him square in the eyes. My heart pounds from the lack of space between us, and he says in a low voice, "It's the adrenaline. When I'm about to take something, my heart pounds, and every fiber of my body feels alive."

Like how I'm feeling being this close to you? Refocusing, I try to think of a time in my life when I've felt something similar, but my mind blanks. I get good grades, do my homework, have a few friends, and love reading. Nothing in my About Me screams excitement, but there's nothing wrong with that… is there?

"Do you still shoplift?" I ask to bring the focus back to his lack of morals, not my lack of rebellion.

Fredrick leans away from me, and I can breathe again. "Not like I used to."

With the added distance between us comes clarity, and with that clarity, my anger spikes. Only this time, I'm mad at myself. I'm mad that I care more about him lying to me than him stealing from people. I'm mad that I want there to be more between us—that I want to feel like he *shouldn't* lie to me. I'm mad that I'm still drawn to him even though he's admitted to doing things that I *know* are wrong. "Why reveal so much, but still lie? What was the point of telling me in the first place? You tell me, but not your best friend? What else have you been lying about?"

His eyes are dark as he answers. "I didn't want to overwhelm you, so I told you what I thought you could handle." He bounces his foot against the floor in frustration. "And I didn't tell Josh because he's a fucking hot head, Paige. He would have turned me in. And you…" His eyes search mine for a moment before looking away and shaking his head. "I don't know why I told you. I shouldn't have."

His last sentence hurts me more than it should. "You think Josh would have ratted you out?"

Annoyance flickers across Fredrick's features. "He tried to."

There's no point trying to hide my surprise, but I look down at my hands anyway. "He didn't tell me that."

Fredrick shrugs. "Yeah, well, I'm sure there's a lot he left out."

"What happened?"

He glares at me, and I sit up straighter. His warm brown eyes almost appear black. Abruptly, he gets to his feet. "Just drop it."

"Why?" I stand too, wanting to keep the playing field even.

"You don't need to know everything. I steal, Josh thinks I'm a piece of shit, and you're stuck in the middle. I get that. But you don't need to know everything."

"Fine," I snap. "But you shouldn't have lied to me."

Fredrick scoffs. "I don't know what you expect. I lie, I steal… maybe you should do yourself a favor and stay away from me."

My mouth falls open as a short, stocky guy walks through the front door. The interruption makes me relax my hands, which I didn't realize I had balled into fists. The guy, who I'm assuming is Fredrick's older brother, Ben, hangs his baseball hat on a hook near the front door. He turns to find Fredrick and me standing in the living room.

Ben raises his eyebrows and opens his mouth to say something, but I mutter, "I was just leaving." I don't look back at Fredrick as I take advantage of the still-open door. I sidestep past a woman and hurry toward my truck, wishing I had parked closer.

Halfway down the driveway, I feel him walking next to me. I didn't hear him come out of the house after me, but I suppose that's to be expected at this point. I ignore his presence and quicken my pace.

Fredrick steps in front of me, cutting me off. I look up and see his face has relaxed since our argument, his eyes now soft with concern.

I let out a sigh. "What? I'm staying away from you."

Tilting his head side to side, he says, "I didn't mean..." His words trail off as he looks around us, and I see his eyes lock on something in the distance. His hand wraps around my wrist. I glance in the direction he's looking, but I don't see anything out of the ordinary. Only a couple casually talking can be seen at the end of the dark and deserted street. Bringing my attention back to Fredrick, I see him staring down at my left wrist in his hand, the silver bracelet reflecting the moonlight.

"What's wrong?" I dip my head, trying to look him in the eye, but his gaze remains fixed.

He scans over me and looks toward the end of the street like he's trying to piece something together. When his eyes fall on my wrist again, he says, "I thought you didn't wear jewelry."

My eyebrows pull together. "I usually don't… what's with you?"

His eyes drift upward, but not to look at me. He looks past me again.

"Fredrick, what's going on?" I ask.

"Come back inside." It isn't a question. This feels like the warning we received at the concert earlier today, so I don't fight him.

Reentering the house, I see Ben sitting on the couch watching TV with his arm resting on the backrest. He has the hair of a surfer, longer and lighter than Fredrick's. He's good looking too, but even though he's older than Fredrick, his light features make him look more boyish.

A woman, who I'm assuming is Fredrick's mom, sits in the same recliner where Fredrick had been reading. She sits with one leg crossed over the other while she flips through a Better Homes & Gardens magazine. Her ashy blonde hair rests in a messy bun at the nape of her neck. I take note of her soft but angled features, making her delicate looking.

Ben looks up from the episode of *South Park* he's watching and nods to Fredrick and me standing in the doorway. "Not leaving, I see." He smirks before returning his attention to the TV.

Fredrick's mom shoots Ben a warning glare as she sets down her magazine and smiles at me. She gets up and walks over to greet us with a warm welcome. "Don't worry about him. Half of what comes out of his mouth isn't worth hearing anyway."

"You have a beautiful home." I manage to spit out. I've never been particularly skilled at hiding my emotions and hope she can't sense everything welling up inside me.

My compliment lights up her face, and I can see she holds a lot of pride in her home. She looks over at Fredrick, still beaming. "Oh, bring her around anytime."

I let out a small laugh, but Fredrick's tight-lipped smile looks forced, his mind elsewhere.

Fredrick's mom holds out a hand for me to shake. "And your name?"

Taking her hand, I smile politely and introduce myself. "Paige. It's nice to meet you, Mrs. Pryce."

Her eyes widen, and she grins. "Oh, *you're* Paige. Well, I've heard quite a bit about you." She looks at Fredrick, who isn't even faking anymore. The woman ignores her son's brooding expression and turns back to me. "Please, for the love of all that is good in this world, call me Kelly."

I glance at Fredrick, my eyebrows pinching together, before bringing my attention back to Kelly. "You've heard of me?"

Ben looks over at us and interjects. "You're the only one he's ever taken on that boat."

I raise my eyebrows and look up at Fredrick again, but he won't meet my gaze. Instead, he speaks to Kelly. "I need to talk to Paige about something. We'll be in my room."

Kelly puts her hands up. "Well go on, then. Don't feel like you have to shoot the breeze with me."

Fredrick starts to walk down a hallway, but Ben calls out, "Wait a minute. How come I can't have some random girl in my room, but he can?"

Fredrick rolls his eyes.

Kelly laughs a smooth, pure laugh. "Because I trust Paige more than I trust you, and I only met her five minutes ago."

Fredrick walks further down the hallway again, and I look over my shoulder back at Kelly. "It was nice meeting you," I say again, not sure what else to say. I turn my head back around and see him holding his bedroom door open for me.

His room holds simple comforts like the rest of the house. However, his grey walls and espresso furnishings give the room a much warmer feel than the bright, airy living room. He has shelves on his wall that look like my own, but his holds fewer books than mine. The rest of the space belongs to athletic trophies and picture frames.

I spot a picture of Fredrick with an older man whom I assume must be his father. His dad's features are dark like Fredrick's, sharing the same dark hair and warm, brown eyes. He looks friendly. It's hard to imagine him as the selfish man Fredrick had described earlier, and I can't help feeling like Fredrick must not hate him as much as he says if he still has it on display.

His bed takes up the center of the room, and a large poster of dogs playing poker hangs over the headboard. *Figures.* Unsure of what to do, I find a seat on the edge of the bed and try not to think about the fact that I'm sitting where he sleeps.

As soon as Fredrick closes his bedroom door, I ask, "What did you see?" My voice is surprisingly even. "When we were outside."

Fredrick paces over to a smaller window on the side of his

room. He peers through the blinds before closing them and returning to sit next to me on the bed. "I might be wrong, but the people at the end of the street looked familiar."

"Like you know them?" I ask.

He shakes his head. "No, they look like the people we saw today." His eyebrows crease together. "They're older," he says, almost to himself.

"What does that matter?" I stare down at my bracelet as I wait for him to answer.

"Older groups are usually more established. They shouldn't be tampering with different territories. I don't understand why they'd be here." Fredrick rubs his temples as he continues to think aloud. "Usually by the time people in the group hit their mid-twenties, they keep to themselves."

My breathing quickens as fear grips me. "What do they want?"

Fredrick shrugs but still shows the same pondering expression. "I don't know."

I look down at the silver around my wrist. "Well, if they come up to me, I'll just give them what they want. My bracelet, wallet, whatever."

Fredrick stares at the space in front of him. "They wouldn't give you the chance."

"Why not?" I ask, feeling confused.

He sighs. "They're not muggers, Paige. The goal is to take it without you knowing, remember? They won't threaten you or try to force you to hand it over. They'll just do whatever they deem necessary." He hesitates. "And if you confront them, they'll either suspect you're in a group yourself, or that you know too much and need to be..." His voice trails off, and I'm grateful he doesn't finish his sentence.

"And what would happen if they thought I was a pirate too?"

Fredrick gives me a side-long glance for using the term before he shakes his head. "Depends on their intentions. If they're trying to challenge us for our territory, things could get bad."

I jump when the doorbell rings. Fredrick gets up too, but not as fast as I had.

I follow him to the door, where we can hear his mom conversing with someone quietly. At first, I can't see who she's speaking to, but once Kelly steps aside, I see him. It takes a moment for me to believe my eyes because inside Fredrick's entryway stands my father, looking furious.

He sees me walk out of the hallway and sighs. "Paige, what were you thinking!"

My eyes widen, and I stumble over my words. "Dad, I'm sorry. I... I know I should have told you where I was going, but—"

He walks over to me. "But nothing. It's a good thing Josh knew where you were. You can't just take off without saying anything." His eyes close as he shakes his head.

Looking past my dad, I can make out Josh's tall silhouette in the passenger seat of my dad's car. Even without seeing his face clearly, I know he's avoiding my stare.

Fredrick steps forward. "I'm sorry. I had no idea."

Dad looks Fredrick up and down with his lips pressed into a fine line.

"This is my friend Fredrick I told you about." I cut in, hoping to smooth things over.

He doesn't look impressed. "We'll talk at home," he says, turning to leave and tipping his baseball cap to Kelly on the way out.

She gives a curt nod, but when she looks my way, her eyes are sympathetic.

"Excuse me, Mr. Lawson?" Fredrick calls out.

My dad stops and turns to face Fredrick. He doesn't say anything.

Fredrick's voice is steady. "Paige parked her truck a few blocks away. Would you mind if I walk her?"

Dad stiffly nods and turns to leave. I watch him as he gets into his car and drives away without a second glance. If he knew there was any chance I may be in danger, I know he would see things differently.

Once the door closes, Ben lets out a slow whistle behind us, and Fredrick and I look at him. Shaking his head, he says, "Daddy drama right off the bat. Not a good start."

My cheeks flush at his comment, and Fredrick gives him the finger before turning to his mother and saying, "I'll be back soon."

After I sheepishly say goodbye to both of them, Fredrick holds the front door open. We leave the house in silence. The awkward tension gnaws at me, but Fredrick seems more concerned with taking in our surroundings.

About halfway to my truck, he looks over his shoulder, his body tensing beside mine. Instinctively, I move closer to him, our arms brushing with every cautious step. The people we saw were at the opposite end of where I parked my truck, so at least we don't have to pass them. I still can't shake the feeling that we're being watched, but maybe it's my overactive imagination.

Fredrick speaks with his mouth in a tight line and confirms my suspicions. "They're following us, but they're keeping their distance."

My shoulders tense, and I force out a slow breath. *Keeping their distance has to be a good thing, right?* I just need to get to my truck and drive home. No big deal. A gust of wind seems to take my newfound relief with it, bringing my paranoia back. "What about now?"

Fredrick laughs breathlessly. "I just looked back not even thirty seconds ago." He humors me anyway by looking over his shoulder. Immediately, his head whips back around. "They're following us, and they're not being subtle about it." His brows furrow. "They must know something…" His voice trails off as he continues to think to himself. A moment later, he grabs my hand and picks up his pace.

My heart pounds, and I'm not sure if it's because I'm afraid or because Fredrick holds my hand in his. I try to match his stride, but his legs are longer than mine, and I struggle to keep up.

Fredrick squeezes my hand. "I'm going to kiss you."

My face pales, and I try to face him. "You're going to *what?*"

He tightens his grip on my hand. "Calm down. Just on the cheek. I can't look back again without making it obvious."

My heart pounds harder, and I keep my eyes straight ahead.

Fredrick leans over and presses his lips to my cheek, making my hand tighten around his. I quickly loosen my grip, hoping he didn't notice.

His lips brush against my ear as he whispers, "Run."

By the time my brain can process what he said, Fredrick has already pulled my hand and started running. I lurch forward, stumbling behind him. It takes everything I have to keep up with him, and even then, I'm still falling behind. His hand holds steady around mine, and I'm able to risk a glance over my shoulder.

Fredrick yanks my arm around a turn, forcing my head forward again. I know a guy and girl are chasing us, but I couldn't catch any details.

My truck comes into view, a beacon of stillness among the chaos. The dark street stirs a memory of my father telling me I should always park in well-lit areas. He's right. I should.

Fredrick picks up his pace, and I fall further behind him even though our hands are locked tightly together. My legs threaten to give out any second, but I push them as hard as I can in this final stretch. I gasp for air, my lungs screaming at me with each step. The drumming of my heart matched the pounding of shoes on the pavement behind us.

Finally, we skid to a halt at the tailgate of my truck. A yell escapes me as Fredrick grabs me and hoists me into the truck bed. In an attempt to collect myself, I kneel in the bed of the truck, the cold metal welcome on my hot skin. I'm still gasping for air and have to grip the edge of the bed to steady myself.

The girl and guy were only a few feet behind us and slow to a jog, stopping a few feet from Fredrick. He was right, they are older, but not by much. They look to be in their mid to late twenties. Both hold sinister smiles on their haughty faces. The tall, thin guy has dull, light-brown hair and small dark eyes, making him resemble a starved rat. The girl, on the other hand, has black pin-straight hair and large, bright green eyes. She's pretty, but the way her dark makeup accentuates the bags under her eyes makes her look haunted.

I can only see the back of Fredrick, but even from this view, he looks threatening. His shoulders are squared, and he's standing completely still. I feel helpless as I watch our attackers move closer. I try to think of something to do, but I know if he thought I could help, he wouldn't have stashed me up here.

Neither of them seems at all fazed by Fredrick. They both come to a halt no more than a few feet in front of him.

After a moment of loaded silence, I blurt out, "What do you want?"

Fredrick tenses at the sound of my voice, but he doesn't tear his eyes away from the two strangers. I know he warned me not to confront them, but I can't sit here and do nothing. The couple both glance up in my direction, and it's obvious they weren't expecting me to address them.

After another moment of silence, I press, "Is it my bracelet? I don't have anything else."

The tall, lanky rat nods at Fredrick casually. "Yeah… my girl likes your chick's bracelet." His voice, laced with excitement, sounds pitchy and unnatural.

The girl smiles at her boyfriend, but it doesn't make her look any livelier. She takes a step toward the right side of the truck, and Fredrick matches her footwork. "Yeah, we saw you two today. I couldn't help noticing. *Very* pretty." She laughs and playfully bats her eyelashes before locking her eyes on me.

Unfortunately, the rat-looking man moves a step in the opposite direction, and Fredrick has to backtrack to match his footwork.

Without wasting time, Fredrick lunges, grabbing the rat-looking man by the neck. He spins and slams him up against the side of my truck, making the truck jolt beneath me. Fredrick doesn't waste any time, and I catch a glimpse of him pulling his arm back for a punch before I remember to bring my attention back to the girl.

She stares at Fredrick and her boyfriend with wide eyes until she looks at me. Her expression contorts into what I can only describe as pure loathing—like her feelings toward Fredrick have been projected onto me. She sprints toward me, and I know in a matter of moments, I won't be in this truck bed alone.

Pulling up on my knees, I scan the street for anyone who might be able to help, but the houses are all dark like they're turning a blind eye. I brace myself, shutting my eyes until the sound of something slamming into metal prompts me to open them. Looking around the bed, I'm confused when it's empty aside from a few leaves and branches. It isn't until I look over the side that I see them. It was the girl crashing into Fredrick that I had heard slam into the side of my truck. He must have jumped in her way at the last minute.

I wonder where the rat-looking man went, but there's no time to ask questions. Fredrick looks up at me, but only for a tenth of a second. The glance was too short to read his face. As quickly as he had appeared, he ducks out of the girl's grasp and disappears to find the guy again. I hear their struggle pick up where they left off and hope Fredrick isn't on the receiving end.

My hopes are interrupted when a petite hand appears on the edge of the bed. She's trying to climb up into the truck, and that's the last place I want her. I do the only thing I can think of: stand up, lift my foot, and stomp.

"Shit!" She curses as she glares up at me. With more determination, she tries again, so I keep stomping.

Everything keeps happening so fast around me, and I'm not sure where Fredrick is anymore. I strain my ears to hear his fight, but all I can hear are the profanities spewing from the girl's mouth.

I'm still stomping on her now red and swollen hand when I feel a surge of shock jolt through my body as she grabs my foot and pulls. With strength unmatched by her appearance, she yanks me off my feet. My tailbone catches me, and I cry out in pain. While I'm in my lowered state, she pushes herself up on one of the tires, positioning her high enough to slam her fist into my face. A piercing pain shoots through my cheekbone like nothing I've ever felt before, making me cry out again. My hand flies up to my face, and I wince at my own touch. Feeling dazed, I search for the girl, but she's gone.

It isn't until I hear someone open the tailgate that I know I'm done for. I force myself to sit up, and that's when I see her. The tailgate is down, and she's pushing herself into the truck bed. Thinking fast, I do the only thing I can from my compromised position. I turn my body and start kicking. I'm not aiming for anything in particular; any contact with her is both a fluke and a blessing.

Amid my flailing, my shoe connects with a larger surface. My eyes open to find my sneaker pressed against the side of her face.

The shock of actually hitting her stills me. Slowly, I pull my leg back in time for her to look at me and spit, "You bit—" but before she can finish, I kick her one last time. This time I aim and hit my target on the nose, literally.

There's a crunch beneath my shoe, followed by the girl screaming. When I look up, I find her clutching her face, bright blood seeping through the cracks of her fingers. The blood takes over my mind, and I'm unable to see anything else. I feel light-headed and push myself backward, trying to create more distance between myself and the gruesome scene. Hugging my knees to my chest to avoid toppling over, I force deep controlled breaths in and out of my lungs.

"Let's go!" I hear the rat-looking man call out, and the girl looks over in his direction, still clutching her face. She glances my way, looking torn. "Misty, let's go!" He calls out to her again, and she turns to me. "You'll fucking pay for this," she spits, before disappearing out of sight.

Fredrick runs into view with wide eyes. It isn't until he sees me through the open tailgate that his expression relaxes. "Shit. Are you okay?"

I nod, still feeling queasy.

Not looking convinced, he says, "You're hurt."

I bring a hand to my cheek and feel the sting of where the girl hit me. It's sticky with half-dried blood. "It's not so bad," I say as I look at my fingertips, checking to see if I'm still bleeding.

He climbs into the bed and helps me to my feet. "Let's get out of here."

As I walk with him around to the passenger side, my legs still shake beneath me. He leans over and fastens my seatbelt before closing the door and walking around to the driver's side.

When he gets in my truck, he turns to look at me. "I need your keys."

I hand them to him. The symptoms from seeing the blood have subsided, but other things are now catching up with me. My legs ache, my tailbone must be bruised considering it's painful for me to sit, and my head throbs.

Flipping down the sun visor, I use the mirror to look myself over. I'm disheveled and tired, but I can handle that. My cheek is red and swollen from where the girl hit me, but that seems to be the worst of it. I look over at Fredrick, who doesn't have a scratch on him. Other than a sheen of sweat and messy hair, everything looks the same as it did an hour ago.

"How can you possibly not have a single mark on you?"

He starts the engine and gives me the same answer to nearly all my questions, only this time, he isn't smiling. "Practice."

11

The sound of raindrops hitting a window wakes me from a dead sleep. My eyes fly open, and I stare at my ceiling for a moment, registering where I am. Last night's events play in my mind like a haunting memory, so I turn over and stare out my bedroom window to clear my thoughts.

It takes a moment for me to realize someone's sitting outside my window. My first instinct is to panic, bringing back last night's adrenaline, but a second look lets me see that it's Fredrick. He's sitting with his back to me, his elbows resting on his knees. His shoulders tense as he rubs the back of his neck, and I can't help noticing the muscles that pull against his t-shirt.

He's here.

Seeing him here comforts me, reassures me, and makes my stomach flutter in a way I didn't think would be possible after last night.

Throwing the blankets off, I hurry to get out of bed.

Fredrick looks over his shoulder at me, and my blood runs cold. Staring at me, are the dark, too-close-together eyes of a man who definitely isn't Fredrick.

Because Fredrick doesn't resemble a rat.

I jump back when the man effortlessly stands and strides toward me with hungry eyes, ducking into my room through the somehow open window.

I try to scream, but no sound comes from my dry, aching throat. My eyes land on my bedroom door which seems so far, but I know it's my only hope.

My feet scramble as I run as fast as I can, still trying to scream with no success. The pounding footsteps of the man flood my ears, and I know he'll catch me. I want to look over my shoulder, but my neck won't move. Forced to stare straight ahead, I sprint toward the door I hope will lead me to my escape.

Fumbling with the doorknob, I'm frantic when it finally opens, and I dart down the stairs. The house is empty. Is my dad at work? I don't know, and I don't have time to find out.

I manage to get to the front door and open it effortlessly. The door doesn't even seem to swing open, but I don't have time to wonder why. I don't have time for anything. Even though I can't look back, I can feel his eyes on me.

My ears pound with either the racing beat of my heart or the relentless thuds of the feet chasing me. I can't control my legs as I run down the driveway, passing my truck. There's no time to check if it's unlocked. I know I don't have my keys anyway. My legs feel weightless—like they could carry me forever. It's probably the adrenaline coursing through my veins.

Even without looking back, I can feel him getting closer.

He's closing in on me.

A hand behind me grabs my shoulder, and I gasp.

Bolting upright in bed, my eyes dart around the dark room. My body heaves as I try to regain my bearings, and I can't shake the feeling that I'm being watched.

There's no one here, though. Everything seems to be in order. My computer sits motionless on top of my desk, my closet doors are shut, and my clothes from the night before still lie on the floor where I left them.

Panting and drenched in a cold sweat, I wipe my hand over my face to move the wet hair stuck to my forehead.

I fell asleep on the ride home and vaguely remember Fredrick helping me into the house. My dad was already sleeping by the time we got back, so I didn't have to face him… yet. That comes later this morning. I groan and hide my face in the pillow, but when I close my eyes, memories of the rat-looking man and his girlfriend vividly come to mind, forcing me to scan my bedroom again.

My clothes stick to my body, so I get up to change. The floor feels cool against my bare feet. Grabbing fresh clothes from my dresser, I freeze as I catch myself in the mirror. I can see my window in the reflection, and my head spins, anticipating the worst, but the night outside stays quiet and still.

The next time I wake, streams of sunlight pour through my window. I squint at the bright light before turning over to face the wall. My nightmare echoes in my thoughts, making it impossible to think about anything else.

I can hear my dad downstairs and feel the immediate dread in the pit of my stomach. Today marks the day for retribution. I'm sure of it.

To avoid panic, I stop and check how I look before going downstairs. The bruising on my face isn't as bad as I thought, but I still dab some concealer on to be safe.

Downstairs my dad sits at the table, waiting for me. I take a deep breath and let the air escape me slowly, my body deflating. He's deep in thought until I pull out the chair across from him, and his tired eyes drift up to meet mine.

Clearing his throat, he mutters, "I don't know where to begin."

If he's going to try to use the guilt route, he's wasting his time. I already regret going to Fredrick's house last night. If I had stayed home, none of this would have happened.

When I don't say anything, he takes a breath. I can tell he's struggling. He rarely—if ever—has to discipline me. My mother had already taken care of that before I moved here. Finally, he groans and slams his hat on the table. "Damn it, Paige! What were you thinking?"

I look up from my hands and decide to tell the truth—or at least part of it. My heart pounds in my chest, but not because he's angry. I'm afraid he'll notice I'm wearing makeup and demand why. Mom would have noticed, but I don't think he will. My words tumble out of my mouth. "I was mad, and I needed to talk to Fredrick, so I left in a hurry because Josh was trying to come with me, and I needed to go alone." I hold my breath as I wait for him to respond.

He rubs his forehead with his hand. "I called your mother."

My eyes widen. "You *what?*"

He throws his arms in the air. "You didn't give me much of a choice, Paige. If you're going to live in this house, you need to be responsible."

My mouth opens, but I have no idea what to say. Finally, I spit out, "Why would you call her? You know she's going to blow everything out of proportion!" I can already imagine my mother getting on a plane and coming here to drag me back to Atlanta with her.

His eyes soften as he says, "Now, calm down. I made sure she didn't overreact but she wants to talk to you."

"She wants to talk to me," I echo with a raise of my eyebrows.

He nods with a tight-lipped smile. "This morning."

I let my face fall into my hands and groan. My dad laughs, and my eyes lift. *He's laughing?*

"Just tell her what you told me. She'll understand. I think you get your temper from her." He gives me a small smile. "You can't take off like that again, though. Okay?"

I nod, but all I can think about is the dreaded phone call with my mother.

My dad leans back in his chair and raises an eyebrow. "Is that boy giving you trouble?"

I scoff and shake my head. "No."

He leans forward, crossing his arms on the table. "Need me to kill him?"

My lips twist as I try to fight my smile. With a roll of my eyes, I say, "That won't be necessary."

Dad stands from the kitchen table and ruffles my hair. I know he's relieved he doesn't need to talk to me about boys. I'm relieved, too. "Don't start causing me trouble, kiddo." It sounds more like a request than an actual threat.

"I'll try not to."

After he leaves for work, I stay at the table for a while. That wasn't as bad as I thought it would be. The phone rings, and I brace myself for what's about to come.

"Hello?"

"Paige!" I'm surprised to hear Leah's excited voice this early. She doesn't waste any time. "Okay, so I'm having a last-minute gathering thing tonight. You'll be there, right?" Her voice comes out as an urgent whisper.

"Why are you whispering?"

If anything, her voice gets quieter. "I'm being incognito."

I hesitate because any *last-minute gathering* that Leah would need to hide from her mom doesn't sound like a gathering. It sounds like a party. Last night drained me physically and emotionally. The last thing I want to do is go to a party. "Oh, I'm not sure..." I struggle to think of an excuse.

"Paaaiiiiiiggggeee." I can hear the smile in her voice and know my attempt is a lost cause. "You don't have a choice. You're coming. I was only inviting you as a formality."

The only downfall to having a best friend is that they know when you don't have a good excuse. I give in and say, "Okay, I'll be there."

"Yes!" She squeals, and I have to pull the phone away from my ear.

I must admit that her overall bubbliness has me in a better mood. "Any news about you and Austin?"

"He hasn't asked me out… yet."

I'm glad she sounds more confident than the last time she brought up the subject. "How do you know he will?"

"Come on, Paige. I can tell. I'm hoping he does it soon, though. The rate he's going, we'll both be dead."

I let out a laugh, and it feels good to laugh after last night. "He's probably just shy."

She groans. "Of all the guys out there, why do I have to like the shy one?" Her voice changes to a hushed tone. "Oh, Paige. I have to go. Mom's giving me the evil eye because I said I would call the pharmacy for her like an hour ago. See you tonight!"

We hang up, and I sit back down at the kitchen table. I wonder what Fredrick's doing. Is he mad? Has he learned who those people are? Will he ever want to see me again?

I picture how he looked while he was sailing, his dark hair wind-blown, his shirt stretching over the muscles in his back as he adjusts the sails, his eyes locked on mine as he gives me a crooked smile. He was so at ease, and I wish I could have had more time with that version of him.

I try to remember how we left things last night, but those memories are a blur, clouded by sleep. An image of me lying in bed as he sits on the edge, his hand brushing my hair off my forehead, comes to mind. Him telling me that our friendship is too dangerous. I remember wanting to protest, but I was so out of it. Now, I don't know if it happened or if it was just a fragment of a dream.

Dangerous.

The word brings a frown to my lips. He mentioned five people in his group, and none of them were his siblings. How is it that his sister isn't a pirate, yet he's not worried about making life too dangerous for her? And didn't Ben say I was the first girl Fredrick brought sailing? That has to mean something, right?

Absentmindedly playing with my hair, I try to answer my chain of questions. There's only one person who can give me answers, though, and I know exactly where to find him.

Running upstairs, I change into shorts and a white t-shirt. I look in the mirror to check how my concealer is holding up. The bruise is still hidden, but I add a little mascara for good measure. I look down at my wrist at the silver bracelet. How is it possible that something so insignificant could cause so much trouble? Quick to unclasp the delicate metal, I leave it on my dresser.

The phone rings again, and the sound makes me jump. I had almost forgotten about my mother's call. I take the stairs two at a time so the machine doesn't pick it up. That would only make things worse.

"Hello?" I say into the receiver and hold my breath.

"Well, I'm surprised you're up so early. It sounds like you had quite the evening."

I can already feel myself shrinking. "I'm sorry, Mom. I was just angry about something. I needed to talk to someone and left without thinking."

There's a moment of silence on the other end of the phone. "Who were you so angry with?"

I don't want to have this conversation. I consider lying, but I don't know how much my dad has told her. "Just this guy I know. There was a misunderstanding."

"Are you dating this boy?" Her cool tone allows me to perfectly picture her raising an eyebrow with a hand on her hip.

"What? No. We're friends." I clear my throat, trying not to imagine what dating Fredrick might be like. "I heard rumors about him and wanted to know if they were true." *They were*, a small voice in my head reminds me, but I push it aside.

My mom sighs. "Don't start pulling stunts like this, Paige. I know your father works a lot and isn't always home. I won't hesitate to move you back here."

I look down at my bare feet against the kitchen tile. Leah painted my toes bright blue a couple of weeks ago, and the polish has chipped. "I know."

"Okay. Well, I have a contractor coming to the house to give me a quote on remodeling the upstairs. He'll be here any minute, but I wanted to call."

"Okay," I say, feeling more defeated than I've felt in weeks. "I'm sorry, Mom. It won't happen again."

Her tone is still all business when she answers. "I hope you're right. Love you, Paige."

She hangs up before I can say anything back.

I stand in the kitchen for a moment and try to digest everything that's happened. All my thoughts circle back to Fredrick. He's the only one who understands what I'm feeling right now. Without hesitation, I grab my keys off the entryway table and head toward my truck.

☠ ☠ ☠

As I drive down the sandy streets lined with palm trees, I pass where I had parked my truck last night. My body tenses when I see the exact spot my fight with the girl happened, and I hit the gas. To ease my mind, I park in the heavily populated public lot instead.

I'm always interested to see the types of people who vacation here. Living in a tourist hot spot is like living in two completely different places depending on the time of year. The peaceful, clean beaches during the fall are nothing like the crowded, loud, littered ones in front of me.

I look around and spot the street that leads to a row of beach houses, Fredrick's included. As I sift through the tourists, I spot a familiar face in the distance. Dan. As my luck would have it, he isn't alone either. Luke stands by his side and sees me before I'm able to make a run for it.

"Paige!"

Luke's voice stops me dead in my tracks. I turn his way and

politely wave.

"Paige, come over here!"

I let out a breath in surrender and head toward Luke and his ominous cousin.

He greets me with a hug, making me uncomfortable. "What brings you to the beach?" he asks as he releases me from his body prison.

I glance at Dan before answering. His eyes are intently on me, giving me the uneasy feeling he can read my mind. I dart my eyes back toward Luke and show my best smile. "It's the middle of summer. Why wouldn't I come to the beach?"

Luke laughs, but Dan's stare is relentless. I wonder if Fredrick told him about the incident. Hopefully, he hasn't. I shudder to think Dan knows what fuels my nightmares.

"Are you going to Leah's tonight?" Luke's voice snaps me back to the present.

"Yeah, she just called before I left the house. Are you?"

He nods with bright eyes. "Of course, I'll be there. I'm glad you're coming."

I give him a tight-lipped smile. "Okay, great." Shifting my weight, I say, "Well, I better get going, but I'll see you tonight!" I make my exit quickly to avoid being stopped again. Dan's eyes burn into me even as I walk away, and I think I'd rather get another hug from Luke.

As I walk, the heat starts to weigh on me, and my forehead glistens with sweat. I'm careful not to wipe my cheek where my bruise hides beneath the makeup.

Trudging through the deep sand brings thoughts of my night-mare back to the surface. I look over my shoulder periodically to keep my overactive imagination at bay. Finally, I see it: the white house with blue shutters. The house looks so serene. I almost feel guilty, knowing I'm likely about to disrupt its peace.

Each step up the driveway makes my heart rate quicken. Once again, I find myself peering through the glass front door, but this time, I don't see anyone. Disappointment weighs in my chest. I should have known I wouldn't be as lucky as I had been last time, finding Fredrick home alone.

As I step back, something catches my attention. Standing in the kitchen are three sets of curious eyes staring at me, none of which are familiar. I look at the outside of the house again. *This is the right house… but who are they?*

The realization hits me. Two guys and a very short, petite girl: the pirates. Or as Fredrick would say, the members of his *group*. One of the guys is tall, reminding me of Josh and Dan.

The other guy is much shorter, and even though he has a buzzed haircut, I can see his hair is a lighter brown, maybe even blonde. He's wearing a tank top that exposes his large muscular arms. On one of his bulging biceps is the unmistakable skull tattoo, but it's surrounded by more ink that travels down the length of his entire arm.

Next to him sits the girl. She's short and petite with long brown hair and piercing blue eyes. Her eyes make me feel like she can see right through me—the dark eyeliner probably adds to that effect. She's wearing the tightest skinny jeans I've ever seen, paired with an equally tight tank top. The bottom of her toned stomach shows, and I can see black lines poking out of the waistband of her jeans. Her tattoo must be on her hip.

Even though I can't see the tattoo on all of them, simple math lets me know who they are. Three standing in front of me, plus Fredrick and Dan makes five. It has to be them. I know the girl must be Melissa, but I have no idea which guy is Carter, and which is Jason. Just as I'm about to back away, Fredrick walks into view wearing jeans and a dark grey t-shirt. He stops when he sees the other three, all staring in the same direction.

At me.

Before he can follow their gaze, I jump back from the door and hurry down the driveway, huggings my arms around myself. My cheeks are hot as I stare down at my feet which aren't moving as fast as I want them to.

I know I've turned to leave too late. I should have left as soon as I made eye contact with the three pirates. Even if I did turn away before Fredrick saw me, they'll fill him in. I know I won't hear him behind me, but I have a feeling he'll be at my side in a matter of seconds, and I desperately hope I'm wrong. I don't want to have this conversation with him in front of an audience.

My thoughts are interrupted when I hear a door slam behind me. The loud smack of the door hitting the frame makes me jump, and I spin around to find Fredrick standing there, his expression unreadable.

I want to run, but my feet won't move. Fredrick marches down the driveway, his jaw clenched.

Seeing him reminds me of my unanswered questions. It reminds me of the simple fact that I don't know where last night leaves us. I barely understand why or how last night even happened.

I open my mouth to speak, but he cuts me off. "What are you doing here?"

I bite my lip as I search his face, trying to gauge his anger. "I need to talk to you."

"There's nothing to talk about." He looks up and down the street before bringing his eyes back to mine. "You could have been seriously hurt last night."

"Okay... so?" I don't know why he's so angry. I haven't done anything wrong.

"So, you shouldn't be here."

I blink. "You want me to leave?"

He nods, his lips pressed into a hard line. "And don't come back."

His words feel like a punch to the gut. "I'm just never supposed to see you again?" I hold my breath as I wait for his answer.

Fredrick crosses his arms cooly. "It would be for the best."

My eyes narrow. I fought that girl last night myself. He didn't rescue me. I'm the one who broke her nose, not him. "But I handled it. On. My. Own."

He runs his hand through his hair. "That's not the point. If anything happens to you because of me..." He trails off and shakes his head.

"Something could happen to me anytime, with or without you," I snap.

He stares at me, and I think he's considering my point until he squares his shoulders, his face harsh. "Paige, don't come here anymore. I don't want you here."

I almost wince at his words but catch myself. It takes everything in me to keep my face blank, but I won't let him know he got to me. "You don't seem worried about your sister getting too wrapped up in this. Ben? Your mom? What's so different about me?"

Fredrick glances back at the house. I know the other pirates are probably watching from inside, but I refuse to break eye contact with him to check. When he turns back to me, he sighs and rubs the back of his neck. "You're right. I put them at risk. I was a dumb kid back then, and we've had to deal with what I did. I've taken precautions with them. I had to. But I'm not a dumb kid anymore, Paige. I won't do the same thing to you."

I bite the inside of my cheek and look down at the ground. I want to fire back with a good point, but Fredrick's voice forces me to bring my eyes to his again.

"So, I'm going to say this one more time." His jaw ticks and I swallow the lump in my throat, bracing myself for what he's about to say. "I don't want you here."

Backing away from him slowly, I nod. Turning on my heels, I start back toward my truck. I'm not someone who gets hung up on other people. Fredrick made it clear he doesn't want me in his life; that fact alone should make me not want him in mine. So, why does this still hurt? No tears fall as I walk away, but I still don't dare give him the satisfaction of seeing me look back.

12

I study myself in the mirror as I listen to the muffled calls of whatever sport my dad watches downstairs. I made chili for dinner, but I'm not hungry enough to force down a bowl. I also don't feel motivated to dress up for the party tonight, so I decide to wear the same white shirt from earlier and change my shorts to jeans. I'd like nothing more than to put on an oversized t-shirt and call it a day, but I can't skip out on Leah's party. I've already had arguments with Josh and Fredrick. I don't think I can handle one with Leah, too.

I'm determined not to think about Fredrick as I comb my fingers through my hair, but despite my best efforts, I can't stop replaying our last conversation. His harsh gaze forever burned into my mind as *I don't want you here* plays on an endless loop. Unfortunately, in the rare moments that I'm not thinking about him, I seem to think about Dan instead—which may be worse. His unwavering stare earlier still sends lingering chills down my spine.

Once I'm downstairs, I sit next to my dad on the couch. "Are you going to be okay for dinner tonight?"

He looks at me with a wry smile. "I would hope so. All I need to do is put it in a bowl. I should be able to handle that." He eyes me with mild concern. "Are you sure you don't want to eat before you go?"

I perk up to try and convince him that I'm okay. "Yeah. They'll probably have food at the party. Save some leftovers for me?"

He nods with a smile. "I can do that." His eyes lock on mine for another beat before he adds, "Have fun tonight, Paige. Laugh a little. You're starting to look older than me."

I shake my head before getting up from the couch and grabbing my keys off the counter. "See you later."

"Alright, kiddo. Drive safe."

☠ ☠ ☠

It barely takes any time to get to Leah's house since she lives a few streets over. I'm still not sure how I feel about going to a party tonight, but less time alone with my thoughts is probably a good thing.

Cars and trucks crowd the street in front of her house. I should have known her party would take over the entire street. Leah doesn't do anything on a small scale.

After finding a place to park, I take my time walking up the driveway. Usually, Leah's long driveway feels like an inconvenience, but tonight I appreciate the long winding stretch of asphalt. Her parents have property like my dad. The only difference is they care about curb appeal. Most of Leah's five acres are wide open, clear of trees and brush. Much different from my dad's house, hidden by forest. Everyone here knows better than to park on the grass. Leah's dad would probably care more about that than his daughter throwing a party.

Standing at the front door, I take a deep breath before ringing the doorbell. No one answers. Muffled music blares inside, so I figure there's an open-door policy. With another breath, I step inside.

This is the farthest thing from a "gathering." I look around for a familiar face but see no one from our circle of friends. The line of cars outside is nothing compared to the number of people here. It looks like most of the soon-to-be senior class decided to show up.

It looks like a rainbow exploded inside—which was probably her intention. Balloons and streamers of every color hang from the ceiling and cover the floor.

Leah catches my eye in the distance and runs toward me, her bouncing, blonde curls looking perfect, per usual.

I can't help grinning back at her. It feels like it has been forever since I last saw her. She wraps her arms around my neck before catching me up on the party happenings. "Mom is out of town, and little bro is at a sleepover! I can't believe how many people showed up!" She looks around at her party with pride before turning back to me. The deafening music forces her to shout, "I hear everything's okay with you and Josh?"

My smile falters. I never told her about Josh and Fredrick. "How did you—?"

She cuts me off with a casual wave of her hand. "Oh, Josh filled me in."

I nod slowly. "Oh…" My thoughts trail off as I search for Josh's face in the crowded room. *What did he tell her?*

Leah doesn't seem to notice I'm distracted. She starts talking about her never-ending guest list. At the sound of Dan's name, my eyes jump to her.

"And Nick, and Juri, and Jenna, and—"

I cut her off. "Why is Dan here?" The music, thankfully, blocks out the slight panic in my voice.

"Oh, he came with Luke." She shrugs offhandedly. "Someone had to bring the beer, and Dan has a hookup or something."

Leah picks up where she left off with the list of names, but I'm no longer listening. Her voice is nothing but a low hum in the background of my thoughts. Every time we see Dan, we're usually at the beach. He has never gone out of his way to hang out with us. *Why would he drive out here for a high school party? I can't be the reason he came here… that would be crazy, right?* The thought makes my stomach uneasy.

I scan the crowd for Josh again, and this time, finding him is easier than I expected. He stands out considering almost everyone here is shorter than him. I spot him at the keg filling up a red plastic cup. "I'm going to go talk to Josh!" I yell over the song playing.

She nods and starts dance-walking through the crowd with her eyes closed.

I walk into the kitchen, and Josh gives me an animated grin. It doesn't take long for me to figure out he must have emptied a few of those plastic cups already. "P! Want to dance?" He shouts over the music as he playfully takes my hand and spins me.

"Absolutely not," I say with a laugh, but Josh just spins me the other way.

"Don't lie. You came over here to dance with me."

After the second twirl, I plant my feet on the ground and shake my head but still can't help the smile pulling at my lips. "Oh, no, no, no."

Josh laughs, well aware of the fact that I don't dance.

"You're drinking?" I ask, even though the answer seems obvious.

He takes a long sip before responding. "Austin said he's not drinking, and I'm staying at his house tonight, so—" he raises his cup in one-sided cheers. "Plus, I figured I can slack off a little until Coach makes us all go to conditioning."

"Do you know Dan is here?"

Josh's face falls. "Who told you that?"

"Leah. I guess he supplied some of the beer." I gesture toward the cup in his hand.

Josh shakes his head, his brows furrowing. "Why would he want to come here? And more importantly, why would he want to come here and give us his beer?" He eyes his cup like it's poison.

His reaction only heightens my concern that I might have something to do with Dan's presence. "Who knows…"

Josh takes another sip, and when he pulls the cup from his lips, he's smiling again. "Well, at least this party is huge. I probably won't have to see his creepy-ass face." He does his best impression of

Dan's brooding expression, making me choke back laughter.

"You told Leah about our fight?" I ask, feeling unsure if I should bring it up.

Josh shifts his weight. "I'm surprised you didn't."

I know why I didn't. Telling her about our fight would lead to telling her why Josh doesn't like Fredrick. "What did you say to her?"

He finishes off the cup in his hand. "Nothing specific. She asked why we didn't ride together, so I said you and I weren't exactly seeing eye to eye."

That's one way of putting it, I guess. I don't have to ask him if he told Leah about Fredrick. If he had, she would have cornered me as soon as I got here. Bringing up our fight makes me uncomfortable, and I'm not sure what to say to my slightly intoxicated best friend.

Someone taps on my shoulder, and I freeze. Turning around, I let out a breath of relief to see *not* Dan but Luke standing behind me. I never thought the sight of Luke would make me so happy. He's wearing cargo shorts and a black t-shirt with a *Metallica* design on the front. I can't help wondering if he listens to their music or if he thinks wearing the shirt will make him look cool.

Before I can say anything, he throws his arms around me, giving me the same uncomfortable feeling his hug had given me earlier. *What's with all the hugging?*

"Uh… Hey, Luke."

He beams. "Dan didn't think you would come, but I told him you'd be here."

I feel the blood drain from my face. "Why?"

Luke shrugs. "Just had a feeling, I guess. He does that some-times."

My mouth falls open, but I quickly shut it. *Why me? Why does Dan have to have a feeling about me?*

Luke's voice interrupts my thoughts. "Want a drink?"

I usually don't drink, but the thought of having something to calm my nerves doesn't sound like a bad idea. I nod and look over my shoulder at Josh, now talking to a girl I've never seen before.

At least he's not far.

Luke hands me a drink, and I ask the question I don't want the answer to. "Where's Dan?"

Luke looks mildly surprised by my interest but points over his shoulder. "I think I saw him near the pizza."

My eyes wander past Luke, and my body locks. Dan's dark eyes stare at me as if he has been waiting for me to look his way. Our eyes meet, and he holds my stare until I force myself to look down at the cup in my hand, taking another sip.

"Are you okay?" I hear Luke's voice, but it sounds far away.

I nod as I scan the room for Josh again, but he's gone. "Do you know where Josh went?"

Luke shakes his head and eyes me with furrowed brows. I pre-tend I don't notice. "Okay, I'm going to try to find him. I'll see you around." I walk away before he has a chance to say anything else.

I try to avoid Dan's gaze as I wander through the house full of people, getting stopped occasionally by people from school who want to catch up. It's all small talk, though. Right now, I'd rather just find Josh.

Finally, I see the back of his head and break away from my current conversation to head in that direction. He's still talking to the same girl, probably trying to get her number using a lame pick-up line from the back of a gum wrapper or something. It doesn't matter what he uses to pick up girls. It always works. I wait impatiently until the girl walks back to her group of friends.

Josh looks at me with a smirk pulling at the corners of his mouth. "Did you see how hot she was?"

I fake a smile before pushing up on my toes and saying in his ear, "Dan's staring at me."

Josh laughs and shakes his head. "I can't help you with that. I've got work to do." He flicks three small pieces of paper, all containing scribbled phone numbers, and walks away. I glare at the back of his head before resolving to find Leah. The only problem is that she could be anywhere, and wherever she is, she probably won't stay there for long.

After a few laps around the house, I give up searching for her. I look out the sliding glass door to Leah's back patio.

It's empty.

A break from telling everyone that my summer "has been great so far," and that I've "been busy, but good," is too tempting to pass up. I go straight for the patio chairs and sit down, still holding my lukewarm beer.

Five minutes of relief is all I get before I hear the sliding doors open and someone walks out onto the patio. I look up, and my eyes widen when I see Dan headed straight for the chair next to mine.

Without a word, he takes a seat, glaring at the house where the party is still in full swing. That's it. He doesn't even look at me. I anxiously take a sip of my beer, regretting it instantly. I don't even like beer. Frowning at my cup, my heart pounds with the growing tension in the air. It eats at me until I blurt, "So, what brings you to Chuluota?"

Dan grunts, still refusing to look at me.

"Okay…" I allow my voice to trail off as I try to think of something else to say. "I've been seeing you a lot lately."

"I'm not following you," he says impassively. I sense a slight tone of annoyance, though.

I stare at him, open-mouthed. "I didn't say you were."

"You were thinking it," he says with more obvious annoyance.

He's not wrong. When I hear someone knocking on the sliding glass doors, I jump. Luke stands on the other side of the glass, beckoning me inside. I glance back at Dan, still gazing off into the distance. There's no point swapping pleasantries, so I get up and walk toward the house without another word.

Opening the door, I ask, "Everything okay?"

He clears his throat. "Yeah. It's just…" He looks over his shoulder at the party inside before bringing his blue eyes back to mine. "It's a slow song."

I blink. "I can see that."

He lets out a nervous laugh, and the back of my neck prickles like a spidey sense for awkward situations. "Right," he mutters. "Well, some people are dancing. I wasn't sure if maybe you'd like to?"

I look past him to Leah's living room which has turned into an impromptu dance floor. My eyes land on Leah dancing with Austin, and I smile. They certainly look like a couple from here. "They make a cute couple, don't they?" I say, nodding in their direction.

Luke hesitates and looks behind him at the scattered dance pairs. "Who?"

I point. "Leah and Austin."

He watches them for a moment and shrugs. "I can see it." Looking back at me, he raises his eyebrows. "So, do you want to dance?"

I glance over my shoulder, where Dan stands a few feet away like he's waiting for us to move so he can go back into the house. He hangs back, giving us some space, but the fact that he's here still makes me uncomfortable.

I sigh. "I don't dance. I'm sorry."

Luckily, the song ends, and I can hear Josh's voice ring out. "Football! Backyard!"

I step aside for the "Teenage Guys Who Love Football" parade to pass. Luke flashes a tight-lipped smile and says, "Maybe next time," before joining them and saving me from more embarrassment.

Leah runs up to me after Austin joins the rest of the guys. "He asked me out!"

Genuinely happy for her, I grin, and it feels like the first real smile I've had in days. "That's great!" I beam at her but then my face falls. "Don't hate me." I grimace. "But I think it's time for me to head home. I have some stuff I need to take care of."

She playfully rolls her eyes. "You are not taking care of any 'stuff' this late at night."

Her eyes meet mine, and I give her a pleading look.

"You're okay to drive?" she asks.

I hold up my still-full cup of beer. "Definitely."

"Fine, get out of here." She says as she takes the cup from my hands.

I glance over my shoulder again. A girl from our school has Dan's attention on the patio. She's laughing and touching his arm, but he only seems mildly interested. His eyes go past the girl and land on me, so I drop my gaze. Sneaking one last peek, I see him look back at the girl and start talking to her again. Slipping into the house, I make a break for it.

☠   ☠   ☠

The roads are clear for my drive home. Driving with the windows down reminds me of the night I had gone to Fredrick's house. My truck cuts through the night air, mimicking the cool ocean breeze.

The dark and quiet house lets me know Dad has already turned in for the night. To avoid waking him, I don't turn on any lights until I reach my bedroom. Flipping the switch, I walk over to my dresser and change into comfortable clothes before going into the bathroom to brush my teeth.

I'm exhausted, but even in my tired state, I can't stop replaying my conversation with Dan. What would he have said if Luke never showed up?

Lying in bed, I notice Dan's face has replaced Fredrick's in most of my troubling thoughts, which is unfortunate only because Fredrick's is so much nicer to look at. Other than that, Dan's memories are less painful; only fear comes from Dan's face in my head, not rejection.

He must be keeping tabs on me. What other reason would there be for his behavior? I replay his words in my mind and remember the tone of annoyance hidden behind them. *I'm not following you.* I cringe back against my mattress to silence the unpleasant memory.

As I sink my body into the heart of my mattress, I hear something move against the wood floor beneath me. I freeze. Straining my ears, I try to listen for any hint that the sound may have been my imagination. I hold my breath and wait.

I exhale halfway and stop when I hear it. It sounds like there may be someone shuffling against the floor.

My tired, even breathing becomes short and shallow. *Could someone be in my room?* My chest rises and falls as my eyes dart to every corner, searching for any sign of movement.

In a desperate attempt to calm my nerves, I force myself to rationalize that there's no reason to be afraid of the dark. I try to convince myself that I am undoubtedly alone, but I can't shake the feeling of something else—someone else.

The noise sounds again, and every joint in my body locks. The only part of me still moving is my rapidly beating heart. If the noise happens again, I won't be able to hear it over the blood pounding in my ears.

Sweat beads down the side of my face, but I refuse to move my arm and wipe it away. I struggle to even blink, afraid the person under my bed may hear it. *Could it be Dan?* The thought grips me, stiff and cold like the dead fingers of a corpse.

Can I run? Where would I go? To get my dad and have him check for monsters under my bed? I'm probably being ridiculous.

Then I hear it again.

Okay, maybe I'm not being ridiculous. I need to get out of here. Maybe if they think I'm going to the bathroom, they'll stay where they are. It's worth a shot, right? I move a shaking hand and gently pull the comforter off my body. Sitting upright, stiff as a board, I throw my feet over the edge of the bed at an abnormally far distance. Pushing my body upright, I start to walk as naturally as I can toward my bedroom door. *Heel, toe, heel, toe.* My knees rattle underneath me as I focus on making my way to the door, my only chance of escape.

I hear a swift movement, but by the time I can register what might be happening, a hand covers my mouth, the other around my neck.

13

Thrashing my body, I try to scream and claw against the hand around my neck, but my attacker's hold tightens. I choke out a painful cough and feel light-headed from the added pressure.

The stranger shoves me out of my bedroom and forces me down the stairs, lifting me by my neck. I can't breathe. Frenzied thoughts take over as black dots creep into the corners of my eyes. I blink, trying to clear them, but it doesn't work. The sounds of my coughing and choking are muffled by the large hands blocking my airways. My feet try to kick, but nothing I do makes any difference. The more I fight, the weaker I feel.

My lungs scream, desperate for air, but I'm helpless. I vaguely know we've reached the bottom of the stairs when my attacker loosens their grip, my feet touching the ground again. The latch to the front door clicks open, and the hand around my throat releases briefly. This would be more of a relief if my mouth and nose weren't still covered. The door swings open, and I'm shoved out of the house by the back of my neck. The person stays behind, making it impossible for me to see their face.

Suddenly, the thought hits me. *Will I live through this?* My chest heaves as I think of how this person could kill me. I thrash in another attempt to break free, but it's futile. Tears stream down my eyes from pain and fear, and I let out a muffled scream against their calloused hand, my voice hoarse.

My gasping must annoy them because their hands shake me by the neck. The sight of my truck in the driveway flickers before me. Letting out another cough, I gasp when the hands release me, trying to get as much air into my lungs as possible. The feeling is short-lived. There's a sting against my cheek, and I cry out in pain, unsure if I've been punched or slapped. My knees buckle beneath me, and the hands are around my throat again before I have time to think.

Darkness engulfs my surroundings, and I no longer see my truck in front of me. My throat aches and begs for air, but I can't fulfill its need. I can't do anything. My struggle stops, and I prepare myself for what's about to come. Everything turns black, and my awareness starts to slip away. My body goes limp in the arms of my attacker. Soon there won't be any pain. Soon there won't be anything at all.

Then, everything stops. My body is free of my attacker's hands. I must have been dropped to the ground when I passed out. With each breath, my throat throbs and burns from being starved for too long. My eyesight starts to clear, and with each passing, painful second, more comes into view.

I roll over, still gasping for air. My elbows dig into the ground, and I try to prop myself up. Taking in my surroundings, my body locks at the sight in front of me.

Fredrick has my attacker pinned to the ground with gritted teeth. His eyes dart from me to the man who had my life in his hands only moments ago.

Fredrick's forearm holds him in place by his throat. He grabs the guy by his collar to lift his head only to slam it back into the ground again. A wave of nausea crashes over me, and I force myself to look away. Shaking from the shock of what happened and the fear of what might happen next, I listen to their muffled fight. They both seem to want to avoid being heard, which I take as a good sign. I hope it means my dad is still inside, giving them a reason to be quiet.

I look back at the fight in front of me and feel my blood run cold. My gaze is met by the dark, too-close-together eyes of the rat-looking man. Fredrick now has him pinned up against the side of my truck, but his beady rat-like eyes lock on me. His expression is full of loathing as he spits in my direction.

Fredrick follows the man's gaze over his shoulder to me. His expression hardens, and he turns back to shove the man harder against my truck.

The rat-looking man shows Fredrick an arrogant smirk before his eyes fall back on me. He blows me a taunting kiss, and I feel sick.

Fredrick looks over his shoulder, meeting my gaze again, and my breath catches. His lingering glance comes across as apologetic, and I bite my lip knowing what he's about to do. The moment his eyes break from mine, he slams his fist into the rat man's face with enough force to make me wince.

I cover my mouth with both hands as a hoarse cry erupts from my raw, aching throat. Tears stream down my face, and I can't tell if they're from shock or the overwhelming pain that wraps my body. I want to look away. I want to close my eyes and pretend this is another nightmare, but I can't.

The rat-man brushes off Fredrick's punch with more arrogance. He picks up his head to look at me again, but this time he sprays vivid, red blood through his lips as he pants. This time, Fredrick doesn't look back before his fist collides with the man's jaw.

I hear a short cry, and it takes me a moment to realize it came out of my own chattering lips. I put both hands over my mouth again to lock in my screams. The last thing I need is Dad waking up and looking outside his bedroom window to find this. I squeeze my eyes tightly shut. If Fredrick is going to make this guy bleed more, I don't want to see it.

I hug my knees close to my chest and let my head fall, and the smell of blood tingles my nose, giving me a headache.

Then, everything goes quiet. There are no more sounds of struggle. No more fists hitting faces. Nothing. Not even the sounds of two guys wrestling in the grass. Lifting my head, I peek over my arm and jump back when I see a figure towering over me. I sigh when it's Fredrick looking down at me with concern.

He reaches out a hand, and I willingly take it. My knees shake as I get to my feet. I look around for my attacker, but the yard is empty.

"He's gone," Fredrick says quietly.

My wide eyes lock on his, and I nod.

He lifts a hand as if to touch my cheek but lets his arm fall by his side, his expression torn. "Are you okay?"

Again, the only response I can manage is a careful nod. I can't find the words, and even if I could, I'm not sure they'd come out.

Fredrick's warm eyes study mine, and I know he's trying to figure out how I'm feeling. If only he knew how impossible it is for me to understand my own feelings right now.

A tear falls from my eye, and this time, Fredrick does bring his thumb to my cheek. "He's gone," he says again.

I nod but another tear falls as I think about what could have happened tonight. Fredrick looks at my house behind me, his jaw set in a hard line. "Come on. I'll take you back to my house. We can't talk here."

I let him lead me down the driveway. Glancing once over my shoulder, my eyes lock on my dad's bedroom window, where he lies in bed, oblivious to everything.

☠   ☠   ☠

My head rests against the window as Fredrick drives down the winding roads scattered with sand. Neither of us has spoken since leaving my house, but I welcome the quiet. Questions weave through my consciousness, but I'm too exhausted to form them into words.

The Jeep comes to a halt in Fredrick's driveway, and I'm relieved to be back at the small white house with blue shutters, where
inside, I'll find small comforts and large bookshelves.

My thoughts are interrupted when I feel Fredrick move next to
me. Turning my head to look at him, I notice he's watching me
intently. His dark brown hair is messier, but again, he managed to
leave another fight without a single scratch to prove it.

His eyes pierce into me, his dark eyebrows pulling together.
Feeling self-conscious, I can't help wondering what he's thinking.

He sounds exhausted like he hasn't slept in days. "Don't
move."

Despite his lack of sleep, he makes sure to come around and
open my door on the other side. He doesn't force help on me but
holds out his arm.

I take it.

As we walk up the driveway, I notice something I had always
thought was impossible. For the first time, Fredrick's movements are
just as slow and imperfect as mine. An outsider might not notice the
difference, but his auditory footsteps and slower pace stand out.

Fredrick places his hand on the doorknob, hesitating before
pushing it open and stepping inside. We enter the house as Kelly
passes through the kitchen archway with a hardcover book. One
glance at Fredrick and I is all it takes for her to skid to a halt. Her
book falls from her hands, smacking against the wood floor. On any
other day, the sound would have likely made me jump, but I don't
even flinch. Everything in me has been spent. I have nothing left.

My cheeks flush with embarrassment when I see her alarmed

eyes zero in on me. I was hoping everyone would be asleep here, but it seems Kelly is a night owl. It must be at least one in the morning.

Snapping her eyes up to Fredrick, she demands, "What happened to her?" Her sharp whisper fails to hide the horror behind her words.

Her reaction catches me off guard, and I wonder how terrible I must look right now.

Fredrick stands back as his mother holds my face between her hands. "I was right." His voice sounds almost ashamed, his eyes only flickering toward me before returning to her.

He was right? Right about what? Questions flash through my mind without giving me enough time to explore possible answers. I want to ask them what they're talking about, but the effort it would take keeps me quiet.

Kelly's already wide eyes amplify as she clasps a hand to her mouth. "Good Lord."

She gently pushes my chin from side to side as she examines my face and neck before running her eyes up and down my entire body. I allow her to lift my arms and prod me as she asks what my pain level is on a scale from one to ten.

After poking every bone and muscle, she reaches for my neck but looks away with tears brimming. Her reaction makes my own eyes burn with the threat of tears. *Why did Fredrick bring me here? Why couldn't he let me stay home and tend to my own wounds? It would have been better than seeing Kelly break down like this.* I look up at Fredrick for solace, but his stony facade is unreadable. He still won't look at me.

"Fredrick, why don't you show Paige where she can get cleaned up?" Kelly's usually smooth voice runs thick. I'm grateful to get away from her. She's wonderful, but I can't handle her transparency right now.

Fredrick gives her a nod and starts down the hallway. He doesn't look back at me until he's standing at his bedroom doorway. Even as he looks in my direction, I can tell he's avoiding looking me in the eye. In his room, I stand and watch as he rummages through a large storage box he pulled from under his bed. The silence is crippling, and I'd give anything to know what he's thinking.

After he collects a handful of first aid materials from the box, he signals for me to follow him into the bathroom across the hall. When he flips on the light, my eyes widen. It's odd to look in the mirror and not recognize your reflection. The tattered girl looking back at me with her bloodshot eyes and bruised neck is someone I've never seen before.

I painfully swallow before opening my mouth to ask the first of many questions. "What were you right about?" The words are rough, and I hold my breath, waiting for him to answer.

Fredrick checks the hallway to make sure we're alone before facing me. Grabbing a washcloth, he runs it under warm water and presses it to my face, dabbing the areas around my eyes and cheeks. The warm cloth stings where I must have an open cut from being hit.

"I can do that," I offer, but he shakes his head without looking me in the eye. After a moment, I ask, "What were you right about?" I try to say it with more conviction, but my voice cracks, and I wince from the pain.

His eyes jump to mine, but it lasts less than a second. Swallowing, he fixes his gaze where he's dabbing the warm cloth. His eyes have always held so much depth. Sometimes they're warm and molten, and other times they're guarded and forboding. Right now, they're the latter. His harsh gaze refuses to meet my pleading stare again. "I'll explain everything later."

"But—"

He cuts me off with a stern shake of his head, and I know trying to get more out of him is useless. There is one question I need to know the answer to, though, and it can't wait. Despite his demand for silence, I choke out, "Is my dad safe?"

Fredrick doesn't break from cleaning my face with the warm cloth. "Jason is over there keeping watch."

My heart races at the thought of not knowing the person responsible for my father's safety, but I'm also relieved that someone is looking out for him.

When Fredrick steps aside, I can see the damage my body suffered. The dirt did a great job of camouflaging the new colors surfacing on my battered skin. Around my neck, bruises have started to form in the shape of the hands that tried to cut off my air supply. I lean toward the mirror to get a better look and tentatively bring my fingers to my damaged neck, wincing at the slightest touch.

Fredrick stands back and watches uneasily, but patiently, as I explore my now unfamiliar body. Each time I flinch, he drops his gaze.

I take out what's left of my ponytail and try to painfully replace it with another, neater one. Once I finish giving myself the once-over, I turn to Fredrick and nod. I'm ready to know everything.

14

The fact that Fredrick was there only minutes after my attacker brought me outside makes me wonder if he knew this would happen. *Did he know and not warn me?*

Without a word, Fredrick holds open the bathroom door for me, and I walk out into the hallway toward the living room. I can still hear his footsteps and wonder how long it has been since he has slept. For the first time since meeting him, it feels comforting to walk in front of him and not have to check if he's still behind me.

As we walk down the hallway, I feel a sinking feeling in the pit of my stomach. Tonight has only proved his theory right: being around him is too dangerous for me. Tonight will likely end with him telling me to stay away from him again. The thought makes my chest heavy as I inch my way closer to the living room where Kelly waits for us in her recliner. She's staring out the dark window next to her chair, her chin resting on her knees. Sitting in the large chair, she looks more like a small child than a middle-aged woman.

Fredrick and I both take a seat on the couch across from her, and her head snaps up to look at us. Her eyes are bloodshot, and her nose is red.

"Does she know?" Kelly asks Fredrick.

I lift my eyes to watch their exchange.

He's sitting next to me on the couch with his elbows resting on his knees. The weight of today's events clearly crashing down on him. His only response to her question is a shake of his head.

Kelly dips her chin slightly and turns her attention back to me with a timid smile. "How do you feel?"

"Mostly confused," I answer honestly. I can't do anything about my physical condition right now, but I can get answers.

Kelly gives me a sympathetic smile before returning her attention to Fredrick. He still hasn't made eye contact with me since we got here.

The two of them exchange a long glance until Kelly finally says, "Fredrick recently told me what happened the other night. If I had known, I would have invited you back here to prepare you for the possibility of that not being the end of it."

My eyes travel up to Fredrick, but he stays focused on his mother, ignoring my stare. I want to know what she's referring to, and I want to know why he won't look at me. Even though there are so many things I want to say, I can't bring myself to say them.

Kelly lets out a small sigh. "Now we just need to figure out how to keep you safe."

As she opens her mouth again, Fredrick cuts her off. "I won't let her get hurt. Not again."

Kelly doesn't look the slightest bit surprised by his objection, which confuses me. *What am I missing?*

She purses her lips in thought. "Well, then I suggest you get started." At first, her comment sounds almost harsh, but when I look at the concern on her face, I know she's sincere.

With a stiff nod, Fredrick stands up and holds out his hand for me.

I stay on the couch. At this point, it's clear Kelly is my best option for answers, so I fix my attention on her. "Wait. What happened tonight?"

She leans toward me from across the room, and there's an underlying sadness in her voice as she says, "Honey, you were attacked."

I shake my head. "I know, but why? How?" I take turns searching each of their faces for the answers I need—the answers I'm not getting.

Fredrick sinks back into the cushion next to me and stares down at the floor for a long moment.

Trying to make myself seem more collected, I straighten my posture and keep my face composed. If anything, I at least need to look like I can handle the truth.

Finally, he says, "To stop our fight the other night, I made a deal with that guy… the same one who hurt you tonight." He hesitates, waiting for my response. When I don't say anything, he continues. "I had promised him that his girlfriend would return safely, in one piece, as long as you did, too. But… you broke her nose." I swear I see his mouth twitch at his last words, but he recovers, looking somber once more. "I thought he might have tried to follow us back to your house, and then I thought I lost him. I guess I didn't. Ever since, he must have just been waiting for the right time to strike. He wanted to get even with you for what you did to his girl-friend."

"Misty," I mutter. He tilts his head at me, and I say, "Her name is Misty."

Fredrick nods in understanding. "Well, the night that it happened, I didn't want to leave you alone. After I brought you inside, I watched your house for the rest of the night to be safe. The next morning, I walked to the gas station and called Jason to pick me up. I didn't want to leave you, but it didn't take long for me to realize I couldn't keep watch all day and night myself. I had to get help from someone. I called Dan and figured it would be easiest if he watched you during the day because you were fairly used to seeing him. I thought he would look the least suspicious."

I can't believe it never occurred to me how Fredrick got home the night of our attack. He had driven my truck, leaving himself stranded at my house.

"Anyway," he says, "with Dan watching you in the day, I kept the night shift. I parked my jeep far enough away from your house, so you wouldn't notice, but close enough that I'd be able to escape if I needed to," he pauses for a moment, "like tonight."

My brain still feels fuzzy. "But you were fighting… and everything stopped… he was gone."

Kelly looks at Fredrick with an expression like my own. Apparently, she's interested in how he got rid of the rat-man tonight as well.

His tired eyes glance between Kelly and me. Finally, he says, "He was harder to fight off this time. I'm sure I could have knocked him unconscious, but then what would I have done with him?" I watch as Fredrick's eyes flicker to Kelly, but he focuses his stare at the wall, avoiding both of us. "While I had one of my hands free, I felt in his pockets and found a switchblade."

Kelly's eyes drop to her lap. Her face pales, and she shakes her head.

Fredrick interprets her reaction and adds, "No mom, it's not like that." He quickly goes on to tell the rest of his story. "I didn't want to use the blade—which I didn't." He pauses and looks at Kelly to make sure she understands. When he sees her relax, he adds, "That's why I took out his blade instead of my own. I wasn't trying to start a knife fight. I needed him to be at a disadvantage."

I can tell Kelly wants to be strong for her son, but as Fredrick explains the possibility of a fight with knives, her eyes brim with tears again.

It hurts to see Kelly so upset. I look at Fredrick, but his head rests in his hands, and he stares at the floor.

In a grave voice, he says, "Once he saw I had his knife, he lost a lot of his confidence. I told him if he ever came back, I wouldn't be the only one waiting for him."

A silent tear slides down Kelly's cheek, but she doesn't bother wiping it away.

This doesn't feel real. I open my mouth but shut it at the sound of Kelly's sigh.

She takes a deep breath and says, "Like I said, now we need to figure out how to keep you safe."

"How?" I'm relieved it hurts less to talk now.

Fredrick and Kelly stare at each other for a long moment like they're having a silent conversation. Finally, Fredrick sighs and turns his attention to me, his lips forming into a thin line. "We need to teach you how to defend yourself."

When I glance at Kelly for a better explanation, she only nods in agreement.

Fredrick resumes his previous quiet frame, and I can tell he isn't pleased with this decision. I try to grasp the reality of his words. "So, you're going to teach me how to fight?" My eyes flash nervously between Fredrick and Kelly as I wait for a straight answer.

Kelly speaks first. She's starting to look less horror-stricken, and more like her usual self. "Well, not me, of course. We're going to have Fredrick's friends help."

At the sound of her last sentence, my body tenses. The only "friends" of Fredrick's I'm aware of are the pirates themselves. I shake my head, but I can't articulate my mental objection into actual words. Fredrick and Kelly stare at me curiously as I struggle to find the nicest way to turn down their offer.

My face must reflect my panic because Fredrick's stone-like composure softens as he leans toward me and whispers, "Paige, what's wrong?" His concerned eyes succeed in easing some of my fears, but barely.

I look back at him and keep my voice low, not wanting Kelly to hear what I'm about to say. "The pirates are going to teach me?"

Fredrick allows a small smile to pull at the corners of his mouth, and the pressure in my chest eases.

"They're good fighters. If you can live through their training, you'll be prepared for anything."

"And what if I don't live through their training?" I blurt out.

Fredrick's smile broadens as he glances over at Kelly, who now pretends to browse a magazine. Meeting my eyes again, he says, "You'll be fine."

Kelly looks up from her magazine. Her green eyes look almost satisfied with how tonight has turned out, but I don't understand why. *What happened to the terror in her eyes that seemed to drain the blood from her cheeks?*

"She should come by tomorrow to meet everyone."

Fredrick nods and says to me, "And someone will keep watch over your house until you feel comfortable."

These are the only words that bring me the slightest bit of comfort. Although, I must admit the thought of having a pirate I don't know or, even worse, *Dan* watching my house makes me uneasy.

My thoughts are interrupted at the sound of a bedroom door opening. Kelly, Fredrick, and I all look up to see a pretty girl around the age of fourteen wander down the hallway toward us. I know she has to be Nicole. Despite her messy hair and big t-shirt, Nicole is as beautiful as the rest of the Pryce family. Her clear and vivid green eyes match Kelly's, while her hair resembles the color of Ben's more so than Fredrick's.

She finally looks up with a hand over her delicate mouth mid-yawn, freezing when she sees the three of us staring at her. Her tired eyes widen, and her hand covering her mouth immediately drops to her side.

After an awkward moment, I realize her eyes aren't locked on the three of us but locked on *me*. I shoot a nervous glance toward Kelly, who stares back at her daughter looking serious.

Nicole finally notices we're waiting for her to say something. She blinks a few times and walks toward us. As she sits down in the second recliner next to Kelly, she keeps her eyes on me, only breaking her gawking stare to turn to Fredrick and ask, "You were right?"

Once again, it seems Fredrick must have told everyone about his concerns for my safety except me. Looking up at him, I notice he now has an unreadable expression. He nods in confirmation, his lips in a tight line. "The guys will be over here tomorrow. She's going to start training."

Nicole gives her brother a blank stare at first but nods. My eyes take turns landing on the three of them as I try to grasp the meaning behind the word *training*. I clear my throat and wince from the forgotten pain. "My dad might notice if I'm gone when he wakes up."

All three of them look at a clock hanging on the wall, and I follow their lead to see that it's two-thirty. I blink a few times and look at it again, thinking that there must be some mistake. *How can it be so late already?*

Fredrick and Kelly look at each other, having another silent conversation, and then he stands. "Follow me." His voice isn't demanding, but I can tell he doesn't expect me to object.

Once Fredrick and I are in his room, I watch him walk over to his dresser. Opening a drawer, he pulls out a grey t-shirt with a boating logo on the front and tosses it my way. Catching it, I stare at him blankly. "What's this for?"

Fredrick hints toward my clothes. "I thought you might be more comfortable in something a little less… tattered."

I look down and realize he's right. Grass stains cover my white t-shirt, and the neckline now lays stretched and misshapen. "I still have one of your other shirts, though," I say, remembering the t-shirt he gave me the day we went sailing. Last time I saw him, he made it clear he didn't want me around. The last thing I want is to burden him more by taking his stuff. He's probably hating the fact that despite his wishes, he's stuck with me coming back here again.

"I don't mind." The intensity behind his eyes makes me catch my breath.

My cheeks flush and I say, "Okay," before turning and walking into the bathroom across the hall. I have no idea where I stand with him right now.

For the first time tonight, I'm completely alone. I stand in the bathroom and stare at the girl in the mirror. I barely recognize her. Studying my features once more, I try to take note of every mark I'll have to hide from my dad. The next few days, if not weeks, will be difficult.

With a sigh, I remove my shirt, thankful that I always sleep in a sports bra. As I throw Fredrick's shirt over my head, my senses flood with his smell, and it gives me a sense of comfort I wasn't expecting.

I walk back into Fredrick's room and see him sitting on the edge of his bed with his face in his hands. When he looks up at me, his eyes linger as he watches me walk in wearing his t-shirt. My cheeks burn, and I know my insecurities are getting the best of me.

"Can we talk?" he says softly.

I sit next to him. He looks apprehensive, and I can see the muscles in his jaw tensing. "I'm sorry about what happened tonight. I was exhausted. I fell asleep while I was keeping watch." He shakes his head as if disgusted with himself. "I should have gotten to you sooner."

"It's not your fault."

His eyes study me, and I'm suddenly aware of how close we are. Fredrick shakes his head, his eyebrows pulling together in frustration. "If I had been awake like I should have been, this—" he traces his fingers from behind my ear and down my neck, "—would have never happened." I flinch when his fingertips brush against my skin, and his hand snaps back.

Keeping my eyes locked on his, I say, "You can't do everything, you know."

Fredrick lets out a hollow laugh. "You might be right, but that's not going to stop me from trying."

He's starting to open up again, so I use this as an opportunity to ask another question that's been bothering me. "Fredrick?"

"Yeah?"

"Why did you tell me to stay away from you?"

"I was trying to avoid this." He gestures toward me, his expression pained.

I nod. "Okay, but now that I did get hurt, I thought you would be even more standoffish… and you're not."

The corners of his mouth twitch. "I can be standoffish."

I roll my eyes at him. "I don't want you to be. I just don't understand why you're acting more like yourself now."

"I'll feel better once I know you can defend yourself." He hesitates, but adds, "That's the only thing that matters right now."

At the end of his sentence, he doesn't stop looking at me. We stare at each other for another moment until we hear Kelly's voice from the living room. "Fredrick, it's almost three."

A torn expression crosses his face, still lingering only inches from mine. "I should probably take you home." His voice is different, lower and rougher than usual. His eyes break away from mine as he stands from the bed.

I nod, afraid if I say anything, my voice might shake.

He goes over to his closet and reaches into the far back corner, pulling out a black hoodie and handing it to me.

I give him a questioning look. "I'm not cold."

Fredrick lightly laughs and shakes his head. "It's to help you hide the uh…" His face falls like he can't bring himself to finish that sentence. He gestures toward his own neck and frowns as he hands me the hoodie.

"More of your clothes," I say with a smile, trying to lighten his mood. I try to hide my pain as I lift the hoodie up and over my head, the smell of him consuming me again.

"They look good on you," he says in a matter-of-fact tone.

His comment surprises me, and my eyes widen. Once I manage to get the hoodie on, I walk over to the mirror and check how well it hides the bruises on my neck. I beam at him with obvious relief. The dark marks are almost completely concealed by the extra material, and I don't hate how I look wearing Fredrick's clothes either.

The only issue is wearing a black hoodie in Florida, during the peak of summer, but I'll figure that out later.

I turn around to find Fredrick watching me, and he looks away as if I've caught him. I go to follow him out of the room, but he pauses with his hand on the doorknob, nearly making me bump into him. My breath catches when I feel him reach for my hand.

Giving my hand a light squeeze, he looks into my eyes. There's something about the way he looks at me that makes me feel like no one has ever really looked at me before. "I'm sorry," he says. "I'm going to make this right."

I hate that he's torturing himself over what happened to me. "You don't have to keep saying you're sorry."

I see his gaze fall to my neck before meeting my eyes again. "Yes, I do."

He releases my hand and opens the door. Kelly still sits in the living room. She has abandoned the magazine and now has a book in her hand. She blinks slowly, and I feel a stab of guilt for coming here and keeping her up half the night.

Setting her book down, she looks up at me and smiles. "You look better."

Fredrick barely looks at his mother. His sister is no longer in the room, and I'm assuming she has gone back to bed, and I envy her.

"I'm taking her home," he says as he grabs his keys from the wall hook.

Kelly's eyes show concern, not for me, I notice, but for her son. Maybe she can see he's torturing himself, too.

Without another word, Fredrick leaves the house, and I'm left standing in the front foyer alone with Kelly.

"Thank you for everything… really." I try to make sure there's enough conviction behind my words. I want her to understand how much I mean them.

Kelly nods and looks like she's fighting back tears again. Her rush of emotion makes me drop my gaze. I'm saved by the sound of a Jeep engine roaring to life, prompting a quick goodbye.

☠ ☠ ☠

The quiet atmosphere in the Jeep is an overdue break from today, and I'm relieved Fredrick welcomes the tranquility as much as I do.

I drift in and out of consciousness for most of the drive. Opening my eyes after another uneasy few minutes of sleep, I notice my familiar street and sit up to get a better look. Fredrick turns off his headlights and pulls over.

"Your dad might wake up if he hears the engine. There's a trail through the woods over here that leads to your side yard."

"Is that how you've been getting on the property?"

"Yeah," he says, "it could be a nice trail too, it's just over-grown."

I'm not surprised. I love my father, but he's known to let things slide. I can hear my mother's voice in my head complaining about how he can't think for himself and has to be told to do everything. I know one of the main reasons Dad bought this property was to evade an HOA breathing down his neck. He mows the grass around the house, but everything else is "left to nature," as he puts it.

Fredrick takes the key out of the ignition. "Come on. Let's get you inside."

I'm worried about sneaking in without waking my dad. I only just got in trouble with him, and this is way worse. If I get busted now, I might as well start packing my bags for Atlanta. The realization makes me hurry to open the door of the Jeep.

Fredrick laughs at the sight of me ready to make a run for it. "Calm down, roadrunner. It'll all work out. I'll get you back in bed before he notices you're gone."

His comment makes my cheeks flush, and I'm thankful the morning is dark enough to hide it. I shoot a glance toward the house hidden by trees and say, "Okay."

Fredrick chooses a slow and steady pace as we walk through the twisting trees. I usually find comfort in our house being sur-rounded by forest, but after tonight, all I can think about is how perfect it is for an ambush.

He easily navigates the path, dodging low lying branches and stepping over fallen ones. He has memorized the trail by now. I, on the other hand, lapse behind him, struggling with each step.

The sounds of our footsteps are suddenly joined by another pair of feet crunching and cracking the small branches.

My feet stop, and immediately the blood pounds in my ears. Fredrick hears them as well and stops. He looks over his shoulder, past me, but it's too dark for me to read his expression.

He must sense my fear because he murmurs, "It's okay." Raising his voice only a fraction more, he adds, "Jason, it's us."

In the dark, I can vaguely make out Jason's figure walking toward us, tall and muscular. I let out a breath and feel my shoulders relax.

"You'd better get her inside. The sun's about to rise." Jason's voice is deep and rough sounding.

"It'll be fine. I'll talk to you after." Fredrick doesn't sound rushed, and I hope he's taking this seriously.

With a single nod, Jason walks away, his footsteps fading with him.

After another minute or so, I can see my house through the trees. Once I see it, my heart aches. I don't want to be here. The rat-man took away the liberty of my home feeling like a home. The realization makes me drop my gaze. I watch my shoes pad through the sandy soil until I walk into Fredrick's outstretched arm.

I stumble backward. "Sorry."

"Is your dad a light sleeper?"

"Not at all."

"I think we can still use the front door."

Fredrick doesn't hesitate once we reach the front walkway. He silently opens the door, holding it ajar for me.

I start up the stairs as quietly as possible and feel Fredrick's fingertips brush the small of my back as he prepares to steady me. I didn't hear him close the front door, but I know he took care of it.

Sneaking into my bedroom, Fredrick closes the door behind him and ushers me with sarcastic urgency. "Quick. Get in bed."

I playfully roll my eyes at him and sit cross-legged on my bed.

He lets out a small laugh as he sits down next to me. "Are you going to be okay here by yourself?"

"I'll be fine," I say reassuringly, desperately hoping I sound convincing.

He studies me and frowns. "You don't have to come tomorrow if you need more time."

It doesn't take long for me to consider his offer. I start shaking my head. The idea of being home alone with my thoughts all day is enough to make my chest tighten.

"I'll be there. What time?"

Fredrick eyes me apprehensively. "The afternoon would work, but Paige, you don't have to."

"Tomorrow at one?" I ask. I'm desperate to have something to do—desperate to not be *alone*.

Fredrick finally nods, giving in to my request. "Okay, tomorrow at one."

He makes his way over to my window, and I watch as he carefully slides the glass open without a sound.

"You're not going to use the front door?" I ask in a whisper.

Fredrick steps through the window and crouches down on the roof outside. As he slides the window shut again, he flashes me a crooked smile and shakes his head. "Too easy."

15

By the time I wake up, light fills my bedroom. The warm sun bakes my cheek, and I roll over, hiding my face beneath the blankets. The sudden blanket-induced darkness brings unwelcome clarity, shedding light on things even the sun can't. Too-fresh memories of Fredrick and the rat man wrestling in my front yard make me wish I could slip back into sleep and escape this new pirate-filled world a little longer.

Pirates.

A word that once symbolized nothing more than eye patches and bottles of rum now changed forever. My foggy mind drifts, and I find myself lost in thoughts of groups, territories, training, and a mysterious dark-haired boy I can't quite figure out.

Training!

Bolting upright, I check the time. It's almost twelve. If I get ready now, I should be fine. I doubt pirates value punctuality, but the stress of running late is enough to get me out of bed.

My stomach tightens as I get closer to leaving the house. It feels like first-day-of-school nerves—if the school only housed criminals. My nerves make me reconsider going, but my new-found fear of staying home alone keeps my feet moving as I walk out the door.

☠   ☠   ☠

When I pull up to the house, Fredrick stands at the bottom of his driveway, waiting for me. I put my truck in park as he walks over and rests his arms on my open window. It amazes me that he can still look good wearing his family's bait shop t-shirt and dark jeans. The thin, gold chain of his trophy tucked into his shirt, hidden as usual.

He looks more rested. His smile reaches his eyes, and I immediately feel less anxious.

"I wasn't sure if you'd show," he says with a smirk playing at the corner of his mouth.

"I didn't think I had much of a choice." Even though I decided to come here today, I didn't have much of a say about the pirates teaching me how to fight. Fredrick and Kelly are the ones who decided that terrifying fate.

Fredrick steps back to open my truck door, offering his hand to help me jump down. I tilt my head before accepting his offer. "Someone's in a better mood today."

He looks down at me and shrugs. "Just trying to see things differently, I guess."

I can't help studying him as we make our way to the front door. I like this lighter, more at-ease Fredrick.

Inside, Kelly, Nicole, and Ben are all in the living room talking amongst themselves. It's nice seeing them under more normal circumstances. Not that this is normal, but something about the way Nicole and Ben are bickering gives me hope that things will feel normal again soon. I guess that's good enough for now.

Then, I see them.

I notice Jason first—probably because he was at my house last night. He stands in the kitchen with his elbows resting on the bar countertop. His face is stern and business-like, but his clothes are the epitome of casual. With his dark grey board shorts and a black tank top, he looks like he's ready to spend the day at the beach. Now that I can see him better, he reminds me of Dan. Only in his features, though. Other than that, Jason seems more personable.

A shorter guy stands across from him in the kitchen, and I assume he must be Carter. Even though he's shorter than the other guys, he's also more muscular, or maybe he just wants to seem that way. His sleeves are cut from his shirt, leaving his arms and the sides of his torso exposed, his left arm covered in ink.

Melissa sits on a barstool at the counter with Jason and Carter. Although petite, the way she carries herself makes it clear that she is far from delicate. Something about her gives me a feeling of unease that I don't feel from the others. She's wearing dark, tight-fitting jeans with a tear at the knee and a black tank top. We're probably the same age, but makeup can be deceiving. Her dark brown, pin-straight hair is a stark contrast against her light blue, kohl-lined eyes, making her stare that much more piercing.

Everyone stops what they're doing when Fredrick and I walk in. Having so many eyes on us makes my face warm, so I look at Kelly, who gives me a slight nod and a reassuring smile.

"Everyone, this is Paige." The lighter version of Fredrick I witnessed outside has vanished. He's all business now.

Ben whistles slowly, taking in my battered appearance. I didn't bother wearing the hoodie because I don't need to hide my bruises from anyone here. "Shit, you've seen better days."

Nicole and Kelly shoot him a warning glare, and he mouths, "What?" I like Ben. If nothing else, at least he's honest.

"It's okay," I say, "he's right."

I look up at Fredrick, expecting him to take the lead and introduce his friends, even though I already know their names. His expression, however, catches me off guard. Fredrick's eyes are brooding and fixated on something.

I follow his gaze, and it doesn't take long to see why he's frowning. Melissa's lips form into a scowl as she glares in our direction.

My direction.

Jason clears his throat, acknowledging the awkward tension in the room. "Well, I'm Jason." He gestures across from him. "This is Carter." Carter nods in my direction. "And this ray of fucking sunshine is Mel." He points to her with his thumb, and Melissa rolls her eyes.

"That's not my name, asshole. 'Mel' makes me sound like a middle-aged mechanic."

Jason looks back at me. "My apologies. This is Melissa, whose name is far too sweet for her overall bitchiness."

Melissa scoffs, hopping down from the barstool. "So, what are we doing here?"

Kelly stands and looks at Nicole. "We have a shift at the shop, so we better get going."

"But Mom," Nicole groans, tossing her head back. "I helped you open this morning. Can't Ben go now?"

With a dismissive pat on her daughter's leg, Kelly quickly says, "Nope. Let's go," and without another word, she walks out of the room.

Nicole gets up, and Ben sticks his tongue out as she passes. She ignores him and rushes over to me with a huge smile. "I'm Nicole. We were never introduced last night, but I'm Fredrick's sister." She beams at me and holds out her hand. I have to admire her confidence. I don't think I would have felt comfortable walking up to a stranger and introducing myself at fourteen. I'm barely comfortable with it now.

I smile back at her. "Nice to meet you. I'm Paige."

Her grin broadens, and her eyes flicker to Fredrick. "Oh, I know. It takes a lot to make this one smile, so kudos to you."

I laugh even though her comment makes my face burn. I don't know where Fredrick's family gets their ideas. Can't they see that he keeps me at arm's length?

Fredrick rolls his eyes and places his hands on his sister's shoulders, turning her around to face the other way. "I'm pretty sure you have somewhere to be," he says, giving her a light push.

Nicole looks over her shoulder, still beaming at me. "Bye,

Paige!"

I can't help laughing as I wave goodbye to her. I didn't know Leah three years ago, but I'm sure she would have been a lot like Nicole.

Ben rests his elbows on his knees as he looks at us. "Where do you guys plan on doing this?"

Melissa chimes in, "Yeah, can someone tell me what's going on?" She's still scowling, but at least she isn't only directing it at me anymore.

Fredrick answers. He may have stopped glaring at Melissa, but his demeanor holds more tension than in the driveway. "I found a clearing yesterday. It's hidden by trees, and the ground is soft."

I almost ask why the ground needs to be soft, but Ben's reply answers it for me.

"Good," he says as his eyes travel from Fredrick to me. "I don't think more bruises is the direction you want to go."

"If she can't handle it, she shouldn't be here." Melissa folds her arms across her chest, her crystal blue eyes trained on me again. My gaze drops to the hem of my t-shirt as I run my thumb over the stitching. Part of me wants to stand up for myself, but the other, much larger part doesn't even want to lift my gaze because I can feel her eyes still drilling into me.

Jason gets to his feet. "Jesus, give her a break Mel." When Melissa glares at him, he adds, "—*issa.*"

Ben ignores Melissa's comment to me and her exchange with Jason. This must be nothing out of the ordinary for him. "Where's the clearing?" he asks Fredrick.

"It's about a mile west of the dock. It won't take long for us to get there, but we should get going."

Ben claps his hands on his knees and pushes himself off the couch. "Good luck my friends." He glances at me again before adding, "She'll need all the help she can get."

I look after him with my mouth open. Maybe I decided I liked Ben a little prematurely.

Melissa lets out a hollow laugh at Ben's comment, and the smug look on her face is enough to make my stomach burn.

Fredrick holds the door open for us to file out of the house, but Melissa takes her time lingering behind. For a fleeting moment, I wonder how hard it would be to trip her as she walks by; she looks light enough. The thought makes me laugh inside, and I have to bite back a smile. She notices this and picks up her pace.

None of us talk as we walk toward an old wooden dock in the distance, but I still try to stay closest to Fredrick and furthest from Melissa. I let myself take in each of the pirates as we walk. They're all so different from how I had envisioned them. When Fredrick first told me about his group, I had pictured four people, all intimidating like Dan.

Wait a minute. Where is Dan?

Catching up to Fredrick's side, I lower my voice to avoid drawing attention. "Why isn't Dan here?"

Before he can answer, a voice behind us says, "He has to take care of something. Should be here soon, though."

I look over my shoulder to see who responded, but neither of the guys gives any indication that they spoke. My eyes shift from one to the other, but I give up and face forward.

The quiet of the group accentuates how audible my footsteps are. They've clearly all mastered Fredrick's furtive habits. Concentrating hard, I try to take each step with more awareness. It works to muffle the sound of my shuffling feet, but I find myself falling behind the rest of the group and give up altogether.

As the sandy road ends, we head into the woods where Fredrick leads us down a maze of brush and trees. Our narrow trail feeds into a clearing, and I know we've made it to our destination. Taking in my surroundings, I can see why Fredrick picked it. Sparse trees circle a wide patch of Florida's sand-like soil, providing us with enough shade to weaken the warmth of the sun, while still giving us enough open space to train—whatever that means. Further outside the clearing, the dense trees keep us completely hidden.

"Are you sure it's big enough?" Jason asks as he walks the perimeter.

Carter steps forward. "Only one way to find out." On his last word, he hitches his leg behind Jason's and, with one fluid motion, brings Jason to the ground.

Flat on his back, Jason groans, "You fucker."

Carter stands over him with a taunting grin. "How'd that feel? Ground nice and soft for ya?"

Jason pushes himself up. "You're a dick."

Melissa rolls her eyes at them both, clearly unamused.

"What's the matter, sis? Can't stand to see people having fun?" Carter opens his mouth to say more, but he's cut off by Jason knocking him to the ground.

Carter's stocky build makes the fall sound that much more painful. He doesn't seem hurt, considering he's… laughing? Deep, hearty bellows erupt from Carter's body as he lies flat in the clearing.

Jason walks over and holds out a hand to help him up, a smile spreading across his lips.

The corners of my mouth pull up as I watch them. I look over my shoulder, expecting to see Fredrick watching their exchange in amusement too, but he's sitting on a fallen tree trunk, wrapped in his own thoughts.

I approach him carefully. "Fredrick?"

He breaks his gaze to look at me, his face still thoughtful.

I hesitate but ask, "Is everything okay?"

He scoffs and says, "Fuck, Paige, look at you." He runs his hand through his hair. "Every time I see those marks around your neck, I wish I had killed that asshole while I had the chance." My eyes widen, and he softens his expression before continuing. "And now you have to do this," he gestures toward the clearing where the three pirates are talking, "while you're still in pain because we can't risk waiting for you to heal." I glance over at the other three, and I'm thankful they aren't paying attention.

His words catch me off guard, but I'm glad he's talking. I'd rather him be cursing and angry than deal with his staggering silence.

"The pain isn't so bad," is all I can think to say.

He gives me a dubious look.

"Really," I add. "My neck hurts at the touch, but the rest of my body is okay."

Fredrick doesn't seem convinced, and I watch as his eyes travel down to my neck. After a moment, he sighs. "Okay, let's get set up then."

As he stands, I ask if he needs help with anything.

He glances back at the other three. When his eyes meet mine again, he looks slightly apprehensive. "No, you stay here." He cuts across the clearing and goes deep into the thick trees on the other end.

I take a seat where he had been, but I'm not alone for long. Noticing the empty seat next to me, Carter bounds over and joins me. "Think you're ready for this?"

I laugh, shaking my head. "I have no idea."

"So, how did you meet Fredrick?"

My eyes jump to Fredrick at the mention of his name. He must have stashed supplies in the woods because he's emerging from the thick trees carrying a stack of buckets.

I bring my attention back to Carter and say, "There was a bon-fire at the beginning of summer."

He raises an eyebrow. "The one here? At the beach?"

I nod. "That's the one."

Carter stretches his arms out behind him, leaning back. "I was at that party. I didn't see you, though." Flashing me a smirk, he adds, "I *definitely* would have remembered you."

His direct approach catches me off guard. I'm more familiar with Luke's futile attempts at spending more time together, and even then, he has never been so blunt. I open my mouth to attempt a response, but thankfully, Fredrick's voice interrupts us.

"Carter, a little help?" His voice sounds casual, but his eyes are dark.

Carter glances from Fredrick to Jason, who happens to be standing next to the stack of buckets, doing nothing.

Fredrick raises his eyebrows at Carter expectantly.

He huffs. "Uh, sure."

I eye Fredrick curiously, but he doesn't meet my gaze. He's too busy watching Carter's every step. My heel bounces against the sand as I watch them set up without my help. Fortunately, it doesn't take long before Fredrick waves me over.

I walk up to find five buckets full of tennis balls set up in a circle. I must look confused because Fredrick says, "I'll explain." Readdressing the rest of the group, he goes on to say, "You all know why we're here. Even though Paige won't be joining us, we've agreed to teach her how to defend herself." He glances at Melissa, giving her a pointed stare before continuing. "To do this, she'll need to undergo a combination of strength-building and self-defense." He looks at me and adds, "We usually start with a baseline strength test, but considering your condition, it wouldn't be a fair assessment anyway." He goes back to addressing everyone. "Today, we'll jump into reflex training. You all know the drill. Everyone, get a bucket."

At that moment, Carter, Jason, and Melissa each stand next to one of the five buckets in a circle, so I do the same.

"Not you, Paige." Fredrick's authoritative voice makes me stop in my tracks, waiting for whatever comes next. "You'll stand in the middle." He points to the open space in the center of everyone. Being the odd one out sets my nerves on edge, and I can feel my heart rate rising.

After positioning himself at the nearest bucket, Fredrick explains, "Before we can teach you how to fight back, you need to learn how to defend yourself. Part of this means studying another person's movements, so you can expect what they're about to do. Today's exercise is simple. Anticipate who will throw the ball next and dodge it before it hits you."

My rising heart rate thuds louder in my chest. I don't play sports for a reason. That reason is that I'm terrible with hand-eye coordination. I'm more of an asset with a book in my hand than a bat. The bruises on my neck ache with the added thickness in my throat.

He must see my mind reeling because he adds, "We'll start with only one person first."

"I call first."

The deep voice behind me makes me jump, and I turn around to find Dan standing no more than a few feet away. I might be able to get used to Fredrick sneaking up on me, but I'll never be comfortable with Dan doing it.

I look over at Fredrick, hoping he'll step in, but he says nothing. He does, however, grip the tennis ball in his hand so tightly that his knuckles are white.

Dan takes his time walking over to the last remaining bucket. He picks up one of the tennis balls and tosses it in the air, a smirk displayed on his face. "Well, of all people, I never thought little

Paige Lawson would be running with our crew."

"She's not," Fredrick interjects.

Dan raises an eyebrow at Fredrick. "She's here, isn't she?"

I look back at Fredrick, but he doesn't say anything.

At the sound of Dan's voice again, my eyes snap back to his intimidating figure. "Man, Luke would never believe this. You. Here with us. Good thing he'll never find out." His last words are a threat; I know it.

When I don't say anything, Dan's lips curl into a sinister smile. "No point wasting time."

He throws the first ball too quickly for me to move out of the way. It strikes me on my left shoulder, but the impact is softer than I thought it would be. He's not throwing at his full strength, and even though I don't know why, I appreciate it.

Before the first ball touches the ground, I'm struck with another. This time it collides with my right hip. Gritting my teeth, I watch Dan intently. He passes the ball from one hand to the other with the dexterity of a magician. I barely see him release the third ball, but it's heading straight for my face. With a yelp, I twist my body out of the way.

Dan's eyes shift to Carter, and he gives him the slightest nod. I spin around to face Carter, but it's too late. The ball he threw grazes my upper arm as it flies past me.

Another, much softer hit meets my back that must have been Fredrick. My eyes scan the five of them feverishly to figure out who will be next.

I notice Jason's foot shift, and I turn to face him. Somehow,

I'm able to dodge the tennis ball at the last minute. He gives me an approving look, and I beam at him.

However, the celebratory moment doesn't last because the impact of the next ball audibly smacks into the front of my left shoulder, making me stagger backward. I grab my shoulder in pain and can't contain the yell that escapes my lips.

"Ow!"

The group laughs, aside from Fredrick, and I see, for the first time, a small smile pulling at the corners of Melissa's lips.

16

The weeks that follow make me feel like I'm leading two different lives. My routine alternates between time with friends and going to the beach for training sessions. I haven't told anyone from school about my time with the pirates. I'm not sure why. I know Leah would be more than excited to know that I see Fredrick regularly. Josh would be less than pleased, but that's not what stops me from sharing. My time with the pirates has been completely mine. My very own secret from the world—well, *my* world.

My bruises from the attack are mostly gone now. Only faint yellow marks linger in some areas. Dad thought I was sick for most of the past two weeks thanks to my insisting on being cold in the house. It was the only way to wear Fredrick's black hoodie without suspicion. Even though I've healed physically, I wouldn't say I survived the attack unscathed. Ever since that night, I think twice before entering an empty room, and unsettling dreams rob me of my sleep.

I don't feel safe at home anymore.

Fredrick and the other pirates usually show up late, so I often spend time with Kelly and Nicole. I enjoy my time with them. Kelly has a way of making me feel like her home is a home for me, too.

Spending time with her makes me think about my own mother. I know my mom would judge Kelly for allowing her son to engage in whatever this is. I can already hear her voice in my head, criticizing Kelly for not having a backbone with her children. The thought makes my stomach uneasy because, based on everything I've seen over the past two weeks, Kelly is a great mom.

Asking her why she doesn't stop Fredrick from stealing isn't something I can bring myself to do, though. It feels accusatory and too personal no matter how I try to word it in my head. From what I've gathered from everyone, Kelly doesn't support it. So, why does she fill her house with criminals? I have no idea.

☠ ☠ ☠

The familiar highway twists and turns under my truck's tires. My babysitting fund has nearly run dry thanks to all the driving I've done on these daily beach trips. My truck may be many things, but eco-friendly is not one of them. If I don't earn some extra money soon, I'll have to start asking Dad for gas money, which I'd rather not do.

I no longer have training sessions with the entire group. Instead, I usually work one-on-one with the pirates. Unlike the others,

Fredrick's sessions usually strengthen me mentally more than physically. He teaches me how to pay attention to things I would normally overlook. Last week's lesson focused on analyzing people and deciphering those preoccupied from those more aware.

"Fredrick, I told you I'm not stealing."

He sighed. "You're not listening. You have to know these things, so you can practice acting casual when you think someone might be following you and when you're following someone else."

"But why would I be following someone else?"

Fredrick shook his head, but I could see a smile tugging at the corners of his lips. "Humor me." His eyes had locked on mine when he added, "Okay?"

I swallowed, still not used to the heat that burns my core every time his eyes meet mine. "Fine."

Pleased with my response, his mouth quirked into a crooked smile. It's the smile I rarely see him give anyone else, and every time it crosses his lips, I'm mesmerized by it.

He's been in a better mood ever since we stopped training with the group. Being around everyone else seems to bring out the worst in him. When the other pirates are with us, he's more irritable and withdrawn. I'm grateful for the shift when we're alone, but one-on-one training means there are some days I don't see Fredrick at all.

His sessions are by far the hardest, but easily the most enjoyable. Compared to my training with everyone else, Fredrick's lessons feel the most academic. They play to my strengths. I've always been good at studying, but I'm just studying people instead of literature.

Melissa doesn't talk to me more than she has to, and it's fair to assume she hates me. The guys will account for the fact that I'm still new to fighting. Melissa usually leaves me with at least two new bruises to hide.

In our last lesson, her eyes were cold as she stared at me with her usual contempt.

She had knocked me off my feet and was towering over me. That's the only way her short frame would ever be able to tower over anyone. "No offense, but you kind of suck at this."

I wanted to say, "No offense, but you're kind of a bitch," but I didn't. I wouldn't say I'm afraid of Melissa, but I would say that considering her size, she's more intimidating than one would think. As a result, our time spent together is usually a one-way trickle of insults—from her to me. If anything, I like to think her lessons strengthen my self-control and give me thick skin.

In our first lesson, it didn't take long for me to learn that Melissa believes in baptism by fire. She came at me with enough force to knock me off my feet.

"Ow!" I looked up to find her staring at me with a smug look. "What was that for?"

Melissa had shifted her weight to one hip and crossed her arms. "Oh, I'm sorry. Did you think we were going to paint each other's nails and talk about boys?"

I don't understand her problem with me. The others tell me not to take it personally, but it's hard not to when she blatantly hates me. Even though she makes me seethe with anger, I can't deny that I learn a lot. I've picked up tons of great fighting moves from her, but I wish she could actually teach them to me instead of just using them on me.

As painful as my lessons with Melissa are, they don't come close to the pain of working with Jason. Neither of us thrives in social situations, which makes for a cut-and-dry experience. Jason is nice, but he lays out the facts and nothing more.

In the same way Jason takes everything too seriously, Carter takes nothing seriously at all. It's easy to forget Carter and Melissa are siblings, especially considering the only thing they have in common is their height—or lack of. At least most, if not all, my lessons with Carter involve him apologizing for his sister's behavior.

Carter's lessons are—for lack of a better word—fun. Whether he's jumping out to scare me or making constant jokes, he always manages to lighten the mood. He still openly flirts with me, but in a playful way. It's funny how Luke's indirect flirting makes me want to run, yet Carter's direct attempts make me laugh and feel more comfortable around him.

Carter yelled, "Hey!"

I jumped back as he sprang out from a nearby tree, my heart pounding. "Stop doing that!"

Carter lifted his chin, looking pleased with himself. "Can't. It's part of your training."

I raised an eyebrow at him, a hand to my chest. "How?"

"I'm desensitizing you." He gave me a proud smirk. "You can't kick ass if you're flinching."

I let out a laugh. "I can't kick ass. Period."

Carter's smile widened. "Don't say that. One day, when we're married, we'll look back on the days before you were badass and laugh."

I had playfully rolled my eyes and looked away. When I didn't hear anything else, I knew he had hidden from me again. I groaned. My eyes frantically scanned the clearing for him, but the forest was still around me. To my left, I heard something rustle in the woods, so I turned in that direction. Carter tackled me from the opposite direction, laughing.

"Damn it, Carter!"

Thankfully, I don't have one-on-one lessons with Dan. He's always too busy doing something more important as head of the group. I have no idea what he spends his time doing, but if it keeps him away from me, I support it.

☠   ☠   ☠

My drive to the beach ends as I pull up to the white house with blue shutters. I sigh at the sight of Jason standing next to Fredrick in the driveway. Another by-the-book lesson from Jason. Fredrick glances my way with a smile but continues to listen to whatever Jason is saying. It's been a few days since I've seen him, and I'm always struck by how much I've missed being around him.

After parking my truck, I walk up the driveway to meet the two of them. "Let me guess," I say with a smile. "I'm with Jason today?"

Fredrick looks at Jason and back at me. "Actually, I was thinking I could work with you today."

I give Jason a questioning look, my eyes asking why he's here.

"I'm starting your session. Fredrick has to take care of some-thing, but he'll teach most of it."

I tilt my head at Fredrick. "What do you need to take care of?"

"Dan needs to talk to me." He doesn't elaborate, and before I can open my mouth to inquire more, he claps a hand on Jason's shoulder. "Take care of her, Jay. I'll see you guys soon."

I watch Fredrick walk away until he rounds the corner and dis-appears out of sight. When I look back at Jason, he's smirking at me.

I know he caught me staring at Fredrick for longer than I should have, but I still ask, "What?"

He shakes his head, but I can still see a twinge of a smile at the corner of his mouth. "Nothing. Come on. Let's get going."

I follow him toward the dock that landmarks our clearing in the woods. As we walk, I stare down at my shoes and study how my feet flex with each step.

"You've gotten better." Jason's deep voice startles me, and my head snaps up.

"Oh, thanks," I mutter, not used to being complimented by him. The fact that he's initiating a conversation with me at all, catches me off guard.

"I mean it. You've come a long way in a short amount of time. You have most of the basic knowledge. You just need to practice."

His last word reminds me of Fredrick, and the corners of my mouth twitch. With a sigh, I say, "Thanks, but I have a long way to go."

Jason still doesn't look at me as we walk side by side but nods slightly. "You'll get it."

Once we're at the clearing, I sit on a fallen log and wait for Jason to tell me what we're practicing today.

I'm surprised when he takes a seat next to me. He rests his elbows on his knees and says, "This is going to sound dumb."

"What is?"

He lets out a sigh before answering. "Luke wants me to convince you to go to this barbeque thing with him."

The mention of Luke brings my eyebrows together. "What? Why?"

He shrugs. "Beats me. He probably wants to ask you out again. You'd think he'd take a hint by now."

I'm so confused. How does Jason even know about Luke in the first place? When I stare at him, he adds, "Please tell me you're aware of his stupid crush on you."

I nod my head slowly. "Yeah, but… how do you…"

He looks at me, taken aback. "Everyone in the family knows how much he likes you. Not that he's very good at hiding it." He rolls his eyes at the thought.

"You're related to Luke?" *How did I not know this?*

"Well, sort of. Dan and I are half-brothers, so… I guess that makes him my half-cousin?"

The similar features between Jason and Dan finally make sense. "I had no idea. I've never seen you with them."

Jason raises an eyebrow. "Can you blame me?"

I don't bother trying to hold back my laughter. "No, I guess not. I'd rather not go to the barbeque."

"I figured as much. I'll make something up. Maybe I'll use

Fredrick as an excuse. Luke has had his suspicions about you two since the bonfire."

My cheeks burn. "He has?" I didn't think Luke had even seen me talk to Fredrick at the bonfire.

"We all have. You may not realize it, but Fredrick is usually pretty closed off."

The heat in my cheeks rises another degree. "Jason, I don't think—"

He cuts me off. "Don't tell me… you two are just friends? Yeah, I know. I hear the same bullshit from him."

The idea of Fredrick talking to his friends about me is enough to make my heart pound, but the fact that he tells them we're only friends simultaneously leaves my chest heavy. I try to remind myself that we *are* just friends. "Carter is the one who talks about having a future with me." I tease to lighten the mood.

Jason laughs. "Yeah, you and every other girl. I think the only two girls he hasn't flirted with are Mel and Kelly." He shakes his head. "No, wait. He's definitely tried to flirt with Kelly."

The idea of Carter flirting with Fredrick's mom makes me shake with laughter.

At that moment, Fredrick walks through the trees toward us.

Jason smiles down at me, and I see something menacing behind his eyes. "Don't worry, Paige. I'll give Luke your message."

Fredrick suddenly looks interested. "What message?"

Jason shrugs. "Ask her about it. I'll see you later." Without another word, he exits the clearing, and I'm left gaping after him.

Fredrick cocks an eyebrow. "What was that about?"

I look up at him, dumbfounded. "I don't really know… Luke wants me to go to a barbeque, and Jason was delivering the invitation."

He takes a seat next to me. "Are you going?"

I look at Fredrick, a little surprised by his interest. "No, I try to avoid awkward situations."

Fredrick nods slowly. "Did Jason tell you why Luke wants you to go?"

I let out a laugh, and even though he smiles, I can tell he isn't sure what I find so funny. I assumed Jason would have filled him in. "You know how Dan told you that Luke and I were dating?"

His smile falters slightly. "Yeah."

"Well," I say, trying to find the right words. "I've never dated Luke, but that's not for his lack of trying. Jason thinks he might want to ask me out again."

He raises his eyebrows. "Again?"

Wringing my hand in my lap, I drop my gaze. "It's a pretty common occurrence."

I can feel him watching me. "But you always say no?"

Still looking at my hands, I nod.

"Why?" he says impassively, making him impossible to read.

I shrug, not sure how to answer. "Luke is… nice, I guess. But I don't think of him that way." When he doesn't say anything, I dare to lift my gaze. "Why isn't Jason teaching me today?"

My question pulls him from his thoughts. Turning to look at me, he says, "I want to talk to you."

His answer makes my stomach flutter and my anxiety spike all at once. "Why? I know I need to improve. I'm nowhere near ready to—"

He raises a hand to stop me. "Paige, that's not why I wanted to talk to you."

I wait.

"I wanted to check in with you. Now that you're working with everyone separately, it's important that you're comfortable with the training."

I let out a sigh of relief. I thought he might tell me I'm a lost cause. "I like training for the most part." I give him a smile. "Carter and I always have fun, and Jason is knowledgeable…" My voice trails off.

"From what I hear, it sounds like Carter enjoys his time with you, too." Something flickers across his face, but I'm not sure what it is.

"Really? He said that?" Regardless of Fredrick's mood, it's nice to know I'm not a complete burden to at least one of the pirates.

Fredrick forces a breath of laughter. "More or less."

"What should we work on today?" I'm eager for today's lesson now that I know it will be with Fredrick.

He smiles, but it no longer reaches his eyes. "Think of it as your day off."

My heart sinks. I wanted time with him. On the other hand, there's a fresh Melissa-inflicted bruise on my right shoulder I wouldn't mind giving time to heal. At the thought of her, I ask, "Do you know why Melissa hates me?"

Fredrick's expression hardens, giving me the feeling that he knows the answer to my question and more.

I press further. "You can tell me."

He sighs. "I've told you. It's nothing against you. She's mad that I told you about what we do without consulting everyone first. She thinks you'll either rat us out or join us."

I frown. "I wouldn't do either of those things. Can't you tell her I have no interest in becoming a part of the group?"

"I have… everyone has. She won't listen. She thinks you'll change your mind."

I try to imagine myself as one of the pirates, but I can't. I can't imagine taking things that aren't rightfully mine. "I don't see that happening."

Fredrick looks torn but ultimately nods. Without saying anything, he goes to stand, and I put my hand on his to stop him. He immediately sits back down, and his eyes drop to my hand on his. I quickly pull my hand back, but my cheeks warm, and I'm sure he can sense my embarrassment.

"I wanted to ask you about something, too." I bite my lip, not sure how he'll react to what I'm about to offer. "Do you think we can space out my training sessions? I haven't babysat recently, and I'm running low on gas money." I grimace, hating that I just admitted to running low on cash.

"I'll pick you up and take you home the days I can."

I gape at him. "I can't ask you to do that."

Those molten eyes lock on mine. "You didn't."

Before I can debate with him further, he stands and holds out a hand for me to take. "Mom is cooking dinner for everyone tonight.

Let's go back to the house."

I consider his offer before letting him help me up and walk with him back through the scattered trees.

☠   ☠   ☠

Everyone is at Fredrick's house when we walk through the glass front door. The only people missing are Ben and Dan. Ben is probably working a shift at the bait shop, but I have no idea why Dan isn't here. I welcome his absence even though I question it.

Kelly stands as soon as I come into view and rushes me into the kitchen. "Thank God. Fredrick, I need her!"

He shakes his head with a breath of laughter. As I'm dragged into the kitchen, I glance over my shoulder, hoping for an explanation, but Fredrick's tight-lipped smile only tells me he's amused.

In the kitchen, Kelly lets go of me to search her cabinets. "Everyone is eating here tonight, but I have no idea what to cook!" She looks a little embarrassed and says, "I figured since you're always cooking dinner for your dad, maybe you can help me think of something?"

"I can try." I laugh. I think Kelly forgets that *everyone* is a group of teenagers who would be happy eating anything.

She forces a smile, but I can still see the anxiety behind her bright green eyes.

I take a quick inventory. "Do you have chicken? I know a good salad we can make."

Kelly doesn't take a break from rummaging through a cabinet

as she answers. "I have lots of chicken, but Dan won't eat salad."

My heart stops. "Dan's coming?"

"Yeah, he's bringing his cousin…" She waves her hand in the air, searching for the name to come back to her. "His cousin…" Giving up, she shakes her head. "Oh, I don't know what his name is, but his cousin is coming."

"Luke?" I ask, and my voice strains in my throat.

"That's the one!" She doesn't notice how her words have affected me. My time with the modern-day pirates has been something I've almost held sacred these past two weeks. Now, Luke will make my two worlds collide.

Kelly stands with the pantry open and calls over her shoulder. "I planned on grilling the chicken, but I don't have time to marinate. Help me pick which seasonings to use?"

Scanning the shelves, I see a few ingredients I can do something with.

Kelly goes back to the counter and hurries to clean the chicken. I don't know why she's in such a rush. It's barely five in the afternoon. We have plenty of time.

"What's the hurry?" I ask.

Kelly wipes her forehead with the back of her arm as she cuts the fat off the raw chicken. "It's the first time I've hosted a dinner since—well, it's just been a while."

I'm not sure what her response means, but once she's done prepping, she huffs. "I need to get one of those boys to man the grill." Kelly washes her hands and leaves me alone in the kitchen, peeling potatoes.

I listen to the endless chatter come to a dull hum as Kelly enters the living room. "Which one of you boys can grill for us?"

She comes back with Jason trailing behind her. I set down the potato peeler. Grabbing the plate of raw chicken, I have an excuse to follow him onto the patio.

"I hear Luke's coming." I'm not sure why I say it but considering it's the only conversation we've ever had, it's all I can think of.

Jason looks up at me from the bottom of the grill. "Is that right?"

I nod. "Dan is bringing him." The corner of his mouth pulls upward. "Wait, you knew?"

Dusting his hands on his shorts, Jason stands and starts turning different knobs on the grill. "I told you, use Fredrick as an excuse."

My jaw drops. "*This* is the barbeque you were talking about?"

Jason grins and puts a hand on my shoulder. "I didn't know Kelly would grill out. That's just a happy coincidence." When I frown, he adds, "Listen, you have nothing to worry about. He already assumes something's going on between you and Fredrick, right?"

I nod, but my eyes narrow. "According to you, yes." This dinner with Luke will be worse than any training session with Melissa.

He beams, loving the reaction he's getting. "Well, Luke doesn't know you'll be here. He'll show up, and it should be pretty obvious that you're here as Fredrick's guest."

None of this makes sense. "But I'm not here as Fredrick's guest."

He pauses. "No?" With a tilt of his head, he adds, "Who are

you here for, then? It's not me." He nods toward the house. "Carter might wish it was him, but it's not. It sure as hell isn't Melissa or Dan." He lowers his head so he can look me in the eye. "The only reason you're here is because Fredrick wants you here."

I shake my head, trying to clear my thoughts. "But you said Luke was inviting me to the barbeque…"

Jason shrugs, releasing my shoulder and returning his attention to the grill. "That part was for Fredrick."

Does Fredrick know about Luke coming here? I want to turn and walk away, but I'm still holding the tray of raw chicken.

Once he finishes throwing chicken on the grill, I get away from him as quickly as possible. Setting the plate in the sink and washing my hands, I dart past Kelly to find Fredrick in the living room. He's sitting with Nicole, Melissa, and Carter, all laughing at Carter's best impression of Dan.

My quick pace made a bigger entrance than I had intended, and everyone stops talking to look up at me.

"Uh… Fredrick, can I talk to you about something?" I'm disappointed by how small my voice sounds.

He looks unsure but nods.

I follow him to his bedroom, where he closes the door behind us.

Without thinking, I blurt, "Did you know Luke was coming tonight and not tell me?" My tone comes out accusatory, but I don't care. Just the thought of him being in on Jason's joke is enough to make my heart race.

Fredrick's expression falters. "What? No."

"You're not in on this with Jason?"

His dark eyebrows crease together. "Jason knows?"

I cross my arms in frustration. "Yeah, he thought Luke coming over here was hilarious."

His eyes darken, and I'm reminded of how intense he can be. "What does this have to do with anything, Paige?"

I wasn't expecting him to turn his anger on me. "I mean, it's your house. Wouldn't you know who's coming over?"

With narrowed eyes, he says in a low voice, "You know, I do have better things to do than try to set you up with someone."

The venom behind his words makes me wish I could take back what I said, and my eyes drop under the pressure of his stare. "I know. I just—I thought you might have been in on the joke."

Fredrick opens the door, a clear signal for me to leave his room. "I'm not in on anything."

With a sigh, I walk out of the room, feeling equally frustrated. Luke will be here any minute, and now Fredrick is annoyed with me. I guess it was only a matter of time before he would shut me out, he always does when a lot of people are around.

I hear a new voice coming from the kitchen. Ben's deep laughter now mixes in with the sound of everyone else.

I turn to Fredrick and say, "I need to call my dad, and then I'll help Kelly." I have no desire to sit anywhere near the pirates right now.

He nods but doesn't waste any time getting back to his friends. Picking up Fredrick's house phone, I call Dad's cell. It only rings once before he picks up the phone and starts reciting his business greeting.

"Hello, this is Dave Lawson from—"

"Dad, it's me."

"Paige?"

"Yeah, I'm using Fredrick's house phone. Kelly is having everyone over for dinner tonight, and I'm going to stay. I just wanted to let you know."

My dad stays quiet for a moment on the other end of the phone. "Listen, Paige, I don't want you staying over there too late, okay?"

Usually, the fact that he still hasn't accepted my friendship with Fredrick bothers me, but between Fredrick's attitude and Luke's pending arrival, I'm more than willing to agree.

"No problem. I'll leave after dinner."

His voice picks up on the other end of the phone like he was expecting me to argue. "Thanks, bud. Have fun tonight."

"Okay. Bye, Dad."

I walk into the kitchen to find a much less frantic Kelly. She's standing in front of a large plate of cooked chicken on the counter and smiles when she sees me. "Do you think you can set this on the table for me, hun? The dining room is just through there." She points to a short hallway off the side of the kitchen.

"Of course."

The dining room has dark olive-green walls, but much like the rest of the house, there's enough natural light from the windows to make the room feel open and airy. The doorbell rings and a flash of dread shoots through me, causing me to set the plate down a little too aggressively. The bottom of the platter smacks the table, but luckily, no one seems to notice. I take a deep breath and brace myself for what's sure to be the most uncomfortable dinner I've ever had.

17

On my way back into the kitchen, I nearly bump into Luke.

He staggers backward, about to apologize, until he sees me. "Paige?"

I do my best to look equally surprised. I smile, but I know it's too much. I feel like I'm showing all my teeth, so I try to dial it back before saying, "Hi, Luke!"

His eyebrows crease in confusion. "What are you doing here?"

I try to ignore Dan standing behind him, eyeing me from over Luke's shoulder. I refuse to give him the satisfaction of meeting his stare. "Fredrick invited me," is all I can think to say, and I hear Jason's laughter ring out from the other room. If I were close enough, I'd kick him for that.

"Oh." His smile falters, but he recovers quickly and beams at me. "Well, I'm glad you're here."

"Thanks. I'll talk to you a little later. I'm supposed to help set the table." I duck out of sight but immediately hear Luke's familiar footsteps trailing behind me.

"Is there anything I can help with, Mrs. Pryce?"

Kelly sounds delighted. "You must be Luke! It's nice to finally meet you. I've heard so much about you from Dan." She gives him a warm welcome, shaking one of his hands with both of hers. "That's so sweet of you to ask. Yes, there is. Can you follow Paige into the dining room and set the dinner rolls on the table?"

Great. As if Luke trying to corner me on his own wasn't bad enough. The last thing I need is for Kelly to unknowingly pair us together. By the time I hear her say my name, I'm already rushing into the dining room to get away from everyone.

I hear Luke answer her behind me. "I'd love to."

My hands grip the bowl of mashed potatoes tighter like my body doesn't know how to handle all of its awkward emotions. I'm starting to think I would have been better off sitting with Melissa. I set down the potatoes to find Luke standing in the doorway, watching me.

Clearing his throat and blinking back to reality, he mutters, "Where should I put this?"

Without looking at him, I reach for the bread basket. "Here, I've got it."

"Oh, thanks."

I want to set down the bread and go back to the kitchen for something else to do, but that's a little difficult when the person you're trying to avoid blocks the only exit.

He's staring at me, and I'm staring back. I have no idea what to say or how to get away from him.

He clears his throat. "Uh, Paige?"

I rearrange some of the silverware, trying to avoid his gaze. "Yeah?" Every time I hear one of the voices from the kitchen or living room grow louder, I hope someone will interrupt us, but no luck.

"So, you've been spending time with Fredrick lately?" His question makes my eyes lift from the table, surprised by how steady he sounds. Maybe all his failed schemes have finally given him the confidence to try a more direct approach. I swallow my nerves at the thought.

I try to answer casually. "I've been spending time with everyone here."

Luke puts his hands in his pockets and rocks back on his heels. "Well, when you have the time, maybe you and I can—"

"Excuse me." Fredrick stands behind Luke with a basket of napkins.

Luke's head whips around before he jumps aside. His shoulders slump once he sees who joined us.

Fredrick neglects to look at either of us as he works on folding and setting a napkin at each seat. I watch him for a moment, hoping he'll say something, change the subject, or start talking about literally *anything*. He doesn't, though. He takes his sweet time placing napkins perfectly around the table.

My attention jumps back to Luke as I try to remember where we left off. "Um, what were you saying?" My voice shakes when I speak now that I'm having this conversation in front of Fredrick of all people. On a regular day, I can barely keep my cheeks a neutral color around him. Now, he's listening to one of my most uncomfortable conversations with Luke. My palms sweat at the thought, and I brush them against my pants.

Luke's eyes jump to Fredrick, and I think he might drop the conversation altogether, but after a moment, he turns back to me and says with complete clarity, "I was wondering if you wanted to go see a movie with me sometime."

Fredrick makes a noise between a snort and a cough, or maybe he snorts and then coughs to try to cover it up. Either way, my eyes flicker to him. I expect him to say something, but he refuses to acknowledge that Luke and I are even here. He must find my embarrassment hilarious because there's a subtle smirk on his lips. Luke probably won't notice, but I read his reaction effortlessly.

Anger burns in the pit of my stomach. I tried to talk to him about this before Luke got here, but he shut me out. He had a short fuse with me, completely dismissing the conversation. He didn't care that Luke was coming here, and he probably wouldn't care if I agreed to go out with him. I mean, he did tell the pirates that he and I are only friends, and friends don't care about stuff like this. My eyes narrow at Fredrick before turning back to Luke. "Yeah, sounds fun!" I know I sound over-eager, and I know my fake smile probably stretches wider than it should, but the words are out, and I can't take them back. I'm not sure why I say it, but as soon as I do, the twinge of a smirk vanishes from Fredrick's face.

Luke blinks at my response. "Really?"

I nod, unwilling to say the words out loud again.

"Cool! I'll see what's playing and get back to you." He glances at Fredrick and then back to me, a huge grin displayed on his face before he leaves the room. As soon as he's out of sight, I turn to Fredrick. "Well, I hope you're happy."

Fredrick's head picks up, and he stares at me impassively. "What?"

I cross my arms and glare at him. "You were smirking! You made me feel like I had to say yes!"

He pauses, his expression darkening as he approaches me. Before I know it, he's inches away from my face, looking down at me. I stare up at him with wide eyes. I hate that even when I'm mad at him, I still feel my breath catch when he moves toward me. In a low voice, he says, "If you don't want to go, don't. You're busy anyway. With me."

He walks out of the room, leaving me alone with my mouth open. I stay there for a moment, not sure what to think. It isn't until I hear Carter's voice yelling, "Let's get a move on this gravy train!" that I snap back to the present.

Moments later, Carter comes bounding into the dining room. At the sight of me, he bows and says, "Hello, Milady." Luckily, he doesn't sense my mood as he takes a seat at the table. He stabs a large piece of chicken with his fork, serving himself a plate, and folds his hands together, impatiently waiting for everyone else.

It doesn't take long for word to spread that the food is ready. Before I know it, everyone stands around the table, passing plates and marveling over Kelly's last-minute homemade meal.

"Paige, sit by me!" Nicole pats the empty chair to her right, and I gladly sit and take it. Unfortunately, Luke takes the liberty of neighboring my opposite side. Once everyone takes a seat, I look up to find Fredrick directly across from me. His eyes lock on mine, and my cheeks flush. I look down, determined to concentrate on pushing my potatoes around with my fork.

Luke talks to me even more than usual. I scan the table as I listen to him go on about the different movie options for our… *date.* Even the thought of the word makes my grip tighten around my fork. Suddenly, it hits me that Dan isn't at the table, but no one says anything about it.

Tonight's conversation feels limited compared to our usual topics of discussion. With Luke sitting at the table, we can't say anything about training, fighting, or piracy in general. Everyone is on their toes, keeping the dinner talk within restricted boundaries. I'm talking with Nicole about how much she would get along with Leah when I hear Jason's voice above everyone else.

"So, Luke, you and Paige are close, right?"

I want to glare at him, but with so many people around, I don't want to risk the wrong eyes seeing. I know this is all a game to him, and I'm more than ready for him to move on to something more interesting.

I glance at Fredrick, who's been quiet for most of the dinner. He's chewing on a bite of food when he hears Jason's question. His expression is impossible to read, but his eyes deliberately look up to meet mine, and I drop my gaze.

Luke beams. "I'd say so. We're always together." He nudges

me for affirmation, so I give him a tight-lipped smile and nod.

Jason puts on a grin that must be as fake as mine has been tonight. "Friends? I swear you two would make the *cutest couple*."

I nearly choke on my piece of chicken and have to gulp down what's left of my water. I expect to see Fredrick focused on me again, but this time, he's glaring at Jason.

Jason looks back at Fredrick with faked innocence. "What? They're both single. It's not like they aren't available."

Carter, oblivious to what's going on, points his fork at Luke. "Don't take Paige from me. I'll fight for her."

"Well, actually," Luke starts to say, and I know he's about to announce our date to the table. Fredrick seems to sense where he's going with his sentence because I swear I catch him rolling his eyes at the sound of Luke's voice.

I start talking over Luke to cut him off. "So, I think the chicken came out great. What do you think, Fredrick?"

He tilts his head at me, and I raise my eyebrows to prompt an answer. My nudge seems to snap him out of his thoughts.

He clears his throat and nods. "Everything's delicious. Great dinner, Mom."

Everyone spouts compliments of the food, and Kelly beams at the head of the table. "You all are too sweet." She waves a hand as if to tell us to stop, but I know she's thrilled with how the dinner turned out. Especially considering how frantic she was beforehand.

When the plates are all but licked clean, everyone helps with dishes before retiring to the living room. This time, I make sure Luke sits down before I do, and only then do I sit—as far away from him as possible.

Trying not to meet Luke's gaze, I take the small space between Jason and the armrest and try to catch up on the conversation. My heart sinks when I realize what they're talking about... *movies.*

Jason praises a new action movie. "...and the guy was a beast! He didn't take anyone's shit."

Luke calls over to me from across the room, and I suddenly wish I were sitting much closer to him. "Paige, we should go see that one!"

I force a smile at him for his suggestion and feel everyone's eyes on me.

Jason's mouth falls open, and I try my best to give him a pleading stare. This is the only topic I wanted to avoid, and it's the second time someone has brought it up.

I glance at Fredrick, but he's staring blankly ahead with his elbows resting on his knees. He doesn't look like he's paying attention to our conversation at all. Once again, his thoughts are more interesting than what's happening around him.

Dan walks through the front door and barks, "Luke, we need to go."

Luke hesitates but ultimately gets up to leave. "I guess I'll see you guys later." Turning to Kelly, he adds, "Thanks for the great dinner, Mrs. Pryce."

Kelly seems taken aback by their sudden departure but displays a smile nonetheless. "Oh, anytime. You're always welcome."

Dan doesn't wait for Luke to follow before leaving without saying goodbye to anyone. Luke opens his mouth like he wants to say something to me, but as soon as Dan starts the car outside, he only gives me a quick wave as he leaves.

Once they're gone, the air in the room feels lighter, even with the lingering tension between Fredrick and me. Although, I'm not sure anyone else realizes it.

Jason breaks the silence. "What the hell was that?"

Carter shrugs.

Fredrick's voice is low as he says, "Dan's been acting… weird lately."

Jason stares at him for a moment before waving him off. "No, not that." He turns to me. "Why the hell are you going out with that kid?"

Kelly excuses herself, and I'm thankful. I groan and rub my face with my hands. "I didn't know how to tell him no," I half-lie. I don't want to admit that my anger got the best of me when I saw Fredrick smirking.

Jason shakes his head disappointedly. "You just look him dead in the eye, he says holding up two fingers toward his own eyes, "and say, 'Fuck no.' That's the only way to get through to someone like him." His eyes flicker to Fredrick before adding, "What about the damn excuse I told you to use earlier?"

At this, Fredrick's head picks up, and he glances between Jason and me. Luckily, Carter interrupts by saying, "Well, I'm heartbroken. I thought we really had something, Paige." He clutches his heart with his hand in fake despair before winking. "Even if you date Luke, we can still have something on the side, you know."

I roll my eyes. "I'm not dating Luke."

"Well, I think it's a great idea if you start dating that kid." Melissa leans back against the recliner with her arms crossed. "Anything that takes you away from here is fine by me."

Shaking my head, I stand up. "Don't hold your breath, Mel." I can't help smiling, knowing how much she hates the nickname.

Jason and Carter bust out laughing, and even Fredrick's mouth quirks.

Melissa holds her middle finger up in my direction but addresses the rest of them. "You idiots are rubbing off on her."

I grab my keys off the wall hook and say, "I told my dad I would come home after dinner. I better get going."

"Goodnight, Paige!" Kelly calls from the kitchen, and I wonder what else she overheard.

Fredrick stands and says, "I'll walk you out."

I'm confused by his offer, but I've been the topic of conversation enough for one evening. Not wanting to give the group anything else to talk about by questioning him, I simply wave and say, "Goodnight," to everyone before walking outside.

Fredrick follows me and closes the door behind us. The night breeze sends a chill through me, and I instinctively hug my arms around my torso. Fredrick remains quiet next to me as we walk down the driveway like he's stuck on whatever thoughts he's been battling with all night. When we reach my truck, I turn to face him.

"I'm glad you stayed for dinner," he says, still looking deep in thought.

I scoff, not bothering to hide the sarcasm from my voice. "Yeah, it worked out really well."

He tilts his head. "Because of Luke?"

I study him, trying to see what he might be thinking behind those molten eyes, but I have no idea.

Fredrick keeps himself locked away, and not knowing how he feels about this makes me fidget with the keys in my hand.

He's carefully watching for my reaction, and when I drop my gaze and say, "Yeah," it comes out barely above a whisper.

"Why?" he asks, pulling my attention back to him, and I suddenly realize how close he is. My heart pounds in my chest. If we were any closer, we'd be touching.

"Because..." My voice trails off as I let my eyes drift away from him. I can't think straight with him looking at me like this.

Fredrick hooks his finger under my chin, forcing me to look at him again. My lips part at the gesture, and my breath catches in my throat. "Paige," he says without breaking his stare, and the way he says my name makes me feel like I could unravel right here. Holding his gaze, I can't speak. My words fail me, and all I can think about is how it feels to have him touching me—like a warm heat has taken over my body from its core. He frowns, the line between his brows deepening. He looks like he's trying to decipher everything I'm not saying, and I hope I can hide the way his touch is affecting me. Letting go of me, he says, "You're not considering going on a date with him, are you?"

As soon as he drops his hand, air rushes back into my lungs. "No," I say too quickly before letting out a breath of laughter, my shoulders sagging. "I don't know." The second part comes out sounding more like a resignation. As much as I would love to cancel my plans with Luke, part of me feels like it might be easier to just go. It's only a movie. I won't even have to talk to him.

Fredrick's jaw tenses as he drops his gaze. I expect him to say something, but after a beat, he nods, swallowing whatever he might have said.

"Training tomorrow?" I ask, hoping for some normalcy between us.

Fredrick shakes his head. "Not tomorrow. I'll let you know when the next one is."

His answer isn't what I expected. "Oh, okay. So…?" I raise my eyebrows. We've always set a time and day for my next training.

"So, I'll see you later." He opens my truck door for me, signaling that it's time for me to leave. My stomach plummets, but I make sure to hide it well as I hop in the truck, shutting the door behind me.

Even though I have no idea what to say, I press the button to roll down my window. I don't want him to let me leave like this. I want to know when I'll see him again. But before I can say anything, he throws me a casual wave and heads back toward the house.

My eyes stay glued to him until he reaches the front door, and he doesn't look back before going into the house. I sit in his driveway for a moment, my heartbeat pounding in my ears. Then I put my truck in gear and head home.

☠ ☠ ☠

Once I get home, I walk into the house and jump at the sight of my father sitting at the kitchen table. "Long dinner, huh?"

I sigh. "Sorry. I helped Kelly clean up."

He nods slowly. I notice in this lighting how tired he looks. Even the laugh lines around his eyes seem to pull downward with exhaustion.

"Paige, I'm not sure I'm comfortable with you always being with this Fredrick kid. Something doesn't feel right about this guy."

I stay silent. I know he only feels this way because Josh is the one who first told him about Fredrick, but I don't exactly have a good counterargument. I know I've been giving Fredrick the benefit of the doubt. *How can a thief be a good person?*

Dad continues. "Josh seemed to have his concerns about him. I just don't want to see you get hurt."

His words almost make me laugh when I think about all the bruises my body has endured over the past few weeks. "Thanks, Dad. Trust me, I'm fine. Fredrick isn't as bad as you think." I know I'm trying to convince not only him but myself, too. He doesn't seem swayed, so I give him another smile. "Josh and Fredrick had a falling out when they were younger, and Josh still holds a grudge. Really, I'm fine."

Leaning back in the chair, he rubs his hands over his face while he lets out a loud yawn.

"Why are you so tired?" I ask.

He shakes his head, trying to wake himself. "Work has been terrible lately. I feel like I've seen way too much of the inside of my office."

I walk over to him and put a hand on his shoulder. "Is there a race this weekend?"

My mention of his favorite sport makes him perk up. "You bet."

"I'll try to be home for it, okay? I'll make nachos like I used to." I give him a quick kiss on the cheek.

This brings a smile to his lips. "Thanks, kiddo." Taking a deep breath, he adds, "Man, I'm beat. Are you going to bed soon?"

"Yeah, I just need to email Mom. It's been a while."

He nods, and I make my way upstairs. I wash my face and brush my teeth in the amount of time it takes my computer to open a single email from my mother.

Her message doesn't surprise me.

Paige,

I'm sorry to say this, but it looks like Trevor and I won't be able to make it to Florida for now. Work has been busy for both of us lately, and we apologize. I wanted to see my little girl! It's not right for a mother to go this long without seeing her daughter!

TTYS Mom

As I write her a response email, I try to sound surprised but understanding. I know it would be a bad idea for her to come here anyway. I don't miss my parents yelling at each other, followed by dramatic tears on my mother's end.

Mom,

Sorry to hear that you and Trevor won't be able to visit. I was hoping I would get a chance to see you before school starts, but I understand how busy you both are. Love you.

Xo Paige

Lying in bed, I can't help feeling dread thinking about my encounter with Luke this evening. I laugh to myself. I've experienced much worse these past few weeks, but awkward interactions with Luke are still what keep me up at night. My mind replays the day's events until I fall into an uneasy sleep.

I'm not sure how long I'm out before I'm awake again. My breath catches when I hear what woke me: a faint knocking on my bedroom window.

18

My heart rate climbs, and my chest heaves with every shallow breath. I cover my mouth with my hand to try and quiet my ragged breathing. The last time I heard a noise in the middle of the night, things didn't end well. Vivid images of the rat-looking man's face come to mind. Part of me wants to run, but I can't bring myself to move.

Someone taps on my window again, this time more urgently. I sit upright in bed and grip the pillow to my chest, looking at my window as if staring at it hard enough will give me the ability to see through the curtains. I try not to blink, afraid I might be attacked again at the very moment my eyes shut.

Another tap.

My fingers squeeze my pillow like it's the only thing keeping me alive. I creep one foot onto the floor and then the other. The cool wood underneath my feet sends a chill down my spine—well, either that or the fear of what's lurking outside my window.

The knocking stops.

I freeze mid-step, my fingers digging into the soft fabric of the pillow hard enough to make them ache. I thought I would feel better if the knocking stopped, but the silence leaves an eeriness in its wake.

I don't know what to do.

Inching toward the window, I lean forward, trying to peer through the crack in the curtains without being seen.

With my face only inches from the glass, the knocking picks up again, this time louder than before.

I let out a small cry, stumbling back and landing on my tailbone. Both hands fly up to cover my mouth, desperate to hold in my yelp of pain. I strain my ears, and the knocking gives way to another sound… laughter?

"Paige! Let me in!"

His tone is no louder than an urgent whisper, but I know Josh's voice as soon as I hear it. Getting to my feet, I hurry to the window and push aside the curtains with still shaking hands. Just as I had suspected, outside in the darkness, Josh's figure sits perched on my rooftop. My body relaxes, and I work on opening the window for him.

He climbs into my room, and I shut and latch the window behind him. The creeping thought that someone else might be out there makes the hairs on my arms stand up straight.

Josh pants as he stands in the middle of my room, the moonlight revealing fresh sweat glistening on his forehead.

"What are you doing here?" I make sure to keep my voice low.

The last thing I need is my dad waking up and finding Josh in my room in the middle of the night. On second thought, it might help him see Fredrick in a better light. My thoughts go back to how he and I left things earlier tonight, and I feel a dull ache in my chest.

Josh sits on my bed and wipes the sweat from his brow before breathing out the word, "Thanks."

"Josh, what are you doing here?" I say, slow and deliberate.

He takes a minute to catch his breath but gives me a taunting smile. "Get a little scared there, P?"

I sit cross-legged on my bed across from him. Despite my head throbbing from the lingering anxiety, I glare at him. "No."

Josh covers up what would have been a loud spout of laughter if it weren't for my dad sleeping downstairs. "So, you just screamed for fun?"

I cross my arms. "And you just hop through people's windows at—" I look at the clock before finishing my sentence. "—two in the morning for fun?" I glance out the window. "Wait, how did you even get up here?"

He leans back on his hands and hints toward the window with his chin. "There's a ladder propped up against the side of your house."

I tilt my head. "What?"

He shrugs. "I don't know. There's a ladder. It looks like good ole' Dave got halfway through a project or something."

Of course. That sounds exactly like my dad. Even if he did finish whatever outdoor project he was working on, the ladder will be there until he needs it again.

Josh grins. "I'll have to thank his lazy-ass tomorrow. He saved me from the cops."

My mouth falls open.

"Please don't freak out. It isn't a big deal," he says with a roll of his eyes.

I look at him, stunned. There are plenty of things that are "not a big deal" but outrunning the police is *not* one of them.

He sighs at my stare. "Look, you know that old barn on Warren Drive?"

"The abandoned one?"

He lets out a low laugh. "Yeah, not as abandoned as we thought. I went out there with Nick and Juri to drink their uncle's homemade moonshine."

My eyes narrow. "Are you drunk?"

He scoffs. "Yeah, I just outran the law and scaled the side of your house completely wasted."

My lips purse. "Okay… so what happened?"

"We didn't get the chance to drink much. Someone must've called us in for trespassing. Two cops showed up with flashlights and started walking the property. We all ran for it."

"Where are Nick and Juri?" I instinctively glance at my window, half expecting to see the two of them peering through the glass.

Josh shrugs, unconcerned. "We all went in different directions. Your house was the closest, so I came here."

"Josh, we live on the same street," I say with my head in my hands.

He lets out a hollow laugh. "Yeah, but your dad would back

me up, and my mom would try to convince the cops to book me overnight or some shit."

I run a tired hand over my face but can't help smiling because I know he's right. "So, you're crashing here tonight?"

Getting to his feet, he stretches his arms overhead. "Definitely. Even without the cops, my mom would lose her shit if I came home this late. At least this way, she'll think I'm saying over at Nick and Juri's. You know, you should sneak out more. Your dad is pretty laid back when it comes to this stuff."

He's right, but he also has no idea how many times I *have* snuck out lately. If only he knew everything that's happened this summer, he would probably lose his mind. I shudder at the thought. "Okay, the couch is all yours."

Downstairs, Josh makes himself comfortable, sprawling out in every direction humanly possible. I'm barely able to fit at the end of the couch where he has generously left a tiny space for me. I sit with my legs crossed and my back leaning against the armrest.

I smooth my hair away from my face and let out a breath. "Luke wants to take me on a date to the movies."

Josh's tone is thick with sarcasm when he says, "Shocker."

I clasp my hands in my lap. "I know, but this time I said yes." I brace myself for his reaction.

Josh sits up with a mocking grin on his face. "You did what?"

"I couldn't say no. I'm running out of excuses, and I don't want to hurt his feelings." My words don't sound convincing as they tumble out of my mouth.

He studies me, still smirking. "Well, that's bullshit. When did this happen?"

I let out a sigh, wrapping my arms around my leg and resting my chin on my knees. "Tonight. I was at Fredrick's for dinner, and Dan brought Luke."

He leans back and folds his arms behind his head. "That must've been fun."

I smile at him, appreciative that he doesn't go off on a tangent about Fredrick for once. "I'm not sure that's the word I'd use."

Josh snorts. "So, tell me. How do you plan on getting out of this one?"

"We didn't set up a date and time." I shrug, giving up. "I don't know."

Josh lets out a laugh and cocks his head. "Not your finest moment, P." He pauses, eyeing me curiously. "I guess this means nothing is going on between you and Fredrick?"

I think about how Fredrick and I left things tonight. His cold goodbye with no plans made for our next meeting. It stands out to me that this is the first time I don't feel my cheeks blush at the mention of his name. The only thing I feel now is a lingering tightness in my chest at the memory. It will be easier to convince Josh that I don't have feelings for Fredrick if I can keep my face its normal color.

"I see him sometimes, but I mostly go out there to see Nicole." I hate lying to Josh, but I can't tell him even the slightest version of the truth.

"Ah, right. Nicole. I'd forgotten about her. I bet she's cute now. Know if she has a boyfriend?"

I playfully roll my eyes at him as I get up from the couch. "Is there anyone you won't try to date?"

Josh laughs. "You never know when cupid will strike, Paige."

"Isn't she like fourteen?" I raise my eyebrows as I give him a pointed look.

He looks up at the ceiling with a coy smile. "Shit, I thought she was only a year younger than us."

I shake my head as I make my way upstairs. "Goodnight, Casanova."

☠   ☠   ☠

The next morning, I find Josh still sprawled out on the couch, snoring lightly. A noise in the kitchen tells me Dad is awake, so he's probably seen our house guest by now.

My dad sits at the kitchen table drinking his coffee. "When did he show up?"

I finish putting my hair in a ponytail and sigh. "Late. I was already in bed."

He raises an eyebrow and asks, "You were sleeping?"

"Trying to." My father eyes me curiously, and I put my hands up. "Take it up with him."

He shakes his head and chuckles. "How long do you think he'll sleep?"

I take a seat at the kitchen table with him. "Probably until you throw something at him like last time."

A boyish grin takes over my father's face as he scans the room

281

for inspiration. His eyes land on the folded newspaper on the counter, and I watch as he reaches for it, wadding it into a thick ball before pelting it at Josh from across the room.

Josh rolls over, glaring. "Screw you, old man," he groans as he sits up and rubs the sleep from his eyes.

After a series of stretches, Josh makes his way to the kitchen table to join us. "There's a party at the lake today. We should go."

My heart sinks at the memory of Fredrick canceling my training, and I welcome the distraction. "I'll go," I say. "You're already here, so we can ride together."

The rest of the morning, Josh and I only see each other in passing. We take turns showering, and he spends time with Dad while I finish getting ready.

There's a pep in my step as I bound down the stairs. Despite everything, I feel good. Having plans with Josh today reminds me of my life before the start of summer.

Before the pirates.

Josh sits on the couch, talking with my dad as the news plays on the TV behind them. I walk over to the two of them and stand behind the couch. "Ready to go?"

"You bet. Later, Dave." He shakes my father's hand as if they're closing a business deal.

As he stands, the reporter on the screen behind him changes stories. "And in local news, a teen was caught in an altercation with police this morning over shoplifting."

The last word catches my attention, and my eyes snap to the television.

The newscaster continues. "The security cameras didn't catch the culprit stealing anything, but the cashier found multiple stolen goods on his person. Police arrived at the scene, and that's when the thief made it clear he did not plan on coming quietly. Take a look."

My heart pounds in my chest as the shot of the news station switches to a poor-quality security stream. My breath catches when I see the unmistakable tattoos, build, and height that I know so well: Carter.

Josh must notice my reaction because his eyes flicker between me and the television. "Do you know him or something?"

I hypnotically nod, my wide eyes staying fixed on the screen.

Josh leans closer to get a better look at the suspect. He curses under his breath before returning his attention to me. "Is that one of the beach boys Fredrick slums with?"

I shoot him a glare.

The news reporter has already moved on to another story, making it feel like it had been a dream—like it had never happened.

But it did happen, and we all witnessed it.

Seeing my father angry is a rare occurrence, but right now, I know he's heated. I can't blame him. His voice is loud when he says, "You mean to tell me your friend Fredrick has been introducing you to people like that?" He gestures toward the television even though the video of Carter is long gone.

I don't know why, but the urge to defend Fredrick takes over. "No! I met Carter at the bonfire at the beginning of summer." I give Josh a pleading look, hoping he won't rat me out. My lie isn't entirely untrue. Carter *did* tell me he was at that party, and I *could* have met him that night.

Thankfully, other than the fuming look on his face, Josh stays silent.

My dad relaxes slightly. "Well, stay away from him. I don't want you hanging around people like that."

Josh nods in agreement.

I decide this is a good time to make an exit. "Come on, Josh. We better get going."

The reluctant look on his face tells me he'd rather let Dad rant on about what a bad influence Fredrick is. Luckily, when I don't back down, he grunts and walks toward the door.

I kiss my father on the cheek. "We should be home for dinner, Dad."

My dad shrugs. "No worries if you stay out later. I'm planning on ordering a pizza. I'll leave the leftovers in the fridge."

Josh seems more than pleased with this and shoots him a thumbs up. "Save me a slice, too."

Dad dismisses him with a wave of his hand. "Get out of here, you two."

"Bye, Dad," I call over my shoulder, already halfway to the door.

Outside, Josh spins around and blocks my path. "Didn't want Daddy to find out your new friends are criminals, huh?"

My eyes narrow, and I say, "You don't know what you're talking about."

"Oh really? Did you miss the fucking news?" He points at the house as if the video were still playing on the TV.

I know he's right, but I refuse to give him the satisfaction. Plus, I like Carter. It's hard for me to connect the dots between the Carter who always makes me laugh and the Carter who was on the morning news. "You don't know anything about them, Josh."

With this, he leans toward me and pokes an accusatory finger. "You know what? You're turning into one of them, Paige. Fredrick said the same shit."

Without waiting for me to reply, he turns and stiffly walks down my driveway. "If you still want to come, I'm driving."

Josh's statement makes me cringe. *I can't be doing the same thing Fredrick did to him… can I?*

Guilt creeps into my gut, and I feel my anger dissolve. We walk in silence to Josh's house, where his truck sits on the street. The tension holds between us as we get in. I expect him to start the engine and continue the silent streak all the way to the party, but he doesn't put the key in the ignition.

When I look over at him, it seems the walk may have dissolved some of his anger, too. His eyebrows crease in concern, giving me a pang in my chest.

"Don't turn into them," he says.

I swallow, hating seeing him this way. "I won't." It feels good to look him in the eye and reassure him honestly. If there's one thing I know for sure, it's that I'm not going to start stealing. Ever.

He nods but doesn't seem completely convinced. "Just keep your head, alright?"

I give him a reassuring smile. "I never thought you'd be the one trying to keep me out of trouble."

He lets out a breath of laughter. "Fuck, you're right. I don't like being on this end."

Laughing, I shake my head at him. "I don't like being on this end either."

19

Josh backs his truck between two others on the grassy field doubling as a parking lot. It's nice to see everyone enjoying their summer in a normal way. I've been so wrapped up with the pirates lately. I've almost forgotten how relaxing summer is supposed to be.

Unbuckling my seatbelt, I notice Luke walking up to my passenger side door. It no longer surprises me to see Dan hovering close behind him. I guess the days of only seeing Dan at the beach are long gone. He and Luke have merged into one person in my mind. Irritating and intimidating in equal parts.

"Hey, Paige! I'm glad you came." Luke opens the truck door for me to step out.

Josh nods to me before joining a group talking near the water. It looks like his helping me with Luke and Dan has run dry. I stare after him, surprised he left without saying anything. Then again, if Fredrick were here, Josh would have all three of the people he hates most in the world standing around his truck, so I guess I can't blame him.

Stepping down and gathering my bag, I answer him. "Me too, Luke."

"Here, let me help." He puts an arm over my shoulder as he reaches past me to grab the cooler, and my entire body tenses.

Ducking out from under his arm, I turn away, calling back a quick, "Thanks!"

People have already taken over the lake in every direction. Portable charcoal grills fill the air with a pleasant smoky scent. Aside from cooking, at least three different sports are happening in the chaos. A group of tall, lean guys kick a soccer ball back and forth along the water's edge, a two-hand-touch game of football takes up the space in front of me, and set further back, a group of guys with lacrosse sticks toss a ball back and forth. Most people would look out over the scene and see only fun, but for me, it might as well be a minefield. The idea of navigating from one end of the lake to the other without getting hit with some type of ball sets my nerves on edge.

Someone has their truck parked on the grass near the water. The windows are down with the radio on full blast. The local radio DJ announces a chance to win tickets to a Brooks & Dunn concert. I never bother calling in for contests because I never win anything, but I love watching people get excited about that type of thing. Even now, a few people with cell phones try to call in.

I spot Leah and Austin under a pop-up canopy and go to set my stuff down by them. Slinging my bag over my shoulder, I make my way through the crowd.

I'm about halfway to them when Leah yells, "Paige! I'm so glad you came!"

Walking up to them, I smile at the new couple. "Look at you two," I say as I set my bag under Leah's lawn chair. I catch Austin's eye and nod in response to a casual wave thrown my way. "Josh is here, but I've already lost him," I say to him with a shrug.

Austin pushes himself to his feet. "Oh good! I want to talk to him about GTA."

Leah and I exchange confused looks. "GTA?" Leah finally asks.

Austin starts walking back toward the rest of the party. "Babe, Grand Theft Auto." He raises his eyebrows at her and turns around to look for Josh.

Leah beams at me, and her cheeks have a little added color. "I'm *babe* now," she giggles.

I shake my head with a smile and take a seat where Austin had been.

"Luke's been talking about you *all day*," she warns.

I let my face fall into my hands and groan. Peeking up at her through my fingers, I ask, "Really?"

A sly smile stretches across her lips. "You've agreed to finally go on a date with him?"

"I never said it was a date." I rub my temples and try to stop the headache that will surely come from this conversation.

She gives me a pointed look. "Well, it must have been heavily implied because he seems to think the two of you will finally get together." She laughs at the thought. "Hey, tell me what happened with the mysterious bonfire guy. Fredrick, right?"

As far as Leah knows, I've only bumped into Fredrick a few times since the start of summer, but the fact that she always asks about him makes me feel like she senses something more. Everyone seems to sense more when it comes to Fredrick. My thoughts bring me back to what it felt like to have his finger hooked under my chin yesterday. His deep, brown eyes searching mine. I wish I knew what he was looking for.

Dropping my gaze to my hands in my lap, I mutter, "There isn't anything to tell."

She sighs dramatically. "I was hoping something would have changed by now. I'd be more excited if you were going to a movie with *him*."

Me too, I think to myself, but I don't have anything to say back to that. I wish Fredrick were here now. I want to know what happened with Carter's run-in with the police. But even more than that, I just want to see him. Between Leah and Austin's branding as a new couple, and Luke's attempts to make us an item, I want to fix the way Fredrick and I left things yesterday even more.

"What's going on over there?" Leah's voice brings me back to the present, and I realize people are yelling. She sits upright in her chair, and I follow her gaze. The color drains from my face when I see the source of the commotion. Josh and Dan are toe-to-toe, looking like they want to kill each other.

Leah looks at me with wide eyes, and we both get to our feet and rush over. Our approach—along with many others who now gather to watch—doesn't seem to faze the arguing guys.

I cut through the small audience to get a closer look. "Josh, what's going on?" I ask as my head snaps between the two of them.

Keeping his stare locked on Dan, he answers through gritted teeth. "Nothing. I was just complimenting Dan on his buddy's fifteen minutes of fame this morning."

I look over at Dan to find his hands balled into fists. "I told you, I don't know what you're talking about."

Straightening, Josh raises an eyebrow as a scoff leaves his lips. "You don't? He's the runt of your litter, right?"

Dan's eyes briefly take in the number of people watching. He manages to compose himself enough but still smirks at Josh with a dangerous glint in his eyes. "What are you going to do, Josh? I'm telling you, I don't know what you're talking about." He takes a step forward. "Follow me for all I care."

Josh snorts but meets Dan with a step of his own. "Don't flatter yourself. Maybe *you* should be keeping better tabs on your minions. What was this one's name? Carter?"

Dan's eyes travel past Josh, and I freeze. His anger has jumped to a new person.

Me.

The look only lasts a fraction of a second, but it's enough to make me swallow the fear in my throat. Dan recovers and goes back to focusing on Josh, but I know I've messed up.

He takes another threatening step toward Josh and growls, "Shut your mouth."

At this, Josh points a finger at Dan's chest, his voice shaking as he says, "I hope his mistake costs all of you."

Dan smacks Josh's hand away. "Get your fucking hands off me," he growls in a low voice.

I want to yell for them both to stop, but how Dan looked at me when Josh said Carter's name keeps me frozen in place.

A few people try to hold Josh back, but he shrugs them off. "All I know is Fredrick never did any of that shit until he started wasting his time with you assholes. And now you're doing the same shit to Paige."

"Josh!" The word is out of me before I even realize I've said anything. Dan's eyes flicker my way again, a dark, low laugh leaving his lips.

Narrowing his eyes at Josh, he says, "Fredrick has nothing to do with this." I know it's taking all his self-control not to bury Josh right now.

He looks my way again. "And as for, Paige. Well, maybe she's not as sweet as you think she is."

My mouth opens, but no words come out.

Josh lunges forward, gripping the front of Dan's shirt with his fists. "You and your low-life friends need to stay the fuck away from her. Do you hear me?"

"You," Dan says, shoving Josh off him, "need to be careful." His chest heaves as he steps away from Josh. "We wouldn't want a repeat of what happened last time, would we?"

"You motherfucker." Josh looks like he's about to go for Dan again, but I catch his arm just in time. He looks down at me, and I frantically shake my head, pleading for him to let this go.

By the time Josh looks back at Dan, he's already stalking away, his shoulders tense.

I let out a breath of relief when Josh doesn't follow him and let go of his arm. He stares after Dan with a downturned mouth and mutters, "Fucker."

Eventually, the rumble of gossiping voices dies down, and everyone gradually returns to whatever they had been doing before. Dan's last statement leaves me with new questions. What happened last time?

Leah gapes at me with wide eyes. I know she's expecting answers, but I spot Josh marching toward his truck and run after him. I reach him as he throws open the truck door.

Panting to catch my breath, I ask, "What are you doing?"

He doesn't look at me as he answers. "Leaving."

"Already?"

He says nothing but slams the driver's door shut with a loud bang.

Resting my hands on the open window, I'm able to stall his leaving enough to say, "What was he talking about?"

Avoiding my gaze, Josh mutters, "Nothing."

"Josh."

At this, his head snaps up, eyes burning. "It's nothing, Paige. Drop it, okay?" His eyes go from harsh to pleading, and something softens inside of me.

"I don't understand why you won't tell me the truth," I say, my shoulders sagging.

Josh's jaw ticks, and for a moment, it looks like he may consider opening up to me, but one more glance at the party shuts him down. "It's not something I'm proud of, okay? Can we just leave it at that?"

I frown, my eyebrows creasing. I want to tell him no. I want to demand that I get the full story, but something in the way he's looking at me makes me say, "Okay."

Visibly relaxing, Josh nods. "Do you want a ride home?"

Now it's my turn to look back at the party. "We just got here."

"See if Austin or Leah can give you a ride then. I can't stay here." He turns the key and barely gives the engine enough time to warm up before throwing the truck in drive and pulling out of the parking lot.

I stare after him, confused and conflicted until he turns out of sight.

Heading back toward the party, I spot Leah again. She's standing with Luke and Austin, talking about what happened.

"I can't believe he just left you here," she says with a frown at the corners of her mouth.

I shrug, not sure what to make of the situation yet.

Austin says, "If he stayed, they would have spilled blood. It's better he left."

Leah's shoulders are still tense. "I'm not mad. I just think it wouldn't kill Josh to be a little more mature sometimes." She then asks the question I was hoping she wouldn't. "What was he saying about Fredrick? And why did he think you were hanging around Dan?"

I let out a nervous laugh. "I have no idea."

Eager for things to get back to normal, I'm about to suggest we sit by the dock when the four of us look up at the sound of footsteps approaching. Dan's towering figure makes its way directly for us. His eyes lock on me, and I suddenly wish I had left with Josh.

Luke takes one look at his cousin and walks away without a word. If I didn't know better, I'd think Luke is mad, but before I can figure out what's going on between them, I hear Dan's booming voice behind me.

"Paige."

An involuntary shudder runs through my body, and when I look back at Dan, he nods to a space nearby. "Let's talk."

I dart my eyes between Leah and Austin, hoping one of them will save me from this. Neither of them proves helpful, though. They're both staring between Dan and me, open-mouthed.

I try to keep my voice casual as I turn to them. "Can you guys give us a minute?"

Leah continues to stare at me in disbelief as Austin pulls her away.

I watch them until Dan stands in front of me, blocking my view. "What did you tell him?" He demands.

His relentless glare makes my voice come out defensive and high-pitched. "Nothing! He figured out I knew him because of how I reacted to the news."

Dan crosses his arms. "How did he know his name, Paige?"

I crack under the pressure. My mouth opens and closes a few times until I can finally spit out, "I—I don't know. I must have let it slip, I guess."

Dan lets out a frustrated sigh as he runs a hand over his face.

"I knew we couldn't trust you."

My words come out just as frantically as my thoughts. "You can trust me! I don't know what I was thinking. I'm sorry." After a moment, I ask, "Is Carter okay?"

Dan rolls his eyes. "He got away without them figuring out who he was. As long as fucking Josh doesn't turn him in, he should be fine."

"Josh won't do that," I blurt out. I'm not sure if it's true, but I hope it is.

Dan ignores my comment, tilting his head, he asks, "No Fredrick to come and pick you up?"

I look away and say, "Not today."

Dan nods slowly as his eyes fall on something behind me. "Did you hear that? Paige has no plans tonight."

My head whips around to find Luke standing by a large oak tree with his cheeks ripening to a bright red. If I wasn't sharing his embarrassment, I would probably feel sorry for him.

I look back at Dan with my eyes narrowed. "Why would you do something like that?"

Dan nonchalantly shrugs. "He's too shy."

"Only because you torture him!" The volume of my voice rises, but I don't bother controlling it. My heart races as I stare at Dan with nothing but dislike. Any redeeming qualities I thought he had are gone.

He lowers his head so he can look me in the eye. In a low voice, he says, "And you're too hung up on a guy who obviously isn't interested."

He didn't say Fredrick's name, but he didn't have to. The words still hit me like a blow to the gut.

I wish Josh had punched Dan in the mouth while he had the chance.

Dan cocks an eyebrow, studying my reaction. "I knew you had a thing for him." He forces a laugh. "Don't waste your time. He just feels bad for you."

Heat flares in my cheeks. "I'm not—*what?*"

Dan straightens, pulling away from me, but a smirk settles on his lips. "Good."

"I have to go," I mutter, eager to get away from him. Turning around, I march over to my friends, kicking around a soccer ball.

I watch as Leah gives the ball a good kick before looking up and seeing me. She immediately runs over.

"What did creepy Dan have to say?" She pants with sweat glistening on her forehead. Yes, Leah's sweat *glistens* in the sunlight. I'm starting to think she's incapable of looking anything less than perfect.

I tell her how Dan embarrassed Luke but make sure to leave out how he embarrassed me, too.

Her hands fly to her mouth. "He what? Poor Luke! I mean, we all know he likes you, but that's harsh."

I nod. "I know. I feel bad."

Leah looks around until she spots Luke sitting alone. "He looks so… embarrassed… and sad."

"Dan can be such a jerk." I study Luke as well. All my usual feelings of annoyance are gone, replaced by the sudden desire to cheer him up.

Rolling her eyes, she nods. "Tell me about it."

Leah and I talk more about Dan and his overall douchebaggery, but I can't stop thinking about what he said about Fredrick.

After a while, Leah wants to play soccer again, so I decide to join. I may hate sports, but if my options are playing soccer or consoling a sulking Luke, I take the road less awkward.

The hours roll on, and everything that happened earlier this morning slips into oblivion. Dan plays soccer too, but I do my best to avoid him at all costs—even if it means losing the game. We end up playing for longer than I would have liked, and I'm relieved when a few of us start to scatter.

I look around for Luke, wondering if he left at some point, but at the sound of his voice, I know I'm wrong.

"Pretty good game."

"Oh—um, yeah."

He stands back for a moment to evaluate the field. "I bet Dan's team will win."

I take a drink of water and keep my eyes on the game as I answer. "I haven't been keeping score, but probably. He's really good," I say almost robotically.

I can feel his eyes on me as he says, "Oh, I was going to say it's because he cheats," he shrugs, "but I guess he can make himself look pretty good out there, too."

A twitch of a smile crosses my lips, and I finally look over at him. "He cheats? At soccer?"

Luke smirks, and I realize he's joking.

"I almost believed you," I say with a small smile.

He lets out a shallow laugh. "I know. It's sad." When I don't say anything, he adds, "It's not sad that you believed me, but it's sad that people can easily see him as a cheater."

"Oh, right."

He clears his throat as if bracing himself for what he's about to say. I wait for the inevitable, like a kid sitting in the doctor's office when they know they're about to get a flu shot.

"I'm sorry about what Dan did earlier. He can get a little carried away sometimes."

"A little?"

"Alright, a lot."

I try to give him a reassuring smile. "Don't worry about it. It's not your fault."

Luke flashes his eyes in the direction of his cousin. Dan is still preoccupied with the ongoing soccer game and doesn't notice us staring. "But if I didn't bring him here, he wouldn't have pulled a stupid stunt like fighting with Josh or making you uncomfortable. I'm starting to feel like his babysitter even though he's five years older than me."

"You're not supposed to have to babysit your twenty-two-year-old cousin."

"Not without getting paid at least." Luke's tone is flat as he watches Dan score another goal.

Unsure of whether this is another one of his jokes, I look out at the field and pretend to be more interested in the game than I am.

"Hey, I know I'm probably the last person you want to hear

this from, but I overheard you telling Dan you don't have a ride home anymore. If you want, I can drop you off."

My heart sinks as I look at Luke. He's catching on to the fact that I don't like him as much as he wants me to. I'm not sure I like this Luke as much as the persistent, annoying one. This one makes me feel guilty.

Something about his expression makes me think he already knows he's setting himself up for failure. His shoulders slump, and his usual optimism has vanished. "Forget it, it's stupid," he backtracks.

It's easier to turn him down when he's annoying, but like this? I don't have the heart to do it. Biting my lip, I hope I won't regret this later. "No, that would be great. Thanks."

Luke's features perk up, but he soon composes himself. "Oh, alright. Well, when you're ready to go, just let me know."

I hesitate. "Are you taking Dan home, too?"

Luke laughs. "Are you kidding? No."

I let out a sigh of relief. "Do you think we can leave… now?"

"I was hoping you'd say that."

Something about Luke's attitude puts me at ease. I never thought I would be happy about getting in a car with him, but maybe I've been too hard on him.

☠   ☠   ☠

Music proves to be an easy conversation starter. I try not to overthink my sudden comfort with him as we drive. If this feeling isn't going to last, I don't want to waste it by worrying.

He turns up the radio. "I love this song."

"I've never heard it," I say.

"What? Seriously, Paige, do you live under a rock?"

I do feel like I've lived under a rock for most of my life. Now that I think about it, I don't think I escaped from the rock until I met Fredrick. I blush slightly when Fredrick's face comes to mind and refocus on my present conversation.

I shrug. "I don't know. Maybe," I say with a light laugh.

Luke laughs too, and the smile I usually have to force with him comes more naturally.

"So, I'm guessing you've been too busy to know *Pirates of the Caribbean* came out today?"

The irony of him bringing up a movie about pirates is not lost on me. His question raises red warning flags in the back of my mind, and the usual tension I feel in Luke's presence becomes abruptly more evident.

I look out the window. "I didn't realize it was out already."

I hear his fingertips nervously drum on the steering wheel. "You have no plans tonight, right?"

I nod slowly. "Right."

"We can go see it—if you want?"

I should have left with Josh.

He must sense my hesitation because he hastily adds, "Or I can just take you home."

His retraction triggers my guilt. "No—it's just that I—" Dan's words echo in my mind.

And you're too hung up on a guy who obviously isn't interested.

He just feels bad for you.

The memory brings back the image of Fredrick walking away from me yesterday, and the once red warning flags turn white. "Okay. Let's go."

20

The car rolls to a stop in front of the movie theater, and I take a deep breath. The drive here was filled with strained small talk that left an uncomfortable silence in its wake. Hopefully, I hide it better than he does.

He takes the keys out of the ignition. "I hope this movie is as good as it looks."

"I hear it's supposed to be funny," I offer to dull the tension.

He smiles, but it almost looks forced. "I heard the same thing."

I can't tell if his behavior stems from nerves, or if he has been hyping this moment for too long, and now that we're here, it isn't living up to his expectations. That's the problem with wanting something so badly. You get fixated and end up only seeing what you want to see. Luke probably hasn't really *seen* me for a long time, and the added pressure of calling this a *date* puts us both under a microscope. Maybe he's regretting this decision as much as I am.

We walk to the box office to buy the tickets. As we're waiting in line, Luke tries to keep a conversation flowing by pointing to the many movie posters lining the brick entrance.

"Have you seen that one?"

I shake my head. "I don't go to the movies much. This is probably the first movie I've been to this year."

His eyes widen as he raises his eyebrows. "Really? Well, this better be a good one, then."

I give him a tight-lipped smile. Luke is a sweet guy. Part of me—a very small part—wishes I did want to date him. He has never told me he doesn't want me around or shut me out for no reason. So, why can't I stop thinking about Fredrick?

Once we reach the window, Luke opens his wallet, and I see him pull out enough money to buy two tickets. I gently tap him on the shoulder. "I'll pay for mine."

His cheeks flush when he turns to answer me. "It's okay. I want to pay for you."

Of course, he does. That's the problem.

I shake my head firmly but make sure to smile. "Really. It's okay. I can pay for myself."

He thinks about it for a moment but puts down enough money for two tickets anyway. "You can get the next one."

Uh, what?

He hands me my ticket, and I mutter, "Thanks."

I don't know what it is about him paying for my ticket that makes seeing a movie with him feel different, but it does. Paying for my own ticket separated us. Now it feels like an actual date, and I want to turn back to the moment I agreed to come here and slap myself.

"Want popcorn?" Luke's voice snaps me out of my thoughts.

"Oh—um, I'm not hungry," I manage to get out. I don't want Luke to spend another dime on me for the rest of the night… or ever.

By the time we walk into the theater, the previews have almost finished. On a positive note, I'm that much closer to getting this not-date over with.

I numbly follow him through the near-empty theater to a couple of seats at the back. I hadn't noticed him leading me to the top row until he steps aside for me to take a seat.

"Are you sure you want to sit back here?" I ask. I should have requested we sit near the closest exit. Even if I've never done it, I know couples sit in the back of the theater so they can make out. Luke and I are not a couple, and we will not be making out. *Why didn't I think to say anything?*

Luke takes a seat at the top of the stairs near the right side of the theater. "Yeah, come on." He pats the seat next to him.

It's just a movie, I think to myself as I sit down.

The lights dim, and we watch *The Curse of the Black Pearl* unfold. Seeing the adventures of Jack Sparrow makes me feel ridiculous for labeling Fredrick as a pirate. Although, there are some similarities. The pillaging, deception, and overall lack of morals, all while maintaining a sense of likeability is almost *too* relatable.

It's impossible to imagine the always-composed Fredrick sloshing around with a bottle of rum. I smile at the thought.

I'm careful to sit at the farthest edge of my seat without it being obvious. Thankfully, Luke hasn't tried to hold my hand or put his arm around me. We only glance at each other when the movie makes us laugh.

The character on screen, Elizabeth, is being proposed to by someone she doesn't like, and she stops breathing and falls off a cliff. As I sit next to Luke on our date, I don't think I've ever related to a movie more in my life.

Especially when Luke shifts closer to me, and I realize I'm holding my own breath.

My body tenses, and I try to watch him out of the corner of my eye. He whispers my name, and the movie doesn't seem as funny as it did a few minutes ago.

I pretend not to hear him. I pretend to be extremely wrapped up in the world of pirates—which I thought would be easier to pull off considering my experience.

"Paige," he says louder.

One of the drawbacks of being one of the few people in the theater is that he can say my name loud and clear. Pretending not to hear him isn't a viable option anymore.

I muster the courage to face him. It takes me a second to realize what's happening, but after that first second, it becomes unfortunately clear.

Luke's tongue is in my mouth. It's sloppy and wet, and not okay. I am *not* okay.

I push against him, but he only leans into me more. Through ragged breaths, he says, "Come on, just have fun."

Is he serious right now? I try to push him off me again. "Luke, stop." It's hard to get the words out. His mouth repeatedly muffles mine.

He shifts more in his seat, giving himself leverage over me. His tongue tries to push past my lips again, only succeeding when I go to ask him to stop. My blood runs cold when I feel his hand on my inner thigh. His fingers fight their way up to the cuff of my denim shorts. I squirm in the seat, but he doesn't care. *Why doesn't he care?*

When his greedy fingers slide under the cuff of my shorts to reach even further up my leg, I gasp. "Get off me!"

My words ring out through the theater, and he finally pulls away. He glances around to see if the few people in the room are looking at us. I have no idea if I've drawn attention to us or not because I'm on my feet before he has the chance to corner me again.

"What the hell, Paige?" He grabs my wrist when I try to take off down the stairs. "You know I've liked you for so long. I've always been nice to you. Why are you being like this?"

My mouth opens as I try to think of what to say. The blood pounding in my ears makes it impossible to think. Finally, I yank my wrist out of his grasp. "Don't touch me," I manage to say.

Luke raises both hands. "Alright, fine. Just sit down, and we can watch the rest of the movie. I'm sorry."

He doesn't look sorry. "I have to go to the bathroom," I say. Without giving him time to answer, I turn and run down the stairs and out of the theater, hoping he doesn't follow.

I cut through the lobby and push open the double doors that lead outside. The warm, humid evening air makes me miss how the air feels at the beach. I'd give anything to have an ocean breeze diffuse how I'm feeling.

Sitting down on an empty bench, I take a deep breath and survey my surroundings. The darkening sky is my only indicator of how long this day has been. Sitting alone makes me wring my hands in my lap, but I know it's better than being stuck inside the theater with him. I can't believe the same Luke I've gone to school with for the past three years is the guy who just made my skin crawl. What would he have done if I hadn't stopped him? I shudder at the thought.

I look up at the softening sky and take a few more conscious breaths. Tears threaten to fall down my cheeks, but I wipe them away before they have the chance. Being stranded at a movie theater with Luke is *not* how I had pictured this day ending. As I peel my eyes away from the sky above, an idling curbside car in the distance catches my attention.

It's a black Jeep Wrangler.

I stand, peering to get a better look. Hugging my arms around my torso, I hesitantly make my way down the sidewalk, wiping my eyes one more time for good measure. Uncertainty weighs on each step until I'm close enough to see an all too familiar silhouette through the passenger window.

Fredrick.

As soon as I recognize him, I pick up my pace and head toward the Jeep. Fredrick rolls down the window once I'm at the passenger door. Resting his elbow on the center console, he leans my way, his eyebrows tilted with mild concern.

Seeing him brings a spur of mixed emotions. He didn't want

me. He's only helping me because he feels bad.

But none of those things compare to what Luke just did—or tried to do.

"What are you doing here?" My words carry some of my frustration with them. I don't even know if it's frustration toward Fredrick or Luke, but the question sounds more like an accusation.

Fredrick cocks an eyebrow. "What are *you* doing here?" he croons.

"I—um—I'm watching a movie…" My voice trails as I look over my shoulder, checking that Luke is still inside.

When I look back at Fredrick his smirk is gone. He's studying me.

"What's wrong?" he demands.

My eyes narrow, and I cross my arms. "Since when do you care?"

"Paige," he warns, his jaw ticking.

"No." I cut him off. "You made your feelings pretty clear yesterday, so why are you here?" My chest rises and falls as I wait for him to answer.

Fredrick opens his mouth like he's about to say something but shakes his head. "Paige," he says again, and when his eyes meet mine his gaze is harsh. "I'm going to ask you again, and I need you to answer me." He leans further across the center console, lowering his head to level with me. "What's wrong?"

"Nothing," I answer too quickly.

His eyes linger on me before he takes his keys out of the ignition and gets out of the car.

Walking around the front of the Jeep, he asks, "You're here with Luke, right?"

My gaze lifts to find his, and I nod.

"Did he do something to you?" His eyes search mine for an answer, but all I can do is tug down the hem of my shorts, still feeling Luke's phantom hand trying to ride them up. I stare up at him, at a loss for words.

Unable to say what happened.

Unable to say anything.

It doesn't take long for Fredrick to read through my hesitation. Cursing under his breath, he says, "I'll kill him," and pushes past me.

Panic brings my voice back with a jolt. "Wait!" I call after him, but he acts like he can't hear me.

My feet scramble beneath me, and I run after him. As he pulls open the door to the lobby, my fingers reach for his arm, desperate to stop him. Fredrick spins around to face me, and I crash into him, my hands bracing against his chest.

Fredrick grabs my arms to steady me, and I freeze. His hands holding me in place are the only thing I can focus on.

"Paige," he says, and I realize I've been staring at my hands on his chest. Snatching them back, I look up at him. He doesn't let go of my arms as he says, "I'm going to ask you again, and you need to tell me the truth. Did he do something to you? Yes, or no?"

"Yes, but—" I'm not sure how I was going to finish that sentence, but it doesn't matter. Fredrick has already let go of me and heads toward the theater.

The poor girl taking tickets watches him with wide eyes. "Um, excuse me. Do you have a ticket?"

"This will only take a minute," Fredrick mutters, sidestepping around her. I hurry behind him, apologizing to the girl as I pass. I make sure to hold up my ticket stub and hope she assumes he has one too.

He yanks the theater door open, wasting no time. It doesn't take long for him to spot Luke in the otherwise empty top right corner. Fredrick takes the steps two at a time, and I try my best to keep up with him. I want to yell for him to stop, but now that we're in the theater, all that will do is draw more attention to us.

Luke sees Fredrick, and his eyes bulge before jumping to me for a fraction of a second. Gripping the armrest on either side, he presses his back into the seat.

He can try to disappear all he wants, but Fredrick shows no sign of slowing down. Without hesitation, he puts a hand around Luke's throat and slams his head back against the theater wall. Towering over Luke, Fredrick is only inches from his face. He keeps his voice low and steady as he says, "I don't know what you did, but if you ever—and I mean *ever*—touch her again, I'll fucking kill you. Understand?"

Luke stares back at Fredrick, his eyes welling like he might cry. His mouth hangs open, but no words come out.

The other scattered theater patrons have started to notice the commotion, turning in their seats and trying to peer through the dark to see.

Fredrick gives Luke's neck another quick shove. "Tell me you understand."

Luke coughs from the added pressure on his throat but manages to choke out, "I understand."

For a moment, I almost feel bad for Luke. I almost forget what he tried to do. For a second, I see him as just Luke, the nice guy who has always had a crush on me. That's not who he is anymore, though, and he'll never be that person again.

Fredrick keeps glaring at Luke, and I think he's considering actually killing him. I've never seen him so angry. The sharp lines of his jaw are tight, and every muscle in his body holds tension as he holds Luke in place.

Hugging my arms around my torso, I say, "Fredrick, I think he gets it. Let's just go." The words leave my mouth with deliberation but get lost in the sword fight happening on screen. I'm not even sure he's heard me, but then Fredrick turns and starts walking down the stairs in my direction. I'm standing only a few steps behind him, and as soon as he reaches me, he grabs my hand, pulling me with him. I don't look back at Luke as we leave.

My eyes stay downcast as we pass the people in the lobby. I figured Fredrick would let go of my hand as soon as we left the theater, but he doesn't. If anything, his fingers wrap around mine tighter. I have to work to keep up with him and stealing a glance his way shows that his expression hasn't softened. I want him to look at me. I want to see what's behind those harsh eyes, but he keeps his focus straight ahead.

He opens the passenger door of the Jeep for me but doesn't say a word.

I stand frozen on the sidewalk. "What was *that?*"

Fredrick rubs a hand over his face and gestures to the empty seat next to us. "Would you just get in?"

Letting out a bewildered laugh, I cross my arms. "Last night you couldn't get rid of me fast enough, and now you want me to come with you?"

He pauses, his eyes piercing into mine. Everything that's happened today left me feeling vulnerable, but nothing compares to how it feels to have those eyes on me. Whatever thoughts were behind that look, he doesn't say. Instead, he blinks, his gaze jumping to the theatre. "Would you rather have your buddy Luke take you home?"

My eyes narrow, and I get inside without another word.

Closing the door, he walks about to the driver's side and gets in without looking at me. The Jeep roars to life, and Fredrick wastes no time pulling out of the parking lot.

"Did you follow me here?" I ask.

He answers without looking at me. "Not quite."

"How did you know I would be here?" *I barely knew I would end up here.*

Fredrick keeps his eyes straight ahead. "Dan mentioned Luke took you home from a party and wanted to take you out tonight."

Letting out a breath, I smooth my hair back, trying to piece it all together. "But how did you know I was here—at *this* movie theater?"

Fredrick's eyes flicker to me before they're back on the road. Scratching the side of his head, he mutters, "I might have convinced

Dan to tell me."

"Convinced?"

He tightens his grip on the steering wheel. "I thought you didn't like Luke anyway."

"I don't," I say, and my defensiveness comes out in my voice.

Giving me a side-long glance, Fredrick lifts a dubious brow. "Yet here we are."

Heat flares in the pit of my stomach. After yesterday, I don't owe him an explanation—even if I had one to offer. Instead, I mutter, "It wasn't exactly planned," and stare out the window.

If Josh and Dan never got into an argument, I would have been home hours ago. I never would have gone to the movies with Luke, and I wouldn't be sitting in Fredrick's Jeep again. The thought makes me look at him again, my mind reeling.

Fredrick registers my stare with a glance of his own but doesn't say anything.

"You didn't have to do that," I finally say.

He swallows with a slight bob of his head. "Yes, I did."

"Dan will flip out once he hears about it," I say quietly, almost to myself.

Fredrick's stoic expression reveals nothing as he says, "Let him."

I run my thumb over the hem of my t-shirt for the sake of having something to do. "Aren't you worried about what he'll do to you?"

He shakes his head. "He won't kick me out. He needs me, or else he would have done that already."

"Why?"

Fredrick's expression remains stone-like. "He doesn't like that I don't give him the same undeserving respect as the others."

"Oh… that's a good thing, though. Isn't it?" From what I've seen, Dan probably doesn't deserve to be the leader of anything.

He shrugs. "Not sure what it is. I just try not to do things I don't believe in."

"Like stealing?" I ask with an expectant look.

He gives me a side-long glance and says, "I had a choice in the beginning, and maybe I chose wrong, but it felt like my best option at the time. I might not like it now, but I don't regret it."

"What made you choose this, though?" I can't imagine why he would resort to joining the group. What could make him justify all the lying, stealing, and deception?

He eyes me wearily. "Not tonight."

His response sounds more like a plea, and the desperation in his tone makes me drop my need for answers. I sigh and look out the window again. "I saw Carter on the news."

When he doesn't say anything, I look over at him. Fredrick's knuckles are white as he grips the steering wheel, and the Jeep accelerates again.

He doesn't look at me. "Carter should have never pulled a stupid stunt like that."

I try to keep my voice calm to ease his anger. "Like what? You all steal."

He shakes his head. "Do you remember when I ran into you at your grocery store?" His voice is tight.

I nod, remembering his strange behavior that day. He had completed my entire shopping list without my noticing.

"Why do you think I was so far from the beach?"

I shrug. "I don't know."

"We never steal from local stores. If we're caught and put on the news, the locals will know to stay away from us. It's hard to pick someone's pocket once you're labeled a criminal. Other groups know this, too. They see it as a weakness—a crack in the system. Seeing that weakness could be enough to make them want to challenge us for our territory."

"Has that started to happen yet? With the locals?"

Fredrick's grip eases, and I feel the Jeep slow. "No, the video was shitty quality. I'm surprised you could tell it was Carter."

"Tattoos."

He nods.

We approach my road, and although his expression remains tense, his lips twitch. "Know how the idiot got caught?"

"How?"

"I'm sure you've noticed, but Carter likes to flirt."

Despite everything that happened tonight, this makes me laugh. "Yeah, I've noticed."

"Right. Well, I guess the cashier at the store was a little more receptive than most. The two of them ended up in a supply closet together, and uh…" He glances at me. "That's when she found the stuff on him."

Holding in my laughter doesn't work. I end up doing a half laugh, half cough. Fredrick laughs a little too, but it doesn't reach his eyes.

I cover my mouth with my hands. "I can't believe Carter did something so stupid!"

Fredrick keeps his eyes on the road with a slight shake of his head. "I can."

We park in front of my house. All the lights are off, but I can see the faint glow of the television through the front window. Gathering my confidence, I say, "Can I ask you something?"

He shifts in his seat to look at me, but he doesn't look so sure when he says, "Yeah."

My gaze drops to my hands in my lap. "Why were you so cold when I left your house yesterday?"

When he doesn't answer right away, I look up to find him rubbing the back of his neck. "Maybe we should talk about that another night, too."

I hitch one leg up, so I can turn to face him, my back resting against the door. My heart pounds, but I shake my head. "I want to know what I did to make you so mad."

Fredrick's eyes soften. "You didn't make me mad. It's just—it's complicated."

I raise my eyebrows, pressing him to keep going.

He glances down. "I can't get into this with you tonight."

My eyebrows crease. "Why?"

"Because I told you, it's complicated." His voice comes out packed with frustration.

I should have known better than to think this would change

anything between us. Rolling my eyes, I go to open the door. "For-get it."

Fredrick stares down at the steering wheel and nods before looking at me. "I'll see you tomorrow?"

I pause, thrown off by his question. "I don't know," I say hopping down from my seat. Before I close the door to the jeep, I can't help turning back to him and adding, "I'd hate to complicate things."

I don't check for his reaction.

I don't hesitate.

Without another word, I march up to the house and slip inside. It looks like Dad fell asleep on the couch, so I quietly latch the lock, turn off the television, and make my way to the kitchen. As promised, a few slices of pizza are in the fridge. Hoisting myself onto the counter, I let my feet dangle as I eat cold pizza out of the box.

I'm not happy with how I left things with Fredrick, but that seems to be the norm lately. I can't keep up with him, and I won't let myself fall victim to his constant mood swings. Being a private person is one thing, but Fredrick's secrets could potentially get me hurt. Shouldn't I know what I'm up against?

The cold pizza helps to dull my anger, and I feel ready to try and get some sleep. Once my head hits the pillow, I'm sure my mind will race with the day I've had. I might as well get an early start. I'm more than ready for this day to be over. Josh driving me to the lake this morning feels like it was at least a week ago. Lately, it seems all my days either leave me feeling charged with adrenaline or completely drained. Tonight, I'm drained.

Opening my bedroom door, I freeze. Fredrick paces my room as he rubs the back of his neck nervously.

He stops when he sees me standing in the doorway. "Okay… let's talk."

21

Despite having just seen him outside, Fredrick being in my bedroom stalls my train of thought. "W-what? How did you get in here?"

"Ladder." He stays frozen in the middle of my room, and I mirror his stillness in the doorway.

I'm about to explain my father's inability to put things away, but the way he's looking at me tells me whatever he came here to say can't wait.

Fredrick returns to his anxious footwork, and I gently close the door behind me before sitting cross-legged on my bed. Watching him cautiously, I try to wrap my head around seeing him this way. He's usually so... composed.

"I don't know what to do," he finally says pressing his fist to his lips. He's still pacing the floor, so I wait for him to gather his thoughts. "I'm used to living selfishly," he goes on to say, "taking what I need—hell, taking what I want, without thinking of anyone else…" Fredrick's words trail off, and he shakes his head. "I don't know what to do."

Leaning forward, I try to keep my voice gentle when I say, "Fredrick, what are you talking about?"

He pauses, those dark eyes locking on me. Even as he looks at me, I might as well be able to see the wheels turning in his head. Taking a seat on the computer chair across from me, he keeps his hands clasped firmly in his lap as he bounces his foot against the wood floor. "I'm selfish, but I don't want to be selfish with you."

I try to understand what he means. "I don't think you're selfish."

He scoffs. "Come on, Paige. I'm not a good guy. Every time you're around me, I'm putting you at risk."

I take a moment to think. Saying the wrong thing might make him push me away again. "I know there are risks… I've known that since the first night I was attacked, but I'm stronger now. I'm learning how to defend myself… because of you."

His eyes fall to the ground. "You were hurt because of me."

I shake my head. "No, I was hurt because that girl wanted my bracelet and made a game out of it. I'm sitting here safe because of you."

Staring down at his hands, he shakes his head. "No, Paige, if you had never met me at the bonfire, you would be safe. But now you've been attacked… twice." He pulls his eyes away from his hands to look at me and holds my gaze as he says, "Who knows what that guy would have done to you the night he broke in here."

It's the same thought I've had countless times, but hearing him say it out loud sends a chill down my spine. Swallowing my nerves, I say, "But I made it out okay *because* you were there."

Fredrick avoids my stare again. "None of this would have happened if I had—"

"No," I say, already knowing what he's thinking. I glare at him. "Cutting me out isn't the answer." When he doesn't say anything, I blurt, "I stood up to Luke tonight because of you." This makes his eyes snap up to meet mine, and my cheeks flush, but I grit my teeth and keep going. "I'm serious. If it weren't for you, I don't know if I would have stood up to Luke so quickly. I don't know that I would have been able to stop him from…" Now it's my turn to drop my gaze. Staring down at my hands in my lap, I shake my head, not wanting to finish the thought. "I don't know."

"Paige," he says wearily like he doesn't believe me.

"No, Fredrick." I look up at him and try to read through the storm happening behind those eyes. "I'm not going to let you keep torturing yourself over this. I'm stronger because of you." The words hang in the air between us. He watches me, his stare never wavering, and I start to feel like I've just confessed something intimate. Quickly, I add, "Jason says I should be in top shape by the end of the summer. You don't need to worry about me."

He nods but doesn't say anything. He's resting his forearms on his knees and looking at the floor again.

"So, what does this have to do with yesterday?" I ask.

For a moment, he says nothing. For a moment, he just stares at me like he's debating what he wants to say. After a beat of loaded silence, he answers, "I hated the thought of you going out with

Luke."

His confession makes me pause, the air catching in my throat. Somehow, I manage to get out, "You did?" and try to ignore the drumming in my chest.

Fredrick scoffs, running a hand over his head. "You can do a lot better than him, Paige."

I let out a hollow laugh. "Like who?" The words are out before I realize what I've said, and I hold my breath for his answer.

He pins me with his stare. "You should be with someone better than all of us."

His answer leaves me disappointed, but I try not to show it. "Right." I should have known he wouldn't say I should be with him. Why would he? Why would he want to be with me? He only sees me as a walking hazard. Even though I know all of this, I can't help imagining what it would feel like to be wanted by him. How it would feel to have him take my face in his hands and kiss me... or feel the warmth of his body against mine.

Fredrick lets out a low laugh, and my eyes snap up, hoping he doesn't notice where my thoughts went. "Whatever you do, don't let it be Carter."

To this, I crack a smile. "I don't know," I say with a shrug. "He's already painted me a pretty great picture of what our life would be like together."

He drops his face into his hands and groans. "Yeah, you and every other girl."

I can't help laughing.

Lifting his face from his hands, he flashes a genuine smile, and

I want to memorize every part of it.

The warmth behind his eyes.

The way his expression softens.

Seeing him this way feels like peeking behind the curtain, and all I can think about is how I can get him to smile like this again.

Our eyes lock, and as much as I don't want to ruin this, the pang in my chest reminds me that I need to tell him what happened today.

"I have to tell you something," I say.

Fredrick's brows furrow slightly, but then he leans toward me. "Okay."

"I messed up," I say in a rush. "I was with Josh when Carter came on the news. I let Carter's name slip. I didn't even realize I had said anything wrong until Josh told Dan. Dan was furious..." My words trail off as the image of Dan at the lake comes to mind, forcing an involuntary shudder.

The smile I loved so much slips away. "Did Dan do something to you?"

"What? No." I say, feeling confused. "He was mad, but he didn't do anything."

His shoulders visibly relax.

"I'm sorry," I say, dropping my head in my hands. "I wasn't thinking. Dan thinks Josh will turn Carter in."

Fredrick deadpans, "He won't."

His confidence surprises me, and I look up at him. "How do you know?"

"Josh hates Dan and me for more reasons than just stealing.

It's not like his moral compass is so different from ours. He won't turn in someone he doesn't know for shoplifting." He rubs the back of his neck. "If it had been Dan or me on the news, he would have turned us in, but he won't do anything to Carter."

I sigh out a breath of relief. "I guess that makes sense."

Fredrick studies me before leaning toward me, giving me his full attention. "You said you wanted to talk. What else do you want to know?"

I almost wane under the intensity of his stare. "Um…" I glance around my room, trying to gather my thoughts. "Why can't you stop?"

Fredrick's dark eyebrows pinch as he considers my question. "Security," he finally says. "They have my back, and I have theirs."

"Why would you need security?" I ask.

He starts to look uncomfortable again. For a moment, I think he might shut down, but eventually, he sighs. "Sometimes other people's mistakes are more dangerous than our own."

At that moment, I hear a shuffle from downstairs. Fredrick's eyes jump to my closed bedroom door, but he doesn't seem worried about my father finding him here. The sound of a door closing calms me down. My Dad must have woken up on the couch and lumbered into his bedroom for the night.

I make sure to keep my voice low. "Whose mistakes are dangerous?"

He gets to his feet and walks over to my dresser, where he holds the picture of Leah and me sticking our tongues out at the camera. "I remember seeing you with her at the bonfire. Is she a good friend of yours?" I give him a dubious look for changing the subject, and he lets out an exasperated sigh. "You're digging too deep, Paige."

"You said we could talk," I remind him.

Fredrick looks at me for a long moment before walking across the room toward me. He sits on the edge of my bed, facing me with one leg bent and the other hanging over the edge. Our knees are touching, mine bare and his clad in his usual dark denim. I try not to think about it.

"Whose mistakes are dangerous?" I ask again, my voice low.

His eyes search mine like he's trying to weigh his options before he says anything. I don't know what he's looking for, but I keep my eyes on his. I want him to trust me, not only with the pirates but with everything.

"My dad's." In those two words, I can tell he finally let out something he has been holding in for a while. He looks away briefly before bringing his eyes back to me, his foot bouncing slightly on the floor. "He runs with the wrong crowd and doesn't have the common decency to be careful about it. He'll piss off the wrong people and then pop in for a visit like he's the father of the fucking year.

"One weekend, he came to see us, and after he left, two men showed up at the house. They wanted to get even for something he did. Ben was working at the shop, Nicole and I were still at school, and my mom was home alone."

My eyes widen, but I stay silent.

Fredrick runs his hand over his head. "My mom didn't know I was in Dan's group then, but I told Dan I was worried something like this might happen. My dad was acting weird on that visit. He's always trying to hide things, but on that trip, he seemed jumpier than usual. Dan and Jason agreed to keep an eye on the house while I wasn't home.

"I'm not sure if the men thought my dad would still be there, or if they wanted to hurt him through us, but they broke in through the back door. My mom was going through a rough time then, so she wouldn't have been able to act quickly enough to get herself out of there. I lied and told her Dan and Jason had a lawn business and not to worry if she saw them around the house. Melissa and Carter hadn't joined us at this point.

"Dan was the one who was there when it happened. He took a beating but was able to stop them from doing any damage. We were still learning how to fight back then, but he did whatever it took to keep my mom safe. I'll never forget that."

I try to process everything he's telling me. "So, after that happened, you had to tell Kelly how you really knew Jason and Dan?"

He nods.

My words come out slowly as my mind puts the pieces together. "And Kelly accepts the group because... she's grateful."

He nods again. "I started doing this because we needed the money. After my dad left, I tried to find a job, but no one would hire me because I was too young. I know I could find a job now, but my dad is still a fuckup. I can't let anything happen to my family."

"Do you still need to do it for the money?" I ask hesitantly.

Fredrick gives me a small smile. "Only because I don't have an alternative."

I consider his situation and try to find a way out. "Why can't you stop stealing and get a job but still work something out with Dan to keep everyone safe?"

He frowns and shakes his head. "I've tried. We pool the cash we steal every week. If I'm not bringing in my share, he won't help."

My anger spikes toward Dan again. Of course, he won't help Fredrick out of the goodness of his heart. I shouldn't be surprised, but part of me thought he might feel inclined to help Kelly.

Fredrick must see my change in mood because he places a hand on my knee, and I immediately snap out of my thoughts. My first instinct is to flinch and pull away from him after what happened with Luke, but there's something so steady and gentle in the way he brushes his hand over my skin. His touch feels nothing like Luke's pawing hands—his touch sets a fire through me. My eyes instinctively fall to his hand. I half expect him to pull away, but he doesn't. He ducks his head low, so I'm looking him in the eye. "It's fine, Paige. This is just my life for now, but I don't want to be like my dad." His eyes fall to my knee, and he moves his thumb in small circles over my skin. His expression is thoughtful when he says, "I don't want to knowingly put you, or anyone else, at risk because of what I'm wrapped up in."

"But…" I struggle to find the words to say. "But don't you want a life? A job? A girlfriend? How are you supposed to have a future like this?"

Fredrick sits back and tilts his head at me. He's no longer touching me, making me regret that I've said anything. "I've had girlfriends," he says with a trace of a smile.

My cheeks turn hot. "Of course—I didn't mean… wait, how?"

A small smirk pulls at the corner of his mouth. "I date. I just can't tell them anything," he says matter-of-factly. "I don't date anyone who lives near the beach, and I always go see her, not the other way around. I keep anyone I date completely separate from everything else." He shrugs. "It ends up ruining the relationship. Girls sense I'm hiding something and stop trusting me."

I'm curious about Fredrick's past girlfriends. What were they like? Did he love any of them? Has he ever had his heart broken? Asking any of these questions seems too personal, so I just nod in understanding and say, "That must be tough."

"I wasn't serious about any of them." His eyes lock on mine, and for a moment, neither of us says anything. His gaze falls to my mouth, and my heart thuds harder in my chest. I bite down on my lower lip to try and calm my nerves.

Not including tonight—I refuse to include tonight—I've only ever kissed two people. I've never had a boyfriend, either—at least not a serious one. My first kiss was at a sixth-grade dance back in Atlanta. Jeremy Fisher. I was mortified because everyone saw it happen. The next day, the entire school wouldn't stop talking about it. I don't think I've ever wanted to disappear more.

The second was at a party Josh dragged me to during our freshman year of high school. He insisted that I "get out there" and "make some friends other than him." When we got to the party, Josh was pulled away by the other guys on the football team, and I was left to my own devices. I remember sitting on a couch for what felt like forever until James Alexander sat next to me. We had geography together, but I never thought he noticed me. He was cute enough, and I liked that he went by James. Most guys with that name end up going by Jim, or Jamie, or Jay. He was nice, and he felt like a safety net at that party. He kissed me at the end of the night, and it was short and sweet. We kept talking for a few weeks after that, but it never turned into anything.

Fredrick isn't even kissing me, he's only looking at my mouth, but I'm already more breathless than I had been with either of the other guys. My gaze drops to his lips. I want to kiss him—I think I've wanted to kiss him for a while—but I don't want to kiss him tonight. Knowing that Luke had his tongue in my mouth only hours ago would taint it.

Suddenly, as if snapping out of a daydream, Fredrick gets to his feet. "I should go."

"You're leaving?"

He lets out another light laugh. "Yeah, I think I need to."

"You don't have to go." I don't want him to leave, but I know he has already stayed longer than he meant to.

"I'll see you tomorrow, Paige." He gives me a crooked smile before ducking out my window. "Lock this," he adds, tapping the frame.

With that, he's gone.

I stay seated on my bed, staring at my open window. "Fredrick?" I bite my lip and wait, but the darkness outside remains still. Dan's words about Fredrick *obviously not being interested* run through my mind again.

Getting up, I head to my open window. He's already gone from the roof, but I catch sight of the ladder being pulled away from the side of the house and it brings a twinge of a smile to my lips.

22

Every morning, there's that moment between sleeping and awake where our thoughts teeter between the subconscious and the conscious. In these last seconds before consciousness, our dreams rapidly slip away, usually without notice, until they're replaced with the reality of a new day.

This morning, all my thoughts—the sleeping and the awake—are of a boy with dark hair and caramel eyes.

My dad's enthusiastic voice booms throughout the house. Checking the time lets me know I've slept later than usual. It's almost noon. I guess more than my mind needed to recover from yesterday. I shower and throw on a pair of denim shorts and a burgundy t-shirt before heading downstairs.

Halfway down the steps, I can hear Dad eagerly talking on the phone.

"Are you kidding me? There's no way Jimmie will come in before Edwards. You watch."

I have a feeling Jim is on the other end.

Dad's laugh bellows through the house. "Why don't you just shut up and get over here."

He hangs up the phone as I walk into the kitchen. Opening the pantry, I grab the cereal and ask, "What was that about?"

My dad takes a seat at the kitchen table. "Jim and I have a little wager on the race today." He raises an eyebrow at the cereal box in my hand. "You sure you don't want to jump straight to lunch?"

I shake my head as I reach for a bowl. "What's the wager?"

He leans back in the chair folding his arms behind his head. "Let's just say he'll be treating us to a pretty nice dinner tonight."

I laugh, knowing he probably bet a steak dinner. "And if Edwards doesn't win?"

Dad grunts, "That won't happen."

I swallow my spoonful of cereal and give him a sly smile. "Of course not."

Jim lives a few houses down, so it's no surprise when the door swings open. He and my dad have been friends for as long as I can remember. Formalities like knocking faded years ago.

I don't have many memories from when my parents were still together, but they used to do everything with Jim and his wife, Sandy. Once mom split and moved to Atlanta, taking me with her, they kept my dad going. I don't know Sandy very well. By the time I moved here, my father was over the divorce, and she doesn't usually join Jim on race days. The years I'm with my dad for Thanksgiving, we sometimes go over to Jim and Sandy's house, but since moving here, that has only happened once.

"Getting my dinner ready, Dave?" Jim yells from the front door.

My dad calls over his shoulder but doesn't get up from the table. "In your dreams."

Jim lets out a hearty laugh. "Johnson's been having a good season. Not even you can deny that."

"I can, and I will," my dad grumbles.

Jim stops in the kitchen when he sees me. "Paige, the nacho queen! I haven't seen you in a while."

Jim is heavier than my dad. Not by much but enough for you to know who's a bachelor and who's happily married. He's taller than my dad, too. Between his booming voice, tank-like frame, and case of Miller Lite always in hand, it's hard to miss when Jim walks into a room.

I give him a smile between mouthfuls of cereal. "Sorry, I just woke up."

Jim looks down at my dad. "I knew having an easy teenager couldn't last with your karma. She's finally starting to party all night and sleep all day." He gives me a wink as he opens the refrigerator and starts storing the beer he brought. My dad opens two beers, and they head into the other room.

I finish my cereal and call out, "Nachos?"

Taking their excited whoops as a yes, I get to work.

A few minutes later, the oven beeps. I check that all the cheese has melted before taking the pan out and walking it into the living room. Both men look almost identical with goofy, boyish grins and their NASCAR t-shirts and hats. The countdown is about to begin, so I set down the tray and head toward the front door for some air. I've never understood the thrill of cars driving around in a circle the way my dad does.

I sit on our squeaky bench swing and look out over the front yard. Everything looks more vibrant under the bright sun. Even with the shade over the porch, I can already feel my body temperature rise.

My thoughts wander to Luke. The memory of his mouth on mine makes me pinch my bottom lip between my two fingers. His lips felt so wrong on mine. The thought of his tongue pushing its way into my mouth sends watered-down waves of panic through me. He was supposed to be my friend. He *was* my friend.

I keep running over what happened. Him smashing his lips against mine, trying to corner me, and sliding his hand further up my leg. I should have done something more. I should have slapped him. Or better yet, I should have used what I'd learned in training against him. It bothers me that I didn't think to do that. At the moment, all I could think to do was push against him. I didn't think to jab, cross, or hook. I didn't think to do anything because I thought I was safe with him. I thought I knew him, and I thought he would never do anything to hurt me. But I thought wrong.

Movement at the end of the driveway catches my attention, and a black Jeep Wrangler makes its way toward the house. I watch, feeling dumbfounded as the Jeep parks in the gravel driveway.

I glance down, wishing I had put on something more appealing this morning. Shaking the thought from my mind, I get to my feet. I'm dressed in my usual shorts and a t-shirt, and he's… Well, he's walking toward me, looking flawless.

I meet him in the middle of our grassy yard. Yesterday he said I'd see him today, but I wasn't expecting him to show up at my house. "You're here," I say with a tilt of my head.

"I'm here." He echoes, looking amused. "I came to pick you up for training."

I hesitate and glance back at the house. A few days ago, I told my dad I would try to stay home for the race to spend time with him. Jim is here to keep him company, though, so there's a chance he may not remember that conversation. "Okay, if Edwards is winning, it won't be a problem."

He watches me curiously as I hurry back into the house.

I feel bad leaving him outside, but I don't need more reasons for Jim to peg me as a "normal teenager." Resting my arms on the back of the couch, I say, "Can I go to Fredrick's house with a couple of friends?" This technically isn't a lie. I'm sure the other pirates will be there, too.

I caught him as he puts a loaded nacho chip into his mouth. He nods vigorously as he chews, and finally manages to say, "Yeah, yeah, go ahead."

"Thanks." I laugh and kiss him on the cheek. Waving goodbye to both Jim and my dad, I walk out the door.

Fredrick looks up at the sound of me slamming the door. His mouth quirks. "In a hurry?"

I shrug, a little embarrassed that I seem so eager. "There's nothing else to do."

He doesn't try to hide his smirk. "Oh, is that it? There's nothing else to do, so you might as well brush up on your fighting skills with a criminal?"

I roll my eyes as I walk past him. "Come on, let's go."

I hear a trace of a laugh behind me and try to hide the tight-lipped smile it brings to my lips.

Once we're in the Jeep, Fredrick starts the engine and pulls out onto the long, winding gravel road.

"Thanks for coming back last night."

"There was nothing else to do," he says in a playful tone.

Laughing to myself, I nod. "Right."

☠   ☠   ☠

As we drive along the sandy road with tall, skinny oak trees, Fredrick's beach home comes into view. Kelly kneels in the front yard with a bandana over her ponytail, her tan gardening gloves deep in the dirt.

Once she sees us, Kelly sets down her trowel, brushes her hands on her knees, and walks over to Fredrick and me as we step down from the Jeep. Looking at Fredrick, she gestures toward the tall trees in the distance. "If you're looking for the rest of them, they're in the woods at that clearing."

Fredrick doesn't try to hide his confusion. "They're all there?"

Kelly shrugs. "They didn't say what they were doing." She

turns to me with a smile. "How have you been? I would hug you but," She gestures to the dirt covering her body.

I let out a laugh, looking past her at the garden. "What are you working on?"

She glances back at the garden and points. "Just planting a few Pentas to spruce the place up. It was starting to look a bit sad."

"I never got that impression," I say. Looking up at Fredrick, I expect to see him rolling his eyes at his mom's comment, but he's rigid next to me, and it looks like his mind is somewhere else.

He places his hand on the small of my back and guides me forward. "We'll be back later," he says to Kelly as he leads me away.

Looking over my shoulder, I wave goodbye to her before quickening my pace to match Fredrick's.

"What's wrong?" I ask.

"Something isn't right," he says with a subtle shake of his head.

I try to ask what he means, but he won't elaborate. He's quiet the rest of the walk, and I find myself wishing we were still back at my house, where he seemed so much lighter.

As the small, dim clearing comes into view, I'm surprised to find Dan with everyone else. He hasn't joined us since my first lesson almost a month ago.

Jason's voice rings out. "And just where have you two been?"

Fredrick ignores the comment and addresses Dan. "What's going on?"

It only takes one look at Dan to know Luke must have told him what happened at the movie theatre. He's standing tall and stiff, his hands down by his sides, and he keeps opening and clenching one

338

of his fists.

This can't be good.

Dan looks like he wants to say something, but his jaw is too tight for the words to get out. Finally, he spits, "What the fuck, Fredrick?"

Fredrick looks over at Dan with a blank expression. "What?"

"You know what." Dan's voice shakes with anger as he approaches him. "You attacked Luke!"

Jason and Carter glance at each other with wide eyes, but Melissa doesn't seem to care. She's sitting to the side, picking at one of the frayed holes in her jeans.

"You attacked Luke?" Jason asks Fredrick, and I can see his mouth twitch with the slightest smile.

Fredrick's eyes flicker to Jason, but he looks back at Dan. "'Attacked' is a bit dramatic."

"Luke told me exactly what happened." Dan pokes a finger at Fredrick's chest, and I tense, expecting him to react.

He doesn't.

Fredrick doesn't back down, but he doesn't do anything at Dan's touch. Instead, he asks, "What did he tell you?"

The volume of Dan's voice climbs. "That he was on a date with Paige, and you stormed into the theater like a fucking psycho. You nearly choked him out for no fucking reason!"

Fredrick cocks an eyebrow. "No reason?" Shoving his hands into his pockets, he shrugs. "That's funny. I thought I had a reason."

I can't believe how calm he seems even though Dan is yelling only inches from his face.

"What was the reason?" Jason calls out from the sidelines. He's doing a poor job of hiding his excitement at this point.

Fredrick's eyes flicker in my direction, but he doesn't tell them what happened. "He pissed me off."

Jason sits on the log with his elbows on his knees, looking absolutely giddy. "Come on, don't hold back on us now."

Carter, who doesn't seem to share the same dislike for Luke, looks confused, his eyes jumping between everyone.

I step to the side, taking a seat next to Jason, but my eyes are glued to Fredrick and Dan the entire time. I can't bring myself to look away.

"He *pissed you off?*" Dan sneers at Fredrick.

"That's what I said."

Carter chimes in with, "Fredrick, just tell us what happened."

Another shrug. He won't tell them, and they won't let it go.

Staring down at my hands, I wring them in my lap. My heart drums in my chest. Bouncing my knees, I can't take the fighting because of me. Finally, I blurt, "It was because of me."

I stare down at my feet, afraid of everyone's reaction. Slowly, I lift my gaze to find everyone staring at me. Even Melissa has stopped what she's doing to stare at me with mild interest, and I swallow the lump in my throat.

"Paige, you don't have to explain," Fredrick says.

Shaking my head, I can't bring myself to look at him. I keep my eyes fixed on the space out in front of me. "Luke sort of… forced himself on me in the theater. I tried to push him off, but he wouldn't listen…" I look around at everyone and hope they don't ask me for details.

"What a pig." I'm surprised to hear Melissa's voice first and even more surprised to see a look of disgust on her face that, for once, isn't directed at me.

"Oh… shit," Jason says. He looks over at Fredrick with complete understanding. "Dan, be glad he didn't kill him."

Irritation flashes across Dan's face when he looks at Jason and snaps, "What?"

Jason puts his hands up. "I'm just saying. When it comes to *this* girl, and him," he gestures to Fredrick, "I'd assume we were all here to plan Luke's funeral."

Carter leans around to look at me. "I would have fought for you, too." He winks, and I give him an embarrassed smile.

Dan ignores the others and redirects his rage to Fredrick. "Why were you even there?"

"It's a good thing I was." Fredrick's words bite into the air around us, and I know he's losing his patience.

I wring my hands in my lap again, keeping my wide eyes locked on the two of them.

"They won't fight." Jason's low voice next to me pulls my attention away.

"How do you know?" I ask. Based on the looks of things, I'd say there's a strong possibility they will.

Jason leans closer to me, so he can keep his voice low. "They'd be breaking the code."

"The what?"

He stares back at me blankly. "The code. The set of rules we follow?"

My shoulders lift, and I shake my head. "Um... I don't—"

Jason brushes me off with a wave of his hand. "Doesn't matter. Point is, we aren't allowed to fight each other. Could you imagine?" He shakes his head at the thought. "They can yell at each other all they want, but they won't hit each other."

My body relaxes, and I turn my attention back to Fredrick, but Dan is the one speaking.

"Come on, tell us all why you were at the theater," he jeers with a taunting smile. "Paige was on a date with Luke, and you were... doing what exactly?"

This catches my attention because I don't know the answer either. When I asked Fredrick how he knew I was at that theater, he said he convinced Dan to tell him... but with everything going on, I never thought to ask why.

"Dan, would you *shut up?*" Melissa gets to her feet and walks over to the two of them. "You," she points to Dan, "need to accept that your cousin is a creep who got what he deserved."

Dan crosses his arms and glares back at Melissa, but she ignores him.

"And you," she turns to Fredrick, "need to figure your shit out."

Fredrick nods, looking serious. "I know."

I give Fredrick a questioning look, but he avoids my gaze.

Melissa claps her hands together, looking pleased with herself. "Okay. Now, can someone please tell me what the hell we're all doing here?"

All eyes turn to Dan.

"Figured I'd see how she's doing," he says gruffly.

This catches Fredrick's attention. His head snaps in Dan's direction. "Why?"

Dan blatantly ignores Fredrick's comment and turns to me. "Let's see what you've got."

23

What I've got? What is he expecting? My eyes land on Fredrick, but he still isn't looking at me. He's watching Dan.

I stammer. "Um, I…"

"Why are you so interested?" Fredrick demands.

Dan shrugs. "Why not? She's been hanging around here long enough. She should know something by now, and I want to see it."

The blood slowly drains from my face, and my eyes widen at the thought of trying to prove myself in front of Dan. Getting marginally better at fighting and becoming a good fighter are two different things. The last thing I want is to become more of a joke to them—especially Fredrick.

Finally, Fredrick catches sight of my pleading stare. I subtly shake my head, hoping he understands my silent cry for help.

His jaw tightens, and when he looks back at Dan, his voice sounds like a warning. "Dan…"

Dan ignores him again. He crosses his arms over his chest and casually says, "She knows everything about us, and for what? What do we benefit from her?"

Everyone is silent, and I watch as Fredrick's eyes narrow. "We were never supposed to benefit from her. We did this to help her."

Raising an eyebrow, Dan replies coolly. "To help her? Or to help *you?*"

I want to ask what he means, but I'm frozen in place. Being the center of attention during my first lesson was overwhelming, but at least they knew how little I could fight. It's impossible to disappoint people when they have no expectations.

Now they expect something, and I know I'll let them down.

Jason steps forward. "Fuck off, Dan."

I'm starting to see Jason in a different light. I always dreaded lessons with him, but outside of that, I think I'm starting to like him more and more.

Irritation flashes across Dan's face. He puts a hand up to stop his half-brother and growls, "Stay out of this."

Jason's features harden, and he looks over at Fredrick, who gives him a reassuring glance. The tension wrapping Jason's body breathes.

After a long moment of silence, Dan leans back against a tree keeping his arms folded across his broad chest. "Face it, she's a waste of our time."

My heart races as his words ignite something inside of me.

Dan continues by saying, "I mean, look at her." He juts out his chin in my direction before adding, "She couldn't fight off a dog."

My pent-up feelings toward Dan pile up to my throat until I blurt out, "I could."

All eyes turn to me.

Dan cocks an eyebrow. "Could you, though?"

Holding his stare, I refuse to give him the satisfaction of saying anything. Instead, I cross my arms and wait.

He leans forward, menacing on all fronts. "Prove it."

"Fine."

Carter fails to hide his smile from Dan, and Melissa and Jason stare at me with their mouths open. I can hardly believe the word came out of my mouth. It's funny how anger can make you brave… or stupid. On second thought, it's probably the latter. *What am I thinking?* When my eyes finally fall on Fredrick, his head is in his hands. His reaction gives me pause. I thought, if anything, he would be proud of me for standing up to Dan, but now I have the feeling he thinks my anger is making me stupid, too.

A loud clap snaps me back to reality. Dan eagerly rubs his hands together and says, "All right, let's get started."

I swallow hard and wait for what's about to come. Dan isn't looking at me anymore, but I keep my eyes on him. I need to hold on to my anger if I'm going to do this. I remind myself of all the terrible things he has done. I think of all the games he has played to get Luke and me together, the embarrassment he's caused me, and how he won't work something out with Fredrick that would let him have a life outside of this. My thoughts spiral deeper until someone blocks my view. My eyes drift up to find Fredrick standing in front of me.

"Don't do this."

Concern brews behind his hardened eyes.

"If this is what it takes to get Dan off my back, I'm doing it." I push past him and walk over to Dan. "Well? What do you want me to do?"

Dan smiles down at me, but it doesn't reach his eyes. "How about a scrimmage?" He doesn't wait for me to respond. Walking to the center of the clearing, he addresses the others. "Each of you will try to fight Paige—except for you, Fredrick. I'd hate for you to go easy on her."

Fredrick sits with his elbows on his knees, hands clasped together, and his foot bouncing against the soft sand. The muscles in his jaw tighten as he watches Dan, but he doesn't say anything.

Spinning around and pointing to Jason, Dan calls him forward with a single hand. "You first."

Jason, however, doesn't move. Instead, he looks past Dan to Fredrick, who nods.

"Paige."

My attention returns to Dan. Jason now stands next to him with an unreadable expression.

Stepping back, Dan says, "Go ahead, Jay."

Jason doesn't break his gaze from mine to look at Dan. He positions himself to fight, and I do the same. Even though we haven't started yet, my chest rises and falls. I try to block out the others watching and focus only on Jason. We do this all the time. It's the same as one of my lessons. *A lesson with an audience*, the voice in my head reminds me, and I try to silence my thoughts. *We're just practic-ing.*

Jason gives a slight nod and takes a cautious step to the left.

I match his footwork.

He looks like he's thinking too hard—like he's trying to figure out an attack he knows I'll be able to block. I appreciate what he's trying to do, but if I can sense it, Dan can, too. I'm not going to convince Dan I can handle myself if he thinks anyone is doing me favors.

Jason tries to paw down the hand I'm using to block so he can get a clear shot at me. I use my blocking arm to jab when I see what he's trying to do, and he's forced to lean back to avoid the hit. I take advantage of his compromised position by striking his lower ribcage.

My fist makes contact, and I don't hold back. One of my favor-ite improvements over the past month has been noticing myself get-ting stronger. In the beginning, Jason would tell me to punch him as hard as I could, and at first, I didn't want to. I was afraid I'd hurt him even though he seemed so confident that I wouldn't. When he finally convinced me to go for it, I found he was right. Despite using all my strength, my punch was useless.

My punches aren't so useless anymore, and Jason folds over from the impact of my fist. He looks at me with mild surprise, but I see the corners of his mouth twitch. Straightening, he advances to-ward me again, his eyes providing the same brief warning.

Our fight continues like this. Eventually, Jason gives me less and less of a warning once he realizes I can handle it. He knocks me off my feet once, but I recover quickly by bracing myself on my fore-arm as I get my legs underneath me to push myself backward, up into a squat. I make sure to keep my other hand up to block any of his blows in the process.

After a while, we both stop and turn to Dan. A feeling of in-competence sweeps over me when I realize I'm panting like a dog while Jason's breathing stays even. I should have taken endurance training more seriously.

Jason says, "I've done enough." Dismissing himself from the center of the clearing, he walks over and sits next to Fredrick.

Dan's eyes are fierce, and I have a feeling he knows Jason was trying to go easy on me. Without changing his expression, he nods to the center of the clearing. "Carter."

The eager expression on Carter's face as he jumps to his feet makes my heart race. There's no hesitation from him—no need for Dan to give him the green light. Carter looks at this as a game, and he's ready to win. Without warning, he charges me, and I have to think fast. Turning to the right, I meet him in the other direction. Fortunately, he's forced to alter his plans with my sudden twist. Even after throwing him off, Carter's next attack comes as swiftly as the first. A strong hit to my stomach leaves me buckled over in pain. He bends low and rushes toward me again, his arms hooking around my legs as he pulls me to the ground.

Carter sees this as a victory, already turning to greet his fans with an overconfident grin.

I know this is my only chance, so I kick the back of Carter's knee from my position on the ground. I have to scramble out of the way before he topples backward and lands where I had been only moments earlier.

I jump to my feet, ready for whatever will come next, but Carter laughs and shakes his head as he holds out a hand for me to help him up. As he exits the center of the clearing, I hear him say, "I fucking love that girl."

Melissa is next, and I try to stifle a groan. Her lessons have always been the worst, and I doubt she'll finally go easy on me with everyone watching. My body begs for a break, but if I quit now, Dan will never consider me as anything more than weak. Closing my eyes, I try to find every ounce of strength in my body. I know this will be the time I need it most.

"Are you ready?" I open my eyes to find Melissa staring at me with a raised eyebrow, her hand on her hip. I take note of the black ink poking out of the waistband of her jeans, where she has the group's symbol tattooed.

Trying to keep my breathing even, I nod.

A sinister smile pulls at her mouth, and I run through everything I've ever learned about fighting. I know I should never turn my back, never assume I know what my opponent is thinking, always remember to block, match her footwork, keep moving, and whatever I do, don't let her get into my head.

Every thought generates too quickly for me to benefit from any of it. Before I know it, Melissa's petite figure comes at me. I try to dodge her, but I'm not fast enough. We connect by way of her fist jabbing me in the stomach. She hits me much harder than a scrimmage warrants. Exhaling a loud breath, I gather as much air around me to rid the wheezing feeling surging through my lungs.

Creating space between us, Melissa prepares to go for my legs—the same way Carter did. She dives, and I push myself backward and flatten to the ground, so she has nothing to grab. Once she's on the ground, I hurry and sprawl onto her back, pinning her. She has used this same move on me more than once, and it feels good to finally be at an advantage. Unfortunately, I make the mistake of internally celebrating early, and she thrusts me off her with one swift movement.

I'm confused when I open my eyes to find her holding out a hand to help me up. I take her offer but keep my untrusting eyes on her to be safe.

Even though Melissa won the round, I can't help feeling relieved at how equal the fight felt. When I first started training, I was her punching bag, but today, for a fleeting moment, I had the upper hand.

"Looks like you've actually learned something." There's an odd satisfaction in Melissa's voice that I don't quite understand.

Is that all it took this entire time? Did she want me to challenge her? Panting and sore, I look up at everyone. Dan stands off to the side, looking pleased. "She's as good as you all were when you started."

I smile at the compliment, and everyone seems impressed with my performance.

Everyone, except Fredrick.

Back at the house, they're all in good spirits. Kelly ordered pizza while we were out. This is only the second time I've had dinner at the Pryce house, but the fact that Luke isn't here makes it better than the first. Part of me is glad Luke showed his true colors. At least I never have to worry about hurting his feelings anymore.

I don't care about how he feels anymore.

Fredrick still won't look at me. I've tried to catch his eye all night, but it's proving impossible. He holds a paper plate with a slice of pizza on it, but he has barely touched his food, and the only person he looks at occasionally is Dan.

Kelly ate a slice with us but has since closed herself off in her bedroom. Nicole and Ben are nowhere to be found, so it's just the pirates and me in the living room. The pizza box rests on the coffee table, and Carter takes another slice. With Fredrick not speaking to me, I've practically glued myself to Carter.

Between bites of pizza, he says, "Man, when you turned the tables on Melissa, I was so excited. If only you could have pinned her. She'd be so pissed right now."

"Maybe it's a good thing I didn't, then," I say as I steal a glance her way. I half expect to find her glaring at me, but she's talking to Dan and Jason about something completely unrelated.

Carter shakes his head. "Oh, she would hate you for it, but she would respect you. I think she already respects you a little more now." He studies his sister from across the room and adds, "Maybe."

I get up from the couch with a laugh. "Doubt it."

When I walk into the kitchen, it's quiet. I throw away my paper plate and open the fridge for some water. Standing against the counter, I take a sip. I still feel tired after today's test and welcome the moment alone.

Fredrick rounds the corner, and I pause mid-sip. He looks mildly surprised like he thought he would be alone. Considering he hasn't looked at me since the clearing, he probably assumed I was still sitting on the couch in the other room.

"Hey," I say quietly.

My voice seems to set him in motion again. "Hey," he says as he makes his way to the refrigerator. I'm standing next to the fridge, and as he opens the door, I can't help noticing the way his shoulder muscles move under his t-shirt. He bends down to get a water bottle from the bottom drawer, and I feel compelled to run my hand down his back to see what it would feel like.

I've come to expect Fredrick to act differently when we're around the group, but he's usually softer when it's the two of us. Not now, though. Even as he steps back with his water bottle in hand, all defenses are up.

I thought he would grab a drink and walk back into the other room without looking back, but he doesn't. He pauses, giving me all of his attention for the first time today, and it makes it harder to think straight.

"Are you okay?" he finally asks. He's still guarded, but at least he's looking at me. The intensity in his eyes makes me grip the bottle of water in my hand tighter.

"I'm okay," I say.

He nods and goes to turn away from me. I don't want him to

leave and go back to acting like I'm not here, so I blurt, "I think Dan was happy with the progress I've made."

He pauses but doesn't turn back to face me. Glancing back at me, he finally says, "That's what I'm afraid of," before walking out of the room.

As luck would have it, Melissa enters the kitchen as Fredrick leaves. She eyes him up and down before she sees me, still standing with my back against the countertop.

I don't realize I'm staring at her until she barks, "What are you looking at?"

"Sorry," I mutter as I look in the direction Fredrick went, but he's already gone.

Melissa follows my gaze over her shoulder, and when she looks back at me, she rolls her eyes. "God, you two are annoying."

"What?" I ask, the confusion obvious in my voice.

She puts a hand on her hip and sighs. "You and him." She nods her head in the direction of the other room.

It suddenly occurs to me why Melissa hates me. My mouth falls open, and I spit out, "Did you two… used to… I mean, if you guys were together at some point—we're just friends." I realize I'm making a mess of this, but luckily, she stops me with a raise of her hand.

"Stop. Just stop." She shakes her head. "There has never been anything between Fredrick and me. He's not my type."

"Oh…" I think for a moment. "So, why do you hate me?"

She laughs, and it confuses me. "You thought I was a jealous ex-girlfriend?"

I shrug and drop my gaze to my bottle of water. For a moment,

I really thought that Melissa and Fredrick had been an item. It would make sense.

"Uh, no," she says sharply. "I don't like how you fuck with his judgment." When I don't say anything, she huffs and continues. "Listen, we have rules, and there aren't supposed to be any exceptions to the rules. Fredrick knows that more than anyone, but for some reason, you're still here."

"I'm sorry, I—"

She cuts me off. "Don't apologize. It is what it is. But if he slips up, it won't just be bad for him. It will be bad for all of us. We can't afford for him to be distracted, and ever since he's met you, that's all he's been."

"I'm not trying to distract—"

"But you do." She raises her eyebrows at me like she's asking me if I understand.

I don't understand, but I swallow whatever questions I may have and nod because I know if I try to say anything, she'll shut me down again.

☠   ☠   ☠

Sitting in Fredrick's Jeep on the ride home, I look over the minimal bruises I acquired during today's test. The thick Jeep tires seem to shape the asphalt as they twist and turn around the sharp bends and narrow lanes of the highway. I don't need to look at the speedometer. I already know he's driving faster than the speed limit.

I don't know why he isn't happy with how the day went. I

thought he would be proud of me for holding my own. We still have a month left of summer to work on my training. If anything, I thought today would make him relieved. If I can make it through a scrimmage with everyone now, I should be twice as good by the end of summer.

"In the kitchen, you said you were afraid of Dan liking what he saw today."

Fredrick gives a slight nod but doesn't take his eyes off the road.

"What are you so worried about?" I ask.

He runs a hand through his hair and sighs. "I've known Dan long enough to know he's hiding something."

My eyebrows pinch in confusion. "But what would that have to do with me?"

He glances over at me, and in a voice devoid of all emotion, answers, "I don't know."

24

The phone rings, waking me from my restless sleep. I hurry to get down the stairs fast enough to answer it and nearly trip. Reaching for the receiver, I answer before the machine picks up.

"Hello?" I answer breathlessly.

"Paige?"

Josh's deep voice surprises me, and I glance at the oven clock to see how long I've slept in. It's only nine-thirty, ridiculously early for Josh to be calling.

"Hey, is everything okay?"

"Yeah, of course… I haven't talked to you since the lake… are you still mad at me?"

His reminder makes me bristle. Not because I'm mad at him, but because I never would have been in that theater with Luke if Josh had taken me home like he was supposed to. "You just left," I say, unsure how to keep my thoughts of Luke at bay.

"I know. I'm sorry. I heard Luke took you home?"

I swallow, and even though Luke technically didn't take me home, I say, "He did."

"How did that go?"

Twisting the phone cord between my fingers, I lean against the kitchen wall. Part of me doesn't want to tell Josh what happened with Luke. Telling him what happened makes it feel too real. The pirates won't see Luke when school starts again. They won't be able to act differently around me when our friends get together. The pirates are a safe enough distance from my regular life. But Josh? Josh *is* my regular life.

"It was fine…" Changing the subject before he can ask more questions, I ask, "Why are you calling so early?"

Thankfully, he drops the topic of Luke and sounds excited on the other end of the phone. "Right! We're going to the beach today, yourself included."

I bite my lip, knowing I will be at the beach today, but for training. "I can't…"

"Why not?" he asks without a trace of suspicion in his voice.

Looking around the house, I try to think of an excuse. I can't go to the beach because of my plans with the pirates, but part of me wouldn't want to go to the beach with him anyway. Luke will probably be there, and he's the last person I want to see. "Dad—he's not feeling well, and um... I don't want to leave him here alone." I hold my breath and wait for him to answer, hoping he believes my poorly delivered lie.

"Damn, alright. Tell the old man I hope he feels better."

I stare down at the ground as guilt washes over me. "Okay, I will." I'm a horrible friend.

"Well, I've got to get ready. I'll see you later, Paige. Try to have fun with the grump-ass."

I let out a light laugh. "You have fun, too."

Heading upstairs, I get ready for my own beach day. Not being home much has its drawbacks, and not doing laundry is one of them. I rummage through the bottom of my drawer and pull out a faded grey school t-shirt from freshman year.

Stopping to check myself in the mirror, I run my hands through my hair and, to help hide how tired I look, add a touch of mascara.

☠ ☠ ☠

The winding beach roads bring comfort in a way I never expected. I hope today's session is more routine than yesterday's. In other words, I hope Dan isn't a part of today's lesson.

I wish I could say that I don't care what Dan thinks of me, but a small part of me does. I don't want him to see me as weak or incapable. He has always doubted me, and I like the idea of proving him wrong.

I'm sitting at a red light next to the public beach parking lot when Josh's eyes meet mine as he lifts a cooler out of his truck. My thoughts go still. The sounds of the radio, ocean, and truck, all fade, replaced by the blood pounding in my ears.

He looks happy to see me until he registers my reaction. My face is hot. I know I look guilty, and that guilt clearly communicates that I'm not here for his beach day with our friends. I'm not here for him at all. I'm here for Fredrick, and I lied about it. I can see his mind going through these steps until he finally lands on the inevitable conclusion. His face goes from happy, to confused, to betrayed in a matter of seconds. At the sight of him looking away and shaking his head, I nearly break down. It isn't until the car behind me honks that I press my foot to the gas too harshly, making my truck lurch through the intersection.

I can't bring myself to look back in my rearview mirror. I don't need to. I can feel Josh's disappointed gaze follow me until I turn out of sight.

Minutes later, I'm parked curbside in front of Fredrick's home. Before getting out of my truck, I sit with my head in my hands and replay the look on Josh's face. Josh is my best friend, and he hates Fredrick—not for bad reasons either. How could I lie to him like I had this morning?

Finally, taking a deep breath, I remove my key from the ignition and step out of the truck, my nerves still on edge. As I walk up the driveway, muffled noises catch my attention. I try to listen and realize voices are coming from inside the house. They don't sound angry, just loud. *Why are they talking so loud?*

Peering through the glass, I slowly knock on the door. It takes a while for anyone to come, but I'm relieved when I see Jason peek around the corner. He sees me, mouths the word "Fuck," and ducks his head back out of sight.

I stand there, feeling baffled. *Maybe I should have gone to the beach with Josh.* Second-guessing if I came here when I wasn't supposed to,

I look up and down the street before turning back to the house. I keep standing there, unsure of what to do.

Finally, Fredrick walks out of the hallway carrying a cardboard box. He looks exhausted. His hair is a mess, and his shoulders don't carry their usual posture. He does a double-take when he sees me standing outside and immediately looks more awake. Setting down the box, he opens the door. "Shit, Paige. What are you doing here?" He doesn't step aside for me to enter the house. Instead, he uses his body to block my view. He looks stressed and tries to smooth his disheveled hair without success.

I hesitate. "Training?" In my mind, I run through our conversation from yesterday, trying to remember if he had told me not to come.

Nope, I'm definitely supposed to be here.

Dan's voice booms louder in the background, and Fredrick's eyes widen. His words come out in a rush. "I'm sorry. I forgot to call you."

I try to crane my neck and look around him, but none of the other pirates come into view. Dan's voice rings out again, and annoyance flickers across Fredrick's face. "Quick, get inside." He grabs my wrist and pulls me through the open doorway.

It doesn't take long to realize why I heard their voices from the driveway. They're yelling across the house to one another. From one end, Dan's voice calls out random household items, and from the other, I can hear the various pirates answering with phrases like:

"Got it!"

"Already packed!"

Or "we need that!"

I look over at Fredrick for an explanation, but he's already carrying his box into the kitchen. I hurry after him, afraid of being left alone as the only person who doesn't have the slightest idea what's happening.

He sets the box on the counter and starts rummaging through the cabinets.

"Fredrick," I say, trying to get his attention. "What's going on?"

He stops and looks at me as if he forgot he had let me into the house. Lightly beating his fist down on the countertop, Fredrick shakes his head. "You know, I knew something was wrong yesterday when he wanted to watch you." He opens one of the kitchen drawers and pulls out a small rag, throwing it into the box.

"What do you mean? What was wrong?"

He doesn't stop packing miscellaneous items as he answers. "Dan. I knew he wasn't telling us something."

"What was he not telling you?" My eyes follow his figure as he moves back and forth between cabinets.

"That we're being challenged. Fucking prick thought it would be better to tell us last fucking minute." He spits out the words like they're hot on his tongue.

I shake my head, trying to make sense of what he's saying. "Wait, what?"

"Challenged," Fredrick growls.

I gape at him, his answer finally sinking in. "By another group? But why? H-how?"

He kneels to open a lower cabinet. "When Carter got caught on the news and broke away from those cops, he must have given some kind of signal to other groups that he wasn't just your everyday shoplifter…" He shakes his head. "but I've seen the tape, and I can't find anything that would have raised suspicion. It doesn't make sense."

I stare at him, unable to blink. "What does this mean?"

Fredrick sighs as he gets to his feet again. "It's fucking barbaric. We meet in a remote place and fight until one group gives up or can no longer fight."

"Do you think you guys will win?"

His eyes harden as he stares down at the box of items. "They have seven, and we have five… It won't be easy."

"What happens if you don't win?"

He runs a hand over his face. "They'll take our territory. We'll either have to join their group and adopt their leader or leave town."

"I want to help." I blurt out the words without thinking, but once they hang between us, I realize how much I mean them.

He finally allows himself to look at me. "No."

I glare back at him. "Why not?"

Fredrick laughs to himself, but his smile is tense. "Paige, you only know the basics."

"Dan said I know as much as you did when you started."

Dropping his gaze, he mutters, "It's different."

"How?" I demand, still glaring at him.

"Will you just drop it?" he says, "I said it's different."

"No, I'm not going to drop it. I'm not useless!"

He rolls his eyes. "I'm not saying you're useless! You don't know what this will be like."

I try to ask my next question without letting my voice rise. "What's so different about this than any other fight? Are they all going to show up with knives and guns or something?"

Fredrick shakes his head, looking serious. "No. No weapons. The Code doesn't allow it."

"What's this code I keep hearing about?" I ask, my hands flying into the air.

Fredrick rubs the back of his neck. "It's a set of rules we all follow… to help keep the peace."

"Well, is there anything in your pirate code that says non-group members can't help with something like this?"

He's distracted and packing the box again. "Yes, but—" He stops mid-sentence.

"But what?" I press.

He doesn't say anything.

"But there's a way for me to help you!"

The sound of footsteps approaching sends Fredrick into action. "Damn it. Come with me." He grabs my wrist and drags me down the hallway. Once we're both in his bedroom, he closes the door behind us. I stay standing where I am and cross my arms. I know if I sit down, he'll tower over me, and I'll lose my confidence. He turns to face me. "Paige, you can't come."

"It's not your decision to make!" He's too stubborn to see how simple this is.

He runs his hand through his hair and snaps, "Didn't you listen to a single word I said the other night? I won't have you get hurt because of me."

I swallow and try to keep my voice strong. "Nothing will happen to me."

He steps around me and pulls a box of first aid items under his bed. "You don't know that. Paige, this isn't going to be like the scrimmage the other day. They won't hold back against you. We have more training and experience and any of us can still get hurt."

"Well, I'm going."

Pausing, he looks up at me with dark eyes. "No, you're not."

"You know what, Fredrick, it's not up to you!" Our eyes stay locked, and the intensity of his stare makes me want to look away, but I refuse to back down. When he remains quiet, I say, "Is this why Dan was there yesterday? Because he thinks I can help?"

My questions take him from stressed to angry in an instant. He stands and kicks the box back under his bed with enough force to make me jump. "I don't give a fuck what Dan thinks. Dan has no say when it comes to you."

I raise an eyebrow. "Oh, but you do? What makes you think you can make decisions for me?"

He tugs at his hair with both hands. "Because I fucking care about you!"

I freeze, the desperation behind his words making my heart race. I watch wide-eyed as he steps toward me, closing the space between us, and I'm forced to look up at him.

"Can't you see that I care about you?" His voice is softer the second time, and his pupils are blown as he stares down at me.

I want to answer, but I can't find the words. My heart thuds in my chest, and my breathing shallows. Fredrick's conflicted eyes search mine for the answer I'm not saying. The longer he looks at me, the harder it is to breathe.

Gently, he holds my face in his hands, and in a fraction of a moment, Fredrick's agonized expression turns to resolve. My eyes fall to his mouth, and my breath catches. "Paige," he says, forcing my attention back to him. His brow furrows like he's not sure how to say what's on his mind. "I don't know what happened… in the theater." Those molten eyes search mine, watching for my reaction. "I want to kiss you, but…" His thumb gently brushes my cheek. "It's up to you. I won't do anything you don't want me to."

My heart goes into overdrive. No one has ever asked before kissing me, but that's exactly what he's doing. He's asking me. He's giving me control, and I don't know why, but my eyes burn because of it.

Fredrick frowns slightly, his concentrated stare reading me too clearly.

Before he can pull away, I put my hands over his, keeping him in place. "I want you to kiss me," I say quietly.

Fredrick moves his thumb over my cheek again, his gaze softening. He leans in, his lips lightly brushing mine, and I feel electricity surge through my entire body. Pulling back, he looks at me, silently checking that I'm okay.

Biting my lip, I nod.

After a brief pause, Fredrick kisses me again, this time with more urgency. The desperation in his voice moments ago, now matched by his lips moving over mine, and I'm lost in him. I clench my fists around the material of his t-shirt and pull him closer to me. He steps forward, gently pressing me against his bedroom door, and my body is on fire at his touch.

I want more.

More of this.

More of *him*.

He breaks the kiss, and his entire demeanor has changed. The corner of his mouth quirks, and he seems more relaxed. His face is still inches from mine as I struggle to catch my breath.

He rests his forehead against mine. "I mean it, Paige. If someone hurts you, I'll lose my fucking mind."

I nod—it's the only response I can generate. After a moment, Fredrick steps back, allowing me to move away from the door. He sits on the edge of his bed and rubs the back of his neck. I notice his cheeks are flushed, and knowing our kiss affected him makes me bite back a smile. "Honestly, having you there tomorrow would only distract me."

I blink. "Wait, *tomorrow?*"

Fredrick rubs his hand over his face. "I told you, Dan let us know last minute."

My head spins with the new information, the aftershock of the kiss, or both. I know Fredrick doesn't want me to help, but I can't sit back and do nothing. I need unbiased opinions. "I'll be right back."

Fredrick's eyebrows pull together in confusion. "Where are you going?"

"I just want to think about this for a minute."

I don't allow him to say anything else. Leaving his room, I'm glad when I see the living room packed with the pirates and the Pryce family—exactly who I want to see. Everyone stops talking when they hear me approach, and all eyes turn to me.

Ben grins at the sight of me. "You guys haven't scared her off yet?"

I ignore his comment and take a deep breath, gathering my nerves. I don't expect Fredrick to stay in the room for long, so I get straight to the point. "I want to help."

Everyone's eyes collectively glance behind me, and I know Fredrick must be standing there.

It takes me a moment to take in their expressions. Melissa looks like I'm wasting her time, Carter has a proud smile on his face, Jason looks deep in thought, and Ben and Nicole look surprised. Dan seems pleased, giving me hope. If I can get Dan on board, everyone will have to listen to him—even Fredrick.

I hesitate before looking at Kelly. I know her reaction will hit me the hardest. She looks even more petite with so many people in the room. The only person smaller than her is Melissa, and that's only if you don't count Melissa's attitude. When I finally meet Kelly's gaze, it's only for a moment. Pity is her reaction. I had expected anger or concern, but pity?

Kelly steps forward and places a hand on my shoulder, her eyes searching mine. "I know you do, hun, but I'm afraid you don't grasp how dangerous these people can be."

I shake her off and step back. "No, I do, and I still want to help."

No one says anything, and all eyes are past me and glued to Fredrick. I expect him to say something, but the voice I hear comes from the crowd standing in front of me.

"So, come if you want to."

At first, I assume the statement came from Dan, but everyone's eyes tell me otherwise. They're all looking at Jason, who shifts his weight, looking uncomfortable. "If you want to go, go. Do whatever the hell you want."

My jaw tightens when everyone looks past me at Fredrick again. It's not like he's my keeper.

"I don't see any reason why she shouldn't go," Dan says in an authoritative tone. "I like what I saw yesterday. She probably has more experience than any of you did at your first fight. I mean, think about it, she's already fought off the girl who attacked her, and that was before she had any training."

I let out a sigh of relief, knowing Dan will help me gain everyone's approval.

"She doesn't know nearly enough to be involved in a claim." Melissa has no problem talking about me as if I'm not standing in front of her.

"A claim?" I instantly regret my question when I see the critical look on her face.

She's looking at me as if I asked how to operate a telephone. "See, she doesn't even know what she wants to fight in."

Carter scoffs at his sister. "Like she's ever heard someone call it that before." He smiles at me. "Don't listen to her, babe."

Melissa rolls her eyes. "My point is, she hasn't been taught how to fight in this situation. She didn't even know what it was called."

Nicole smiles at me. "I wish I could go, so I say go for it."

I beam at her appreciatively.

Kelly's expression holds nothing but sadness at the sound of her daughter's words. I'm sure the thought of having another child involved in this lifestyle is enough to send her over the edge.

Ben must sense this as well because he walks over to Kelly and puts an arm around her shoulder. "Come on, Mom. You look like you're about to break down or something."

Kelly shakes her head but allows Ben to lead her into the other room, and I can't take my eyes off them.

Once they're in the other room, Ben calls out, "Nicole, get in here."

She frowns but sighs and follows her mom and brother out of sight.

With Fredrick's family gone, I'm left with only the pirates. Looking around the room, I realize I already have most of them on my side without Dan having to convince them. For the first time since walking out here, I dare to look back at Fredrick. He casually leans against the wall, deep in thought. I'm again caught off guard by how good he looks, even in this tired state. Thoughts of his lips on mine fog my focus, and I find myself wishing I had stayed in the room with him a little longer. He's the person I want to sail smoothly with, yet here I am, making waves.

Fredrick's eyes find mine, and I look away. I hadn't realized I was staring.

"Paige, why do you want to fight?" At the sound of Fredrick's voice, I look up to meet his gaze again. He doesn't look angry like I thought he might. That's a good sign, I guess.

I lean against the opposite wall and try to gather my thoughts. Finally, I say, "You went above and beyond to help me." I look around the room at the other pirates. "You all did. Most of you were helping me before you even met me. You kept me safe when I didn't realize I was in danger. You watched over my home, looked out for my dad, and—as if that weren't enough—you've all dedicated your time to teach me how to better myself." I look back at Fredrick. "What type of person would I be if I didn't return the favor?"

Melissa scoffs. "I don't know. Maybe a smarter one than you're being now." She looks around, waiting for someone else to piggyback her comment, but everyone stays quiet. She huffs, "I don't have time for this." With a final, judgmental glance my way, she leaves the room.

When we hear her slamming cabinets, Carter grimaces. "I better go defuse the bomb."

I'm not sure what Carter's definition of *defuse* is because he can be heard scolding his sister in the other room. "You're a real pain, you know that?"

"Don't be stupid, Carter; you know she shouldn't come."

"I know, but—ugh, never mind, Melissa. Just know that you're a real pain in the ass."

"If being a pain means being the only one with common sense, fine."

Jason clears his throat. "I better tell them we can hear what they're saying…" His voice trails off as he rushes into the kitchen.

Only Fredrick, Dan, and I remain. I had almost forgotten about Dan's presence. I'm not used to him being so… quiet. This is the first time I've realized how tired he looks too. He eyes Fredrick and shrugs. "I figure you're the one who took her in, so this one is up to you."

Not the delegation I had hoped for.

Dan leaves the room, and I mutter, "He's wrong."

"About what?" Fredrick asks in a low voice.

I look up at him but keep my voice down. "It's not up to you. Shouldn't I be able to make my own decision?"

He considers this for a moment and slowly says, "Yes, but not with something like this. I need you to trust me."

"But—"

With a stern shake of his head, Fredrick cuts me off. "I want you to go home, and I don't want you to come back here until I call you."

"You want me to leave?" I hate how wounded I sound.

Fredrick's jaw ticks, but after holding my stare for a beat, he nods. "Yeah."

My eyes narrow, and without another word, I march outside to my truck. I'm about to open my driver's side door when I feel him catch my wrist in his hand. I try to shake him off, but it's no use. Spinning around, I don't try to hide my frustration. "*What?*"

"Promise me, Paige."

His eyes are too intense for me, so I look away as I open the truck door and get inside. Right before I slam the door, I answer his request. "I'll think about it."

25

For the rest of the day, my mind swirls in a fog. To help the pirates or not to help the pirates. They're not just *the pirates* anymore. They've become my friends throughout the summer—maybe not Dan and Melissa, but the rest. I may not have strong feelings about keeping their territory, but I don't want them hurt in tomorrow's fight because they're outnumbered. Then again, if my being there will only distract Fredrick, I don't want to be the reason he gets hurt, either.

Leah has tried to call the house a few times, but I've been avoiding her. I know she'll try to get to the bottom of what happened this morning with Josh. I should talk to Josh about everything, but I have no idea what to say to him.

When Dad and I ate dinner, he kept the conversation going, so I only had to nod and react appropriately. Now that I think about it, I'm not even sure what he talked about. Even as he enthusiastically went on and on about… something… I could only think of the elusive *them* and what they're up against. Imagining the pirates preparing for what's to come while I'm stuck here eating pork chops leaves me restless.

I try to read before bed, but my eyes keep scanning the same sentence. I'm reading the words on the page, but my brain reels with other thoughts until I set down the book and fall into an uneasy sleep.

I don't know how long I've been asleep when I hear a tap on my window, making me jolt upright. I wait, listening for the sound again. Another knock comes, and I jump to my feet. Inching my way toward the window, I whisper, "Fredrick?"

"No…" The voice trails off, and I stop in my tracks until I hear, "It's Jason."

My eyebrows pinch as I slide open the window for him.

Jason may be taller than most, but he has no problem climbing through the window. Before I know it, he's standing in the middle of my bedroom, smirking at me. "Why did you think I was Fredrick? Does he come in through your window at night or something?"

"What? No. I'm just tired." My cheeks flush, and I'm thankful for the dark. "What time is it anyway?"

"A little before five."

I guess I slept longer than I thought. It feels like it's still the middle of the night, not the early morning.

Rubbing my eyes, I ask, "What are you doing here?"

Jason sighs. "I don't know what's going on between you and

Fredrick, but he's acting irrationally. We need your help."

Taking a seat on my bed, I say, "What do you mean he's being irrational? Dan didn't seem to think I'd be much help, either—considering he left the decision up to Fredrick." The bitterness in my voice surprises me.

Jason scoffs. "Dan doesn't want to get his ass chewed out by Fredrick again. He flipped the fuck out when Dan waited so long to tell us what was happening."

I finally say what's been on my mind for weeks. "It doesn't seem like Dan is a good leader."

Jason lets out a forced laugh. "He's not. The only one who could make him step down is Fredrick, but he won't do it."

His words pique my interest. "He won't?"

He shakes his head. "Fredrick doesn't even want to be in this as much as he is; there's no way he would go deeper."

My conversation with Fredrick about his dad and keeping his family safe comes to mind.

"Do you really think I can help?"

"It's a numbers game at this point." His expression is thoughtful. "They have more people than us, and I think you can hold your own well enough to not die."

I laugh because I think he's joking, but his stern expression doesn't crack. Recovering quickly, I ask what the next step is.

"Get changed," he says. "Dark jeans are good if they're not too tight and you can move in them. Wear a dark shirt, too. Do you think you can make it out of the house without waking your dad?"

I nod. "Yeah, but I'll have to leave a note." I try to think of an excuse, but it's early, and I'm tired, and I come up with nothing.

As if reading my mind, Jason walks back over to the window. "Pick a friend and say that friend dragged you out for a midnight movie showing or something and that you're sleeping over after. Say you'll be gone most of the day. Meet me at the end of your driveway. I'll wait for you there."

Without another word, he ducks out of the window and disappears.

I stand there, stunned. *Did that really just happen? Am I even awake right now?* It takes me a moment to shift my mind into gear, but I do as I'm told.

Using Jason's template for an excuse is easier than I thought. I tell my dad that Leah insisted I go with her to the midnight release of the newest Harry Potter book. The release was last week, but it's close enough to make it believable. My father knows that Leah and I both read the books too, so that helps.

I change into a black t-shirt and my darkest pair of functional jeans. Ready to go, I hold my breath as I tiptoe to the staircase and make my way down the wooden steps. Luckily, I dodge the areas that creak, only leading to squeaks here and there.

If my dad hears me walking down the stairs, it wouldn't concern him anyway. He would probably assume I was getting a glass of water or something. The front door poses another challenge altogether. Even though Fredrick seems to have no issue opening this door without a sound, I haven't been able to master it.

My palm sweats against the metal doorknob, and I hold my breath until I hear the faint *click* of the latch coming undone. As slow as I can, I push the door open. My ears strain for any sound coming from my dad's bedroom, but it's impossible to distinguish anything over my rapidly beating heart. I only open the door wide enough for my body to slip through. With shaking hands, I close the door behind me and cut across the grass, making sure to duck under my father's window.

Jason waits for me at the end of the driveway like he said he would. "Took you long enough." He doesn't wait for me to respond. "Come on. We need to go."

I struggle to keep up with him. "Are we late?"

"No, we're early." Giving me a sideways glance, he chuckles. "But Fredrick will lose his shit when I show up with you, so we need enough time for that."

"Oh," is all I can bring myself to say. He's right. Fredrick is going to be furious with me.

I swallow at the thought.

We reach Jason's silver Toyota Corolla parked on the street, away from my house. He opens the driver's side door and pauses to look at me. Seeming to read my thoughts, he says, "Paige, I can handle Fredrick."

Biting the inside of my cheek, I can't help doubting him. Instead of voicing my concerns, I nod and get in the car.

Jason and I don't talk most of the drive, and the silence only heightens my anxiety. As I gaze out the window, I keep playing out hypotheticals in my head of how Fredrick will react. I can see this going one of two ways: he'll either be angrier than I've ever seen him, or he'll be so wrapped up in everything going on, he won't have the energy to fight this. I hope it's the latter, but the knot in my stomach suggests otherwise.

It's barely six in the morning, but the lights are on in Fredrick's house when we arrive. I take a deep breath and step out of the car.

Before I've closed the passenger door, Fredrick storms out of the house. "What the fuck is she doing here?" He snaps at Jason as he gestures toward me with an outstretched arm.

Jason holds his hands up as Fredrick marches straight for him. "You know we need her. We can't lose this over something as stupid as being outnumbered. We have to do what's best for—"

Jason's sentence is cut short by Fredrick grabbing fistfuls of his shirt and slamming him against the car. "She's not supposed to be here!" Keeping Jason pinned in place, Fredrick's eyes look past him and land on me. I stare at him wide-eyed, unable to look away. "Paige, go inside." His voice is tight, and I know he's struggling to control himself.

I don't move. He's looking at Jason the same way he looked at Luke in the movie theater, and I'm afraid of what he might do.

"Get in the house, Paige!"

The sheer shock of being yelled at only makes it more impossible to move. His eyes jump to me again, his expression softening. Dropping his shoulders, Fredrick runs a frustrated hand over his face. "Please, Paige. Go in the house."

My chest rises and falls as I watch the two of them, my eyes jumping from Jason to Fredrick. Nodding, I turn around and hurry toward the house. I'm halfway up the walkway when Dan flings open the front door, stopping me in my tracks.

He looks at the two guys struggling near the car, and then at me. "Shit," he mutters and heads down the driveway to pull Fredrick off Jason. As his hand lands on Fredrick's shoulder, Fredrick shakes him off. "Calm the fuck down. You're drawing attention to us, asshole."

Dan's words must trigger something inside him because Fredrick gives Jason one last shove against the side of the car before dropping his hold.

Dan's shoulders relax. "We'll deal with this inside."

Fredrick paces up the driveway, passing me without acknowledging my presence. I flinch when the door slams behind him, and my eyes turn to Jason and Dan, still standing in the driveway, looking bewildered.

"Let's go." I jump at the sound of Fredrick slamming the front door again. Now, with keys in hand, he grabs my hand and pulls me down the driveway toward his Jeep.

My sneakers skid against the pavement as I try to pull away from him. "Fredrick, stop."

He pivots, and his eyes pierce into me. "You promised."

"No, I didn't!"

He runs a stressed hand through his hair. "I'll take you home. We still have time."

Dan approaches with Jason close behind. "I said we can deal with this inside," he says with gritted teeth.

Fredrick stares at Dan for a long moment, his jaw clenched like he's debating what to do. "Fine." He places his hand on the small of my back, his hand shaking with anger. He must notice this because he moves his hand to my waist and squeezes me a little tighter to steady himself.

As soon as we're inside, Fredrick lets go of me and turns on Jason. "What the hell are you thinking bringing her here?"

Jason's mouth is a thin line as he speaks. "I'm thinking of what's best for the group, and we need her."

"He's right," Dan adds, squaring his shoulders.

Fredrick fumes as he looks at both of them, but he doesn't say anything.

I want to speak up, but I don't want him to yell again. I look at Jason for help, but his eyes stay locked on Fredrick.

Finally, Fredrick turns to me. "So, this is it then. You're coming?"

I look up at him, sinking my teeth into my bottom lip, and I nod.

Without saying a word, he nods and walks out of sight into the kitchen. As soon as he's in the other room, I hear him hit his fist against the countertop.

Bringing my concerned gaze back to Dan and Jason, Dan keeps his composure and says, "I'll handle him."

After he leaves, Jason and I look at each other with uncertainty. Scratching the scruff on his cheek, Jason sighs. "Well, that didn't go well."

I let out a breath of laughter even though my chest is tight.

Jason lets out a slow whistle. "I've never seen him like that." He eyes me up and down. "What have you done to him?"

My cheeks flush, and I shake my head, equally baffled.

Jason laughs at my clueless response. "Come on. We still need to gather a few things from the pharmacy."

I tilt my head. "The pharmacy?"

He walks to the other end of the house to a room I've never been in before. Looking over his shoulder, he says, "Yeah, that's what we call Kelly's bathroom."

"Why do you call it the pharmacy?" I ask as I follow him.

"Well, as you probably already know, Kelly used to be a nurse, so she has a lot of medical stuff." His last sentence comes out rushed.

I didn't know Kelly used to be a nurse, but I also don't find it surprising. She has the perfect bedside manner for it. I'm about to ask Jason why she isn't a nurse anymore, but I'm distracted by the stunning room we've walked into.

The master bedroom isn't huge, but the walls are lined with windows like the rest of the house. The large bed in the middle looks perfect with a collection of throw pillows. It looks like something out of a magazine with rich walnut furniture and touches of ivory and sage green. Even though the sun has barely risen, I can imagine how beautiful the room must look when it's full of light.

We walk into Kelly's bathroom, and I understand the nickname. A collection of pill bottles lines the countertop, and I find the sheer quantity alarming. I soon learn that the bottles on display are nothing compared to the different medications, ointments, creams, and bandages that fill her bathroom closet.

Jason doesn't touch the bottles on the counter as if they're off-limits. *Are they off-limits because Kelly uses them regularly?* The thought makes me uneasy.

Jason must notice my eyes lingering on the bottles because he says, "Those are mostly holistic supplements now that she's in—well, now that she's more holistic."

My eyes scan over the collection of bottles again. "Holistic supplements for what?"

Shrugging, he says, "Life, I guess?" He reaches far back into the closet. "This is what I was looking for." He holds it up for me to see.

I raise my eyebrows at him. "Really? Hydrocortisone Cream?"

Jason looks at the tube in his hand with an enthusiastic nod. "Hell yeah. One time, we camped out, and I got poison ivy. I'll never go into the woods without this stuff again."

I let out a laugh and gesture to the room we're in. "Out of all the stuff in here, that's all you need?"

He reaches into the closet once more and shakes a bottle of pills. "And the extra-strength Ibuprofen." Tossing and catching the pills, he adds, "We got most of the serious stuff together yesterday. These two are just my personal favorites."

"Where is Kelly anyway?" I've been so preoccupied with Fredrick's reaction to my arrival, I didn't even notice her absence until now.

Jason pockets the small bottle of pills before answering. "She doesn't like to be here for stuff like this, and she doesn't like it when Nicole and Ben witness our shit. Mostly Nicole for obvious reasons. They all went into the bait shop early today."

"Nicole wants to be a part of the group, doesn't she?" The

question only now occurs to me, but I think I've known the answer since meeting her.

Jason's face hardens. "Yeah, but it will never happen. Kelly won't let her get caught up in this. Fredrick got into it without her knowing, and then by the time he told her, she figured the best way to help was creating a safe place for us to go." Scanning The Pharmacy one more time, he gives a sharp nod. "Let's get back out there. The others should be back soon."

His comment reminds me that I haven't seen Melissa or Carter since I got here. "Where are they?"

"Bagel run." He laughs under his breath. "I told Melissa to include you in the headcount, and she looked like she wanted to bitch-slap me. Hopefully, she brings you back something."

Even though it's still early, my stomach feels empty after being awake for so long, and I hope she does too.

Back in the family room, Fredrick and Dan are nowhere to be found. I turn to Jason and say, "I'm going to see if I can find Fredrick."

He nods as he places his two newly collected items into what I assume is the general first aid box.

I'm relieved when I reach the end of the hallway and see that Fredrick's bedroom door is open. He sits on the edge of his bed with his head in his hands. Feeling unsure, I timidly knock on the door frame, and his eyes lift to meet mine.

I keep my voice low, not wanting to be overheard by anyone else in the house. "I just wanted to see how you were doing."

Holding my gaze for a beat too long, he says, "I've been better."

I carefully enter the room and sit next to him on the edge of his bed. "I'm sorry."

Fredrick shakes his head, his eyes falling back to the ground. "It's not your fault. I figured this might happen. I just didn't want it to."

Taking a deep breath, I say, "I want to ask you something, but I don't want you to get mad."

Fredrick's eyes meet mine. "Well, I'm already mad, so you might as well ask."

His response isn't exactly the vote of confidence I had been hoping for. I look down at my hands. "Does the reason you steal have something to do with your mom?"

Fredrick doesn't shut down like I expected him to, but his face pales slightly. "What did Jason say?"

I shake my head. "Nothing. He showed me her bathroom." I hesitate before continuing. "He said she used to be a nurse, but something felt off."

Fredrick's face hardens for a moment. Finally, he sighs. "When I was thirteen, my dad left. That was hard. But then, a few months later, my mom was diagnosed with breast cancer. Ben tried to get a hold of my dad, but that proved to be impossible, and I was worried about what type of trouble he'd bring back with him anyway. Even with the help we got from the hospital, we were barely getting by. No one would hire me because I was too young, so when I met Dan and Jason, and they offered me money and security, I jumped at the opportunity to join them."

"Is Kelly…"

He finishes my sentence for me with a nod. "In remission."

I sigh out a breath. "I'm sorry. I had no idea."

Fredrick gives me a faint smile. "I would have told you. It's just not my favorite thing to talk about." He shrugs. "I guess it's better that you know."

We're interrupted by Carter's voice bellowing throughout the house with his best attempt at a New York accent. "Bagels are heeya! Get ya bagels!"

Fredrick stares in the direction of Carter's voice and shakes his head. "We better go out there."

When Carter sees me trailing behind Fredrick, his face lights up. "Well, hey there, beautiful!"

Fredrick looks over his shoulder to roll his eyes at me but doesn't say anything. He walks over to the kitchen table and grabs a bagel from the bag.

Melissa's eyes dart from Fredrick to me in disbelief. She puts her hand on her hip and directs her question to him. "You're seriously letting this happen?"

Fredrick responds by shrugging her off. He starts to spread cream cheese on his bagel without a word.

Walking back to the bag, she reaches for a bagel and tosses it to me.

I catch it and look back at her, feeling confused. "Thanks?"

"Trust me, you'll need it."

2 6

We all pile into Kelly's van, stuffed full of anything we may need. I have no idea why or how we might need a jar of coconut oil or the other seemingly random items the pirates have collected, but I trust they have a good reason.

Dan drives, and Melissa rides shotgun. She insisted. The middle row holds Jason and Fredrick, and Carter and I sit in the back. Carter leans over the seat in front of us to tell Jason and Fredrick about a new girl he has been dating. He made sure to preface the conversation by looking back at me and saying, "Don't worry. I'm just killing time until you're ready for me." Which made me laugh, but I had stopped paying attention to the conversation since then.

I lean my head against the window and can't stop thinking about Kelly. A new, even stronger dislike for Fredrick's father wells inside me—even though I've never met him. I can't imagine how lost the Pryce children must have felt back then with their father gone and their mother sick. I can see how a thirteen-year-old Fredrick may have found solace under Dan's wing.

Glancing over at the guys talking, I notice Fredrick watching me, his brow furrowed with concern. I give him a faint smile of reassurance. I know he's worried about how I've been handling everything and how I'll handle what's coming next. If I'm honest, I'm concerned too.

Melissa turns down the radio to make herself heard. "Okay, we need to go over everything we know about the other group."

Dan nods. "They have seven members." He shrugs. "We don't know much more than that."

"We know this is only happening because Carter is a horn dog," Jason says dryly.

Carter leans forward and playfully pushes Jason. "Don't be jealous."

Fredrick keeps his eyes on me as he addresses the group. "I did some digging, and even though they're older, they don't have their own territory. That's why they're so interested in ours. They might be a newer group. If that's the case, we can use it to our advantage."

The other members comment on this, but Fredrick keeps his eyes on me. He raises his eyebrows, and I give him a slight nod to signal my understanding. For the rest of the drive, I look out the window and focus on my breathing—trying to get a grip on my nerves.

After driving for nearly an hour, we turn down an obscure dirt road. Dan follows the bumpy, winding path until the trees on both sides are overgrown. No one has been back here in a while. Eventually, the trees become too thick for the van, and Dan says, "This is as far as we can go. We'll have to kill time here. We have a little over an hour before we need to walk to the clearing."

I sit up straight and look around, but all I see is the forest. "Have you all been here before?"

Carter answers my question. "About a year ago, we had another group challenge us. They were less of a threat, but we met them here too."

"Oh, okay." I'm not sure why, but the fact that they've been here before eases my mind a bit.

We unload the essentials from the van: mostly snacks, water bottles, and bug spray at this point. As I'm setting down a box of granola bars, Fredrick walks over with his hands in his pockets. "Take a walk with me?"

I look around at everyone else. "Don't we need to help?"

He lets out a light laugh. "This is it, Paige. Now we wait."

As I look around, I can see that he's right. Carter and Jason have set up a pop-up table and shuffle a deck of cards while Melissa stretches. nearby, and Dan paces the clearing looking grim.

Fredrick watches me study the others. "We all have our ways of preparing. Come on. I want to show you something."

"Okay," I say as he leads me away from everyone else.

The sun hides today, adding to my impending feeling of doom. As I walk in the wake of Fredrick's footsteps, I find myself hyperaware of every noise. The squirrels, the breeze, and the leaves crunching beneath my feet all add to my anxiety. It looks like there was a trail here once upon a time, but now we're left with a snaking line of sand hugged by ominous bushes.

Fredrick glances back at me. "It's just up ahead."

I can't imagine what he could want to show me out here. It seems like no one has been back here in decades. Regardless of the direction I look, we're surrounded by nothing but trees. We walk for another minute or so, and then I see it. The trees thin, and in front of us stands a massive plantation house. It's abandoned, but that doesn't make it any less impressive. The house has two-story columns covered in vines that line the front of the once white estate. Steps lead to an elevated front porch flanked by a decorative railing on either side. I'm surprised to see it doesn't look vandalized, but then again, I'm not sure anyone would even know it's back here.

I stare at the sight ahead of me in awe. "How did you find this?" I can't break my eyes away from the old house.

I can feel Fredrick's eyes on me as he answers. "Like I said, everyone has their way of preparing. I usually take a walk to clear my head. The last time we were here, I found this. We can't get inside, I've tried, but the best part is over here anyway."

He walks out of the forest in the direction away from the house. I had been too busy looking at the architecture to notice the lake. Near the edge of the water are two things: an old weeping willow, and a white gazebo, also in a state of decay. Like the house, its neglect hasn't hindered its beauty. Much like the rest of the property, overgrown grass lines the edge of the lake, allowing it to sway in the breeze.

Fredrick steps onto the gazebo and extends a hand to help me do the same. The view of the water and nearby willow is breathtaking. I can only imagine how beautiful this scene must be with more sunlight.

"This is amazing," I say as I take in the view.

Fredrick rests his forearms on the railing as he overlooks the water. "I thought you'd like it."

After a moment of silence, I turn to him. "Thank you."

He gives me a questioning look. "For what?"

I look out at the water again, but I can feel his eyes on me. "I know you didn't want me here. I guess I'm just glad you're not shutting me out."

"I didn't want you here because I wanted you to be safe. Now that you're here, holding on to my anger would only make things worse." Looking over at him, I see his expression darken, and my thoughts flash back to Dan saying he would *handle* Fredrick back at the house. I can't help wondering if he's repeating the words that were spoken to him.

"Well, I appreciate it," is all I can think to say.

Fredrick turns to face me. "Paige, I may not like your being here, but you're a good fighter. Once we meet up with the other group, make sure you don't let your guard down. We don't know what we're dealing with. Remember to use your non-dominant hand to block—sometimes you forget. And make sure you breathe while you're out there. Your reflexes will suffer if you don't remember to keep a steady—"

I don't know what comes over me, but at that moment, I kiss him. He seems taken aback at first, but I feel him lightly laugh against my lips. He leans into me, suddenly serious, and my body melts against his. The stress and anxiety tied to today unravel as he grazes my bottom lip with his tongue. My breath catches, and when my lips part, I feel his tongue slide over mine. The only person to ever kiss me like this was Luke. With him, it felt invasive, but when Fredrick does it, my knees go weak.

My back rests against the railing, and Fredrick's lips move down to the base of my neck. He takes his time, working his way to below my ear, and a soft sound escapes my throat. Embarrassment clouds my mind, but as soon as the sound escapes me, Fredrick pauses, and his grip on my waist tightens. He pulls away and gently kisses my lips before letting the corner of his mouth quirk. "See, I knew you'd be a distraction."

My head falls against his chest, and I let out a laugh. "Right. Sorry." Taking a step back, my lips twist as I try to fight my smile. "What were you saying?"

He smiles, and it's one of the rare, real ones. My heart flutters at the sight, and it takes all of my self-control not to kiss him again.

Luckily, he nods and goes back to giving me pointers for the fight.

Eventually, Fredrick tells me it's time to go back. At the edge of the trees, I look back at the peaceful lake view and hope I can hold on to this feeling. I know everything is about to change.

The thickening clouds provide little light as we follow the abandoned trail back to the others. At some parts, I lose sight of the path completely, but Fredrick always seems to know where to go.

I'm more relaxed now, and maybe that's why I don't notice it right away when our footsteps are joined by others. Fredrick stops dead in his tracks, and I try to perk my ears to listen. At first, I don't hear anything, but I notice the sound of walking lingers after both of us have stopped. Fredrick glances at me for a fraction of a second, and that's all it takes for me to know something is wrong.

I don't have time to consider what's happening because I'm slammed to the ground. When I roll over, someone jumps on top of me, holding me down. I look up into the eyes of my attacker, and it feels like all the air has left the forest. Staring down at me with loathing are the sinister green eyes of a girl with a now slightly crooked nose. I can't tear my eyes away from her nose. Seeing the damage I caused all those weeks ago distracts me from realizing the reality of her being here.

The corners of her mouth pull up into a small smile. "Surprised to see me?"

Her voice snaps me back to the present, and I frantically look around her for any sign of Fredrick. I can't see him anywhere. But I can hear him struggling with someone. I kick the girl in the stomach from my position on the ground, causing her to stagger backward off me. Getting to my feet, I scan my surroundings and see Fredrick pinning someone against a nearby tree. The man's beady eyes find mine, and I feel sick. The rat-like man sneers at me the same way he did the night he broke into my house. Fredrick follows the guy's gaze over his shoulder to me, and his face falls. "Paige!"

I spin around in time to block the girl's attack. My fist catches her in the ribs, and I hear her curse under her breath. I can see something moving off to the side, but I don't have time to look at what it might be because I have to block a blow from the girl headed straight for my face. I notice fighting her feels different now. Her movements seem slower than they did the night we fought in the bed of my truck. I can see what's coming and think quickly enough to respond in a more calculated way.

She tries to aim for my face again, and I have a feeling she's trying to even the score for her broken nose. I duck under her swing and hook my leg around hers. She falls to the ground with a thud but grabs my ponytail on the way down. I make sure to block my face now that I know what her target is. Using my free hand, I grab her hair and pull as hard as I can, giving her a taste of her own pain. Blocking my face with one hand and gripping her hair with the other, I use my leg to kick her.

Someone new grabs me from behind, putting me in a headlock and releasing me from the girl's grasp. I can't see who he is, but as he holds me in place, I try to comprehend everything happening around me. Fredrick works on fighting off two guys at once, but it's obvious he's starting to struggle. In the past, watching Fredrick fight usually meant watching him deliver most of the blows, but now my chest aches as I watch him buckle over in pain more than once. I groan when I see more figures coming through the trees to where we are. There's no way we can escape so many of them.

It isn't until I realize the new figures belong to Dan, Jason, Melissa, and Carter that I feel the slightest bit of hope. None of them waste time diving into the action. Melissa immediately goes for Misty, Jason runs over to Fredrick and takes on one of the two guys he had been battling alone, and Dan and Carter take on three more pirates from the opposing group.

I try to escape my opponent's grip, but the more I squirm, the tighter he holds me against him. The way his arms wrap around me feels uncomfortably intimate. I can feel his hot breath against my ear, making me cringe. "Now, how is it that a pretty little thing like you has caused so much trouble?"

I claw the back of his forearm, but it's no use. Even though he's not choking me, I'm still reminded of the rat-like man's hands around my neck all those nights ago. My breathing becomes shallow as panic takes over.

The man's voice sounds in my ear again, making me want to vomit. "Maybe you and I should go somewhere, so I can teach you how pretty girls are supposed to behave." His rough hands slide under the hem of my shirt, and I tense. His hand grazes across my bare stomach as he walks backward, dragging me further away from the fight.

Fredrick no longer battles with the rat-man. He's now fighting a tall guy with bright red hair. As I watch him, I'm reminded of what he said to me at the gazebo. *Remember to breathe.* Fredrick's voice rings through my thoughts, and I force myself to take a deep breath. At first, the panic has its nails dug into me too deeply, but after a few concentrated efforts, I start thinking more clearly.

My captor still drags me further away from the fight, but now I'm reminded of a lesson I had with Carter. It was weeks ago, but Carter had put me in a headlock from behind. I remember him teasing me about my hate for strength training. With his arm wrapped around my neck, he had said, "Sometimes it's not about strength. It's about movement. If you can outmaneuver someone, you'll be fine."

Remembering Carter's words gives me the extra boost of confidence I need. I elbow my attacker and use my free hand to twist his pinky finger as hard as I can. He howls out in pain. "You bitch!" Hooking my ankle around the back of his, he stumbles backward. I fall too, but I'm able to get out of his grip in the process. I try to crawl back toward the fight, but he grabs my ankle. I turn over, trying to kick myself free, but he takes it as an opportunity to hold his body over mine.

I stare upward, and for the first time, I can see his face. He has light brown hair and large brown eyes. His pointed chin makes me think he may be related to the rat man, but he was fortunate enough to get human eyes. I struggle to get free, but he has me pinned down. He growls, "You're going to regret that." His fist connects with my cheek, and I yell out in pain. The blow disorients me, and I squeeze my eyes shut, anticipating another hit. *Breathe, Paige. Breathe.* I repeat the words in my head like a mantra. I know if I blackout, I'm done. He drags me further again, my back scraping against the wooded floor. I know I'm being scratched and cut, and I know those scratches and cuts should probably hurt, but all I can think about is how far he's taking me from the others. We stop moving, and he kicks me in the stomach, making me roll over and gasp for air. I scramble to my feet and run, but he grabs hold of my ankle, and I land hard on the ground again.

"Not so fast, sweetheart."

I can't see the fight anymore. I can hear it, but I can't see any-one. I'm alone with this man who wants to hurt me, and I'm starting to think Carter was wrong. Maneuvering isn't everything. Some-times you just need brute strength.

In a final, futile attempt to get free, I lift my head as fast as I can and head-butt my attacker's face. We never went over how to properly head-butt someone during training, so my head falls back to the ground throbbing, but I hear the man curse in pain as well.

When I open my eyes, fresh blood drains from his nose, and I feel nauseous.

"Fuck!" He yells as he brings a hand to his face, the other still holding me firmly in place.

I try to look away, but his face is inches from mine, and there's nowhere else to look. I twist my body to try and get out from under him, but he has me pinned with his knees. He's rougher with me than he was before. His hand runs over my chest and down my body until his fingers slide into the waistband of my jeans. I try to turn out of his reach, but it only makes him press me into the ground harder. He yanks at the button of my jeans, and my pants loosen. I squeeze my eyes shut and try to squirm away from him, but it's no use.

My eyes fly open when I feel his weight pulled off me. At first, I don't see anything other than the dark thundering sky above, but when I look to my right, I see them. Fredrick sits over my attacker, punching him relentlessly. He doesn't stop to see how effective his last hit was before delivering another blow to the man's face. I watch open-mouthed, unable to look away.

"Fredrick, stop!" The words come from Dan, who's now running over to us. Dan tries to pull Fredrick off the man, but it's like Fredrick can't see or hear anything. He keeps hitting the guy without pause. Dan yells, "You'll kill him! Fucking stop!"

This makes me get to my feet. I run over and kneel in front of him. "Fredrick." I make a conscious effort not to look down at the man's face, probably covered in blood.

He glances up at me and pauses for a moment. He's breathing hard, and his knuckles are stained red. I stare at him wide-eyed and shake my head. Fredrick looks down at my attacker and gets to his feet, still looking furious. The guy on the ground rolls over onto his stomach and groans, blood spraying from his mouth. The sight makes me light-headed and I clench my fists, letting my nails dig into my palms to give my brain something else to focus on.

Fredrick's breathing is hard, but it doesn't stop him from kicking the man in the gut before cupping a hand around the back of my neck and pulling me to him as he leads us away.

One of the people from the other group runs over to help their bloodied teammate. Dan keeps a careful eye on Fredrick like he's worried he'll run back for more.

Letting go of me, Fredrick wipes the sweat from his forehead with the back of his arm. His eyes stay on the man he brutally beat. It isn't until I step closer to him that he finally looks at me. His gaze immediately drops to my unbuttoned jeans, and I quickly fasten them.

I try to open my mouth to say something, but he shakes his

head. His chest rises and falls with anger as his eyes land on his victim again. For a second, I think he might go back for more, but he stands there, his blood-stained hands clenched into fists.

When I look at what's left of the fight, I can see it's nearly over. Misty has her palm pressed to her cheek to stop it from bleeding, and a man with dark dreads sits on the ground next to her, tending to his ankle. It takes me a moment to recognize the emotion on their faces, but I think it's fear. They're both watching Fredrick with wide eyes like he's a rabid animal.

Melissa kneels next to Carter, who seems to be hurt but not terribly. Jason knees the rat-looking man in the stomach before the guy falls to his knees and holds up his hands in surrender. Dan squares his shoulders and stares at the man who looks like a rat. "We're done here."

The rat man hesitates, and I hear the green-eyed girl call out to him. "Duncan, let's just get out of here." Misty still holds her face as her wide eyes flicker to Fredrick.

The rat-man, now Duncan, looks up at Dan as he gets to his feet. "We're done," he spits.

I let out a breath of relief as I watch them walk away through the trees, and the pirates and I get together to assess the damage on our end.

"Hey, Pryce!"

Fredrick's head whips around to find Duncan and Misty standing at the edge of the clearing. The rest of their group has already disappeared through the trees.

Once he knows he has Fredrick's attention, he smirks and says,

"Next time you see your old man, tell him this isn't over." As soon as the words are out, he and the girl take off into the woods.

At the mention of his father, Fredrick looks as though he's seen a ghost. He lunges to go after them, but Jason and Dan hold him back.

27

Packing the van takes longer than it did to unpack it. We're all worn down after the fight, and it shows. No one says anything, but I wish they would. I'd welcome any distraction at this point because winning feels more like a relief than something to celebrate, and the gravity of Fredrick's father somehow being tied to this weighs heavily on us all.

Carter tries to put away one of the folding chairs with only one arm. He's holding his left arm close to his body as if it were in an invisible sling. I walk over to him and take the chair, and he gives me a weak smile. "Thanks."

I look down at his arm, noticing his swollen wrist. "Do you think it's broken?"

Carter looks down and frowns. "No idea, but it doesn't feel great." He sighs. "Kelly will know what to do."

At the mention of Kelly, my chest tightens. I wonder if she fully understands her son's reality. I know I didn't. I only understand now because I've experienced it firsthand. Nothing could have prepared me for what happened here today.

Jason cleans a cut on Melissa's shoulder blade. She doesn't wince once, and I have to admire her strength.

"Paige."

Hearing Melissa say my name startles me. I spin around to look at her, assuming I've done something wrong in her eyes.

She tosses me a water bottle from the cooler next to her. "Good job today."

I catch the bottle. My brain doesn't know how to process a compliment from her, so I end up just staring.

Jason laughs and shakes his head. "Nothing like a close call to bring out the best in even you, Melissa."

She rolls her eyes and glares at me. "Well, don't make it weird by just standing there."

I let out a light laugh, holding up the bottle. "Thanks."

We go back to using first aid items and packing them in the van. Most of us need the same few supplies, so we take turns handing different antiseptics and ointments to each other until our sullen silence breaks.

"I didn't know!"

At the sound of Dan's voice, we all look over to where he and Fredrick stand, Dan with his hands up defensively.

The rest of us rush over to see what's going on.

"What's wrong?" I ask.

Fredrick glances at me before bringing his eyes back to Dan.

"I'm sick of Dan being an idiot."

Dan lowers his eyes at Fredrick. "Watch it."

Ignoring him, Fredrick turns back to me. "This whole time, he told us we were being challenged because of Carter. He said it with absolute confidence, but it was all bullshit—like everything else that comes out of his mouth."

Dan takes a step toward Fredrick. "I said, watch it."

Even though I know they have a code, I'm grateful when Fredrick doesn't advance toward Dan. Instead, he staggers backward and runs his hand through his hair. "You had communications with their group. You knew this wasn't about Carter."

I'm surprised when Dan stays quiet.

"Dan, how much did you know and not tell us?" Jason's eyebrows crease as he studies his half-brother from a distance.

We all keep our eyes on him, all wanting to know the answer to Jason's question.

Finally, Dan sighs. "I knew it wasn't about Carter. When I met with the head of their group, Duncan, or whatever the fuck his name is, he mentioned having a run-in with a couple from our group. I knew Melissa hadn't had trouble with anyone and figured he had to be talking about Paige and Fredrick."

"And you didn't think it would be a good idea to tell us that?" Fredrick spits the words with nothing but contempt.

Dan glares at him. "If I had, you wouldn't have been the only one worried about bringing Paige. Carter and Jason would have been against it, too. Everyone's too soft when it comes to this girl."

Fredrick fumes as he stares at Dan. "And you didn't think that shit couple having it out for Paige and me was important?"

Dan shrugs, starting to look less concerned with the fact everyone is angry with him. "We needed another person. They would have outnumbered us."

I look over at Fredrick. "I still would have wanted to help."

He ignores me.

Jason adds, "What about this stuff with Fredrick's dad?"

This makes Dan look less at ease. "I didn't know anything for sure… but I had my suspicions."

"You motherfucker," Fredrick growls as he rushes Dan, but Jason stands between them, pushing him back.

Jason looks over his shoulder at Dan and demands, "What made you think Fredrick's dad was involved?"

Dan, stone-like and unreadable, says, "This group didn't seem familiar with our way of doing things. They were older, and established, but didn't have their own territory. I knew something wasn't right. They seemed to be operating under a different set of rules." He pauses, his eyes jumping to Fredrick. "The only other person I know who follows rules like that is Fredrick's old man."

I don't understand anything coming out of Dan's mouth. I thought Fredrick's dad left his family to live on a boat, but I guess I should have known nothing is that simple. Jason no longer needs to hold Fredrick back because his arms have gone limp at his sides. He's looking at Dan like his worst fears have been confirmed.

Jason speaks up and looks at Fredrick and me. "That explains why you guys were ambushed."

Fredrick's jaw tightens, and he nods.

I tilt my head at Jason. "Was that not normal?"

He shakes his head. "The whole point of setting up a time and place is to make it a clean, fair fight. No weapons, no surprises, just fight. And may the better group win."

I nod slowly in understanding.

Melissa says almost to herself, "At least they didn't break the weapon rule." Her eyes are wide at the realization of how easily today could have been worse.

There are murmurs of agreement from everyone.

"Look," Dan says, "who would have known their connection with your dad would make them abandon the rules?"

Fredrick's eyes narrow, and he takes a step toward Dan. "I would have. I would have fucking known."

Jason steps toward Fredrick, eyeing him warily. "Alright, it's over. No point dwelling on what could have been. Let's go home."

Fredrick's eyes linger on Dan for another moment. I think he might blow up again, but he walks over to the van without another word. The others look relieved and follow.

I take my same seat in the back row, but this time Fredrick sits next to me. I know under normal circumstances Carter would have cracked a joke about Fredrick getting in the way of our love or something dramatic, but he doesn't say anything. Everyone stays quiet.

Fredrick doesn't look at me or say anything as the van bumps back down the path toward the main road. I place my hand on his, but he pulls away. His rejection stings until his hand slowly wraps around mine, squeezing firmly.

The overwhelming silence on the ride back to Fredrick's house makes it feel longer than it should. I don't mind. He keeps his fingers wrapped around mine, his thumb tracing small circles on the back of my hand. I don't know if he's trying to calm me or calm himself, but either way, it seems to be working.

When we finally pull up to the white house with blue shutters, I see Kelly sitting in her recliner near the front window. By the time we pull into the driveway, she's on her feet and anxiously waiting to assess today's damage.

We leave everything except for the first aid supplies in the van. Jason sets the box of items from The Pharmacy on the counter, and we all find somewhere to collapse in the living room. I let my body sink into the soft leather couch. The obvious tension in the van and Fredrick's hand on mine had helped me stay alert until now. I close my eyes, but I'm immediately interrupted by Kelly's voice calling out to me.

"Paige!"

My eyes fly open to find her standing at the other end of the room, frowning. "No one sleeps until I make sure there are no concussions."

I sit up straight and nod. Carter approaches Kelly first, holding out his swollen wrist. She looks at him with pity in her eyes and sighs. "Come with me."

I watch them walk toward her bedroom and assume she's taking him to her bathroom. Dan and Melissa each sit on a recliner in front of me, looking as tired as I feel. Jason seems more alert. He's sitting on the armrest of Melissa's chair, staring off in the direction Carter and Kelly just disappeared. I look to my right and see

Fredrick sitting a few feet down from me on the couch. He has his elbows resting on his knees as he stares at the floor. He looks deep in thought, so I'm surprised when I hear him say, "Today was too risky."

Dan's eyes darken, making me nervous. "It was my call, and it's done. Get over it."

Fredrick looks like he's biting the inside of his cheek to avoid saying what's on his mind. Finally, he shakes his head and looks back at the ground.

Dan's lips curl into a small smile. "Face it, Paige has a lot of potential to become a decent…." He glances at me and says, "pirate? Is that what you call us?" He laughs, "If you think we're pirates, what would you call—"

"Dan…" Jason's voice warns.

Fredrick looks at Dan and shakes his head. Dan doesn't finish his sentence, but he doesn't give up either. He changes tactics by saying, "Come on, Paige, you're practically one of us. All that's left now is some ink and something shiny that catches your interest."

I shift in my seat as I listen to him. Joining them was never part of the plan. I don't want to steal, or fight, or get branded like cattle to match the rest of the herd.

Fredrick doesn't look up but says, "Shut up, Dan."

Melissa looks me up and down, her arms folded across her chest. "She's not like us. Someone like her has no business with people like us."

I cock my head at her. "What do you mean?"

She rolls her eyes and gestures to the three guys in the room.

"All their dads are pieces of shit. Dan's dad knocked up Jason's mom two years after Dan was born. He lived a double life for a while until Jason's mom found out. Then, he left both of them." She points to Dan. "He got double jeopardy because his mom is a piece of shit, too." My eyes dart to Dan, and I'm surprised he doesn't cut Melissa off or get angry, but instead, he just sits there, listening. Melissa continues, "As soon as his dad left, his mom expected him to pick up the slack, so he had to figure out a way to get money." She points to Jason. "His mom had to work three part-time jobs to make ends meet, and he got sick of watching her struggle." She nods her head in Fredrick's direction. "And I'm sure you know his story by now."

I nod, and she sits back in her chair like she's done explaining.

"What about you and Carter?" I ask.

Melissa hesitates, and for the first time since meeting her, she looks vulnerable. "Carter and I had shitty parents too, and then we had a lot of shitty foster parents."

I want to know more, but I know better than to ask Melissa too many questions. The room falls quiet until Fredrick's low voice utters, "She's not joining."

Dan stretches his arms behind his head. "That's a real shame, man. She's a decent fighter, and she'd be the least suspecting." He eyes me up and down in a way that makes me want to hide. "Everything about her screams 'goodie-two-shoes virgin.' No one would pick her out of a lineup."

My cheeks burn at his comment. I'd give anything to disappear right now. Fredrick glances at me with an unreadable expression, which only makes my cheeks flush hotter.

"You're a dick, Dan," Jason says as he shakes his head and gets up from the chair.

"It's not broken!" Carter sounds back to his old self as he comes bounding around the corner with a bandaged wrist. He takes inventory of the room and frowns. "Who died?"

Jason walks over and claps Carter on the shoulder. "We were worried you wouldn't pull through, man."

Carter's brows pull together, but at that moment, Kelly walks into the living room with a weary smile. "Okay, who's next?"

I stand up, maybe a little too quickly. Everyone's eyes fly in my direction, and I feel my lingering embarrassment flare up again. Kelly gives me a warm smile and waves me over. "Come into my office."

Once we're in Kelly's bathroom, I sit down on the edge of the bathtub, feeling numb. I know better than to look at my reflection in the mirror, so I keep my eyes locked on the wall in front of me. She stands at the counter, rummaging through a box for something. Her eyes glance down at me. "So, how are you feeling?"

I meet her gaze. "Okay."

She gives me a sympathetic smile. Finally, finding whatever she had been looking for, she kneels in front of me. "I'm going to look at your pupils, okay?"

I nod.

Once she's convinced I don't have a concussion, she relaxes a bit. "It looks like you made it out alright. Your cheek is a little swollen, and you have a few minor cuts and bruises on your back, but other than that, I think you got through this with minimal damage."

"Yeah." My mind replays flashbacks of the guy trying to drag me into the woods. His hands groping my stomach and fumbling with my jeans. "Minimal damage," I repeat. I can't stop thinking of what might have happened if Fredrick hadn't looked up from his own fight when he did. I swallow at the thought and try to push my feelings down with it.

Kelly studies me. "Hang in there, Paige. You're stronger than you think."

Her words bring a pang of guilt. Here I am, consumed by hypotheticals when she's the real survivor. My thoughts can't form into words right now, so I simply say, "Thank you," and hope she can sense how much I mean it.

She follows me back into the living room, where everyone still sits. As soon as I walk into the room, they all fall quiet, and Fredrick gets to his feet. "I'll take you home."

"Not so fast," Kelly says in a motherly tone. "Let me look you over. Then, you can take her home."

Fredrick's eyes linger on me for a moment before he nods and follows his mother into the other room. I look to my left and see Dan, Jason, and Melissa in the living room, looking grim. I don't have to wonder where Carter is because Kelly and I passed him in the kitchen. I'm relieved to have an escape from Dan and turn back into the kitchen to sit with Carter.

He looks up at me with his mouth full as I walk into the room. He's eating a double-stacked peanut butter and jelly sandwich, and the sight brings a smile to my lips. "Hungry?" I'm relieved that my voice sounds steady.

"Mm-hmm," he says, still chewing. He swallows and grins at me. "And now I have dinner and a view, so thank you." He holds up his sandwich with a slight bow of his head.

I let out a small laugh, rolling my eyes at him. "You sound like you're feeling better."

He gives me a mischievous grin. "Kelly gave me drugs." His face falls, and he asks, "Are you okay?" He gestures to his own cheek to mirror where I was punched.

Without thinking, I bring my hand up to my cheek and wince. It's swollen. "Yeah," I say, "I've had worse."

Carter takes another bite of his sandwich and nods. "True. That." He jabs the sandwich in the air with each word for emphasis.

"Ready?" A hand touches my arm, making me flinch. I guess I'm still a little on edge after our day. I look over and see Fredrick eyeing me with concern.

I give him the best smile I can muster. "Ready."

☠ ☠ ☠

We pull up to my driveway, and Fredrick cuts the engine. As always, he wasn't much of a conversationalist on the drive over. I'm starting to get used to his thoughtful drives, but when so much needs to be said, I find myself trapped in my thoughts.

Because the day started so early, it's still only four in the afternoon. Dad will be at work for another two hours, so I don't have to worry about hiding my swollen face... yet.

Fredrick turns to me, his lips pressed together in a fine line.

I hold up my hand. "Stop."

He cocks an eyebrow at me. "I didn't say anything."

I let out a sigh. "I know, but you're going to. You're going to try to push me away again because of Dan and because of what happened today." I look down at my hands, dreading the inevitable. When I don't hear a response right away, my eyes lift, and I find him staring at me with traces of amusement pulling at the corners of his mouth.

"What?"

Fredrick shakes his head. "I was going to ask if you're okay. You haven't said much."

"Oh." My voice is small. "You're not going to tell me I should stay away from you?"

He studies me for a moment but shakes his head.

"Fredrick," I say carefully, "what kind of stuff is your dad caught up in?"

He sighs, and I know I've asked him the one thing he doesn't want to talk about. But out of all my questions, this is the one I want answered most. He runs his hands over the steering wheel as he gathers his thoughts. "My dad and his... friends... they uh, make enemies easily." His eyes flicker to me before he adds, "They take what they can and give nothing back."

Realization comes over me, and I say, "They're pirates." I've always referred to Fredrick and the group as pirates, and I think I always will, but I've known they were more of a modified pirate—a modern-day version of the word. It sounds like Fredrick's father shares the label in a more traditional sense.

Fredrick's eyes finally meet mine, and he rubs the back of his neck. "Yeah, I guess they're pirates."

"Do you think…" I almost refer to him as the rat-looking man until I remember his name. "Do you think Duncan and his group will be back?"

He shrugs. "He said this isn't over, whatever *this* is."

I clasp my hands together in my lap. "What will you do?"

A sweet smile forms on Fredrick's lips. "What I've always done. This doesn't change anything."

I fall quiet, unsure of what to say.

He lets out a low laugh. "Honestly, after today, I figured you'd be running the other way."

I look at him, and our eyes lock. His are softer now, making him more vulnerable than I've seen before. Without thinking, I unbuckle my seatbelt and climb over to the driver's side. My legs rest on either side of him, and he stares up at me with wide eyes. Dan's voice echoes in the back of my mind, *goodie-two-shoes virgin*, and it drives me to be bold.

He rests his hands on my thighs, his pupils dilating. "Paige what are you—"

I cut him off. "I'm not running the other way."

Fredrick nods, and I notice his eyes drop to my lips before meeting my gaze again. His tongue wets his bottom lip, and my heart rate rises.

"I think you should stop training," he says quickly, and my heart sinks as I realize this is the other shoe dropping.

"Oh," I say, disappointment evident in my voice. I go to move off him, but he grips me tighter, keeping me in place.

He puts a hand on my good cheek to guide my eyes back to his. "I don't think I can handle having you around Dan and the others right now. They're getting their lines crossed with you, and I don't want you wrapped up in this more than you are."

"That reminds me," I say, "how was I able to help the group if I'm not one of you? You said the code said something about that… but I still fought."

Fredrick grazes his fingers over my hips where he holds me, and it spreads goosebumps over my skin. "We can't get outside help, but the other group assumed you *were* one of us. That's why they approached us so openly that first night—and why they didn't think twice about seeing you with us today."

"So… they still think I'm one of you," I say softly.

His expression is thoughtful. "That's why I was so adamant about you not coming. If we showed up without you, they might have realized their mistake, but now we've only confirmed their thinking."

Knowing there are dangerous people out there who assume I'm on the same level makes my heart pound. "But I don't want to be one of you."

He lets out a hollow laugh. "Trust me, hearing you say that is a relief. I don't want you to join us either. That's another reason I think you should stay away for a while. If anything happens, I don't want other groups having more reason to believe you're in this."

I take in his words slowly. "So, will I still see you?"

His eyes travel to meet mine, and he says, "Every chance I get."

He presses his lips to mine, and my body feels electrified again. His tongue grazes my bottom lip, and I tighten my grip on his t-shirt. No one has ever kissed me the way Fredrick does. There's so much meaning behind his kiss. All the things he can't say come through in the way his lips move with mine. I let out a soft moan, and my cheeks burn, but my body's reaction to him seems to fuel him more. He weaves his fingers through my hair and gently pulls downward, lifting my chin to expose my neck. His lips trace my jawline and nip at my neck, and my breathing turns ragged. Feverishly, he brings my mouth to his once more, and I gently bite down on his bottom lip. He groans into my mouth and moves his hands down to my hips, squeezing me harder. He pulls away from me, and we look at each other, both catching our breath. His lips are swollen from kissing me, and I can't stop replaying the sound he made in my head.

He lets out a breathless laugh. "We should probably stop." His words disappoint me even though I know he's right. He must sense my feeling because he adds, "Your dad will be home soon, and you should ice that cheek."

My hand finds my swollen cheek, and I nod. Crawling back into the passenger seat, I open the Jeep door.

As I hop out, I hear his voice. "Hey, Paige." My eyes look up to find him looking at me intently. He smiles, and I'm breathless. "You're beautiful."

My face warms, and I can't help smiling back at him. I want to ask him when I'll see him next or how we'll juggle separating me from the group. I want to figure out a plan for next time, but I know he doesn't have the answers. Not yet, anyway.

As I walk up to my front door, something catches my eye. Once I get closer, I see an envelope sticking out of the door-jam with the world *Girl* scrawled across the front. I stand there, staring at the message that can only be for me. My hand trembles as I reach for the paper and slide my finger under the seal.

Inside, I find a short note written in the same sloppy handwriting on the envelope. My palms sweat as I read:

Convince Pryce to do the job, or he won't be the only one to pay Freddie's debt.

Staring at the words on the page, my mind jumps back to Duncan calling Fredrick by his last name after the fight. If in this note, Fredrick is *Pryce*, then *Freddie* must be…

My head snaps up, ready to call out to Fredrick, but by the time I turn around, his Jeep is already turning onto the main road.

GIVE NOTHING BACK

HEATHER GARVIN

FREDRICK'S CHAPTER

Scan the code below to claim your copy of Fredrick's chapter! It was a night like any other… until he saw her.

ACKNOWLEDGMENTS

A huge thank you to the team of people who helped make this book a reality. If it weren't for the dedicated editing and critique work of Katryna Arias, Corey Wys, Sydney Gabel, and my own "Deeda" Peter Garvin, I can assure you, this book would not have reached its full potential.

Now, lovely reader, I'm going to acknowledge each of these incredible people directly.

Katryna, my maid of honor, dearest friend, beloved coworker, and, as it would turn out, kick-ass editor, I can't thank you enough for all of the hours of hard work you have put into this book. And yes, I picked a sentence with the most commas possible on purpose. In fact, part of me hopes some of those commas are grammatically wrong because I know it will drive you crazy. But on a serious note, thank you. Thank you for giving me line-by-line edits. Thank you for circling all of my commonly used words. Thank you for your overly-excited reactions anytime Fredrick would say, "Jesus, Paige" because it truly made the writing process that much more fun. I could probably write another ten pages thanking you, but I've got other people to get to. Don't be greedy.

Corey, you are one of the people in my life that I put on the highest of pedestals. I absolutely adore you, and having you involved in this process made it that much better. One day, when you publish a book of your own, I look forward to returning the favor. If it weren't for you, Chapter 20 would still be "boring," and Fredrick would never have confronted Luke inside the theater. This chapter is now one of my personal favorites thanks to you. Your honesty made me strive to do better, and I love you for it!

Sydney, I'm so glad we reconnected through this book! When we were in high school together, pretending to look busy in TV Production and playing dance games on your Wii, I never would have thought we'd be editing this book together from opposite ends of the country ten years later. Your editing suggestions were always spot on, and you helped me look at my own book differently. Not to mention all the times your Google Docs comments made me snort with laughter. Your support and friendship means the world to me, and I could never thank you enough.

Last, but certainly not least, I have my wonderful father to thank. Who would have thought that your English degree would finally come in handy through ways of reading your daughter's book? After I wrote the original manuscript for Take What You Can when I was in high school, you always suggested I do something with it. FOR YEARS you suggested I do something with it. I never listened. If anything, I felt embarrassed by it. You would bring it up fondly and my brain would react with something like *Oh my God, Deeda. Don't bring up the fact that I isolated myself and wrote a book. That's so weird and embarrassing!* Of course, you were right all along. Finally doing something with this story has brought me so much happiness, and I can't imagine doing any of it without knowing you were in my corner every step of the way.

I feel so grateful to have friends and family willing to give me their honest opinion because there is truly nothing more valuable to a writer than the reaction of her readers.

☠ A Special thanks to Courtney Grifo, who single handedly helped me re-edit Take What You Can in preparation for its new cover! Your insight and willingness to dive deeper into the story is greatly appreciated. Thank you! ☠

ABOUT THE AUTHOR

Heather Garvin works as a nationally certified sign language interpreter by day and writes a variety of romances in her spare time.

Aside from working and writing, she's also a wife, mom, and a fur mama to two dogs, two cats, and Tuskan: the horse who inspired the logo and name for her publishing company, Tuskan Publishhing LLC.

There's nothing Heather loves more than hearing from readers. Connect with her on Instagram!

heathergarvinbooks